The Tomas Dearlove Chronicles
Book One

Caractacus Plume

For more information about the adventures of
the paranormal investigation agency of
Lyons & Hound
(est. 1895)
and to join the Caractacus Plume mailing list
and receive a free short story from
The Lyons & Hound Casebook
visit
www.caractacusplume.com

Silvatici Publishing
silvatici@outlook.com

ISBN 978-0-9935105-0-2

For Catrina

With thanks to:

Andi

Dr H

David

George

Kit

Olivier De Beventine

&

Percival

PROLOGUE
The Wizard Earl

Petworth, Sussex, England.
1587

Henry Percy, 9th Earl of Northumberland, looked down at his trembling hands with all the practised indifference that might be expected from one of the most powerful men and (of far greater interest to this story) most inquisitive and scientific minds in the Kingdom.

Is it fear or excitement that makes me shiver so? he mused to himself, as he adjusted his grip on his horse's reins for the umpteenth time. *Perhaps a strange marriage of the both*, he concluded, though he could not decide which emotion was the more dominant.

With an almost physical effort he lifted his gaze and, in so doing, drew his purpose back once more to the matter at hand.

It was approaching midnight. A brilliant full moon cast down a glorious yet ghostly glimmer that glanced off the treetops on his country estate and made the swaying grass fields shimmer like a silver sea.

The splendour of Nature, reflected the young Earl. *So precise, so ... perfect. How strange to be shown such beauty on this most dreadful of nights.*

A full moon: a *Hunter's Moon* – but who was to be hunter and who was to be prey?

Henry shifted in his saddle and turned to appraise his companions – seventeen in all: twelve on foot (mostly *volunteers* from the local village); five on horseback (his dear friends and close comrades).

What a sorry party we do make, he thought. *Pray God that we prove worthy to this challenge.*

He studied the expressions of the men around him.

The villagers huddled nervously together; confused, uncertain, wide-eyed. Their faces echoed the grey and pallid landscape. The moonlight trickled eerily from the tips of their spears, making them look more like fragile pagan-spirits exiled from the *Faery Lands* than the terrified but determined country-folk that they were.

Thank God that his good friends, mounted and gathered about him, were cut from a different cloth. Henry could sense the air of exhilaration smouldering beneath the nonchalant expressions that they wore like courtly masks – camouflaging their fervent anticipation and, if they felt anything like he did, concealing the ever-growing feeling of excited dread that was throbbing through their bones like a waking fever.

To his immediate left were his closest companions – Thomas Hariot, mathematician and astronomer; Walter Warner, physician; Robert Hues, geographer. Hardly men of action, rather they were scholars – men of books and of science. Books, science and ... *magic*. That, in part, is why they were here. All of them were fascinated – *No, be fair, "obsessed" was closer to the mark!* – by the occult. Little wonder, then, that they had become known throughout the gossiping circles of Queen Elizabeth's Court as the Earl's 'Three Magi'.

But then he himself, Henry Percy, 9th Earl of Northumberland – twenty-three years old and less than two years into his title – delighted to be known by his nickname of 'The Wizard Earl'.

To his right sat old Bartholomew Scrimshaw, his bodyguard and master-at-arms (so-called *Black Bart* – very quietly and behind his back – by the other members of the Earl's retinue), a dour, stony-faced and world-weary man who had been in the service of the Percy family for over thirty years. In all that time no one had ever seen a hint that he even understood the meaning of the words *"fear"* or *"uncertainty"* ... until now.

Next to him, awkwardly mounted, but looking as keen as the proverbial mustard, was the venerable scholar, scientist and sorcerer, Dr John Dee – possibly the most learned and brilliant mind in all of England.

Whilst recently visiting Petworth House (*How opportune!*) to peruse through the Earl's ever-growing library – only bettered, it was rumoured, by Dee's own in Mortlake – the dear Doctor had got wind of this *adventure* and was adamant that he must participate, despite his advancing years and ill-health. And who could blame him for his desire? Dee was one of Europe's leading experts on magic and the occult, and what an unprecedented opportunity this was to come face-to-face with a creature from the darkest nightmares of the human mind – a monster that had stalked the fringes of man's imagination since time immemorial.

It had begun a month ago as little more than rumour. And then, all too soon, the rumours had manifested themselves into hard and horrifying realities. Slaughtered sheep were found. A herd of deer decapitated. Mistress Latham's milk-cow was discovered with its legs and jaw pulled off – not killed and eaten for food, but ripped and tortured by a wild and odious thing.

The villagers grew nervous. They whispered of witches and *Faerie-Hounds*, *Black Dogs*, *Gilly-trots* and *Devils*.

But worse was soon to come.

The wife and three young daughters of Will Shirley, the village blacksmith, were found – their bodies barely recognisable, mauled and mutilated as they were. Will himself was missing, feared dead.

Old Bob Cobber swore blind that he had seen a demon racing into the woods around Petworth House under the light of the last full moon, the limb of a man-child clenched in its murderous jaws. And Bob was a *straight man,* they said down in the village, a *church-man – no drinker, no liar was he*. (Although Henry couldn't help but wonder what the old rascal had been doing out so late – and on the Earl's land, no less? Rabbits for the pot perhaps? If it were venison that Old Bob was after, then he would be for the stocks.) Now people talked in hushed tones and locked their doors at night. "*The devil is abroad!*" they hissed.

With the waning of the full moon the dreadful incidents had ceased, but all – villager, scholar and young Earl alike – counted down the nights and waited, with a nervous trepidation, for its return.

To the educated man – the mystic, the scientist, the occultist – the nature and the name of the beast was apparent. And now, with the full moon returned, here they were, huddled together in taut and trembling anticipation. Here they had gathered, on the edge of midnight, to destroy a monster that was no longer myth nor fairy tale.

They had come to kill a were-wolf.

Blue-grey clouds swirled and whispered in front of the Circean moon, leaving them all, for a moment, in an uncomfortable, hushed and inky darkness.

The nervous silence was harshly cracked by the sharp jolt and snap of chains.

Master William Tiggs, the Earl's head-gamekeeper, struggled to control two mighty wolfhounds straining at their leads. Fearsome creatures – lean, agile and massive. Beloved by the Earl, who had raised them himself from pups: Dindrane – with a coat as fiery as cinnamon – and her brother, Percival – the colour of ripened wheat. Wolf-killers. Man-hunters. Fierce and fearless. Their ancient kind had been bred over the centuries for war and for the chase, and was prized the world over for its strength, bravery, loyalty and fighting-spirit.

Well, thought the Earl, *this beast from Hell won't have it all its own way at least, for we have raised monsters of our own.*

The clouds passed, revealing the silent silver beauty of the night.

Almost immediately the fleeting tranquillity was broken by a soul-quaking howl ripping across the silhouetted skyline.

All present buckled to the very core of their being.

The horses whinnied and shied.

The two dogs growled deep in their throats, as if affronted by the sound. Lurching forward they broke free of Tiggs' fumbling grip and hurtled in deadly silence towards the trees.

This is it! thought young Henry, mastering both his nerves and his agitated steed. *This is it! Courage, Henry! Courage. Think straight, think fast, and hold firm to your course!*

'The chase is on, my boys!' he cried. 'Look to your hearts and no man here shall be found wanting! Come, lads! On! On! In the name of all the blessed Saints, let us drive this devil from our land and raise a cheer for England!'

And with the breath of his battle cry still hanging like mist in the air, he drove his rearing horse forward, leaving the startled and worried shouts of Thomas, Walter and Robert, breathless in his wake.

The earth thundered beneath his horse's hooves.

The chill of the night air snatched his breath.

He stole a glance backwards, to see his companions struggling to control their anxious mounts – only old Bartholomew even beginning to follow after him.

Good old Bart, thought Henry, and he smiled as his heart filled with a fierce and ancient joy.

'No! No, my Lord!' he heard Thomas cry out. 'We must stay together! We must stay together!'

But the thrill of the chase fired through the young Earl's blood and filled him with a hot wildness, and he laughed and laughed and laughed, half-crazed with excitement.

Ahead of him he saw a long low shadow flit from one group of trees to another with an effortless yet unworldly grace, and knew his quarry.

Is it a beast more like a wolf in form, or more like a man? he wondered.

Never mind, he would know soon enough.

In one hand he tossed and re-gripped his father's old boar-spear, recently reset with a wicked blade of pure silver. And he felt the comforting heft of the pistol jammed against his leg – tucked firmly into the saddle and primed and loaded with a silver bullet.

The chase! The chase! Oh Lord!

In all his years! This is what it meant to be alive!

He crouched forward, whispering encouragements into his horse's ear, and together, as one, they surged onwards.

Before him the two hounds, Dindrane and Percival, coursed silently like ghostly-driven javelins, disappearing into the woods hot on the trail of the hell-beast.

To his left a herd of deer darted out from among the trees, scattering in panic to vanish into the silver-blue shadows of the night. Henry forced his mount forward and followed the dogs, entering into the woods and ignoring the fading cries of warning screeching behind him.

Among the trees he soon found himself in near-total darkness.

He slowed his horse and picked his way cautiously towards a clearing.

Moonlight seeped through the treetops like water.

The wind died.

No creature stirred.

The trees seemed to hold their breath.

Silence – as solemn as an empty church.

As soundlessly as he could, the young Earl dismounted and drew the pistol from his saddle, still tightly gripping his father's spear in his right hand – as if he were once again a frightened child holding onto the old man's hand for reassurance. But no sooner had his feet touched the ground than his horse reared and bolted. Henry cursed and tried in vain to catch the reins, but the beast was panicked and in its flight bumped into him, sending him sprawling to the floor.

And then he heard it – a long, low, muttering snarl.

Young Henry's blood ran cold, but, as he frantically rolled to his knees, his heart froze further still.

There, not twenty yards from him, stood the monster itself – following the horse's terrified flight with hellish, blood-dipped eyes. Seven feet tall it stood. Wicked as the Devil's heart. A mouth of polished daggers, poised wide open. Dark saliva dripped from its elongated muzzle. Half man. Half beast. Pure malice.

O brave new world! That has such creatures in't ...

The monster slowly turned to face him.

Lifting its grotesque head the man-beast cast from its dreadful claws the broken, limp and lifeless body of the great hound Dindrane.

Henry stumbled to his feet. His limbs felt like syllabub. Somehow he had the time to think that this fear shamed his warlike ancestors. He cursed himself for a coward and, with all the might that he could muster, hurled his father's spear towards the beast.

The creature disdainfully swatted it away – as if it were a reed thrown by a small boy – and slowly, with measured tread, prowled menacingly towards him.

Henry staggered back, his face agog – a mask of rigid terror.

And then, from nowhere, old Bartholomew rode into the clearing.

The creature pounced, vaulting over the startled veteran, snapping and engulfing the poor man's head in its hideous jaws in one foul swoop.

Bartholomew's horse screamed and bolted, its eyes white with terror as it ran into the woods, taking with it the decapitated corpse of the old soldier; disappearing into the silver-dappled forest as a newborn nightmare – a ghastly headless horseman.

The were-wolf landed elegantly on its hind legs and raised itself, man-like, to full-height. It spat out Bartholomew's bloody skull. The old man's grizzled head smacked against a tree with a muffled thud, then rolled and came to rest, staring directly at the Earl.

'*Why?*' the dead man's eyes seem to ask. '*Why this?*'

The creature padded forward. Upon its hideous muzzle it wore a cruel and callous grin. Henry's hand shook uncontrollably as he raised his arm to take aim with the pistol, but, faster than an adder's strike, the beast sprang, ripping him across the belly with a twisted paw of murderous talons, sending Henry tumbling backwards into the brambles and the pistol spinning from his grip.

The breath flew from his lungs. It felt as if his ribs had been crushed. If not for the near-priceless Milanese breastplate that he wore the young Earl knew he would be dead ... or worse.

But no matter, he thought. *Not long to wait. As comes the creature, so comes my death.*

'Oh all the Saints commend my soul,' he managed to whisper, immediately regretting his words and knowing that this was a stupid, wasted breath. *With what words should an Earl meet his doom?* he wondered. Not begging, that was for certain. And fleetingly he was relieved to be alone, with no one else to see him die so poorly.

The monster towered over him. Warm blood dripped like crimson honey from its rippling snout, spattering the young Earl's face. Henry, in a last act of bravado, clenched his hands into fists, looked the hell-beast in the eye and roared with every ounce of defiance that he could summon.

The wolf-man threw back its head and howled at him, seeming to delight in the exchange of war cries.

The bushes to his right suddenly exploded.

Like a flashing golden blade, the giant hound, Percival, leapt onto the creature's back, sending it crashing to the ground. Tearing, slashing, snarling and snapping, the two beasts rolled and wrestled, bristling with fury – the battle almost too fast for the horrified Earl to follow. Percival pinned the monster down by its throat and ripped and tore with relentless ferocity. Blood sprayed in all directions as the man-wolf howled in agony – a pitiful, ugly, hell-born music that made the Earl's ears bleed.

But this was a creature of the supernatural. No wounds, however gruesome, were enough to end its days. The monster cruelly lashed out, flipping Percival over, and sank its murderous fangs into the huge hound's shoulder. The dog jerked backwards, wobbled gingerly on watery legs, and then flopped in slow motion to the floor.

The wolf-man lurched to its feet, resting its weight upon the knuckles of one lethal hand, the terrible wounds making its fury even more terrifying to behold. It fixed Henry with a baleful gaze and snarled, seething with an outraged spite and malevolence.

The hell-beast sprang forward, and the Earl, having located and retrieved his pistol while the two creatures fought, fired point-blank into the monster's heart.

The were-wolf dropped without a sound, a surprised expression on its face, as if to say '*How could you?*'

Henry sunk to the floor and rolled onto his back.

Any moment now, he thought, *and I can breathe again.*

Soon, how soon he knows not, the area is a bustle of activity; men on horseback followed by wide-eyed and breathless villagers on foot. Thomas and Walter dismount and rush to Henry's side, worriedly checking him for wound or injury. Robert fires another bullet into the prostrate monster. Dee bustles forward and examines the creature's corpse with a childlike fascination.

Henry brushes off all assistance and staggers to the body of the fallen were-beast.

As he watches, the creature morphs and slowly withers into the shape of a man. The lifeless face still wears its expression of surprise but now (or so it appears to the young Earl) it is mixed with one of horror – an understanding of the monstrosity of its actions.

Perhaps, reflects Henry. *Or do I just project my own imaginings?*

'Sweet Jesus!' whispers Old Bob Cobber, gasping to catch his breath. 'It's Will ... Will Shirley!'

Dear God! thinks the Earl, remembering the warmth and loving joy with which he once saw the blacksmith play with his three young children. *What wicked world would make a man so cursed?*

But his thoughts are broken by a low, soft whimpering.

Percival, the great and loyal hound, lies in a pool of blood, his ribcage weakly rising and falling.

The Earl stumbles to his wolfhound, kneels and gently caresses the great beast's massive head.

The poor dog feebly wags its tail.

'Master Warner, Dr Dee, are you not the very best of physicians?' he rasps. Unintentionally his question comes out somewhere between a command and a threat.

The two scholars stare at him with saucer-eyed uncertainty.

'You will do everything within your powers to cure this animal. He saved my life ...' whispers Henry Percy, 9th Earl of Northumberland, his voice catching, his throat suddenly taut and dry, 'perhaps my very soul.'

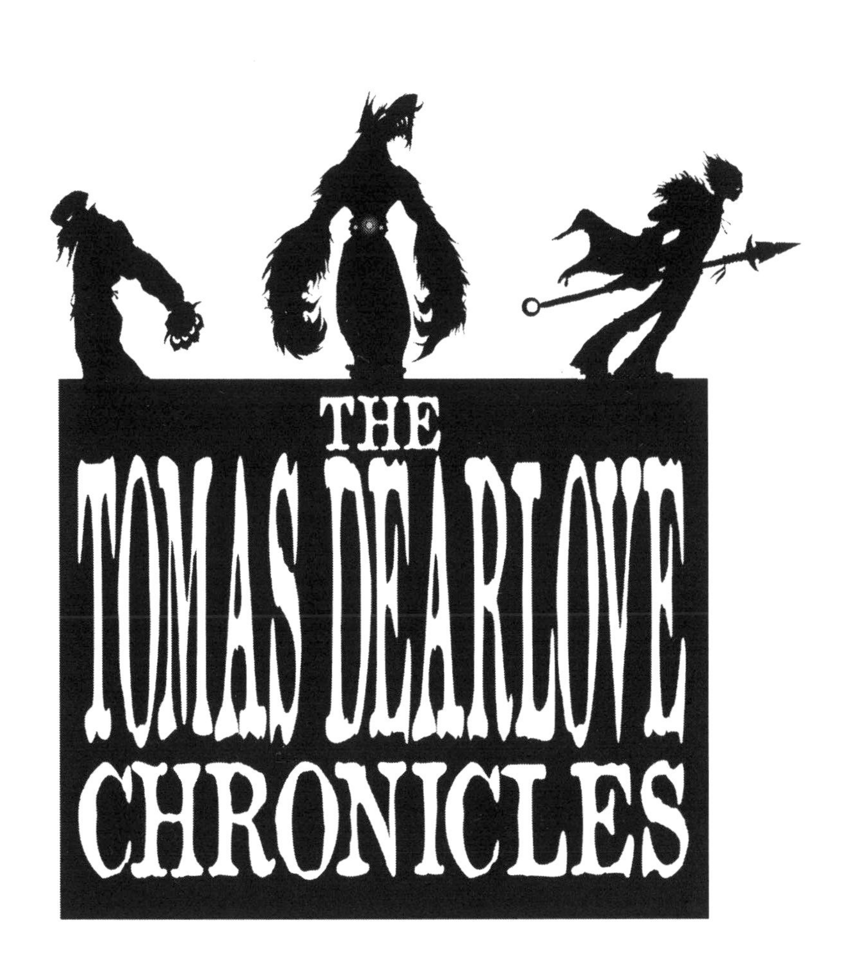
THE
TOMAS DEARLOVE
CHRONICLES

The Wild Hunt

“When I carefully consider the curious habits of dogs
I am compelled to conclude that man is the superior animal.
When I observe the curious habits of man
I confess, my friend, I am puzzled.”

Ezra Pound

1. One Punch Cottage
2. Uncle Cornelius
3. The Study
4. The Perilous Art Of Eavesdropping
5. The Muse-asium
6. The Ear-Shaped Eye-Stone
7. The Reveal
8. The Hound Who Hunts Nightmares
9. The Origin Of The Species
10. The Apprentice
11. Peculiarities In Petworth Park
12. Stay Put In Your Grave
13. An Unexpected Return
14. The Curious Chase Of Spring-Heeled Jack
15. A Very Victorian Vignette
16. The King Of The Downlands
17. The Mysterious Incident Of The Hunters Of Hollingbury Ring
18. Were-Lions! Were-Tiger! Were-Bears! Oh My!
19. The Battle Of Hollingbury Hill
20. The Prisoner
21. The Society Of The Wild Hunt
22. An Extraordinary Elizabethan Enigma
23. The Dark Curtain
24. The Sinister Threads Of A Most Diabolical Tapestry
25. The Witches Of Frederick Gardens
26. The Night Of The Smack Faery
27. The Art & Science Of Exhibition-Skirmishing
28. The Devil's Huntsman's Daughter
29. The Council Of The Elves
30. Three Princesses
31. Four Jacks & A Queen

32. The Brighton Boy
33. Dr Chow's Carnival Of Curiosities
34. Kidnapped!
35. The Visitor
36. We Are Siamese If You Please
37. The Reunion
38. The Grabbers' Secret
39. Hoodwinked
40. Courage & Shuffle The Cards
41. The Wild Hunt
42. False Endings

ONE
One Punch Cottage

Brighton, East Sussex, England.
2010

Tomas Dearlove reshouldered his bag and walked up and down Black Lion Lane for the umpteenth time. It was really barely worthy of such a grand title as 'Lane', being no more than a tiny passageway that Tom could easily have touched both sides of by slightly extending his elbows. A "twitten" in the local parlance, he would later learn: *twit ten*. Tom wondered what would happen if two people were walking along it in opposite directions? Surely one party would have to reverse all the way back out. That, however, seemed most unlikely in Brighton, where, from what he had observed so far, people seemed to take umbrage at the very notion of a backwards step. No, they would have to try to squeeze past, side by side, he concluded. Very intimate. Very ... *Brighton*.

Black Lion Lane had been hard enough to find in the first place, but now, at the very end of his journey, Tom was finding his final destination frustratingly impossible to locate.

Surely there must be some mistake?

He was here to stay with his *uncle,* Cornelius, during the school holidays. Not something that he relished, since he had only a very vague recollection of the man – having briefly met him once, four years ago (when Tom was barely nine), at his granddad's funeral (Tom's granddad, that is, not Uncle Cornelius').

Though he was called "Uncle" by everybody, Tom wasn't quite sure exactly what Cornelius' relationship to the family was. His mum had instructed him to call the old fellow "Uncle" (and he was most definitely not Mum's brother!), what's more, she, in turn, also-called him "Uncle" ... so that must mean that he was probably Tom's great uncle – or something equally stuffy like that – but from which side of the family no one seemed to be quite able to pin down. Uncle Cornelius' surname was *Lyons*; Tom, his mother, and all other known relatives were *Dearloves*. And it seemed most unlikely that the old codger was from Tom's father's branch of the family (whoever *he* was and wherever *they* might be).

Rarely seen by anybody, except at christenings and funerals, Uncle Cornelius had become a bit of a family myth. He was, by all accounts, widely travelled, a historian, a collector of antiques and, in his youth, had reputedly been a well-respected boxer. Always immaculately dressed and always immaculately absent from family gatherings. On that account at least, thought Tom, the decrepit old bugger showed some remarkable good sense.

Tom's mum was working some much-needed extra shifts over the holiday period and so had suggested that, instead of idly kicking his heels at home, Tom might like to go and visit Cornelius down in Brighton. She seemed to think that it would be good for him to get away and have a holiday somewhere "different and exciting" – as if they'd ever *actually* been on holiday ... anywhere ... ever! Brighton was a fabulous place, she insisted – by the seaside, full of cafes and parks and every type of shop imaginable (as if she'd ever *actually* been here herself!), with lots of things for young people to see and do. And it would be a fine chance, she insisted, to get to know Uncle Cornelius a little better.

"We don't see him much but he's always been very good to us, he has. Very kind."

What she really meant was, that if Tom stayed at home, unsupervised, he'd get himself into all sorts of mischief. *Guilty Ma'am*, he had to admit. Still, he'd liked the sound of it – Brighton that is, not the staying with some near-dead, distant and doddering relative. But at least the old fellow would offer him somewhere to kip while he *kicked up the dust* and found himself all sorts of delightful shenanigans to pursue.

His mother had provided him with an open-return ticket ("Just in case it doesn't work out, Sweetie" – *!!?!!*), a crisp £50 note and a pocketful of change for spending-money (*ho-ho, ha-ha and thank you very much*), and, as a *thank-you present* for his coffin-nudging host, a box of Turkish Delight (an unwanted gift, left over – unopened of course – from Christmas; on account that neither he nor his mother liked to eat sweets that smelled and tasted like old peoples' clothes [not that he'd ever tasted old peoples' clothes, you understand, just that ... well, that's how he imagined that they might taste ... if he was ever, somehow, forced to taste them – though he didn't even want to begin to imagine what awful circumstance might have to befall him to be put in such an appalling situation]).

With an almost physical effort he forced his mind back to more immediate matters and looked down, once again, at the scrunched-up piece of paper in his hand. It read –

> Onepunchcottagestopblacklionlanestopfromstationwal
> ktoclocktowerstopturnleftcrossroadstopfindshipstreeto
> nrightstopwalktowardsseastopblacklionlaneonleftoppo
> siteshipstreetpassagestopexpectingyoustop

'For crying out loud!' snorted Tom, 'Who sends a frickin' telegram in this day and age?'

To be fair the directions had been pretty accurate, once he'd deciphered the bloody thing. Fortunately for all concerned, Tom had spent many a weekday afternoon ~~bunking off school~~ studying diligently at home and watching old black and white movies (mainly Westerns) – in which the use of said telegrams was essential for passing on dramatically dreadful news – and so he'd only missed Black Lion Lane on account of it being so minuscule and ... hhhhmmmm, how to put it? ... Ah, yes – IMPOSSIBLE TO FIND!!! (Also there was the slight detour to the amusement arcade on the pier to take into account – he was on holiday after all. But that had been cut short by the menacing appearance of a gang of menacing-looking local lads, trying hard to act 'hard' and 'trying' – all dressed in impossibly trendy clothes and sporting cutting-edge [ho-ho] haircuts. Tom was only too well aware that he, by comparison, was dressed like the proverbial country bumpkin – and let's not even begin to discuss the merits of Mum's attempts at DIY hairdressing for boys. Thus, thinking that discretion was the better part of valour, he had decided to make himself scarce before they tried to fleece him of his holiday funds.) And so, after a few tromps up and down Ship Street he'd finally discovered the elusive Black Lion Lane. But of his uncle's house, the intriguingly named *One Punch Cottage*, he could find neither a sign nor trace.

There were three small houses along the lane, none of which bore any name, only numbers (unsurprisingly, and rather unimaginatively – 1, 2 and 3, respectively). There was also a slightly sinister-looking wooden gate – definitely locked and with no bell or any visible means of access.

Oh dear Lord, thought Tom, with growing dread, *I'm going to have to* [gulp] ... *ask someone!*

The tiny twitten, however, was completely and utterly bereft of anyone to ask.

Summoning up his courage, he decided that the only course of action now open to him was to knock on the door of one of the three houses and make an excruciatingly embarrassing enquiry.

Which one to start with, though? he mused, in a vain attempt to delay the inevitably humiliating task of talking to complete and utter strangers.

With that thought still rattling in his head, he suddenly became aware of the presence of a little old lady standing beside him. How she had got there unnoticed, Heaven knew. He certainly hadn't heard her creeping up on him. That was slightly unnerving, but, well, she did look very kindly. In fact she was probably the sweetest-looking little old lady that he'd ever seen. That settled it. He'd ask her.

'Excuse me, Miss,' he began, in his most polite voice.

She looked up enquiringly at him (*My, she was tiny!)* – two chubby, peachy cheeks gurning under watery eyes as green as a summer-sweet orchard.

'I'm looking for a house called *One Punch Cottage*. It's supposed to be in this street but I can't seem to find it.'

She squinted at him quizzically.

'What's that, Ducky?' she croaked kindly, her eyes boring into him like two home-baked apple pies.

'ONE! PUNCH! COTTAAAAAAAAAGGGHHHHHHHHHH!!!'

The reason for Tom's unusual pronunciation of the word "cottage" was this: as he'd begun his 'deaf sensitive' repeat of the question (especially reserved for the hard of hearing senile old git) a gnarled, fat little hand had appeared from within the sleeve of the tiny crone's musty antique coat, swiftly followed by the uncurling of a gnarled, fat little sausage of a finger, which proceeded (moving faster than a damp cobra with its tongue caught in a plug socket) to poke him most painfully in the eye.

‘Ow, ow, ow! Jesus frickin’ H Christ! What did you do that for, you horrible old hag!’ howled Tom, hopping in agony and clutching his weeping peeper.

Winking like a cat’s bottom, he frantically peered around. The shame and humiliation, coupled with the realisation that he might be being mugged by somebody’s great-great-great-grandmother – and only hours into his first day in a big city (*My God, what were these people like?!*) – adding unbearable embarrassment to his understandable physical pain. But, to his surprise and relief, the vicious little harridan was nowhere to be seen.

Confused, and more than a little worried, he quickly checked his belongings. Thankfully, everything appeared to be in place. When he was absolutely certain that his vertically challenged, wizened and wantonly wicked assailant was no longer anywhere in the immediate vicinity, he ground the heel of his palm into his weeping eye in an attempt to ease his discomfort.

It was then that he noticed something quite extraordinary out of the corner of his ‘good’ eye.

Where a moment ago there had been nothing but wall, there now stood an enormous wooden gate. And written to the side of said gate, in a flowery antique script, were the unmistakeable words – *One Punch Cottage*.

Tom blinked and blinked again, and rubbed both eyes in disbelief.

‘Don’t look like no bleeding cottage to me,’ he muttered angrily to himself (partly to regain some sense of being in control of events after the embarrassment of having clearly missed such an obvious and large an edifice as a house, and partly on account of his astonishment at having been grievously assaulted by a geriatric midget).

To be fair, his observation was indeed an astute one. One Punch Cottage towered above the surrounding buildings in a most un-cottage-like way – sprouting upwards and outwards between its neighbours like a giant, greedy and crooked weed.

Swiftly collecting his composure, Tom looked suspiciously about him (just to make sure that he wasn’t about to be *shanked* by members of the local pensioners’ Tea Dance Society) and slowly turned the handle of the gate.

The latch lifted with a satisfying click.

Tom pushed open the heavy, creaking door and walked through the sweeping archway.

The gate automatically groaned shut behind him and he found himself, much to his astonishment, standing on the edge of a rather lovely-looking, well-kept country garden.

At the far end of the garden hunched One Punch Cottage itself, brooding and twisted like a sinister, wind-swept tree. Four stories high, with a razor-sharp slate roof and a wobbly chimney balancing at an almost impossible angle.

Old-fashioned – certainly, thought Tom, shockingly immune to the peculiar, foreboding and, all in all, rather forbidding appearance of his uncle’s abode.

Would benefit from a lick of paint, he observed, noticing the flaking paintwork on the lattice windows. *But, on the whole, pretty acceptable. Perhaps this trip was beginning to look up, after all.*

He crunched his way along the winding gravel path, his eye weeping like a hysterical budgerigar, until he stood before the huge, blood red coloured front door of his uncle's house. On inspection, no doorbell was to be found but, in its stead, a weighty bronze knocker in the shape of a snarling dog's head.

Tom looked around him, having the unusual feeling that he was being watched, but, as far as he could tell, the grounds appeared to be completely deserted.

He boldly gripped the knocker and gave three hearty raps.

At first there was, perplexingly, no sound from the knocker – and then the house hurled back a resounding BOOM! BOOM! BOOM!

It was, Tom thought, like three heavy stones being dropped down a hundred-foot-deep wishing well.

The last boom faded into silence.

Tom waited.

Nothing.

And waited.

Still nothing.

'Oh for Christ's sake, come on!' he hissed to himself in exasperation, suddenly realising that he didn't even have the incontinent old nudger's telephone number. 'Please be in. Please be in.'

He was about to reach for the door knocker again when he heard the heart-gladdening sound of footsteps from within and then a voice, as rough and warming as his mother's cooking brandy (apparently) calling out – 'Missus Dobbs! Missus Dobbs? The door, Missus Dob– oh ... bugger it!' More footsteps and then the rasping sound of a grille being whipped open.

Tom did his best to control his twitching orb and look both endearing and politely normal whilst under inspection from the invisible gaze, until, finally, after an uncomfortable infinity, the grille was hurriedly snapped shut again.

'No, Bess. Back you get, old girl,' the voice cooed, swiftly followed by the sound of a closing door, yet more footsteps and then a short eternity of the unlatching of locks, bolts, chains and the turning of many keys.

Eventually the door swung open and there, filling the doorframe like a partially shaved grizzly bear stuffed into an antique tweed suit – long of limb, shoulders like a wardrobe and hands like battered shovels – stood Uncle Cornelius.

TWO
Uncle Cornelius

Uncle Cornelius could, Tom considered, have been anywhere between fifty and seventy years of age. Dark, fierce grey eyes under thick grey eyebrows and a head of short grey hair, from which sprang enormous sideburns and connecting moustache (a 'Newgate Knocker', he was later proudly informed). He was dressed, to Tom's imagination at least, like an Edwardian country squire – a snappy tweed suit and matching waistcoat, with a heavy, golden fob watch chain dangling weightily across his midriff. The appearance of respectability was slightly marred, however, by a shining black eye and raw-looking grazes across the knuckles of both fists.

Good grief! thought Tom, in alarm. *What is wrong with this town and its hooligan pensioners?* Had there, he wondered, been a ruckus over the last cream tea at the local bingo hall?

'Tim,' said Uncle Cornelius, warmly.

'Tom,' said Tom, coldly.

'Tom,' beamed Uncle Cornelius, extending a massive and misshapen mitt (that looked and felt like it had been carved [badly] out of aged oak) and firmly pumping Tom's hand. 'Good to see you, son. Been expecting you. Find us all right, did you?'

Tom smiled weakly, struggling to control the quaking spasms in his still weeping eye.

'Cor blimey, just look at you,' chortled the old man, tilting his head to one side in order to observe Tom's disturbingly ticking visage (which was fluttering like a dying fluorescent lamp). 'My, you've ... grown ... since I last ... saw you,' he continued, desperately trying to drag his gaze away from Tom's convulsing peeper. ''Ow's your ma? Very fond of your mother, I am. Always 'ave been. Lovely girl. Nothing like a run of bad fortune to make you feel compassionate towards a person, is there?' he frowned, looking Tom up and down. 'Poor little Abigail.'

Tom wasn't quite sure what the tweedy old soup-dribbler meant by that particular remark, but he was quite sure that he didn't like the implication.

'Well don't just stand there, come on in, son, come on in.'

Tom squeezed past his uncle's cast iron bulk and entered into the vestibule.

Frantic scrabbling noises came from the other side of the closed storm door. Tom waited nervously for Cornelius to finish locking the front one – which was no small task, since the enormous thing was covered from top to bottom in locks, bolts and catches. Tom's (good) eye was drawn, with first wonder and then horror, to the antique blunderbuss that was mounted over the doorframe and then to the umbrella stand – which was crammed not only with the odd umbrella and sturdy-looking walking stick, but also with wooden clubs, metal bars, at least four battle-axes, a brace of maces, what looked like a tomahawk, and a cricket bat with a wicked array of nails sticking through it.

Good grief! gasped Tom, swallowing hard and feeling slightly sick. *He's some sort of geriatric crime-lord! No wonder we never see him, he's probably in and out of prison ... or constantly on the run from Interpol!*

'You all right, son?' asked Uncle Cornelius, staring with a morbid fascination at Tom's uncontrollably winking orb, 'You look a little ... pale.'

'Er ... yes, Uncle. I ... er ... aye, I, eye ... I've just been poked in the eye by a horrible old lady. Bit shocked, that's all.'

''Ave you now?' enquired Cornelius, peering down with some concern. 'Looks all right to me. Best not to meep, son.'

Tom wasn't sure what "meeping" was, exactly, but it didn't sound like an activity that was looked upon kindly in this house, nor did he like the insinuation that he might be a "meeper" or one who "meeped".

'Oh, no. I'm fine, thank you,' he lied. 'Just thought I'd ... mention it, that's all.'

Uncle Cornelius smiled and opened the storm door.

Tom was immediately assaulted by an enormous grey dog the size of a pony. The monstrous beast hurtled forward, slammed both of its horrific front paws onto his shoulders (making Tom's legs buckle and his knees a-quiver) and began to lick him enthusiastically about the face.

'Aaaaghhh!' meeped Tom, wailing with near equal panic and disgust.

'Down you get, girl,' chuckled Uncle Cornelius, seizing the great hound by its collar and dragging her from the trembling wreck formally known as Tomas Dearlove. 'Now then, Bess, this 'ere's Tom. 'Es 'ere to stay with us for a while, 'e is,' he informed the bouncing, tail-lashing monster – whilst wagging a finger like a melted church candle in front of the giant dog's nose. 'You'll get used to 'er, Tom. Wouldn't 'urt a fly, would you, girl? Wolf'ound she is, Tom, right beauty an' all. Got any dogs yourself?'

Tom, wolfhound drool sliding from his chin and eye twitching like a rabbit's nose at a carrot-growers' convention, informed the callous old bastard that he didn't.

Thinking to restore some semblance of self-respect, he fumbled in his bag, drew out the (now slightly crumpled) box of Turkish Delight, and handed it awkwardly to the old man.

'A present ... from my Mum. A "thank you" ... for having me.'

Uncle Cornelius eyed the box suspiciously.

'Turkish Delight?' he sniffed. 'Gave a box identical to this one to your mother, only last Christmas. Didn't know you could get this make over 'ere. Yes, well, thank you very much. Very kind, I'm sure.'

He tucked the box under his arm while Tom forced a stale and mortified grin.

'This way then, son,' smiled Cornelius, briskly bouncing away and leading Tom into the hallway.

What a sprightly old codger, thought Tom to himself, benignly.

'Cojer-time,' cried Uncle Cornelius over his shoulder.

'You what?!' spurted Tom, having the instant horror that he had just been speaking his thoughts out loud.

'*Cojer-time* – old Sussex expression – means *lunchtime*. Now then, I reckons that you must be starving 'ungry after such a long journey, an' all.

'Missus Dobbs, the 'ousekepper, seems to be out at the moment – shopping I 'spect. She's very keen to meet you she is, Tom. Oh-ho, very keen. 'Ow's about I rustle us up some tucker? Egg an' sausages sound all right?'

Tom nodded.

'Why don't you go drop off your bag an' make yourself at 'ome, son. Your room's on the second floor up, third door on the right, next to the bathroom. I'll give you a shout when the grub's ready.'

Tom smiled weakly and nodded again.

'Thank you,' he managed to reply in a trembly voice, as Uncle Cornelius and Bess bounded down the hallway (presumably towards the kitchen).

Tom forced himself to take some deep breaths.

'Everything's just fine,' he tried to convince himself. 'It's all good. No need to panic.'

Wearily, he hoisted his bag to his shoulder and began his ascent up the long, crooked staircase.

Signed pictures and photographs of ancient boxers lined the wall. Tom read their names as he made his way upwards: *Gentleman* Jackson, Jem Belcher (*The Napoleon Of The Ring*), Henry Pierce (*The Game Chicken* – !?), John Gully, Jack Randall (T*he Nonpareil*), Dutch Sam, Tom Cribb and Tom Moulineux, Tom Spring, Young Dutch Sam, Nat Langham, Jem Mace, Billy Edwards, Peter Jackson, Bob Fitzsimmons, Albert Griffiths (*Young Griffo*), Joe Gans (*The Old Master*), '*Peerless*' Jimmy Driscoll, George Dixon, Jimmy Wilde (*The Ghost With A Hammer In His Hand*), Joe Walcott (*The Barbados Demon*), Packy Mcfarland, Sam Langford, Ted 'Kid' Lewis, Mike Gibbons (*The St Paul Phantom*), Gene Tunney, Harry Greb (*The Human Windmill*), Benny Leonard (*The Ghetto Wizard*), Tommy Loughran. Their faces seemed to scowl at him as he walked past.

'*Meeper!*' he imagined them crying out, accusingly.

Bog off! thought Tom, remembering his mother's sound advice to never listen to men dressed in tights.

By the time that he reached the foot of the second set of stairs, Tom felt decidedly out of breath and so decided to take a breather and study the huge portrait that loomed down at him from the top of the next flight. The painting was of a handsome and imposing middle-aged man, who sat with his head resting elegantly on one hand, garbed in (what Tom assumed to be) Elizabethan clothing, and sporting a long, aristocratic beard. The man's eyes conveyed a look of insatiable curiosity, accompanied by a striking and steadfast certainty of purpose.

'Henry Percy, Ninth Earl of Northumberland,' Tom read aloud, as he started up the stairs again. 'Hello Henry.'

The third step from the top creaked noisily beneath his foot and Tom tore his eyes from the Earl's hypnotic gaze, stopped and looked down.

Always worth remembering a creaking step, he thought to himself – the veteran of many a secret midnight jaunt whilst his mother slept, peacefully and unawares, in her bed.

When he looked up again he almost tumbled back down the staircase in fright, for he was eye-to-eye and nose-to-nose with a second ginormous hound. But where Bess had bounded and lolloped good-naturedly this one sat bolt upright, stock-still, ears erect, looking like some grotesque and carnivorous gargoyle.

The monstrous beast stared at him with unflinching and unfathomable black-rimmed, walnut-coloured and almond-shaped eyes.

Though obviously of the same(ish) breed as Bess, this dog was wheat-coloured (bar the almost reddish ears, with the faint hint of white spots on them) and appeared to be slightly smaller and stockier – and looked all the more dangerous for it.

'Good girl ... er boy?' offered Tom.

The hound stared at him with a look as unforgiving as rust.

'Come on now, out the way, you stupid old mutt.'

Another contemptuous and merciless stare, and then the giant dog reluctantly relaxed and lowered itself onto its elbows.

Tom took his opportunity and cautiously hurried past.

Along the landing he came to the third door, opened it and went in.

He was pleasantly surprised to find a very pleasant and surprisingly tidy room, furnished with a wooden chair and a large bed – with a multi-coloured bedspread draped over it – that looked like it hadn't been slept in since the Boer War. An immense (and immensely ugly) vase full of yellow flowers was perched on top of a small chest of drawers (*A nice but unnecessary touch*, thought Tom), over which was hung a yellowing engraving of yet another active-looking chap in tights.

Tom threw his bag down onto the chair and then tested the springs of the mattress.

Pretty good. To be honest – better than I'm used to.

Not a bad place to crash at all, if a little too 'Famous Five' for his liking. He would soon, he felt sure, be being offered *lashings of ginger beer*. The whole house seemed to be in some kind of bizarre time warp.

He sprawled across the bed for a moment and then sat up and peered out of the window, looking down onto the garden that he had just walked through. Perhaps the glass was warped, for the edges of his vision seemed a little blurred and he couldn't quite see beyond the garden walls. He also noted, with some curiosity, that the window had been nailed shut from the inside and that a thick line of chalk had been drawn around the frame. Probably, he concluded, some builder's mark to show that it needed replacing.

Tom got up from the bed and ambled over to the picture hanging on the wall. The muscular-looking man portrayed in said picture was sitting down, naked from the waist up, with what looked like a spotted scarf tied around his middle. Underneath the fading engraving it read – "*Tom Sayers, 'The Brighton Boy'. 1828-1865.*" He had a nice face, Tom thought, and looked far too kind to be much of a fighter.

'Hello, Tom,' said Tom, 'Nice to meet you. Looks like we'll be rooming together. My name's Tom, by the way.'

'Grubs up, Tom!' hollered Uncle Cornelius, and Tom, suddenly realising just how hungry he was, rushed downstairs – silently thankful that the great wheaten-coloured wolfhound was nowhere to be seen – in eager anticipation of a hot plateful of sausage and eggs.

Sitting at the large oak table in the enormous kitchen (which looked, as did the rest of the house, like the set from a BBC Victorian period drama), Tom – his eye having (thankfully) returned to some normality – finished the last of the sausages and drained dry a mug of hot, sweet tea. The food was wonderful. *Must be the sea air*, he thought.

During their meal Uncle Cornelius popped incessant questions at him – about his journey down (*What was there to be said about five hours of tedium? ... Really?*), school, and life at home in general – to which Tom replied as best he could without ever coming too near to anything like the truth.

Tom and his mother lived in what must be, Tom genuinely believed, the most desolate and isolated place in the country. Theirs was the only house for miles around: their nearest neighbour (the diminutive, doddering and decidedly stinky old tramp, Bob Goodfellow – along with his two psychotic dogs; the aptly named Nipper and Snapper [allegedly Airedale Terriers – but who looked more like the bizarre and alarming offspring from the mating of an ill-disposed teddy bear and a psychopathic alligator, who had then been raised on a diet of raw meat and illegal steroids]) being a good half-a-mile hike away. No shops, no cinema, no Internet, no nothing. Oh, how the long winter evenings flew by! School was little better, an unwelcome distraction at best: an hour's walk to pick up the school bus (assuming that his mum was unable to give him a lift, that is) followed by a further forty-minute bus ride to even get to the miserable place. In consequence, Tom rarely had the opportunity to establish and cement any lasting friendships on account of his constant travelling. It was, he concluded, a lonely existence and barely worth talking about.

Uncle Cornelius gave his last sausage to the grateful Bess – who had spent the whole meal gawking begrudgingly at their every mouthful with '*lost a pound and found a penny* eyes'.

'God 'elp us if they ever develop psychic powers,' chortled Cornelius, wiping his enormous whiskers with a napkin.

'Where's the other one?' asked Tom.

Uncle Cornelius raised an eyebrow.

'Oh, you've met 'im 'ave you?' he sniffed, distractedly. ''E'll be skulking 'bout somewhere, no doubt. Don't mind 'im, Tom. 'E's getting on now an' a bit of a grumpy so-an'-so in 'is old age. Bess 'ere, why, she's as friendly as a summer's day, but the old fellow likes best to be left alone, Tom, if you follow me.'

'Understood, Uncle,' replied Tom. 'What's his name anyway?'

'Eh? Oh, er ... Percy, I suppose. Not that 'e ever answers to that these days, mind. Bit deaf. Ah, 'ere comes Missus Dobbs.'

A pile of rubbish tottered into the kitchen on stick-thin legs buttressed by a pair of gargantuan hobnail boots. Actually, on second glance, it was a vast collection of shopping bags, boxes and packages supported by the tiny frame of a little old lady, her face hidden beneath the small mountain of groceries that she carried in her arms.

She sidled by, placed the bags down on the floor and turned to face them both.

Googly green eyes, as sweet as a summer orchard, beamed towards Tom.

'Tim,' she croaked warmly, holding out a gnarled, fat little hand.

'Tom,' said Uncle Cornelius.

'Tom,' cooed Missus Dobbs, her kindly orbs boring into Tom like two home-baked apple pies nestled over a crooked, toothless grin.

Tom felt his eye begin to twitch uncontrollably as he recoiled in horror from her approaching pointy claws. He snatched up his chair like a lion tamer and jabbed an accusing finger at her from behind it.

'You!' he hissed. 'You! You poked my eye!'

'Now, now, Tom,' tutted Uncle Cornelius.

'Hark at him, Professor,' gurned Missus Dobbs sweetly to the old man. (*He's a professor!* thought Tom.) 'Ooh, he's a one,' she cackled. 'No need to meep, Ducky.'

'Best just crack on,' chimed in Uncle Cornelius.

'Let me make you both a nice cup of tea,' she clucked.

Now it was Uncle Cornelius' turn to leap from his seat.

'NO! No, no. No need, Missus Dobbs. Ha ha. You get the shopping away an' I'll sort us all out with another brew. More tea, Tim?'

'Tom!'

'Tom.'

'Yes. Thank you. That would be ... *lovely*,' sneered Tom, curtly, lowering his chair and staring suspiciously at the wicked old hag.

'Right you are then, m'Ducks. I'll get this lot away in the pantry, er, I mean the ... re-frid-jor-ray-tor,' cackled Missus Dobbs, rolling the syllables around her gummy mouth like a giant gob-stopper, and looking at Uncle Cornelius as pleased as punch – rather like a small child who has just learnt a new word and is using it for the first time. Uncle Cornelius shot her a congratulatory wink. 'And then I'll get started on supper. Steak 'n' kidney pudding all right for you, Professor?'

'Lovely, Missus Dobbs.' beamed Uncle Cornelius, bristling with a look of pure pride. 'Lovely.'

Missus Dobbs busied herself with unpacking the shopping bags while Tom watched her like a hawk, expecting any minute for the evil old harridan to bimble over and scrape the heel of her savage-looking boot down his shin while no one was looking.

When she had momentarily pottered from the room under an armful of packages (all neatly wrapped in greaseproof paper), Uncle Cornelius sidled over to him and whispered urgently in his ear.

'Whatever you do, son, don't let her make you a cup of tea! Wonderful 'ousekeeper she is, but tea ain't 'er strong point. God knows she's tried, Tom, but she's never seemed to be able to quite get the 'ang of it.' And with that he lurched away and back to his tea-making duties just as Missus Dobbs returned to the room.

'Ooh, Tom,' she chortled, 'almost forgot. I got you some lovely bottles of ginger beer.'

'Smashing!' smiled Tom, as sarcastically as he dared.

THREE
THE STUDY

With teapot, strainer, and cups and saucers balanced precariously on a delicate silver tea tray, Uncle Cornelius led the way up the stairs to *The Study,* followed by Bess (bounding with perilous enthusiasm) and Tom (bringing up the rear with an apathetic mooch). On entering the room, the wolfhound artfully dived onto a large, comfortable-looking sofa and instantly made herself at home – sprawling out like an oil slick and leaving little space for anyone else to even think about sitting beside her. Uncle Cornelius placed the tray on the small table that stood before a magnificent fireplace, and then plonked himself down on a beautifully crafted leather armchair. Opposite this stood another armchair, identical in design but built to far more impressive proportions.

Tom made to sit down on the giant chair.

'Not there, Tom, if you don't mind,' frowned Uncle Cornelius.

'Oh? ... Sorry,' replied Tom, mid-squat, and (hovering like a guilt-ridden slalom skier) looked frantically around for an alternative. Bess thoroughly occupied the sofa (and he didn't fancy his chances of moving her!) so all that remained was a small, tatty footstool. Tom hastily retrieved said stool and gingerly placed it before the fireplace.

Trying to make himself comfortable, he took stock of his surroundings while Uncle Cornelius poured the tea. The room was high ceilinged (as was rest of the house) and painted a deep olive-green, with portraits and photographs (some of which, Tom couldn't help but notice, were intriguingly turned to face the wall) swarming in an effort to take over all available wall-space. At one end of the room was the largest bookcase that Tom had ever seen, crammed full of ancient-looking tomes with cracked leather spines (not a paperback in sight!). Against one corner stood a rather magnificent grandfather clock (ticking softly with an unerring and rather comforting resonant precision) and in another were propped a vintage banjo and a contraption that Tom could best describe as being a cross between a mandolin, a model pirate ship and a pasta-making machine. A row of battered filing cabinets lined another wall, on top of which stood a shiny and antique candlestick phone. And finally, perched majestically before a large bay window, stood a sturdy writing desk with various collections of files and papers scattered like an unruly sea around the island of an old-fashioned typewriter – on which was balanced a large, spiked metal ball-and-chain on a stick.

'There you go, son,' smiled Uncle Cornelius, handing Tom a cup and saucer. 'Your good 'ealth, an' 'ere's to a pleasant stay.'

'Uncle Cornelius?' asked Tom.

'Yes, Tom?'

'What, exactly, is it that you do? I mean ... no one seems to know ... anything much ... about ... what you ... do ... exactly.'

'Hhhmm,' replied Uncle Cornelius, sipping his tea and considering the implications of Tom's question carefully. 'Well, Tom, that's a fair enquiry.'

Tom waited for him to continue, but the old man seemed lost in thought and showed no inclination to speak any further on the subject.

'So...? What ... do you do?' Tom asked again, trying not to sound too irritating.

'Oh... Er ... This an' that ... mainly.'

Uncle Cornelius darted a hopeful glance towards Tom and, seeing that his answer was clearly inadequate, hastily sipped more tea.

'*This and that* ... being ...?'

'... Well, ... Tom, ... I suppose you would say that I am in the business of ... *security*.' The crafty old swine mumbled the word "security" very quickly and very quietly, but not nearly quickly or quietly enough to get past the eagle-eared Tom.

'Security!' gasped Tom, excitedly. 'What kind of security?'

'Oh, um ... *Prevention* ... *Detection* ... *Protection*. That sort of ... thing ...'

'Protection! Detection! Of what?' asked Tom, thoroughly enthralled.

'Well, Tom, ... sometimes ... *things* ... need to be found an' then ... returned.'

'*Things*? What sort of *things*?'

'*Things* that 'ave become ... lost ... An' ... er ... an' sometimes ... *things* ... that should 'ave stayed lost an' shouldn't 'ave been found in the first place. Or *things* that ... turn up where no ... *thing* ... has a right to be. When that 'appens then my, our, job is ... to put ... *things* ... right.'

Uncle Cornelius offered Tom a sprightly, slightly awkward smile and hurriedly slurped more tea.

'My, that's a lot of ... *things*,' mused Tom, utterly confused.

'Oh, you're right there, Tom, an' that's a fact. It is indeed ... a world full of ... *things*. Well now, listen to me rambling on,' continued the slippery old nudger, hastily. 'It's been a long old day, Tom. A rare old day. I think that we should be giving your mum a call, don't you? Tell 'er you got 'ere safely, like.'

'Yes. Yes I suppose we should,' muttered Tom, disappointed and frustrated to have the conversation so decisively swung away from him.

Uncle Cornelius pushed himself from his chair and glided over to the writing desk. He pulled open one of the many drawers and, after a moment of frantically scrabbling about, produced an antiquarian mobile phone the size of a large brick and an even more antique-looking address book. The old fellow held the phone at arm's length and eyed it suspiciously. After a long scrutiny he gingerly jabbed a button with a gnarled finger. The mobile phone trilled into life and Uncle Cornelius shot Tom a look of elated triumph. Having flipped open the leather-bound address book to the appropriate page, he then set about tapping in Tom's mum's phone number – pressing each digit as if he were slowly and deliberately squashing an unpleasant bug.

Having successfully entered the number, he tentatively held the phone to his ear.

'Oo! It's ringing,' he cried, sounding both surprised and delighted, and passed the phone to Tom as quickly as he possibly could.

' –llo?' said Tom's mum's voice. 'Hello? Who is this?'

'Hello, Mum, it's me.'

'Hello, Sweetie. How's everything? You get there all right?'

'Yes, Mum.'

'How's Uncle Cornelius? Did you give him the Turkish Delight?'

'Yes, Mum.'

'Listen, Tom, I'm just about to start my shift, so call me a bit later, when you get the chance. Be a good boy. And have fun!' she said, making it sound like a good-humoured order.

'Yes, Mum.'

'And, Tom ...'

'Yes, Mum?'

'... love you.'

'Love you too,' mumbled Tom, as the phone went dead.

'Everything all right there, then, son?' asked Uncle Cornelius, ensconced snugly back in his armchair.

Tom assured him that it was.

Bess snored loudly from the sofa.

'So, what would you like to do now, Tom?' asked his uncle, eyeing the slumbering hound enviously. 'Time for my afternoon nap, so you'll 'ave to amuse yourself for a bit, I'm 'fraid.'

Uncle Cornelius scrutinised his *nephew*, expectantly.

'Do you have a computer?' asked Tom.

'*Com-pew-tor* ...?' mused Uncle Cornelius. 'No.'

'A television?' Tom asked, with sinking dread.

'*Atelly-vision*? ... Let me see now.' The old fellow pulled his whiskers hard in thought. 'No.'

A gaping silence, as wide and as deep as their generation gap, stretched between them.

'Got a wireless,' Uncle Cornelius offered at last, hopefully.

'A what?'

'A wireless, you know a ... er ... what do you young'uns call 'em? ... Ah ... a 'ray-de-o'. One of them 'dig-it-all' whatnots. Test Match Special. Cracking stuff.'

Uncle Cornelius looked very pleased with himself until he saw Tom's forlorn expression.

'Why don't you take Bess for a walk?' the old man suggested. Bess popped open a hopeful eyelid and wagged her tail. 'No, 'ang it all. Can't do that.'

'No, I'd like to,' said Tom eagerly, but his uncle would have none of it.

'Storm's coming,' sniffed the old man. 'Best not to go out now, son.'

Tom looked out of the window onto a bright, cloudless sunny afternoon, and sighed inwardly.

'I know!' piped Uncle Cornelius. 'I'll have to forgo me nap, mind ... but ... let's play some cards! Got any money on you, Tom? No, no – forget that I said that!'

They whittled away the hours of the afternoon playing a game called 'Old Maid' – very easy to learn, Tom conceded, and surprisingly good fun. The only downside being that all attempts by Tom to question his elusive uncle further about his curious occupation were firmly side-stepped with a 'Not now, son, I'm thinking.'

Finally Missus Dobbs appeared and informed them that supper was ready.

Supper consisted of the afore-promised steak 'n' kidney pudding, which was strange to Tom's taste but not bad at all (if a little *heavy*), followed by a local delicacy called *Sussex Pond Pudding* (which was exactly the same thing as steak 'n' kidney pudding but with the steak and kidney replaced by a lemon and half a ton of brown sugar).

'I didn't put no tadpoles in it today, Ducky,' cackled Missus Dobbs.

To Tom's infinite relief, Uncle Cornelius informed him that the "tadpoles" where in fact currents and/or raisins.

When all was done, Tom and Uncle Cornelius waddled slowly – and with some considerable discomfort and difficulty – back up the stairs to The Study. Tom honestly thought that if he ate another mouthful he would explode. On reaching The Study he flopped to the floor in front of the fireplace, rubbing his bloated belly and resting his head against the footstool. He was (he was forced to admit) very tired, and he let out a long and gloriously lazy yawn.

"S'all that sea air. Sea air an' proper food. Not used to it, I 'spect,' chuckled Cornelius. 'Why don't you take yourself off to bed, son? Big day tomorrow. Early start, an' all that.'

'Would you mind if I borrowed a book?' asked Tom, who'd been eyeing the bookcase with some fascination since his first visit to the room earlier in the day.

'Course not, son. 'Elp yourself'

Tom rose slowly, tottered like a heavily pregnant woman over to the bookshelf, and began to peruse the shelves with a keen interest.

One group of shelves seemed to be dedicated to books concerned with ancient fencing – including such ripping page-turners as: "*His True Arte of Defence*" by Giacomo Di Grassi, "*Vincentio Saviolo; his practice*" by (unsurprisingly) Vincentio Saviolo, and "*The Academy of the Sword – The Mystery of the Spanish Circle in Swordsmanship and the Esoteric Arts*" by Girauld Thibault d'Anvers. Below these was a section concentrating on books about boxing and boxers – featuring such magnificent bedtime reads as: "*Scientific Boxing*" by Gentleman James J. Corbett, "*The Art of Boxing and Manual of Training*" by Billy Edwards, "*Physical Culture and Self Defence*" by Robert Fitzsimmons, "*Fifty Years a Fighter*" by Jem Mace, and "*Arms for a Living*" by Gene Tunney. Next up – row upon row of volumes with titles of unfathomable nonsense, among which nestled such international bestsellers as: "*Monas Hierolglyphica*" by Dr John Dee, Giordano Bruno's "*De Vinculis in Genere*", "*Artis Analyticae Praxis*" by Thomas Hariot, and Robert Hues' all-time classic "*Tractactus De Globis Et Eorun Usu*". And then, finally, on the left-hand side of the bookcase, the titles took an even more bizarre turn – including such literary wonders as: "*The Rise & Decline of the Great Troll Dynasties of*

Western Europe – 910-1463" by G. Gillespie Livermore, "*The Book of Spell Recognition*" by Dame *Ginty* Parsons, "*Werewolves, Warlocks & Wampyres*" by Professor Viktor Von Vasso, "*In Search of Ailuranthropes*" by Dr Walter Octavius Hyslip-Campbell, "*The Ungrateful Undead: My Life as a Familiar*" by Dr S. Benedict Walsh, "*Greymorris' Field Guide to Monsters (updated edition with extended appendix and new introduction) – 1982*".

Tom pulled out the weighty "*Werewolves, Warlocks & Wampyres*" (mainly because it had a picture of a cool-looking monster on the spine) and idly flicked through it. The book flopped open at page one hundred and seventy-two.

Alongside a series of detailed sketches, the text began –

Were-Wolves & other Were-Beasts

Of all the monsters that continue to haunt our world and our imagination, the Were-wolf is certainly among the most terrifying, persistent and powerful. Confirmed sightings have become ever more rare over the last one hundred and fifty years – with the exception of certain parts of Eastern Europe (see page 213), the afore-mentioned 'organised packs' of New England, and the Ulfhedinn of Sweden (see Appendix iii.). However, those in our profession must be ever alert to the possibilities of an encounter with such dangerous and cunning qua...

The book was gently plucked from his fingers and snapped shut by Uncle Cornelius.

'You don't want to be reading that one, son. Give yourself nightmares,' he smiled. ''Ow 'bout this?'

The old man handed Tom a brick-sized book with a faded brown hardcover that had a crown and the letter "L" embossed in gold on the front.

'Cracking read ... as far as it goes.'

Tom turned the book in his hand and opened it.

The Lonsdale Library
Volume XI
BOXING
A Guide to Modern Methods by Viscount Knebworth
With a contribution by W. Childs, Coach to the Cambridge University Boxing Club.
With over fifty
ILLUSTRATIONS
London
1931

'Er ... Yeah ... that looks ... uhm ... *thrilling? ...*' winced Tom, carefully closing the book and trying to mask his abject disappointment. 'Thank you.'

Uncle Cornelius beamed warmly at him and ruffled his hair.

'G'arn then, off to bed with you, you young rascal. An' don't be up reading for too long. Big day tomorrow, we 'ave. Early start. You'll be needing a good night's sleep.'

Tom bade the old lunatic goodnight and crawled his way up the stairs and to his bedroom, the book tucked firmly under his arm.

Twenty minutes later and Tom was lying on his bed staring at the ceiling and mulling over the peculiar events of the day (whilst trying to digest a serious overdose of suet pudding). His uncle was clearly some sort of criminal, but he couldn't help but like the eccentric old duffer. Even so, as eventful and weird as the day had been, he was feeling more than a little homesick. Lying on this antique bed, in this bizarrely old-fashioned room, in this strange and crooked house (mystifyingly hidden in the heart of this busy, bustling city), he was overwhelmed with uncertainty and not a little fear.

Going to be a funny few weeks, he thought to himself.

Struggling to sleep, he reached out for and randomly opened "*The Lonsdale Book of Boxing*, 1931". His eyes rolled down the page and were caught by the lines –

> *The greatest welter weight of all time, and a really great boxer, was the American, Joe Walcott. That is, if the days of the prize ring are excluded. For there was probably never anyone so good as Tom Sayers.*

Tom rested the book gingerly on his drum-like stomach (wincing a little as he did so) and looked over to the portrait hanging above the chest of drawers.

Flicking through the book again he was surprised to come across a reproduction of the very same picture.

"*Tom Sayers*" it read underneath. "*Born at Brighton in 1828, Sayers did not weigh more than 10 st. 8 lbs., yet he fought and beat all the best heavy-weights of his day.*"

'That must have been quite something, Tom,' he said softly to the portrait, with a genuine admiration. 'I wish I had half the courage that you had.'

And with that thought he rolled over and sank into a deep and heavy slumber.

FOUR
The Perilous Art Of Eavesdropping

Tom was woken by the noise of the storm. (So the old fellow *had* been right – eventually.) Rain pattered against the window like fiercely drummed fingernails, and a torrid wind whistled eerily through the nooks and crannies of the crookedy old house. He lay listening to the rhythm of the storm for a while and then decided that he could do with a drink of water. Flicking on the antique bedside lamp (which hummed slowly, and possibly unwillingly, into life) Tom made his way to the bathroom for a few gulps of ice-cold, slightly chalky-tasting water from the bulbous and vintage taps.

He was about to return to his bed when he heard the sound of two voices coming from The Study downstairs. It wasn't quite an argument, more of a scolding really, and from the sound of it Uncle Cornelius was the one being reprimanded.

Tom was down the stairs in a flash (being careful to avoid *creaky step number three*) and, crouching against the banister, held his breath in wide-eared anticipation as he strained to listen to the conversation.

'This is an intolerable inconvenience, Dandy,' barked the stranger – in a voice that was impossibly deep and with the short, clipped tones of a 1930s BBC newsreader. 'Intolerable. Have you any idea how much this compromises me?'

'Well, I'm truly sorry for that,' sniffed Uncle Cornelius, 'but it can't be 'elped. What's done is done.'

'And just how long is he going to be staying here?' asked the stranger, in an exasperated tone.

Good grief! realised Tom, *They're talking about me!*

He strained his ears even harder.

'Just the school 'olidays ... initially.'

There was a short pause and then the stranger's voice exploded.

'Initially! What do you mean – *initially*!?'

'Keep your voice down!' hissed Uncle Cornelius. Then he seemed to relax a little. 'Look, sit down, 'Aitch, shut up, an' pass me that bottle. There's something that I've been meaning to talk to you about.'

There was a dull clinking sound of glass on glass, followed by glugging.

'Well?' demanded the stranger.

'Listen, 'Aitch,' sighed Cornelius, taking his time and obviously choosing his words carefully, 'I'm getting old. I'm not as good as I once was. I'm slowing down. Past me best.'

He was curtly cut short.

'Nonsense, Dandy! I saw the look on that old knucker's face when you clocked him with that famous right hand of yours last Tuesday. He didn't know what decade he was in. It will be a good while before he sticks *his* head above water again, I can assure you. No, no need to fear there, old stick. You've still got the old magic. Best right-cross since John L. Sullivan – I've always said it and I still believe it to be true.'

Uncle Cornelius chortled. 'So *shake the 'and what shook the 'and of the great John L* (despicable rogue that 'e was, mind).'

There was the light clinking of glasses and then Uncle Cornelius continued, returning to a more serious tone.

'Well that's all very kind of you to say so, 'Aitch, but I knows m'self ... an' I can feel it. I'm getting on. Wearing out. Pretty soon I'll be a liability ... No, hear me out! Now, I knows that I'm fitter an' 'ealthier than any man my age 'as any right to be – an' I'm grateful for that, I truly am – but it can't go on forever. We needs to be thinking 'bout the future. The time is fast approaching when you'll be needing someone to take over from me, an' so why not start that process as soon as we can?'

There was a long, unsettling silence.

'You can't possibly mean Tim?'

'Tom,' replied Uncle Cornelius. 'An' yes, I do.'

'But have you seen that nervous facial tick? I'm not sure that the lad has it in him.'

Tom racked his brain trying to think of anybody else that he'd met since arriving at this madhouse.

'That's no nervous tick. Missus Dobbs gave 'im the old *Wodin Poke* earlier on.'

'*Wodin Poke*?' mouthed Tom in silent confusion, as his eye suddenly began to flutter uncontrollably.

'I believe that 'e's a good lad, 'Aitch,' his uncle continued. 'A stout lad, 'less I'm mistaken. Just what's needed.'

'But he's so young,' the stranger (*Aitch*? *Haitch? H*?) protested.

'Yes, 'e is. An' that, as you very well know, is what 'as protected 'im so far. But what 'appens when 'e reaches 'is majority, I ask you? Can't 'ide the lad away in the middle of nowhere forever, now, can we?'

'I am very well aware of that. But just think for a moment. Just consider the trouble that this could bring our way.'

'Well you've ain't never been one to avoid trouble – an' neither 'ave I. No, 'Aitch, I've thought this through an' it's for the best. We knew very well what we was doing fourteen years back when this 'ole sorry mess 'ad to be sorted out. Now it's time to take responsibility for what was done an' pick up the slack, so to speak. So we'll take 'im in. Teach 'im the ropes. Apprentice 'im, if you will.

I've spoken to Abigail 'bout it an' she's more than 'appy with the arrangement. Take a load off 'er mind, an' that's a fact.'

Tom almost squealed – his mouth a perfect circle of indignation and horror.

'Oh, Dandy. I'm just not sure about this,' growled *Aitch*.

'Well I am. 'E's my blood, 'Aitch. 'E's Abigail's boy. An' that should count for something. An' where's safer for 'im to be than 'ere, where we ... where *you* ... can protect 'im.'

'Protect 'im ... him!' hissed Tom to himself, squeaking from both ends. 'Protect him from what?'

'So what now? I'm just to *reveal* myself am I? Well what better way to convince the lad that "*it is indeed a world full of ... things*"? Brilliant!' scoffed the stranger, sarcastically.

'Oh, so you was eavesdropping was you? Wondered what you was up to.'

Aitch snorted.

'You've done it before,' Uncle Cornelius continued, curtly. 'You know 'ow to 'andle these kind of *things* better than I do. Now, I'm off to bed. Good night!'

'I'm not happy about this, Dandy. Dandy! ... Dandy?' the stranger pleaded.

Tom heard his uncle's footsteps approaching The Study door and silently bolted back up the stairs like a startled moorhen (carefully avoiding aforementioned *creaking step number three*), making it back to his bed and flicking off the flickering lamp before Uncle Cornelius had begun his ascent of the second flight.

He listened to the old man's surprisingly light tread, and heard him pause momentarily outside the bedroom door.

Cornelius gave a heavy sigh and then headed upstairs towards his own room.

Tom lay in his bed, his heart racing and his eyes wide-open, not knowing what to think.

Tomorrow, he promised himself, *tomorrow he'd make the conniving old rogue answer every blooming question that he had, or he'd run back home on the first train that he could get on!*

Home?

Home to his mother, who'd willingly agreed to have him "apprenticed" to a geriatric crime lord? Home to a place that was deemed 'unsafe' by his wicked old uncle and his mysterious partner?

The world was falling apart.

Outside a bolt of lightning cracked the sky open and the rain pounded even harder against the window, like a monster trying to claw its way inside.

But the windows are nailed shut, Tom reminded himself. *Ain't nothing getting in.*

Nor, he realised with mounting horror, nothing getting out.

FIVE
The Muse-asium

'Wakey-wakey, Ducky. Shake a leg.'

Tom startled out of a deep sleep to find himself staring into the rheumy green orbs of Missus Dobbs, as she loomed over him, gurning with a terrifying joyfulness. He stifled a cry of horror as his eye began to flutter like an electrocuted chaffinch, while she busied herself putting down a mug and flinging open the curtains.

'Made you a lovely cup of tea, Ducks. The Professor's waiting for you down in the basement. He gave me these for you to put on.'

She indicated a pile of neatly folded garments under a pair of ancient-looking plimsolls at the end of his bed.

'Ten minutes, mind, or I'll be back to dress you myself,' she chortled, as she bimbled jovially from the room.

That thought alone was enough to make Tom spring out of bed like an invigorated salmon. He peered bleary-eyed out of the window. The storm had abated but it was still pitch-black outside. He looked down at his wristwatch. Five-thirty.

Five thirty! Good grief! What kind of people would do such a thing?

Absent-mindedly he picked up the mug, took a sip and immediately retched it back out.

Spewed tea hit the windowpane like a bucket of bilge water hurled by a burly seaman. Tom gagged painfully.

'Everything all right in there, Ducky?' peeped Missus Dobbs.

'Yes, ... Missus Dobbs,' he wheezed. '*Smashing*.'

'Don't keep the Professor waiting now, Ducky. He's very keen to get started.'

Oh is he? thought Tom, with vicious indignation. *Well, whatever he's got in mind, he's in for some hard interrogation and no mistake.*

He eyed the pile of clothing at the end of the bed suspiciously and, hearing Missus Dobbs loitering about in the hallway, decided to get changed and on his way as quickly as he possibly could.

Three minutes later Tom was standing in the basement doorway, his eyes wide with amazement. He was dressed – much to his embarrassment (but who was going to see him, so what the hell!) – in an enormous pair of billowing maroon-coloured shorts (that flapped majestically around his skinny knees), a vast grey vest (that, when tucked into said shorts, stuck out beneath the legs-holes of said shorts like the folds of a milkmaid's petticoat) and a pair of ancient plimsolls that resembled two hard-boiled eggs.

He felt, to put it politely, like a prize twit.

The sight of the basement, however, was enough to stop him feeling so self-conscious and make him gawk with an impressed awe.

It was a gigantic room – that must have run not only the whole length of the house but probably stretched out far beyond on either side. His eye was briefly drawn to one dark corner in which there appeared to be a Wild West-style gaol! However, the whole room could perhaps best be described as being somewhere between a museum and a gymnasium (a "mym" or perhaps a "muse-asium"?). Antique training equipment was dotted about willy-nilly – decrepit-looking punchbags; ropes; various sets of, what looked like, tenpin bowling pins; not to mention a full-size boxing ring(!) – while a small armoury of vicious-looking weapons hung on the walls, glistening like hungry bats.

Standing in another corner, mounted on a colossal wooden frame, was a huge, misshapen suit of armour after the fashion of a Conquistador (that had, quite clearly, been made for a deformed giant). Tom stumbled forward, coming to stand, gape-mouthed, before an enormous sword – the blade of which was wider than his fist and almost as tall as he was, with curling hoops and bars at the hilt.

'Morning, Tom,' chirped Uncle Cornelius, cheerfully. 'Step away from the sword, son. Let's not be 'asty. Body first – weapons later. Get a good night's sleep, did we?'

Tom narrowed his eyes and shot the evil old swine a withering look.

Uncle Cornelius was bobbing around, dressed in black vest and tights (ha!), rolled-down white socks and dainty black leather ankle-boots. His feet seemed to kiss the ground like leaves caught in an autumnal gust, as his arms (like slabs of marble crafted by an over-enthusiastic one-eyed Greek sculptor) pumped the air like pistons, and his head bobbed back and forth and from side to side like a nodding-dog car ornament being driven at high speed over cobbles.

'Look at you, Tom,' he beamed, 'smart as paint. All raring to go then?'

'Uncle, could I talk with you for one moment?'

'Course you can, Tom – after we've finished our session. Best way to start the day, eh? Get the body an' mind sorted. Busy day a'ead, son. Come on, lad, bit of shadow boxing. Follow my lead. Let's get moving!' barked Uncle Cornelius gleefully, and Tom, seeing that the old git was not to be distracted, forced himself to whip out his skinny arms in a woefully pathetic display of enthusiasm.

'Come on, son. Put some vim into it!' snapped the old man, looking on with an expression of concerned disappointment.

And then Tom heard him mutter 'God 'elp us if the Germans ever kick off again,' under his breath.

Right then, he thought, *I'll show you, you wicked old scoundrel!* And he flung himself into the task, flailing his arms about as quickly as he could, head held back and tongue sticking out in concentration.

'That's the ticket, son,' chuckled the old man, skipping around Tom like a Whirling Dervish who's eaten too many red Smarties. 'Smart straight-left, Tom. Right 'and tucked in tight an' 'igh. An' keep them jooks moving.'

Apparently a "jook", Tom learned later, was a clenched fist: hence the expression "*put your jooks up*" not "*put your Dukes up*" – which is what Tom had always thought that belligerent cowboys said when challenging each other to fist fights in black and white Westerns (rather confusingly, it has to be admitted – who, after all, carries a collection of European aristocracy around with them [well, by choice anyway]?).

After what felt like a good half hour of shadow-boxing, Uncle Cornelius decided it was time for a proper warm up. (*Warm up!?!* wheezed Tom to himself. *Then what the frickin' Hell had they just been doing?!*) Stretches, jumps, and floor exercises (which involved lying on the floor – a promising start soon ruined by the abject disappointment and agony of having to pump, hold, lift and twist his legs in all manner of unnatural directions).

'Right then, Tom, done any *Milling*?' grinned his uncle, keenly (and not even slightly out of breath).

Tom, the very picture of youthful athletic dignity, forced himself to look up from his position of resting his hands on his knees and gasping like a fifty-a-day smoker, to see his uncle standing with one foot on the bottom rope of the boxing ring whilst hoisting its neighbour on high with a ham-sized hand and beckoning Tom to enter with the other. The heartless old bastard was beaming heartily, as if he were inviting Tom to enter Santa's grotto.

'Eh?'

'Fisticuffs, lad. The Sweet Science. Boxing.'

Tom politely informed the callous old cretin that he hadn't. (In fact, he'd never so much as even got into any sort of fight. Being an outsider at school, he'd soon learnt the invaluable life-lesson of being as invisible as he possibly could and had, in consequence, generally been left alone.)

Uncle Cornelius threw two antique, brown leather boxing gloves at him.

'Not a fan of the mufflers m'self,' he twittered, 'tend to teach a chap too many bad 'abits. But still, don't think your mum would thank me too much if we sent you 'ome with a broken nose now, would she.'

The old swine flashed an unbearably jovial grin and put on a pair of equally ancient-looking gloves.

Tom slipped his hands into the gloves. They were soft, warm and unpleasantly damp, but all he was thinking, as he glowered at the gurning old villain, was – *My mother? My mother, who'd sell me down the river like some Dickensian urchin to this ... this ... this modern day Fagin, what would she care?!*

Tom stepped between the ropes with a look of grim determination engraved on his face.

The old man bounced in after him.

'Now then, son, the secret of pugilism is in the 'ips an' feet. Keep moving an' keep the 'ands in position, with the elbows tucked in nice an' tight. Use the shifting of the 'ole body to get power, an' punch from where the jooks are; don't be pulling them back. Right then, Tom, off we go. Try an' 'it me.'

With pleasure, thought Tom, his face morphing into an expression of righteous and wicked retribution.

Uncle Cornelius bobbed and weaved like a battling top, calling out encouragement and pearls of confusing advice. 'Weight on the back foot, Tom, that's the spirit. Oo – that was a good one, son, almost shaved me whiskers, ha-

ha. No, no, no! For 'Eaven's sake don't crouch down, lad! We don't want none of that American nonsense.'

Tom flailed away savagely, but, try as he might (and he tried with all his might), he couldn't have hit the infuriating old codger with a handful of rice.

Right then, thought Tom, behind a wheezing grimace of frustration, *let's see what you make of this, you shifty old duffer!* And with that, he swiftly spun around and aimed his best roundhouse kick (as executed by all his favourite martial arts and action-movie heroes) at his uncle's midriff.

He couldn't be sure if he'd actually blacked out or not, but the next thing he remembered was looking up at his uncle's concerned and perplexed face.

'We'll 'ave none of that French skulduggery 'ere, son. Get yourself killed trying that sort of thing.'

Tom hauled himself gingerly to his feet and immediately hurled himself forward, lashing out a clubbing right hand to Cornelius' face ... only for the blow to be parried with a sharp and impossibly pointy elbow, before the old man skipped lightly forward and gently sunk a sledgehammer-sized fist into the pit of the poor lad's stomach.

Tom collapsed like a crushed beach ball and melted towards the floor, gasping for a breath that he was incapable of taking.

'The old *Fitzsimmons shift,* Tom. Good lad was old Bob. Crafty bugger. Out of the very top drawer 'e were. Used that very blow to take out that old rake, *Gentleman Jim,* for The Title, he did. Teach it to you tomorrow, son. Well, that's enough of that for today.'

'Oh thank the gods,' gasped Tom 'Thank you ... thank you,' though the words were unintelligible, on account of his having no air in his lungs.

'Right! On with some skipping,' cried Cornelius, vaulting over the ropes with maniacal enthusiasm.

'You have got to be kidding!' sobbed Tom, as a surprisingly hefty and tattered leather jump rope plopped heavily on his head.

He dragged himself up using the ring-ropes for support.

'Skipping?' he gasped.

'Does wonders for the footwork, son,' chimed Uncle Cornelius, who was bounding over the canvas floor like a six-legged cat on hot-plate – accompanied by the sound of a high pitched whirling as he twirled the rope so quickly that it was practically invisible.

Tom tried a few unsuccessful attempts of his own, looking like a three-legged nag with gout in a steeple-chase, while his uncle jauntily bounced around him, singing –

'Oh it really is a very pretty garden
An' Chingford to the Eastward could be seen
Wiv a ladder an' some glasses
You could see to 'Ackney Marshes
If it wasn't for the 'ouses in between.'

I hate you! thought Tom.

After several eternities of pain – from both the attempted jumping and the regular whippings received from his own rope to the legs and back of the head – his uncle mercifully called a halt to proceedings and helped Tom from the ring, where he stood gasping and a-meeping, with jelly-arms and jelly-legs, in a completely wretched state.

'Punchbag!' announced Cornelius, gleefully, as he chaperoned Tom's husk to stand before a gnarled-looking, long leather bag of spite and malevolence. 'Good for the arms. Good for the wind. Strengthen you up, son. Don't 'it the bottom of the bag, though,' cautioned his uncle, sagely, 'on account that it's a bit old an' all the sawdust 'as settled to the bottom.'

Tom, with 'bag-mitts' encasing his tender hands, tried a few feeble punches and felt his forearms buckle under the impact.

'Go on, son,' enthused the malicious old swine, ''it it! 'It it!'

Next, the *Indian Clubs* – which were the bowling-pin-like implements that Tom had noticed earlier. While Tom could barely lift the wretched things, his uncle twirled his about like a cocktail-barman having an epileptic fit.

After fifteen minutes' worth of stretches for a warm-down, Cornelius finally called an end to this hellish misery.

Tom seeped to the ground like a drunkard's vomit.

'We'll call it a day there, son, seeing as it's your first go an' all,' sniffed Cornelius, having the audacity to sound slightly disappointed. 'We'll carry on tomorrow, though. You did good, Tom. Showed a lot of bottom there, son. Can't ask more than that.'

Damn these shorts, thought Tom, though he hurt too much and was too exhausted to feel any more embarrassment. (Later he would learn, much to his relief, that his uncle used the word "*bottom*" to describe *pluck, spirit, grit* and *courage*.)

'Jump upstairs an' 'ave a shower an' then I'll meet you in the kitchen for breakfast in twenty minutes,' chirped Cornelius. And with that, the old codger bounced up the steps, three at a time (with a pristine white towel tucked jauntily under his arm) warbling to himself in a sprightly fashion –

'An' 'Endon to the Westward could be seen
An' by clinging to the chimbley
You could see across to Wembley
If it wasn't for the 'ouses in between ...'

Tom lay in a wrecked heap on the floor, panting furiously.

His only thought, as he watched the jovial old swine bounding effortlessly up the stairs, was – *You vicious, sadistic old bastard.*

Twenty minutes later found Tom seated at (and with forehead slumped upon) the kitchen table, feeling as if all his bones had been surgically sucked out of his body.

Having managed to haul himself up the stairs like an inebriated serpent, he had forced himself into the shower (ice-cold – the bloody merciless sadist!), determined to make sure that he was ready and waiting to give his wicked-old-goat-of-an-uncle the grilling of a lifetime.

Bess lay expectantly at his feet, wagging her tail in anticipation, whilst trying to give the impression that she had just been passing through and decided that she'd sit a little while beside her dear old pal.

Missus Dobbs tottered in carrying a collection of silver dishes, and arranged them neatly on the table.

'Breakfast's ready, Professor!' she hollered towards the stairway.

To which came the hasty reply – 'Don't worry about the tea, Missus Dobbs. I'll get that!' from Uncle Cornelius.

'How'd it go then, Ducky?' asked Missus Dobbs, sympathetically, addressing Tom as if he'd just returned from a dress rehearsal for his own funeral.

Tom wearily raised his head and smiled humourlessly.

'Nice breakfast'll sort you out, Ducks,' she gurned, pointing to each dish in turn. 'Hearts. Kidneys. Liver. Build your strength up.'

Good grief! gasped Tom, unable to disguise the gagging sound that emitted from his mouth.

Missus Dobbs watched him with a look of hurt and utter bewilderment.

Tom felt a pang of remorse, despite himself.

'Do you have anything else? I'm not feeling too well. Cereal, perhaps?'

Missus Dobbs chewed her whiskery lip and studied the ceiling.

'Got some of them there *corn flakes*,' she offered, doubtfully.

'Cornflakes would be marvellous, Missus Dobbs. Thank you.'

The tiny hag trotted off and returned, with an alarming rapidity, clutching a greying box of cornflakes (that looked like it had last seen action during the D-Day celebrations) and a jug of milk.

Tom poured the cereal into his bowl. The flakes slopped down with a wet squelching sound, landing like homeless whelks.

His stomach churned and lurched into his throat.

Missus Dobbs poured lashings of milk on top of them, presumably, Tom thought, to make sure that the bloody things were drowned before being eaten.

'Er, Missus Dobbs ...'

'Yes, Ducky?'

'This milk's warm.'

'Course it is, Ducky, its milk.'

'Don't you keep it in the fridge?'

Missus Dobbs looked worried and confused.

'Er, I mean the re-frid-jor-ray-tor.'

'Whatever for, Ducks?'

'Oh? Er ... no. No, never mind. Just a thought.'

Missus Dobbs scuttled from the room and Tom quickly offered his bowl to the optimistically eager Bess. As he was doing so, the old yellow dog, Percy, entered the room. Tom reached out his hand to give him a stroke but the rangy mutt gave him an indignant look and curled his lip.

'Don't mind 'im, Tom,' sniffed Uncle Cornelius, carrying in a large shiny brown teapot. 'Miserable old sod 'e is these days. Don't know quite what's gotten into 'im. Thinking of 'aving 'im neutered, I am.'

The old man and the dog seemed to swap a frosty look as his uncle sat down and helped himself to large quantities of various semi-cooked organs.

Right, thought Tom, slyly. *Now that I've got you, you horrible old thing, let's see how you play this hand.*

'Uncle?' he asked, sweetly.

'Yes, Tom?'

'Are you a criminal?'

A half-eaten kidney flew silently across the room and was instantly pounced upon and snaffled by Bess.

'Whatever do you mean, Tom?' spluttered the old man. ''Oo gave you such an 'orrible notion as that?'

The old git did, Tom had to reluctantly admit, sound more than a little hurt.

'Well, it's just that you seem so very secretive about what you do, and well, you know, I was just wondering. I don't mind if you are. Be quite cool really.'

'Well you bloody well should mind!' snapped his uncle. 'There's nothing "cool" about it, Tom. An' for the record, I am most certainly not a criminal. In fact I'm the exact opposite.'

'So are you some sort of policeman? What with all that *detection and protection* malarkey?' pursued Tom, cunningly.

'No, you're not listening, son. I told you, I'm the opposite of a criminal.'

Tom was a little confused by his uncle's answer.

The old man busied himself picking up the immaculately pressed newspaper that was placed by the side of his plate, and curtly and loudly and deliberately unfurled it, firing a disappointed scowl in Tom's direction as he did so.

Round two, thought Tom. *The elephant in the room.*

Tom knew absolutely nothing about his father. Over the years all his attempts to find out anything about him had been fumbled clumsily aside by relative and family friend alike. On the few occasions that he'd asked his mum, she would simply take him in her arms and say "Oh, Tom ..." and then start sobbing. In consequence he'd stopped asking but, naturally, he remained inquisitive. And he was sure that Uncle Cornelius knew the answers.

'Uncle Cornelius?' began Tom, casually.

'Yes, Tom?'

'Mum said that you'd tell me about my father,' he lied.

'No she didn't,' came the immediate response.

'Did you know him?'

'No.'

'What was his name?'

Uncle Cornelius took a deep breath from behind his broadsheet. 'Don't know. Jim, Jack, John – something like that. Can't rightly remember.'

Liar! thought Tom. *Liar, liar, liar! All right then, you slippery old eel, let's see how you handle this one ...*

'Uncle Cornelius?' asked Tom, as innocently as he possibly could.

'Yes, Tom, what is it now?'

'What's a *Wodin Poke*?'

'... A what?' came the high-pitched squeak from behind the wobbling newspaper.

'A Wodin Poke,' repeated Tom, gleefully.

Uncle Cornelius lowered his paper slowly and fixed Tom with a fearsome glare.

'An' where did you 'ear such a phrase as that? 'Ave you been eavesdropping, Tomas Dearlove?'

'And what if I 'ave ... I mean – have!' cried Tom, rising from his seat and making Bess startle backwards. 'What if I have?'

'Well if you 'ave,' growled the old fellow, with a rueful shake of his head, glancing fleetingly at the great yellow hound (who was sitting like a massive gargoyle and suddenly staring inquisitively at the pattern on the carpet with large sad eyes the colour of ancient walnuts), 'if you 'ave, then I suppose that it just about changes everything.'

SIX
The Ear-Shaped Eye-Stone

'Now, Tom, you've a right to feel aggrieved, no question 'bout it, but just 'ear me out a minute,' said Uncle Cornelius, trying to calm Tom down.

Tom reluctantly sat back down, glowering his full frustration and anger (with brilliant effect) at the kidney dish.

'Don't know 'ow much you 'eard last night, nor 'ow you 'eard it, but I'm sure that what you did 'ear must 'ave sent your 'ead a-spinning. Now, I've no doubt that you got all manner of questions, an' I'll give you all the answers that I can – in time. But I'm going to ask that you believe me when I say that everything that 'as been done, 'as been done with your best interest at 'eart. Your mother, Abigail, God bless 'er, she loves you very much, Tom, an' all she wants is for you to be safe, that's all.'

'Safe from what?' snapped Tom.

'Safe from being too sharp for your own good, that's what,' sighed Uncle Cornelius. 'Small steps, son. One bit at a time.'

'All right. Who were you talking to last night?'

'My ... er ... business partner.'

'He didn't sound very keen on the idea of me being here.'

'Bit of a shock, that's all. Things ain't as straightforward as they could be, Tom. 'E'll come round, though. I'm sure 'e will.'

'So, are you going to tell me anything at all?' rasped Tom with frustration. 'And why was he calling you *Dandy*?'

Uncle Cornelius grinned.

'Well, when I was a young fellow, Tom, I was a bit of a dresser, you might say; sharp clothes an' whatnot – tie pins, fancy 'ats an' silver-'eaded canes. Bit of a flash cove really. A "dandy" some might 'ave called me. An' they did. Dandy. Dandy-Lyons. *Dandylyons. Dandelions.* You know, like the flower.'

Tom snorted, humourlessly.

'Anything else I should know, "*Professor*"?'

The old yellow hound slowly hauled itself from the floor and sauntered casually from the kitchen.

Uncle Cornelius watched its departure with what might have been a look of envy, took a deep breath and stroked his ample whiskers.

'Tom, I'm going to ask you to trust me for the moment an' be patient. There's a task that I'd like you to do. 'Elp us all out.'

'A task? What task? Would you like me to hold your hat and coat while you beat the living daylights out of some poor impoverished squatters?'

'No I would not!' barked Uncle Cornelius, looking more than a little mortified. Then he beamed gloriously and produced a plastic bucket and spade from under the kitchen table. 'We're going to the seaside. Ha-ha!'

‘I’m a little old for a sandcastles, don’t you think?’ sneered Tom sarcastically, slightly offended but growing a little pleased at the thought of getting out of this infuriating madhouse.

‘Bucket and spade’s for Bess, Tom. She’s a big girl and, well ... it’s just not right to leave a mess, is it.’

‘We’ll take the back route,’ suggested Uncle Cornelius, struggling to get Bess (who was quivering with excitement like an overwound clockwork hopper) still enough, long enough to put her collar on.

‘What about Percy?’ Tom asked.

‘Oh no, we’ll leave ’im ’ere. Miserable old sod. Wouldn’t enjoy it any’ow. ’E can sulk ’bout in the garden, if ’e’s a mind.’

Uncle Cornelius marched purposefully along the hallway and then stopped in front of the door of the understairs cupboard.

‘This way, Tom,’ he chortled, as he opened the door and ducked inside, squeezing himself through the slender opening.

Slightly bewildered, but not totally surprised (this was, after all, he was rapidly coming to realise, a nuthouse full of the rarest of nuts), Tom tentatively followed his uncle.

They stood under the stairs, huddled together in near total darkness like prematurely tinned sardines – tweed-suited, mutton-whiskered, eccentric lunatic; enormous, over-excited, tail-lashing and giggling wolfhound; scowling, mightily miffed thirteen year old boy, muttering ‘Why me?’ to himself.

Uncle Cornelius mumbled, and fumbled through his jacket pockets.

‘Ah! Got ‘em!’ he exclaimed, pulling out a set of ancient-looking keys and jangling them with theatrical delight in front of Tom’s startled visage.

‘Well come on then!’ chuckled Cornelius, disappearing through a small door that had mysteriously appeared at the back of the cupboard.

Lights were flicked on and Tom, intrigued and excited despite all his misgivings, followed after him.

He found himself standing at the top of a large wooden spiral staircase, that seemed to descend, at a leisurely angle, for an eternity. Delighted and fascinated, Tom hurried to catch up with the old man and the bounding hound.

‘Old smugglers’ tunnels,’ explained Cornelius, when the goggle-eyed Tom had caught up with them at the foot of the steps. ‘’Ole town’s riddled with secret passages like this one.’

‘Cool!’

They walked along a damp, and surprisingly spacious, passageway hewn straight from the rock. The subway slowly twisted ever downwards and to the left, until it eventually came to a square and rusty metal door (that might once have been painted turquoise) set deep into the stone wall.

Uncle Cornelius wrestled once more with the keys, unlocked the door and led them into a capacious lock-up with a high, arched ceiling.

The room looked like it was the setting for a retiring antique dealer's closing-down sale. Piles of old junk, bric-a-brac and clutter were scattered willy-nilly in all directions. Six other rusty, turquoise metal doors fanned around the walls. Tom wondered to himself just where they might lead. In the middle of the room stood a large and vintage car ("*automobile")* would perhaps be a more fitting description) that looked somewhere between Chitty-Chitty-Bang-Bang and a 1930s Chicago gangster's getaway vehicle (complete with dark tinted windows).

Following his uncle and stepping through a small door set into a much larger one (and therefore, mystifyingly, called a "Judas gate") at the far end of the lock-up, Tom found himself on a wide road only a few feet from the pebbled beaches of Brighton.

To his right was Brighton Pier (which Uncle Cornelius repeatedly called the "Palace Pier" – invariably accompanied by the word "monstrosity") and to his left he could see the jutting walls of the Marina.

Having carefully locked the *Judas gate* behind them, Uncle Cornelius cried out 'This way!' and – resplendent in tweed, coachman's bowler hat, and with twirling cane – began to saunter along the promenade like a geriatric Bill Sykes after a lucky night at the casino. Bess gambolled joyfully behind him in crooked sweeping circles, nose pressed excitedly to the floor.

This was only the second time that Tom had ever seen the sea (the first time was yesterday, on his visit to the Brighton Pier amusement arcade – *My God! Was it only yesterday?*) and he was bewitched.

When one hears the word "beach" one perhaps thinks of stretches of golden sand with crystal-blue waters lapping gently beneath a scorching, cloudless azure-coloured sky. Brighton beach however was more a collection of painfully sharp shingle, flint-grey waters and a sea breeze that hit you in the face like a bowlful of salty soup thrown by an indignant waiter. Tom loved it.

They promenaded along the promenade, past a small flotilla of fishing boats and pleasure crafts hauled to safety on the shingle's edge – the rigging slapping against the masts like an orchestra of impatient cooks beating out the *"foods up; come and get it!" anthem* – until they stood before what could best be described as the looming skeleton of a sinister giant octopus, frozen forever in its last agonizing thrashes of death.

'That's what's left of the West Pier, Tom,' his uncle explained, waving his silver-topped cane in the direction of the wreck. 'Should 'ave seen 'er in 'er pomp, son. That was a thing that was. Bands playing, theatre, tearooms an' dancing. Thing o' beauty she was. Now look at 'er.' He shook his head ruefully. 'Ah well, what's done is done, I suppose. No use meeping after what's been lost.'

He shot a baleful grimace of regret towards the Brighton Pier (which bustled vibrantly with gaudy lights, whirling rides and the muffled plastic beats of muffled plastic music) and resumed his stroll, stepping onto the pebbles with a hollow crunch and heading towards the sea through a row of tall and imposing metal pillars rusted to black.

Bess hurtled gleefully towards the water's edge, sending small stones flying dangerously in all directions, and jigged and barked frantically at the lapping waves. A large, sturdy and sodden Chocolate Labrador bustled gingerly over to join her, and – after a few stiff-legged bristling sniffs, sharp waggings of the tails, and the all-important mouth and bottom inspections – they began a stuttering and joyous dance, wrestling and cuffing each other playfully.

'Now then, Tom, I want you to do something for me,' began Uncle Cornelius.

Tom tore his gaze away from the Labrador's hasty retreat (a few gentle cuffs from Bess' gigantic paws had sent him bowling like tumbleweed, and he was enthusiastically withdrawing from the scenario, sending the occasional furtive glance back towards the disappointed-looking Bess that seemed to say – "*Lovely to meet you but, er, must be going now ... Um ... do, please, stay in touch ...*", whilst searching frantically for his owner with a look of "Help!!" tattooed in his eyes).

'Yes?' replied Tom, all ears, staring at the horizon and not meeting his uncle's fierce gaze.

'I want you to find me a stone.'

Tom looked down and around at the millions upon millions of pebbles surrounding them.

You are frickin' joking!

He dashed his uncle a sour, humourless smile.

'A stone?' he said, managing to keep his voice both polite and steady, as if he wasn't talking to a complete and utter imbecile.

'Not just any stone, mind. Gotta be a *special* one, son,' purred Cornelius, with deadly serious intent.

'Really? Hhmmm. "*Special*". Yes ... Yes of course. I see. What was I thinking?' replied Tom, his despair flooding back faster than the incoming tide.

'A stone with an 'ole in it, that's what you're after. One what you can look through. An *'oled-stone*, a *seeing-stone*, an *eye-stone,* or an *'ag stone*, as some call 'em – a looking-stone.'

Tom sighed.

'Oh good grief!' he whispered into his hands, as he wiped his face in as natural a fashion as possible.

Right then, he groaned inwardly, *let's just get this over with as soon as possible.*

'So then, Uncle,' he said, with a look of considerable resolve, 'let's get this straight. You want me to find a *stone* ... with a hole in it ... among the pebbles on the beach?'

'That's right, Tom.'

'And then ...?'

'Well, me an' Bess'll be up in that café over yonder,' answered the tweedy old moron, nodding towards a small, hut-like building huddled like a crab against the elements. 'An' then you come an' find us an' we'll 'ave a cup of tea an' ... a chat, like.'

'A chat?'

''Bout ... *things.*'

'Good,' sniffed Tom, with curt restraint. 'I'll see you in a minute, then.'

And with that, he marched stoically away – as far from the psychotic old cretin as he could possibly get – and began his search.

Forty-five minutes later and Tom was still frantically searching ... well, let's say "half-heartedly" searching. OK, he was sitting, legs dangling over the edge of one of the jutting groynes, absent-mindedly daydreaming and watching the waves crash against the slippery black rocks beneath him. The sea air was exhilarating and, sitting there with the wind ruffling his hair majestically (he thought), he imagined himself the hero from some far-flung myth, riding masterfully across the oceans on the bow of a speeding dragon ship; crashing through the waves as he hurtled towards epic adventures.

His fantasy was broken by the arrival of a pair of fat-necked and worryingly enormous herring gulls, who, upon landing, squawked menacingly and eyed him accusingly; disgruntled (and no doubt offended) that he was in possession of no food for them to bully from him.

Ah well, thought Tom, *best get back to the daft old duffer. "Sorry Uncle, I tried and tried and tried but I just couldn't find a stone 'special' enough",* he rehearsed in his head.

'Stupid old git!' he snorted out loud, as he kicked out at a pleasingly spherical pebble.

The stone ricocheted off the wall (sending the two gulls scurrying into the air with a screech of indignant dismay), collided with another pebble, which in turn shunted a third stone, which slowly rolled to rest in front of his still-raised foot.

'Oh, that is just too weird!' groaned Tom, as he reached down and picked up the orange pebble – which was the size and shape of an ear, and with a small hole in it just where the small hole in an ear-shaped stone should be.

He held it up to his eye, looked through it (framing a large and swanky-looking yacht that was edging its way towards the Marina) and chuckled.

'Well, that's sorted that then,' he grunted.

And he hurried off to find his uncle.

Uncle Cornelius was seated (determinedly) at a small plastic table, placed (determinedly) outside the café (the wind buffeting his tall hat and making it wobble – as if he'd stowed a brace of agitated weasels beneath it), and surrounded by an impressive array of teacups and a hefty pile of empty cake plates.

Bess wagged her tail as Tom approached and bounded to meet him, almost knocking him off his feet.

'Tom,' grinned the old fellow. ''Ow'd it go?'

Tom made a low, courtly bow and produced the orange, shiny, ear-shaped *eye-stone.*

'Well done, son. Looks like a real cracker, does that!' exclaimed Cornelius. 'Now, 'ow about some chips?'

They walked back along the promenade, eating deliciously crisped and salty chips from cones of white paper made soggy by lashings of vinegar.

'Now then, Tom,' said Cornelius, 'guess we need to talk. Let's 'ead back 'ome, via Black Lion Lane, an' make sure that that old stone of yours ain't a duff.'

Tom eyed his uncle suspiciously as they climbed the steps up to the main road, waiting for the old man to continue.

'Been thinking long an' 'ard 'bout this, an' it's the best that can be done. Should 'ave done it a while ago, I s'pose, but everyday life always seems to take its toll an' get in the way of the important things. So, 'ere goes ... 'Ow'd you like to be my apprentice? Be 'ard work, mind, years of study, practise, an' patience.'

'Apprentice what?' asked Tom, through a mouthful of chips.

'Well, Tom, we, I, am, like I said before, in the business of security, an' we'll ... I'll ... be needing a young chap (much like yourself) to manage things an' take up some of the slack now that I'm getting on a bit, so to speak.'

'Does that mean that I won't have to go back to school?' asked Tom, hopefully.

Uncle Cornelius chuckled.

'One step at a time, son. One step at a time.'

They wound their way – a hop, skip and a jump, really – up Black Lion Street and onto Black Lion Lane.

'Now then, Tom,' sniffed Uncle Cornelius, stroking his whiskers thoughtfully, 'let's see if that stone of yours cuts the mustard.'

'I don't really understand what you're talking about, Uncle,' muttered Tom, as they began their walk down the tiny twitten.

'Find One Punch Cottage for me, will you, son,' asked Uncle Cornelius, with a wicked grin bristling beneath his startlingly bristling whiskers.

Tom sighed and looked up and down the alleyway.

There must be some kind of mistake! he thought, more than a little alarmed.

Just like yesterday, he could see no sign of his uncle's house.

He looked towards the old man, utterly baffled.

Cornelius nodded his head sagely.

'That's right, Tom. An' no, you ain't going mad. You can't see *'er* 'cause *she* don't want to be seen.'

'I ... I don't understand. It was here. I was here. The gate! The garden! The wobbly chimney!' he whimpered, looking up at a distressingly empty sky.

'Now, I told you that my business is one of security,' growled Uncle Cornelius, jabbing a sausage-sized finger firmly at Tom (making the poor lad leap backwards, eye a-twitching, in unpleasant and petrified anticipation). 'An' that business can, at times, be dangerous – an' more than beyond. Over the years, I've ... we've ... made more than our fair share of enemies, Tom – powerful enemies some of them, nasty folk – an' so we needs to take precautions, so to speak. Protect ourselves, if you follow me. Make sure that only friends can find us when they 'as to. So One Punch Cottage is protected by ... well, by ... er ...'

'By amazing, high-tech, state-of-the-art, incredible super-spy technology!' whooped Tom excitedly, in utter rapture. 'Of course! Coo-el!'

'Er ... well ... well, yes ... yes, something like that, son, that's right,' mumbled Cornelius, sounding slightly put out and beginning to look a little uncomfortable.

'Well, show me then!' cried Tom, bursting with expectation and excitement. 'Oh, this is the best thing ever, Uncle!'

'Well ... er ... take the stone ...'

'Yes, yes!'

'... put it to your eye ...'

'Yes, yes!'

'... and, er ... well ... look through it.'

Tom dropped his hands to his side, feeling like a child who'd been promised a BMX bike for Christmas only to receive a rickety old bone-shaker, complete with wicker basket and stabilizers.

He stared disappointedly at his uncle.

'What sort of high-tech, state-of-the-art, super-spy technology is that?' he withered.

'Just do it, Tom, an' quickly, 'fore anyone comes along,' urged Uncle Cornelius.

Feeling like he'd been conned by a cruel practical joke, Tom slowly lifted the stone to his eye and looked through it.

'Good grief!' he managed to gasp, as his jaw slowly dropped open.

He looked through the *ear-shaped eye-stone* again and there, unmistakably, was One Punch Cottage – enormous wooden gate with a yew hedge sticking over the top of the high, sturdy walls; the cottage itself growing upward and outward, like a crooked sunflower into the cloudy, windswept sky. Several more looks through the stone (and whip-like turns to Uncle Cornelius) and Tom shook his head, blinking wildly in disbelief.

'I don't understand,' he wheezed, half to himself and half to his uncle. 'How can this be?'

'Don't worry 'bout that, son,' crooned the dapper old man. 'One step at a time, remember. It is what it is – right? And that,' smiled Uncle Cornelius, lightly tapping the orange stone in Tom's hand with the tip of his cane, 'is the best an' safest security known to man.'

SEVEN
The Reveal

Tom bounded up the stairs after his uncle, bombarding the old fellow with questions: 'So how does it work?' 'Is there some sort of electronic cloaking device activated by the molecular structure in the make-up of the stones, perhaps?' 'Is the hole in the stone absolutely necessary?' 'What other cool stuff have you got that I can get my hands on ... I mean ... see?' etc. etc.

'Don't be 'asty, Tom,' was all his uncle would say. 'One step at a time, son. One step at a time.'

On reaching The Study, Bess nosed open the door and walked over to greet the old hound, Percy, with a soft nudge of her head, before diving artistically onto the sofa. The great yellow dog himself was sitting in his usual gargoyle pose, carefully watching the arrival of Uncle Cornelius and Tom. Without moving his massive and elegant head, he followed the old man's path with mournful eyes and let out a huffing, one might almost say *resigned*, sigh.

'Close the door will you, Tom,' said Cornelius, as he turned and half-sat, half-leant against the writing desk, arms folded across his chest.

Tom closed The Study door and excitedly turned to face the old man.

'Tom, there's somebody that I'd like you to meet.'

'Cool,' said Tom, looking expectantly looking around the room.

Uncle Cornelius looked towards the giant yellow hound and nodded.

'Yeah? ... I've already *met* Percy ... Remember?'

'Yes, but I don't think that you've been properly introduced, son.'

The great wolfhound sighed once again and then pierced Tom with a weighty and ancient stare. There was a five-second cacophony of sharp snapping sounds (like popcorn popping in a covered pan) accompanied by a fluid and graceful morphing (like a plant's growth captured on a time-lapse camera and then played back in fast-motion) and there, before Tom's very eyes, stood a ... seven-and-a-half feet tall ...

'W ... w ... w ...were ... w ... w ... w ... werew ... w ... wo...'

Tom passed out.

When he opened his eyes, the first thing that Tom saw was Missus Dobbs' uncomfortably close face gurning concern down at him.

Over her shoulder Uncle Cornelius loomed into focus.

'You all right there, Tom?' he enquired, jovially.

'Got a nice cup of tea for you, Ducky,' beamed Mrs Dobbs, scampering off to retrieve said tea from the writing desk.

Uncle Cornelius leaned in closer and whispered in Tom's ear. 'Don't worry, son, made it myself.' As if that was the most important concern in this whole affair.

Well, come to think of it ...

No! thought the calm, rational part of Tom. *No, no, no, no, no. It's not, because ... I've just seen a ...*

'WWWERE-WWWOOOOOLLLLLLLLLLFFFFFFFFFF!!!' he wailed, at the top of his lungs.

He was up on his feet faster than a startled ninja with piles, casting saucer-sized eyes around the room. And there, ensconced in the enormous armchair, wrapped in a dark red silk dressing robe, sat the beast itself; crossed-legged, with Uncle Cornelius' morning newspaper delicately clutched in its huge, monstrous hands...paws...talons: a creature of nightmares, fairy tales and tacky B-movies. Genuine. Irrefutable. A were-wolf!

The beast turned its monstrous head and looked at Tom, as if considering what to have for lunch. The semblance of a smile (it was hard to tell) crafted itself onto the long snout, revealing a mouthful of teeth like drawn dirks.

'A *cynanthrope,* a *were-hound,* a *dog-man* would perhaps be closer to the mark,' it said, in an impossibly low voice, and with the clipped tones of a 1930s BBC newsreader, 'but even that would, in fact, be an incorrect assessment. A *wolfhound-were-wolf* would be the ticket. However "*were-wolf*" is an understandable mistake, Tom. Do sit down and have your tea, old chap, you look positively all at sea.'

Tom's legs buckled under him and, if not for the quick-thinking Missus Dobbs placing the tattered footstool beneath him, he would have crashed to the carpet like a dropped glass of milk.

He sat, slack-jawed and whimpering, while Missus Dobbs thrust the cup of tea into his quivering hands.

'Ttthh...tth tthhank yyyoyou,' he managed to say, sounding like he'd inhaled the contents of several large helium balloons.

'So,' drawled the monster, casually discarding the newspaper and looking down at Tom like a disapproving schoolmaster dressed up as the villain from Little Red Riding Hood, 'Dandy, here – I mean, your Uncle Cornelius – has a mind to take you on as an apprentice to our little firm. What do *you* have to say about the matter?'

Tom looked up at the creature and his heart quailed, but then, thinking things through – and it's amazing how fast the mind *thinks things through* when the sudden realisation hits you that the terrifying nightmare in front of you isn't actually intent on eating you (just yet) – decided that there was no reason (apart from the obvious) to quail. The monster seemed, if not overly-friendly (and that, on reflection, would have been even more terrifying!) at least *well disposed.* A quick glance towards Uncle Cornelius confirmed that the wily old duffer was positively at ease, if a little concerned about Tom's immediate response. Missus Dobbs was gurning encouragement with misty, happy-go-lucky swirling orbs. And Bess was fast asleep on the sofa, farting for England. Things certainly weren't half as bad as they had first seemed – and that was no small matter, when you considered that he was sitting only three feet away from a were...*thingy.*

Tom stood up and, with faltering gait, stepped towards the monster and began a cautious examination (as only a young chap who has just survived the fright of his life – and whose natural inquisitiveness and passion for all things weird and wonderful has been a constant source of despair to all who know and care about him – could).

The creature must have stood around seven-and-a-half feet tall, still retained its yellowy, wheat-coloured wiry fur, and loosely resembled an enormous shaggy man with an elongated dog's head. The black-rimmed, almond-shaped, walnut-coloured eyes blazed with an intense and unfathomable wisdom. The long, powerful snout ended with a large black nose. Beard and whiskers like nails. Teeth like a set of daggers (canines like polished gladii) beneath thin black lips. Huge, reddish pointy-up ears, with the faintest trace of white spots on them. A gracefully arching and powerful neck. Impossibly elongated and muscular limbs – running to long, almost delicate, fingers and toes (all coming to an end with the most lethal-looking talons) – and a long sabre-like tail (currently curled artfully around, in a perfect picture of sartorial elegance).

The monster suffered the inspection and then raised a shaggy eyebrow.

'Well?' it asked, stiffly.

Tom tried to find his voice, and then, once found, did his best to try to steady it before he spoke.

'S..s..s..so wwwwwhat do I c...c...c...call you ttttthen? P...P...P...PPercy?' he asked, trying to sound as nonchalant and unfazed as he possibly could.

The beast tapped a finger like a longshoreman's loading hook against its muzzle.

'No,' it replied, 'you do not. The name *Percy* is used only as a *cover* when I am in 'dog-form'. My first (and only) master christened me *Percival,* but there are only a few to whom I now allow that privilege. You,' he said, holding Tom's eye in a terrible gaze, 'may call me *The Hound.*'

'*The 'Ound 'Oo 'Unts Nightmares,*' piped in Uncle Cornelius, sounding as pleased as punch.

The creature motioned for silence with an elegant spiralling wave of its vicious-looking claws.

'Well, Tom? What will it be?'

'So th...the...then ... Th...Th...Th...The H...H...Hound? Wwwwhat is it that you wwant me to d...do?' asked Tom, unable to tear his eyes away from the monstrous teeth only inches away from him.

The creature, as far as he could tell, seemed to be dog-like from the neck up, man-like from shoulders to waist and 'hound-ish' again from the 'knees' downward.

'As your *uncle* has so eloquently informed you, *we* are in the business of *security*. And, as you have just recently become only too well aware, young man, this world is full of more mysterious and supernatural entities than you could have ever thought possible. The creatures of myth and fairy tale do exist and, on occasion, our two worlds collide – not always in the most harmonious and congenial of manners. When the boundaries are crossed, when the *Nightmare* slips into the waking hour, when the *Darkness* creeps towards your door, we are the ones who put *things* right.'

'Just like what I told you, Tom,' beamed Uncle Cornelius.

'And yyyou wwant me to h...h...h...help you...?'

'I cannot promise you that it will all be *fun,*' continued The Hound. 'You will have to work more diligently and study a great deal harder than you have so far managed to do during your brief, but *illustrious*, school career,' he sneered, staring down his hellish snout like a High Court judge reprimanding the village ne'er-do-well caught weeing in the church font (again).

Tom gulped. *Whatever do you mean*! he thought, indignantly – though he knew exactly what he meant ('Buck up, son!' is what he meant) – and, more importantly, wondered *how* he knew?

'Nor can I ensure that you will always be safe from harm,' frowned the were-hound, as if he could read Tom's every thought. 'It is a dangerous path that we walk; one that is fraught with peril. You will see things that you will wish to forget, but will never be able to do so. It is a lonely existence, with few friends and even fewer with whom you will ever be able to share your experiences. But I give you my word, Tomas Dearlove, that I will do everything within my power to protect you, that you will see and explore a world that few are privileged to even glimpse, and that you will lead a life that can only be described as ... *extraordinary*.'

Tom stared at the were-wolfhound, who sat keenly before him (like the plucky captain of the *big school* cricket team interviewing a prospective first year batsman), at Uncle Cornelius (biting his lip in eager anticipation), at Missus Dobbs (doe-eyed and chewing frantically on the knuckles of her twisted, gnarled little mitts), and he heard the comforting trump of encouragement as Bess 'let one go' from the sofa.

Well, thought Tom, *what's a boy to do?*

'All right,' he said at last, beaming an uncontrollable grin. 'Be my pleasure.'

'Ha-ha!' cried Uncle Cornelius, clapping his hands in delight and storming over to slap Tom heartily on the back. 'Good to 'ave you aboard, son. Know you'll be a credit to us all.'

Missus Dobbs whinnied with delight and planted a wet, furry kiss on Tom's cheek (which was rather like having someone squash an overripe apple in your face). 'Oh, Ducky, I'm so made up. Ooh, it's wonderful news it is!'

Bess opened an eye and lashed her tail against the sofa cushions, beating out a military-style tattoo.

The were-wolf-wolfhound smiled (possibly) a lop-sided grin and extended an enormous hand like a kitchen knife rack. Tom gingerly took it, and his hand was engulfed and pumped in a warm, firm grip that Tom felt could have crushed his own like a sparrow's egg.

'Splendid!' growled The Hound. 'Welcome to the illustrious firm of Hound and Lyons.'

'Lyons an' 'Ound,' beamed Uncle Cornelius, his whiskers bristling with joy. 'Paranormal investigators extraordinaire.'

'I expect high things of you, Tom,' glowered the were-hound. 'Don't disappoint.'

Tom assured him that he wouldn't.

'Missus Dobbs, I think that this calls for a celebration. Toasted cheese sandwiches all round!'

'Right you are, Mr Hound,' she cried, bimbling at joyous full tilt from the room.

'I'll get the tea, Missus Dobbs!' barked Uncle Cornelius, hurriedly, before looming beside the overwhelmed and idiot grinning Tom.

'Might as well begin your education right 'ere an' now, son. Most important thing that you'll be needing to know for the moment, an' that's a fact. With me, Tom, with me. At the double!' he bellowed in good humour, as he marched towards the door. 'Going to teach you the great mystery of 'ow to make a *proper* brew.'

EIGHT
The Hound Who Hunts Nightmares

'Your duties will begin first thing each morning with a minimum of at least two hours physical training,' continued The Hound, as they sat around the writing desk in The Study later that afternoon. 'What use is a keen mind without a firm body at its disposal? Cornelius will instruct you in manners of self-defence and unarmed combat and I, in time, will educate you in the science, art and philosophy of arms.'

'Cool!' squeaked Tom.

'Try not to interrupt, Tom,' grinned Uncle Cornelius.

'Where and whenever possible, the rest of the day will be taken up with the study of all things *supernatural*; a sound grounding and understanding of the worlds that we inhabit is vital, not only for your development as a detective of the paranormal but also for your very survival. You will also be expected to perform various household tasks. When given a request, command or order you will not hesitate to perform it. Hesitation in our *game* can lead to death – or possibly worse. Do you understand?'

Tom assured The Hound that he did.

'Now, Tom, I am sure that you must be bursting with all manner of questions, but I will call upon you to be patient. One step at a time, as your uncle so rightly cautions. However, perhaps the most burning concern that you might have right now is of my own nature and very presence, and so, as a precursor to your apprenticeship, I will tell you all that you need to know regarding this matter.

'Perhaps we should make ourselves more comfortable,' suggested the were-hound, elegantly flicking a claw towards the armchairs. 'We must have another chair ordered, Dandy, we can't have the poor fellow squatting on a stool for the rest of his life. And,' he continued, running a disparaging eye over Tom, 'it will be necessary to arrange an appointment with a good tailor as soon as is convenient. *Anderson and Sheppard* will do.'

Tom looked down in befuddlement at his best jeans and brand spanking new trainers.

The Hound leant back in his enormous armchair, closed his eyes, pressed the tips of his talonous fingers together as if in prayer, lifted his snout, took a deep breath and so began his tale.

He told of how he had been born in the year 1585, and of what he could remember of his early days as a pup – the companionship of his siblings (one brother and two sisters) and the comfort and protection of his darling mother. Of how he, along with one of his sisters, had been presented as a celebratory gift to the newly titled Earl of Northumberland – the young Henry Percy. And of how the young Lord had delighted in them and loved them both. Of long, gambolling walks through the Earl's estate in Petworth, of their hunting expeditions together among the great deer herds that roamed those woods, and of his early training with Master Tiggs – the Earl's huntsman and master-of-hounds.

And finally, he told Tom of that fateful night in 1587; when the villagers and gentry of Petworth gathered together and stalked a rampaging were-wolf by the light of a Hunter's Moon. Of that dreadful affair when he had fought the monster – with tooth and claw and every ounce of his strength – to save his master's life.

'Dr Dee and Master Warner did everything that they could to cure my terrible injuries. The young Earl kept me by his side both day and night. And, to everybody's great surprise, my wounds healed. And how they healed – far faster and far better than both Dee and Warner knew that they had any right to. And what had, at first, been joy at my recovery, soon turned to suspicion and fear. I had, after all, survived an attack by a *beast from Hell*, and the nature of the curse was not unknown to them. Oh yes, I had been bitten by a monster, and I could feel its unholy rage coursing like poison through my veins – and they soon began to swap strange, furtive glances. "What if?" they whispered to each other. "What if ...?"

'As the new moon approached, I (now fully recovered and feeling fitter and stronger, and more *aware*, more *curious*, than I had ever felt before) was moved to a remote barn and housed within a cage – one crafted from the sturdiest iron and set both firmly and deeply into the middle of the floor. Dee was fascinated, the Earl was concerned, and his 'three magi' were, to put it mildly, intrigued. Here was a chance to observe, to bear witness to, the creation of a myth and monster.

'But what would that monster be?

'If a man cursed with the were-wolf's bite transformed into a man-like wolf creature, then how would a dog, so afflicted, change?

'They crowded into the barn on the night of that full moon, their faces bursting with curious excitement and eager anticipation. Only the Earl showed any real concern for my well-being and, unlike the others, only reluctantly took the pistol (primed with a silver bullet) that was offered to him. And, with the coming of *Artumes*, my first transformation happened. It was agonising, lasting much longer than the one that you observed only a short while ago, Tom. But, eventually, there I stood before them, in the centre of the cage, in the very form that you see before you now. The wide-eyed, startled scholars gawped at me in horror and retreated hastily from the cage, weapons primed and pointed. But I knew them all, was fond of them. I staggered, uncertainly, to the cage bars on strange new limbs, gently offered an extended hand, smiled and wagged my tail; used every sign of friendship that I could imagine.

'And I *could* imagine, Tom. My mind rippled with wondrous new thoughts and expectations.

'Well, as you might appreciate, I was a wonder to these men of science. They began to talk excitedly amongst themselves, and, to their astonishment, I tried to ape their sounds. The gift of speech was, of course, new to me; the physiology felt terrifying and awkward, and, at first, frustratingly clumsy, and, quite naturally, I had to learn to speak as would a child.'

'So,' interrupted Tom, 'if you only changed ... shape ... with the full moon, how come you can do it now, with no full moon and in the middle of the day?'

'A fine question, Tom. A fine question, without doubt. To begin with, I did indeed only take on this *were*-form with the coming of the new moon. The ability to transform at will was acquired much later and I shall explain that episode in its turn.

'But to continue: month by month, full moon by full moon, Dr Dee, the Earl and his '*three magi*' would instruct me how to behave as a man and not as a dog. I learned to dance. To understand music and appreciate the arts. I learned to read, and discovered the joy of literacy before I ever found my voice (as I have already said, that took many decades to completely master, I must admit, and in dog-form I am unable to speak). I was tutored in the sciences by Dee, Warner, Hues and Hariot. I was taught (and developed a great passion for) the art of arms by the great soldier and master of fence, *Vincentio* Saviolo. Everything, in fact, that was necessary for the education of the Elizabethan gentleman, (with the exception of riding – horses, understandably, have never much liked me, and besides, I could travel far faster and further than they ever could).

'Of course, I was at first nothing more than a miraculous novelty, but they soon noted how eagerly I learnt and not only *longed* for my lessons but *excelled* at them.

'Think on it, Tom! They were the first men, perhaps in all of history, to be able to converse with a being from another species ... I say, where are you off to, young man?'

Tom was up and out of his seat, flying to the bookcase and rifling through the shelves.

'I recognise those names,' he said over his shoulder.

And indeed, there they were – the works of Dee, Warner, Hariot and Hues.

Tom ran his finger along the cracked leather spines of the books.

'You knew all of these people?' he asked, looking around in wonder.

'Yes, very well indeed,' responded The Hound, patiently. 'They were, I suppose, family to me.'

Tom pulled out the leather-bound copy of "*Vincentio Saviolo; his practice*".

'And him?' he said, holding the book in one hand and pointing excitedly at it with the other.

'Vincent? Yes, he and I were firm friends. Good chap. Into some dubious activities perhaps, but a thoroughly decent sort. Married Warner's daughter, Elina ... at the end.

'At the end of what?' asked Tom.

'Another story, Tom, for another time,' replied The Hound, softy, intently watching the young man.

Tom nodded and carefully opened the book.

It read –

VINCENTIO
SAVIOLO
his Practife.
In two Bookes.
The firft intreating the ufe of the Ra-
pier and Dagger.
The fecond, of Honor and honourable
Quarrels.
Both interlaced with fundrie pleasant Discou-
ses, not vnfit for all Gentlemen and Cap-
taines that profeffe Armes.
AT LONDON
Printed for William Mattes, and are to be solde
at his fhop in Fleete ftreete, at the figne of
the hand and Plough.
1595.

Under this, written in a beautiful swirling script, where the words –

To Percival,
My most extraordinary friende & scholar.
Always readie at your service & at your commaunde.
V. S.
{P.S. –"Love me, love my dogge."}

Tom blew out a silent whistle.

'Now, if you would be so kind as to put it back, Tom. It is very old and, as you will no doubt appreciate, it has great sentimental value to me. Come, sit back down and I'll continue with my tale.'

Tom did as he was told, suddenly feeling very conscious that he was handling a book that was over four hundred years old.

'Now, where was I?' considered The Hound, when Tom had settled back onto the stool. 'Ah, yes.

'It is a terrible thing, but undeniably true, that some men's hearts are dark and wicked places, and there were those who, discovering of my existence, thought to use me for a dreadful design. "*What,*" they reasoned, "*if we could create an army of such monsters? Think how the world would tremble before us!*" But, thankfully, it was not to be. On the one occasion that I was tricked into biting some poor soul, nothing ever came of it. My *victim* remained, and lived his days, as a man – a man with a terrible scar it is true, but a man and nothing more. (Just for the record, Lord Henry had the vile instigators removed from his service.)

'The world aged around me, and yet I seemed unaffected by the passing of the years. Dee grew old and died. My beloved lord and master, Henry, departed all too soon. Oh, Tom! How the spirit of England was changed by the demise of such men. The age of *enquiry* passed into one of *inquisition*. And though I retained the goodwill, support and affection of Henry's children (especially his heir, my dear, dear friend, Algernon), a creature such as I would not, could not, be tolerated by this *new* society. Besides, I was under no illusion that my survival had always, at best, been somewhat precarious.

'With the help of some close acquaintances of Robert Hues – who had connections with the, then newly discovered, continent of what is now called America (Robert had, in his youth, sailed with Raleigh to settle the colony of Roanoke in New England, and still maintained strong contacts with that newfound land) – it was arranged that I would travel to the New World. As I prepared for my exile, I was advised and counselled by my closest friends to make my own way in the world and keep as far away as possible from the society of men.

'And so I did, and headed deeper and deeper into the uncharted wildernesses of that remarkable continent. Happily I lived, partly as a dog and – when the moon was in Her splendour – partly as a creature neither man nor hound (yet perhaps, somehow, a little more than either). I spent decades simply living and hunting with the native wolves and avoiding all human contact whatsoever, for I had grown saddened by the bewildering nature of men. For, as the poet Ezra Pound was to remark – "*When I carefully consider the curious habits of dogs I am compelled to conclude that man is the superior animal. When I observe the curious habits of man I confess, my friend, I am puzzled.*"

'I roamed and explored, in awe, the bountiful and wondrous glories of Nature. But my upbringing and education had had its effect, and eventually I came to realise that I missed the company and conversation of humans.

'In time I met, and was befriended by, a shaman of the Cheyenne people. His name translates as *Man-Whose-Spirit-Walks-Beside-The-Wolf,* and he was a shape-shifter – delighting in nothing more than his transformation into a wolf. And so we met somewhere in the middle: a man who could change himself into a wolf, and a dog who was turned, on occasion, into the semblance of a man.

'It was he who taught me to control my transformations, so that with time, under his tutelage, it became as natural and as easy as the singing of a song for me to change between one form and another.

'I stayed with the Cheyenne for years as they continued their slow migration ever westwards towards the Great Plains. However, when Man-Whose-Spirit died, I decided that it was time for me to head back east.

'And so, the last decade of 1700s saw me make my return to Europe.

'With the giant leaps forward being made in technology at that time, modern science had begun to enter into realms that had previously only been the domain of *Magic*. And the '*Old Powers*', it appeared, were *kicking back*.

'The world of magic has long been in slow decline, and there were those from that realm who suddenly became fascinated by the vibrancy and dynamism of the society of *modern* man. Likewise, in the western world there grew a newfound and heightened interest in the realm of the supernatural and the occult – and the names of *Dracula* and *Frankenstein,* and of the *Vampyre* and the *Wolf-man* entered firmly into the public consciousness.

'I was still remembered and documented in certain quarters, and so I discretely made myself known to them. In time, my unique skills were sought out and I found myself hired by those who faced unwanted and *unnatural* problems; problems that no mortal being could hope to solve. It was, Tom, as if I had stumbled onto the reason for my existence. As a dog, my kind had been bred over the centuries to fight for and protect man from his enemies; now, as this 'creature', I could serve the very same purpose but contest on a far deeper, deadlier field.

'I became, as Cornelius so poetically phrased it, *The Hound Who Hunts Nightmares.*'

'But,' pondered Tom, fondly recalling his favourite horror films, 'I thought that all were-wolves, were-creatures, were ... cursed, vicious, bloodthirsty monsters whose hunger for human flesh is insatiable? Like the one that attacked you.'

'Alas, dear boy,' sighed The Hound, clicking the tips of his claws together and running an enormous tongue over his enormous polished teeth, 'there is an element of undoubted truth in your statement; though it is well to remember that there are several different types of *were-wolf.*

'*Were-wolf* – from the Anglo-Saxon: *Wer* (meaning *man*) and *Wulf* (meaning, quite naturally, *wolf*). Or, *Lycanthrope* – from the ancient Greek: *Lykos* (meaning *wolf*) and *Anthropus* (meaning *human*).

'Firstly, there are those who are shape-shifters; sorcerers who voluntarily turn themselves into the shape of a wolf or a dog (sometimes creatures of extraordinary size) – men such as Man-Whose-Spirit, for example. Then there are those who are able to shift at will into a humanoid-wolf form; men such as the *Ulfhedinn* of Scandinavia. There are also communities where the power to shift shape is hereditary – such as the *Neuroi* of the Baltic, or the *Conroicht* of Ossory in Ireland. To some cultures these "Turn-Skins" are thought of as creatures of evil, but it is well to remember that in other societies the were-wolf is regarded as a protector and guardian. In Ireland, for example, were-wolves (or *Faolch)* were considered to be the defenders of children and of lost and injured folk, and, during times of war, were actively recruited by the kings of Ireland to fight in their armies.

'As recently as 1692, in Livonia, an old peasant by the name of *Thiess* was tried by the local Inquisition – accused of being a were-wolf. *Theiss* did not for one second refute the charge, and proudly testified that he, along with others from his village (clearly other members of the *Neuroi*), were were-wolves. It was they, he claimed, who protected the crops from evil sorcerers and, on occasion, even travelled down to the plains of Hell itself to do battle with witches and demons (as, he insisted, did the were-wolves of both Germany and Russia). And he was adamant that when he died, his soul, and those of his brethren, would be welcomed into Heaven as reward for all of their good services. (For the record, Tom, the judges ordered that *Thiess* be punished with ten strokes of the lash for his idolatry and superstitious beliefs.)

'There is also a fabled race of dog-like, or *dog-headed,* men said to inhabit certain inaccessible regions of Southeast Asia and parts of India – so-called the *Cynocephaly* by the ancient Greeks, or the *Nacumerians* by the explorer John Mandeville.

'Then, throughout the world, there are wolf and dog *spirits*, who, on occasion, take on human-like form (for the most part solely for their own amusement; *Reynadine* – the *English* Fox-Spirit, for example).'

'Sly old bugger,' chortled Uncle Cornelius, with a rueful shake of his head.

'But these,' continued The Hound, 'are immortal spirits.

'In the Shetland Islands there once lived a strange were-wolf-like beast known locally as the *Wulver*; a creature of kindly disposition, known to be both protector and provider for the unfortunate. But the Wulver does (or did) not shift its shape, and again is perhaps best described as a spirit of nature – a creature born of the Faery Worlds (though it is probably safe to assume that the most recent sightings can be attributed to a fishing vacation that I took a few years ago).'

'Miserable 'oliday that was,' grimaced Uncle Cornelius, as he slurped his tea.

'So, are you immortal?' asked Tom.

'Good grief no,' chuckled The Hound. 'I am very long-lived indeed, but I am most certainly ageing. And I can most definitely be harmed ... and killed.'

'By silver bullets and the like?' pursued Tom, eagerly.

'Later, Tom, later,' said The Hound, patiently. 'Let us return to your original point concerning the modern representation of the lycanthrope, or, as you so rightly phrased it - "*the curse of the were-wolf*".

'You are in so many ways correct, Tom. For when most people think of were-wolves they imagine the poor unfortunates as you have so imaginatively described them. And, alas, as I have made all too plain, these creatures do indeed exist. Cursed and *turned* by the coming of the full moon; wretched beings, utterly unable to control their dreadful impulses or the horror of their actions.'

'So how come you're so ... so ... so *civilised*? asked Tom, intrigued. 'What I mean to say is – why didn't ... why don't *you* have any of that hunger and blood lust? You don't, do you?' squeaked Tom, with a sudden gut-wrenching alarm.

'Most certainly not!' frowned the were-hound.

Tom gulped in relief.

'Then why,' he hastily continued, 'aren't you evil and wicked and ... and all that?'

'It is well to remember that it is not the *wolf* in the *were* that makes the beast a killer, it is the *were* in the *wolf* that makes the monster so,' replied the were-hound.

'Uh?' Tom pulled an expression of confusion.

'Wolves, *Canidae*, are not by nature *evil*. They can, of course, appear to become so over time (if that is how their experience shapes them); but evil is, in the natural world at least (and I am sorry if this is news to you, Tom), the sole property of man.'

'Hang on a minute!' cried Tom, feeling like he should at least stand up for his *species*. 'Everybody knows that wolves and the like are indiscriminate killers who, given the opportunity, will kill everything and anything they can. Like foxes in a hen-house –'

'Absolutely not!' interjected The Hound, with a derisive snort (which almost made Tom wet himself with the truly abysmal concern that he might have caused offence – and who, to be honest, really wants to piss-off a seven-and-a-half foot tall were-wolf-wolfhound?). 'Let us examine the incident of the *"fox in the hen-house"* to which you have just alluded.

'The fox, out hunting, comes across a flock of hens penned and sheltered in a bewildering enclosure. The hens, partly through their domestication and partly through their unnatural surroundings, behave strangely, having nowhere, and no opportunity, to flee. The fox – knowing through painful experience that finding and providing enough food is a difficult and rarely certain activity – on discovering such *easy* prey, kills all of the hens with the intent of caching what he cannot immediately eat for the lean times that invariably lay ahead. Naturally, he is only able to carry one or two chickens at a time and so is forced, by necessity, to make numerous trips to and from the scene of his hunt. On one such return to the hen-house, he realises that his activities have been discovered by the farmer, or chicken-keeper, and so is unable to complete his task. The *owner* of the hens is justifiably angry and naturally appalled by what appears to be an unnecessary, mindless slaughter, and thus labels the fox a savage, wasteful killer. The truth, however, is quite the reverse.'

'Hhhhmm?' conceded Tom, though he was, truth be told, very fond of the foxes that lived around his and his mum's house. 'But,' he continued, not wishing to push his luck or anything, but being a naturally inquisitive sort, 'what about the were-wolves that you just mentioned – they *are* killers aren't they, and even if they're men turned into wolves or dogs or wolf-like monsters, it's the wolf in them, the wolf's ... powers, its weapons, its predatory nature, that makes them such effective and horrific killers. Isn't it?'

'Is it indeed, Tom?' sighed the were-hound. 'I wonder.'

The Hound stood up and started to pace around the room, hands held behind his back, his massive, pointy snout tilted skyward.

He turned to look at Cornelius and then at Tom, as if making a weighty decision.

Tom eyed the door and wondered if it was even worth trying to make a bolt for it before he was shredded into a million pieces? (His mother had always warned him that his almost Tourette-like curiosity would get him killed one day, but he bet that she never thought it would be at the hands of a shaggy yellow were-wolf-wolfhound with a plummy accent, dressed in a red silk bathrobe!)

'Perhaps it is time to begin your education in earnest, Tom,' continued The Hound, at last.

Tom inwardly sighed and unclenched his buttocks.

'Part of our work is the identification, tracking and capture of the creatures of the supernatural world. And, in order to do that, we must, like all good hunters and detectives, try to understand our quarry. More often than not, Tom, the best place to start is at the very beginning. So let us for a moment reflect upon – to use a well-worn phrase – *the origin of the species.*'

There was another long pause while The Hound seemed to be collecting his thoughts.

'I'll go put the kettle on,' sniffed Uncle Cornelius.

'Excellent. We shall desist until your return, Dandy,' replied The Hound, graciously.

amazon.co.uk

A gift note from Victor Francisco:

Enjoy your gift! From Vic Francisco

Gift note included with The Wild Hunt: The Hound Who Hunts Nightmares - Book One

NINE
The Origin Of The Species

Ten minutes later, with hot tea and Jaffa Cakes passed around, The Hound continued with his discourse.

'When mankind first came down from the trees and chose to walk a *different* path, the creature that inspired him above all others was the wolf. They were of a similar size, hunted similar prey, and relied on teamwork and communication to achieve this. The wolf became, if you will, a mentor.

'It is known, for example, that many of the earliest Indo-Europeans adopted tribal names that can be loosely translated as *The Wolf-People* or *The People of the Wolf*; thus specifically identifying themselves with that animal. Among many of the indigenous tribes of North America the wolf was, and is still, regarded as a teacher.

'Over time, as is their – as is *your* – nature, the hunting and survival skills passed on by *wolf-kind* were abused by *man-kind*. The wolves became confused and upset by man's wanton and wasteful actions. They therefore reasoned that man must have somehow misunderstood the fundamental function of the hunter and thus misinterpreted his place in Nature. And so, resolved to redress this terrible wrong, they sent representatives to live with man and re-educate him. These noble *ambassadors* were the ancestors of the domestic dog. However, man would not, or could not, amend his manners – still could not understand, or perhaps refused to see, the consequence of his ill-considered actions. Over time, many (but I would like to think not all) of these *ambassadors* became, for want of a better word, *corrupted*, both mentally and physically. The wolves became angrier still. Harsher action was needed. *How*, they wondered, *could they make man comprehend?*

'The answer, they thought (with hindsight, in their innocence), was to make man understand how it felt to be *like* a wolf. Then surely, it was reasoned, if carefully chosen individuals could be made to *see* like a wolf, *feel* like a wolf and even *think* like a wolf, then they would be able to impart this wisdom to the rest of their kind. And so, with a magic that has long been lost, certain men were chosen by the wolves and given the *gift* to be able to spend a part of their lives *as* a wolf. The *spell* was passed on by the bite from (for want of a better description) a "wolf-mage". The intention was that the beneficiaries of this wonderful gift would spend the nights of the full moon (the very best time for hunting) living as a wolf.

'But the power, the nature, the essence, and the arrogance of man was far stronger than the wolves could ever have imagined, and instead of becoming wolf, the inner-spirit of the man demanded that the wolf become like he. And so, in the struggle between the two great hunters, the *were-wolf*, the *wolf-man*, was born.

'Feeling the strength and the power of both man and wolf multiplied tenfold, those poor creatures so afflicted went mad; crazed by their own being, maddened by their twisted knowledge of the world, and by the arrogance of their newfound power. Instead of educating their brethren, they cruelly turned upon them – longing to consume, craving to destroy and to devour all that was most dear and sacred to them.

'And so the thing that was given as a *gift* became a *curse*, passed on from one victim to another, or, in some cases, as a hereditary blight.'

'So, what about you?' asked Tom. 'Where do *you* fit in to all of this? Are there others like you, other ... you know, canine-thingy-ma-jigs?'

'Cynathropes,' muttered Uncle Cornelius.

'To the best of my knowledge, Tom – no,' sighed The Hound, 'not exactly. I, for whatever reason, appear to be unique in all of existence; for I am a canine who takes a man-like form, rather than a man who adopts the physical characteristics of a wolf.'

'But how? And why? Why no one else? Why aren't there others animals, dogs, who survived a were-wolf attack and became human...ish ... I mean ... man-like ... I mean ... like you?'

At this point Missus Dobbs appeared at The Study door.

'Sorry to interrupt, Duckies, but supper's ready. *Toad in the hole.*'

TEN
The Apprentice

The next few weeks were probably the most fatiguing and fulfilling of Tom's life. Every morning, at the *"crack of sparrows"*, he was awoken, by Missus Dobbs, with a kindly cup of tea (which, for the benefit of humanity, was carefully smuggled to the bathroom and tipped hastily down the plughole). Then he would drag himself down to the gymnasium for the daily pounding of his exhausted carcass.

Under Uncle Cornelius' patient and enthusiastic supervision, Tom was beginning to *educate* his left hand and was exploring such marvels as the "chopper" and the "pivot blow", the "shovel hook" and the "corkscrew punch".

On occasion The Hound would appear and cast a disparaging eye over Tom's progress. During one truly terrifying session, while trying to explain the use of (mind-bogglingly complex) footwork in relation to the movements of the heavy punchbag, The Hound had accidentally "lamped" (to use a phrase from Uncle Cornelius' vernacular) the bag so hard that it had walloped into the ceiling and made the whole house shudder.

Perhaps, Tom had considered, *it was called One Punch Cottage because that's all it would take to bring the crookedy old thing crashing down!*

'You're a fistic wonder, Tom,' his uncle would chuckle at the end of each session, as he beamed over the panting, dribbling husk of the boy known formerly as Tomas Dearlove.

And, to be honest, Tom could feel himself getting fitter, stronger and growing in confidence daily. He was, he felt almost afraid to admit, actually enjoying himself.

After a huge breakfast (he was eating so much that he was sure that it was only the gargantuan workout sessions that kept him from looking like a walrus sucking on an air pump) he would spend the rest of the morning reading through books that were carefully selected and given to him by The Hound and/or Cornelius. These consisted of – old case files; histories of magical people, peoples and creatures; survival-guides for the paranormal investigator; and books on magic and spell recognition (Dame Ginty Parsons' *"The Book of Spell Recognition"* being, he was reliably informed, the definitive work on the subject). From this fount of mystical knowledge he had discovered much; for example –

> **Wodin-Poke** – a spell awarded to the *uninitiated* to give them the short-term ability to see through *Glamours* [Elven spells of masking, misdirection and/or hiding (UK.)] See ***Glamour.***
> The name ***'Wodin-Poke'*** coming from:

Wodin - [noun] the leader of the Teutonic Gods, who plucked out his eye in order to obtain wisdom
and
Poke - [verb] to push with (the end of) a finger.

If someone had told Tom a few weeks ago that he would not only be spending all his hard-earned holiday hours in hard earnest study, but also loving it, he would have laughed in their face until his tongue fell off. But love it he did. He found himself fascinated.

Amazing how you could apply yourself when suitably stimulated, he mused, thinking about his woefully uninspired school, classmates and teachers.

After *cojer-time* he would walk Bess (armed with bucket, spade and stoic grimace) and then help with household chores – such as sweeping the gym floor, or helping Uncle Cornelius in the garden, or polishing the old lunatic's collection of antique brass knuckle-dusters. After a colossal supper, he and Cornelius would walk Bess again (at a slow, sometimes painful waddle) and then (his favourite part of the day) he would sit in The Study and listen to his uncle and The Hound swap tales and reminiscences of past adventures, while he slowly and warmly crumpled into drowsiness and then hauled his weary self to bed.

He'd also had a couple of phone calls with his mum. They had been painfully awkward at first, but she (as always) had taken everything in her stride. She'd known of The Hound from before Tom was born, had met him on several occasions, knew he was a "good sort", was very pleased to hear that he and Tom were getting along so well, and that Tom was enjoying his visit.

"We'll talk more about you being apprenticed when you get back, Sweetie. Incredible opportunity for you, it is, Tom. Make the most of it, won't you? And, oh, Tom, I'm so proud of you."

Tom was a little amazed and, at first, more than a little miffed that she had kept such a huge and astoundingly brilliant secret from him for so long, but then, if you thought about it, what else could she have done?

Being an inquisitive, determined and resourceful sort of chap, Tom had also discovered a little more about his fellow housemates (or *inmates,* as he often found himself referring to them).

Missus Dobbs, he learned, was the daughter of *Master Dobbs*, a famous Sussex *House-Fairy* (or *Brownie*) who had disappeared from the *world of men,* sometime in the 1830s, after a dispute over a hat: the tale being that Master Dobbs (who always wore a tattered old hat) had helped a struggling farmer during a particularly difficult harvest, and the grateful farmer, in return, thought to reward the little fellow with a brand new one (hat, that is). Leaving it out for him that evening, he heard the enraged Brownie rant – "*New 'at! New 'at, iz it? Dobbz will never do no more good!*"

Master Dobbs was never seen or heard of again.

A *Brownie*, according to *Greymorris' Field Guide*, was described as follows:

BROWNIE

House-Elf; House-Fairy – "*The Good Neighbours*".
A (usually) helpful *house-spirit* of the United Kingdom. Similar in appearance to an Elf or Goblin – a Brownie is sometimes described as being to a Goblin what a dog is to a wolf.
Not dangerous, unless they feel they have been slighted.
Can be attracted, and sometimes pressed into service, by 'shiny things'.
As to their origins there has, over the years, been much speculation. The two predominant theories being that they are either:
(i) A Goblin tribe or clan who, at some point early on in the history of Man's arrival into the British Isles, attached themselves to the society of Men.
(ii) The descendants of a slave population (possibly Goblins who had been captured by the Elbi during their colonization of Albion) who, upon the arrival of Man, chose to offer their services to Humankind instead of remaining with their Elven masters.

Bess, he was rather relieved to discover, was a wolfhound and nothing but a wolfhound. The Hound himself saying that he always kept a wolfhound or two, being – for obvious reasons – very fond of them. He had, in fact, when the breed was in danger of dying out in the late 1800s, been of great assistance to a gentleman by the name of *Captain George Augustus Graham* in his efforts to re-establish what is now known as the Irish Wolfhound. Besides that, though by nature gentle giants, when roused they were, in The Hound's opinion, the best guardians possible – and that was a comforting thought when he and Cornelius had to go away on *business*.

He had almost, almost, almost-almost-almost, got a hold on his slippery-old-goat-of-an-uncle.

One afternoon, while Tom was reading in The Study and Uncle Cornelius was resewing and reloading his *one-shot-stab-proof-anti-mugger-waistcoat* (a glorious Victorian garment of self-defence for the well-to-do gentleman about town – designed, with one yank of a button, to blast away any assailant who crept up on you from behind!!!), he found himself in a position to corner the wily old duffer.

'Uncle?' he asked, carefully laying his brilliant trap.

'Yes, Tom?' replied his uncle, distractedly.

'I've just been reading *Greymorris'* field-notes on the Wulver.'

'Oh aye? Lovely creature, so I'm told; very friendly.'

'You've never actually met one, then?' Tom asked, in seeming innocent rapture.

'No,' growled his uncle, ruefully. 'The 'Ound did a lot of searching a few years back, but 'e could find neither 'ide nor 'air of the poor old fellow.'

'But you *were* on the fishing holiday with The Hound when he might have been mistaken for the Wulver, weren't you?'

'Bloomin' well was! Miserable 'oliday that were an' all. Rained for a fortnight, with no rest nor respite for man nor beast. An' we caught next to nothing, as I remember,' reminisced the old codger, squinting in concentration as he attempted to rethread a needle.

'It says here,' said Tom, tapping the copy of *Greymorris' Field Guide,* and with the trace of a wicked grin pulling at one corner of his cunning mouth, 'that the last confirmed sightings of the Wulver were in the first decade of the Twentieth Century.'

'That'd be about right,' answered Uncle Cornelius, absent-mindedly.

'But you think that what they actually saw was The Hound, while the two of you were on a fishing holiday together?' Tom continued, innocently.

'*"Long sodden coat, miserable expression"* – aye, that were 'im all right.'

'So ... that would mean that you would have to be over a hundred years old! I mean, if everything is true and you were really there of course.'

Uncle Cornelius laughed and put down the needle and thread.

'Well, you're a sharp one an' no mistake, aren't you, Tomas Dearlove. Well, yes, it is true that I'm a little bit older than what I looks, but then I put that down to lots of exercise an' a proper diet (none of this modern 'ealth-food nonsense). That an' 'anging around *magic-folk* for so long, if you gets my drift. Now, you get back to your studies, young man,' he chuckled. 'Crafty little bugger.'

Now that the were-wolf-wolfhound was out of the bag, so to speak, the *refused* pictures in The Study had, mostly (most intriguingly), been righted to their intended positions, revealing numerous old photographs of Uncle Cornelius in various pugilistic poses – including one of him as a youngish-looking man, standing with his arms folded over bare-chest, slicked back hair and glowering, with muscular ferocity, over a huge handlebar moustache; and another of him, looking slightly older and with his beloved 'Newgate Knocker' firmly ensconced, standing proudly before a table jammed-full of sporting trophies, cups and what looked like several championship belts. There was also an antique photograph of what could have been a Victorian international cricket XI, featuring Cornelius and The Hound – both resplendent in stripy and tasselled *schoolboy* caps. The most impressive picture, however, was a large and cracked old oil painting of a stern-looking The Hound dressed resplendently in Elizabethan-style armour (similar to the one, or perhaps even the very same suit, that was in the Muse-asium) that glistened with martial vigour against the deep-dark background. There was another, smaller, portrait of The Hound (in dog-form) sitting with an expression of devotion and patient loyalty next to the imposing figure of a man who, Tom thought, looked a lot like the chap from the painting in the hallway, and must therefore be Henry Percy, 9th Earl of Northumberland.

Tom had also made great use of his *Seeing Stone*, which he kept in his pocket at all times – attached to his belt by an old shoelace. He had, for example, discovered that the chalk lines drawn about his bedroom window (and all the other windows and doors of the house) were, in fact, on closer examination through the stone, lines of tightly packed letters and symbols in a mysterious and archaic script. These, he was informed, were charms to protect One Punch Cottage from unexpected, unwanted and unpleasant (!) visitors.

Early one evening, Tom was rudely awoken from the little nap that he was taking – (it had been a particularly exhausting day – the morning spent manfully pummelling the living daylights out of various sorts of shifting bags and swinging balls, followed by an extended period of hard study [reading about the *fascinating* political manipulations that had instigated the devastating *Troll Wars,* and which, in turn, had led to the collapse of the great Troll Dynasties of Alpine Switzerland {see G. Gillespie Livermore's absolutely riveting "*The Rise & Decline of the Great Troll Dynasties of Western Europe – 910-1463*"}], and rounded off by a painfully long afternoon of weeding in the garden with Uncle Cornelius [mercilessly murdering anything that looked like it wasn't supposed to be there – though Tom got the distinct impression that his uncle was about as clueless as he regarding the whole matter and might have been making things up as he went along]) – by a truly horrible sound.

Good grief! he squawked in alarm, rising like a startled partridge from his slumber and rushing towards the bedroom door. *Missus Dobbs has caught Bess' tail in the mangle!*

He pelted downstairs, full of mortified concern, only to realise that the dreadful sound was emanating from The Study, and that now the fast metallic plinking of a banjo could be heard bouncing jauntily around the cries of pain of the poor, wailing, tortured beast. Suddenly the appalling din was accompanied by a brace of hearty voices, rolling and heaving like a couple of tone-deaf drunken pirates spending their leave in a karaoke bar.

'Our boots and coats is all in paaawwwwn
*[**Go down you Blood-red roses!**]*
And it's flamin' draughty round Cape Hooooorrrrn
*[**Go down you Blood-red roses!**]*
Ooowh, you pinks and posies
*[**Go down you Blood-red roses! Go down**!]*
Oh, my old mother she wrote to meeeeeeee
*[**Go down you Blood-red roses!**]*
My darling son, come home from seeeeeaaa
*[**Go down you Blood-red roses! Go Down!**]*
It's drown you may but go you must
*[**Go down you Blood-red roses!**]*

If you graft too hard your head they'll bust
[Go down you Blood-red roses! Go down!]
Ooowh, you pinks and posies
[Go down you Blood-red roses! GO DOWN!]'

Tom, full of fearful imaginings, pushed open the door of The Study ... to see, to his almighty relief, Bess sitting with her ears pinned back and a look of pig-eyed concern on her face (but otherwise unharmed) and lashing her tail gleefully like the second-worst drummer in history.

Seated in their respective armchairs were his uncle (armed dangerously with a banjo – the old duffer had the uncanny ability to make anything in his hands look deadly) and The Hound (huddled over the peculiar implement that Tom had first noticed on his arrival – the curious mandolin/model pirate ship/pasta-making machine – and furiously churning away at the handle like a demonic organ grinder after an overdose of Sherbet Dip-Dabs).

Both The Hound and Cornelius had their heads thrown back in rapturous joy, "singing" (that was the closest word that Tom could think of, although to call it *singing* felt like some sort of injustice) their happy hearts out: The Hound gibbering in a soft howl with his mouth quivering like a sock puppet.

'Ah, Tom,' cried The Hound, gleefully, on noticing Tom's arrival. 'You are, I hope, a connoisseur of the hurdy-gurdy?' (For so was named the terrible contraption.)

'Come on, son, join in,' chortled an ecstatic Uncle Cornelius, his fingers flying over the fretboard of the banjo like a man trying to stamp out an ant colony. 'Go an' get that Riddle-drum over there an' put some *ump-pa-pa!* on it, lad. The Tipper's behind it.'

Dazed and confused, Tom followed his uncle's directions and gingerly went to pick up the large circular shield-like drum that was leaning against the wall; the skin of some long dead animal stretched tightly over its wooden frame. Behind it he found a double-headed wooden beater (the 'Tipper'?) – invented, no doubt, to trounce the poor, long-suffering creature beyond the grave, in an eternal act of punishment.

'Come on, son!' roared Uncle Cornelius, joyfully. 'It's like trying a German sausage – what's the *wurst* that can 'appen.'

Well, how hard can it be? thought Tom, giving the drum a quick testing thrash.

And so, sitting himself down on the tatty footstool, Tom did his best to join in. And, in so doing, was introduced to the world that is called – by some with awe and by others with horror – *Folk Music.*

ELEVEN
Peculiarities At Petworth Park

Tuesday morning found old man, were-hound, boy and eternally optimistic wolfhound sitting around the breakfast table scoffing hot muffins (don't dare say "English muffin" to Cornelius or you'd be given a stern half hour lecture) dripping with butter and cheese.

The Hound suddenly swept down his newspaper.

'Bored, bored, bored, bored!' he muttered to nobody in particular, whilst drumming his claws on the edge of the table.

The were-hound sighed heavily and looked to both Cornelius and Tom.

Tom offered a weak but sympathetic '*sorry out of my depth on this one*' muffiny-butter-chinned smile, while Uncle Cornelius remained firmly and silently ensconced behind his own newspaper.

The Hound rippled his talons against the table once more, threw a sideways glance in Cornelius' direction and blew out his cheeks.

Cornelius edged a hand around his newspaper and delicately retracted his teacup.

'That's a shame,' he muttered from behind his paper, and then slurped tea loudly before returning his cup to the table.

The Hound glowered briefly at the newspaper (held steadfastly between them like a barrier) and continued to tap out a frustrated rhythm whilst looking distractedly about the room.

'S'pose it might be quite nice to take a little jaunt out Petworth way this evening?' offered Cornelius, eventually, paper-barricade held firmly in place.

'Do you think?' sniffed The Hound, whose attempt to sound nonchalant was ruined by the sudden vigorous whip-like wagging of his sabre-like tail. 'Well, it has been a while, I suppose. Yes. Yes I think that would be most agreeable, Dandy.'

Uncle Cornelius lay down his paper and gave Tom a wink. 'Worst poker player in 'istory,' he chuckled quietly to Tom.

'Right then, son,' he continued, 'let's you an' me go get Old Nancy ready then.'

Old Nancy, Tom soon discovered, was the vintage automobile that he had spied earlier in the beachside lock-up, and he spent the rest of the morning polishing and cleaning the old crock while Uncle Cornelius fluttered around tinkering with various spanners and pots of oil.

'Don't really understand the bloomin' things m'self, but I s'pose that'll do,' muttered the old man at last, anxiously chewing his lip and eyeing his handiwork with some suspicion.

From beneath a pile of clutter, Uncle Cornelius drew a large, thick plastic sheet and arranged it carefully so that it covered the interior of Old Nancy's extremely spacious boot.

'Much as 'e won't admit it, 'Is Nibs always grows a bit restless when there's a full moon on its way. Gets a bit tetchy like, a few days before'and. An' Petworth, well, it's 'is 'ome I s'pose, 'elps calm 'im down.

'*Proud Petworth, poor people; 'igh church, crooked steeple.*'

Sundown saw the *One Punch Cottage Crew* pottering along winding country roads and through small, picturesque villages on their way to Petworth. Tom sat up front in the passenger seat, with Uncle Cornelius at the wheel – the old codger resplendent in tweed, a scarf that looked like it belonged to a First World War fighter pilot and a (needless) set of antique driving goggles nestled (needlessly) around an archaic-looking stovepipe hat. (Tom, to his eternal gratitude, had so far avoided the trip to the tailors.) The Hound was stretched out in the back seat with Bess resting her elegant head blissfully across his lap. The were-hound himself was dressed in a long grey duffle coat with an enormous hood, and a pair of immense baggy shorts that were tied up at the *knee* (making him look like an Elizabethan were-wolf – which, Tom supposed, was pretty much what he was) and held up with a wide leather utility-belt (fastened with an enormous circular buckle) strapped around his waspish waist.

Tom wondered whether the concept of modesty was one of the first changes that had happened during the process of becoming *human-like* or if it was just an awful attempt to *blend in*. Anyway, he was thankful for Old Nancy's dark tinted windows as she pootled through the Sussex countryside.

They drew up at the edge of the high stone wall that runs around the large estate of Petworth Park, and parked under the branches of a billowing willow tree.

Uncle Cornelius switched off the lights and cut the engine.

Tom peered out at an eerie world, dimly lit by the full moon.

'Right then, Tom,' smiled Uncle Cornelius, 'you an' I'll sit tight 'ere, with a flask of 'ot tea an' a packet of Jammy Dodgers, while 'Is Nibs an' Bess go for a little *walk*.'

'Can't I go with them?' Tom asked, rather disappointed.

'No you can't,' came the quick response. 'You stay 'ere with me, an' that's an order.'

'Right then, chaps,' said The Hound, eagerly leaning over and checking the time on the clock set into Nancy's polished walnut dashboard, 'be as quick as we can. Tip-top. Two honks of the horn, Dandy, if there's any ... *inconveniences*.'

And with that, he opened the back door, sidled out of the car and disappeared into the silver-blue shadows, keeping Bess closely under control by his side.

Tom looked out of the window after them and could just about make out The Hound gently hoisting an embarrassed and mortified-looking Bess under one arm and then bound, like a monstrous puppy-napping gibbon, up into the branches of the overhanging tree, before swiftly disappearing over the wall. There was the softest of thuds as they landed on the other side, followed by a hushed 'Good girl, Bess', the gentle clink of a belt being undone and the rumple of clothes being removed and folded, a five second cacophony of popping, and then ... silence.

'What's going on, Uncle?' asked Tom, suspiciously.

'Just out for a walk, that's all,' replied Uncle Cornelius, seemingly deep in concentration as he wrestled with the Jammy Dodger's wrapper. 'Good to let them off the lead once in a while. Run wild an' all that. Can't be nice being cooped up all day, now, can it?'

'So, ... *Uncle*?' continued Tom, rather uneasily. 'I was reading that Petworth Park is famous for its herds of deer. That is right ... isn't it?'

'Is it?' sniffed Uncle Cornelius, in a high-pitched gruff.

'... And the plastic sheeting in the boot of the car? What's that for then?' pressed Tom (with a firm suspicion that he already knew the answer).

'Arrh ... That's for ... uhm ... in case it ... er ... *rains* ...'

'You're poaching!' wailed Tom, somewhat amused and totally flabbergasted.

'Poaching? Keep your voice down, Tom. Poaching!' hissed Cornelius, a picture of innocent indignation. 'We is most certainly not ... *poaching*! I've never 'eard the like ...'

Tom shot his uncle an expression overflowing with disbelief.

'We got a licence an' everything,' the old man protested.

'Oh really?' replied Tom, with loaded scepticism. 'Let's have a look at it then,' he chirped, gleefully delighted to have the old duffer on the ropes.

Uncle Cornelius blustered, reluctantly handed Tom the Jammy Dodgers, pulled open a small door in the dashboard and fumbled around in the glove compartment. Some minutes later, after much mumbling and muttering under his breath, the old codger produced an ancient and yellowing scrap of parchment.

Tom took it gently from the old man's uncertain grasp and unfolded it. It felt like a moth-eaten, floppy leather glove.

Scratched in a fading hand was the script –

I

hereby decree that
the Bearer
of this letter is to be given
Free range & accesse
to my Landes {& all the Game therein}
to exclusively include
the Estate of Petworth Park -

As is seene to bee most fit, & profitable, for all concerned.

Algeron Percy,

Earl of Northumberland

the 2nd day of February – in the year 1632

'This ran out three hundred and seventy-eight years ago!' blasted Tom.

'No it never! Where's it say that it's run out?'

'Ha!' Tom snorted, loving every minute of it. 'I'm going for a hedge inspection.'

'You what?'

'I need a wee.'

'Oh, right you are. Don't stray too far now. An' 'and back those Jammy Dodgers!'

Tom sidled out of the car.

'An', Tom ...' whispered his uncle.

'Yes Uncle?' Tom whispered back.

'Try and be ... discreet.'

'Course I will.'

His uncle smiled thankfully.

'*Poachers,*' chuckled Tom, shaking his head in mock exasperation as he gently closed the car door.

Still chortling to himself, Tom made his way along the grass verge until he turned a corner and found a suitable amount of vegetation to hide modestly behind.

Poaching, who'd have thought it? Crafty old buggers. ... Crikey, must be all that tea ... he mused, trying to wee in near total darkness with as much stealth as this whole preposterous situation seemed to demand.

'*Tom!*' hissed a voice, urgently.

'Uh!' yelped Tom, as he leapt into the air, turning and peeing with frantic alarm in all directions.

'*This way!*' the voice whispered, insistently.

'Uncle Cornelius? Is that you? What's up?' hissed Tom, fixing his trousers and looking hopelessly around him.

'*This way ...*' the voice repeated.

It seemed to be coming from behind the wall.

Still, best check, he thought.

Tom stuck his head out from behind the bushes. Nothing to be seen apart from Old Nancy, camouflaged rather expertly in the shadows – if you didn't know she was there you'd have been hard pressed to have spotted her. Tom had to admit that his uncle certainly knew his business. But what the devil was the mad old duffer up to now?

'*Tom ... this way. Hurry!*'

Tom redrew his head into the bushes and edged towards the wall. It was then, just as the sweeping clouds uncovered the moon, that he noticed it. How odd that he hadn't seen it before. Right in front of him was a slight gap in the wall where the bricks had crumbled; just wide enough for him to squeeze through, if he ducked down and contorted himself a little.

'*Hurry, son, hurry,*' his uncle's voice rasped again.

Tom pressed himself through the gap and found that he was standing among closely packed trees and shrubbery. The light from the full moon gave the tips of the branches a spooky, silvery blue tint and, despite his best efforts, Tom shuddered a little.

'Where are you, Uncle?' he hissed. 'What's going on? Has the gamekeeper turned up?'

Blimey, they'd be for it now. He could just imagine it –

"It was then, M'Lud, that I discovered The Accused amblin' frantically frew the woods among the terrified 'erds of deer, wearing wee-stained trousers [see Ex'ibit A] an' an expression like a guilty ferret. Wiv 'im were two monstrous deer-'ounds [one attired in duffle coat and outrageous pantaloons], an' a partially shaved geriatric gorilla [dressed up like a villainous 'enchman from an episode of Sherlock 'Olmes]. Their mode of transport was revealed to be a gangsters' vintage getaway ve'icle – what looked like it might 'ave been purloined from Wacky Races' The Anthill Mob – an' wiv, what could only be described as blood-proof plastic sheetin' carefully coverin' the interior of the boot of said automobile.

On being apprehended, The Accused produced a mangy scrap of old leather, claiming it was an 'unting permit, that the suspect 'ad clearly not seen fit to renew in over free 'undred an' seventy-eight years ..."

Good grief! We'll be transported!

'Uncle Cornelius!' he hissed again. 'Uncle Cornelius!'

But there was no reply.

The moon suddenly disappeared, slinking behind dark clouds, and Tom became disturbingly aware that he couldn't even make out where he had just come from, let alone where he was going. He stumbled gingerly forward ... and recoiled in horror as he felt thin branches brush across his face and seemingly clutch frantically at his arms and legs.

Pluckily sweeping them aside, he forced his way forward, entering deeper and deeper and deeper into the darkness of the woods.

After only a few minutes he knew that he was totally lost.

Where, oh where, was the doddering old bugger? And just what was the incontinent cretin up to?

If it wasn't for the growing feeling of fear that was rapidly rising from the pit of his stomach, he would have been furious with the infuriating old rascal and this whole ridiculous, illegal and (probably) immoral expedition.

The moon suddenly broke free from the clouds and lit up the faint outline of a path beneath his feet.

If he followed it long enough, he reasoned, it must eventually lead out onto the grass fields (he was in Sussex after all, not the Amazon). From there he'd at least be able to get some sense of how to get out of this blasted park.

He followed the path as it snaked its raggedy way through ever-denser, ever-older, ever more foreboding trees; the flickering moonlight making it look like they were shuffling clumsily towards him, their swaying limbs beckoning and terrifying.

It was useless! He was totally lost. The path had disappeared, and now he was surrounded by sinister-looking yew trees that seemed to want to reach out and suck his flesh into their roots.

Where, oh where, was his uncle? whined Tom inwardly, both terrified and furious. And what the devil was the daffy old nudger up to?

'The stupid, frickin' idiotic, badger-faced, inconsiderate old fart!' cursed Tom, under his breath.

'This way!'

'Ah ... Uncle!' gasped Tom, with joyous relief (silently praying that his mutterings had been inaudible to the old swine). 'Where are you? I ... I can't see you.'

'This way ...'

His uncle's voice was definitely coming from behind the most gnarled, twisted and massive of the ancient yews. Tom swiftly headed for it, circled its warped and enormous trunk ... and nearly had a heart attack.

There, magically lit by the dappled moonlight, that fluttered like silvery butterflies through the treetops, was a clearing. And in the middle of that clearing lay a giant millstone, that looked like it must have weighed half a ton – if not more. And thrust through the middle of said millstone was an enormous metal spike, with weeds (loaded with blue-black, poisonous-looking berries) clawing and spiralling their way up it. And pinned facedown beneath that stone, impaled by the stake, was the remains of a deformed skeleton of what had once been a man. A very, very large man indeed. The bones that could be seen (the hands, feet and skull) looked like they had been melted and then badly remoulded into shape again. The long skeletal fingers and toes splayed out like twisted hooks from the quarters of the stone wheel. The empty eye sockets, set deep within the bubbled skull, stared pityingly outward, cutting straight through Tom like an icy knife. The flickering shadows of the swaying branches above made the hideous skull look as if, for one moment, it wore an expression of abhorrence and desperate surprise, before suddenly shifting to one of exuberant and unexpected hope, and then flit back again.

Tom forced his heartbeat back down his throat and took a step closer.

There was a sudden flash of movement and Tom turned to see Bess coursing towards him.

But no. No it wasn't Bess ... it looked more like ... The Hound. Tom's heart lifted in a momentary glorious balloon of relief, only for it to burst with the ferociously freezing realization that it wasn't The Hound at all, but a savage doppelgänger – silvery rust-red, almost spectral in form.

As the beast bounded closer, snarling dangerously, Tom thought he could make out terrible gaping wounds on its neck and chest.

He turned to run.

A spear smacked into the tree just inches before his eyes. The shaft quivered with the force of the impact and, for a fleeting moment, Tom saw his own horrified reflection wobbling back at him in the polished silver blade.

Tom yelped – meeping like a professional meeper at the Annual All England Meeping Championships – and turned to run, but the ghostly hound had him pinned against the tree, snapping at him with loud, lightning-fast, razor-teethed jaws. He could almost feel the crunch of its fangs ripping the air around him to shreds.

A horse whinnied.

Tom spun to see a mounted horseman rearing up in silhouette.

In one hand it held a long, wickedly edged sword that caught the moonlight like a ghost-mirror, and in the other, held high to the night sky like a terrible trophy, was a severed head ... its own head! Man and mount bucked and reared, looking for all the world like a Comanche warrior who'd overzealously scalped himself.

The headless horseman screamed a blood-curdling cry, whirling his detached bonce about him (thus making a sound somewhat like the most uninviting ice-cream van on the planet) and then hurling it towards Tom.

The head spun and swerved, driving through the air like a spinning cricket ball.

Tom caught fleeting glimpses of its face, contorted with rage.

'YOU!' it screeched, floating and spiralling around Tom. 'You CANNOT be here! You cannot BE here. You cannot be HERE!

'YOU CANNOT BE HERE!'

TWELVE
Stay Put In Your Grave

'Stand down, Master Scrimshaw,' said Uncle Cornelius in a calm, steady voice. 'Been an unfortunate occurrence, an' that's all. We'll be going now, if that's all right with you.'

The spectral hound stopped its snapping and backed, massive head lowered menacingly, towards the horseman's side. The spinning skull ceased turning, and tilted, with a look of indignant surprise, towards Uncle Cornelius. It floated to within a few feet from the old man's grim, stern face and eyed him suspiciously.

'But he cannot be here,' it snarled firmly. '*He* cannot be here.'

'You've never been more right, Master Scrimshaw. I'll be giving 'im a good talking to when we get 'ome, an' no mistake. Come on, Tom, let's be going.'

Tom performed the fastest run on wobbly legs ever recorded in history and hurled himself into the long, safe-secure-most-welcome-sight-he'd-ever-seen arms of his uncle.

'But, Dandy,' the headless horseman pleaded, sounding most confused, 'he cannot be here.'

'I know that, Bartholomew, course 'e can't. Won't 'appen again I can assure you. Now, good day to you, sir, an' we'll be off.'

Uncle Cornelius half-pulled, half-lifted Tom from the clearing and back into the trees.

As they were leaving, Tom looked back to see The Hound (in dog-form) and Bess racing through the undergrowth and towards the scene. Bess hung back at the edge of the trees, her ears flattened and her tail wagging uncertainly, but The Hound shot forwards like an arrow towards the cinnamon ghost-dog and they capered together in a dance of pure joy and delight. Then he turned and high-trotted proudly to the horseman (head now tucked firmly underarm) who leaned down and playfully scratched the great dog's ears.

'Now then, Percival,' growled Bartholomew Scrimshaw, 'what's all this skulduggery?'

As Cornelius led him by the hand and drew him through the woods, Tom's eyes were drawn again to the enormous, twisted skeleton lying pinned beneath the giant stone. In his imagination the empty sockets seemed to follow his departure; the fluttering shadows from the twitching treetops casting strange and mournful movements on its hideous countenance.

When they had finally left the woods, Tom sank to the grass, quivering on his haunches, and retched.

'It's all right now, Tom. No 'arm done, son,' said Cornelius, hunkering down beside him and patting him on the back.

Tom shot the callous old idiot an incredulous glower.

'I've just been physically threatened by an exceedingly miffed, psychotic headless horseman,' he rasped, 'and that's all right is it?'

'Well, you've 'ad tea an' crumpets with a were-wolf-wolf'ound so what's the big deal?' replied Cornelius, trying to make light of events. 'Plus you can now add to that – a ghost-dog, an 'eadless 'orseman, an' an 'Ouse-Fairy ... not a bad collection in a couple of weeks, if you think 'bout it.'

'No, no I suppose not,' muttered Tom, trying to get his thoughts together and sound as matter-of-fact as his uncle.

'What the 'ell were you doing running off like that for anyway? I told you not to wander, an' the next thing I know you've scaled the walls an' are bolting through the woods like an escaping convict. 'Ell of a job I 'ad catching up with you.'

'I ... I thought I heard you calling me ... from behind the wall.'

Uncle Cornelius stood up straight, tugged his whiskers and looked back towards the woods.

'Did you now?' he growled softly, with such seriousness that it startled Tom almost as much as the two ghosts that he had just seen.

'Come on, Tom,' sighed the old man, effortlessly hoisting Tom to his feet. 'Let's get you back to the car, son.'

At that moment The Hound (in were-form) and Bess joined them.

Bess playfully nudged Tom back to the floor and cleaned his face with a wet tongue like a warm flannel.

'Are you all right, Tom?' asked The Hound, bristling with concern.

Tom nodded and hugged Bess, burying his face in her coarse, soft fur, and trying not to cry.

'What the blue blazes is going on, Dandy? Why is Tom even in the grounds?' demanded the were-hound, sternly.

'Young Tom 'ad the urge to water the 'edgerow, so to speak, got lost, an' then thought 'e 'eard me a calling 'im,' Cornelius replied steadily, giving The Hound a hard and loaded stare.

The Hound took a deep breath and looked about him.

'Let's get Tom home, Dandy. Bess and I are done for the night. We'll meet you back at the car in five minutes.'

And with that he sprung away at an impossibly fast canter, with Bess, leaping at joyous full tilt, chasing after him.

When they were back in the car and driving homeward (with Bess snoring softly next to The Hound in the back seat, and a large, carefully wrapped, deer carcass stowed in the boot) Tom found that all he could think about was the piteous, dreadful skeleton crushed beneath the millwheel with an iron stake driven through its heart.

'He must have done something terrible,' he said quietly, to no one in particular.

Uncle Cornelius sent him a concerned glance.

''Oo's that then, Tom?' he asked, gently.

‘That man. The man who was buried under the stone. He must have done a horrible thing for someone to have done that to him.’

There was a long, awkward pause while Cornelius studied the rear-view mirror and then, in a sad and strangely weary voice, reluctantly replied.

‘That ’e did, Tom. ’E was a wrong’un, an’ no mistake. Bad to the bone. Too wicked to stay put in ’is grave, ’e was. Best forgotten. Least said ’bout ’im the better.’

‘But who was he?’ Tom asked in a hushed tone.

Uncle Cornelius stiffened and watched the road with a deliberate concentration.

Tom looked on in fascination as the corners of his uncle’s mouth turned downwards into a fearful grimace.

‘’Is name was Johnny Grendel,’ hissed the old man, and his words were hard and cold. ‘Now let that be an end to the matter.’

And they drove all the way back to One Punch Cottage in silence.

THIRTEEN
An Unexpected Return

'Nice cup of cocoa'll set you right, Ducky,' gurned Missus Dobbs, as she handed Tom a large mug that was bubbling noisily with a thick, mud-coloured liquid.

Behind her back Uncle Cornelius gave him a quick thumbs-up, assuring him that it was safe to drink.

And it was: lovely, hot, sweet, thick, glorious, drinking chocolate.

'Sounds like you've had quite an evening of it, Ducks. Poor love. Get that inside you and then off to bed.'

Tom nodded and smiled in thanks as he reclined comfortingly in Uncle Cornelius' leather armchair, but he was actually feeling much better. Cornelius had been right; if you thought about it (and he'd spent the whole journey back doing just that!), after being chastised by a were-wolf-wolfhound only a few days ago for not holding his cutlery correctly, and having spent the last few weeks avoiding poisonous cups of tea foisted on him by an eye-gouging House-Fairy, what, after all, were the horrors of being chased by a monstrous, salivating ghost-dog, and having a razor-sharp hunting spear thrown at you by an enraged and deranged headless horseman?

The skeleton trapped under the millwheel still bothered him, though. And he felt sure that, however hard he might try, he would never be able to forget the sad, haunted, and hateful expression worn by the shadowy, warped and hideous skull.

'Got something for you, Tom,' said his uncle, sitting beside him on the arm of the armchair and putting an enormously long arm of his own around Tom's shoulder. 'Was going to give it to you in the morning but, well, after all that's 'appened, seems only right an' fitting that you should 'ave it 'ere an' now. *Baptism of fire,* an' all that.'

He handed Tom a book-shaped parcel wrapped in brown paper and tied up, in businesslike fashion, with smart-looking string. Tom put down his mug and looked to his smiling uncle and then to The Hound – who might have attempted (it was hard to tell) a comforting smile of his own as he languished, ankles artfully crossed, in the chair opposite, studying Tom intently.

Tom slowly opened the package – delighting in the sound of the thick, crisp paper – to reveal that the book-shaped present contained ... not one but two books! Who'd have thought it?

One was a Moleskine notebook and the other a copy of *Greymorris' Field Guide: 2010 Edition (updated with extended appendix concerning South American travel).*

Tom opened the cover and read –

To Tom,
Welcome to The Firm.
All the best,
Uncle Cornelius
&
Percival T. Hound

'Thank you,' said Tom, with genuine delight. 'That's fantastic.'

'Keep it with you at all times, young Tom,' advised The Hound, still staring intently at him. 'Always pays to know exactly what you're up against. Do everything that you can to stack the odds in your favour and then you might just be able to predict just how the cards will fall.'

'Yes, yes I will. Thank you again, it's ... it's marvellous!'

Uncle Cornelius ruffled Tom's hair and then joined The Hound and Missus Dobbs as they entered into a deep conversation on the variety of splendid ways to prepare venison.

Tom eagerly flicked through the pages of his new book.

H ... H, he mused, as he skimmed through the pages. ... *'Harpie'... hhhmmm ... H...E ... Aahh ... 'Headless'... 'Headless Coachman' ... 'Headless Ghosts' ... 'Headless Horseman' ... Ah-ha.*

HEADLESS HORSEMAN

(See **HEADLESS HORSEPERSON**)

Oh good grief!

HEADLESS HORSEPERSON

Ghost (usually malevolent).

The vengeful (and often downright spiteful) spirit of a horseman, or woman, who has met their death via decapitation – usually by supernatural means.

Famous examples include:

1. ***The Hessian Horseman***

Sleepy Hollow, New York, USA.

The ghost of a German mercenary in the employ of the British, killed during the American War of Independence.

2. ***The Wild Huntsman***

Dresden, Germany.

The Huntsman lures his victims into the forest, and to their doom, with a blast from his hunting-horn. Those who hear the *Huntsman'*s horn are said to encounter their death imminently.

3. ***Black Bart***
Petworth, Sussex, UK.
Black Bart haunts the grounds of Petworth Park, accompanied by his faithful & monstrous dog.
Of interest, Sussex can also boast
4. ***Squire Powlett (Paulett)***
St Leonards, UK.
Powlett is unusual in that he prefers to ride pillion on other peoples' mounts, grasping the unfortunate rider around the waist with one hand and thrusting his head (howling with wicked delight) in their face with the other.

The ancient phenomenon of the headless horseman is, quite naturally, becoming ever more uncommon, being replaced, as it is, by the more modern occurrence of the **HEADLESS MOTORCYCLIST** (see below).
(Also see **DULLAN**.)

The antique candlestick phone suddenly rang out loudly, making Tom jump.

Missus Dobbs trotted over to the phone and (after quickly brushing down and straightening her clothes, followed by a brisk clearing of her throat) answered the call.

'Lyons and Hound Investigation Agency – established 1895,' she squeaked slowly into the mouthpiece (in an outrageously plummy voice). 'To whom am I speaking and how may I be of assistance?'

She cast a proud and jubilant gurn at Uncle Cornelius, who winked back encouragingly.

There was a slight pause and then her face wrinkled into a smile and her voice melted back to its *normal* croak.

'Oh hello, Ducky, how's tricks? ... Yes, mustn't grumble ... I'll just pass you over.'

She held the earpiece to her chest.

'It's that lovely Inspector Jones of the D.S.C.,' she whispered loudly.

Uncle Cornelius gracefully bounced to the phone, while The Hound pricked one alert ear and kept his eyes fixed firmly on Tom.

''Ello Inspector, an' what can we do for you at this ungodly 'our?'

Uncle Cornelius' face creased into a frown.

'Oh, I see ... A group of students were attacked outside the Bystander Café ... Yes ... Well that's most unfortunate but not really our department ... What's that? ... The assailant was over eight feet tall ... dressed up like the Phantom of the Opera ... with a white, devilish face ... talon-like 'ands ... an' spitting blue flames from 'is mouth ...'

The Hound's second ear joined the first and his eyes sparkled and danced with an excited curiosity.

'... an' 'aving what can only be described as a *fiendish demeanour* ... When challenged 'e sprang away ... clearing a distance of near twenty feet! ...'

The Hound was up and at Cornelius' side in an instant.

The two of them locked eyes.

'We'll be there in a jiffy, Inspector ... What's that? Right you are then. See you in a mo.'

Cornelius hung the earpiece back on its stand and set the phone back onto the filing cabinet.

'Says 'e's sending a car round to get us. Constable Tuggnutter will escort us to the scene.'

Four minutes later and Tom, The Hound and Uncle Cornelius were being shepherded into the back of an unmarked police van. Uncle Cornelius had tried to convince Tom that he should go to bed, but Tom was in no mood to miss out (on anything!), especially after the earlier events of the evening (and in any case, he really didn't fancy the idea of being left on his own). The Hound, however, had thought it a capital idea for Tom to accompany them.

'Can't mollycoddle the boy forever, Dandy,' he'd said. 'Besides, it will undoubtedly help Tom's state of mind to keep occupied ... particularly when one considers recent proceedings.'

With that, the matter was settled. Tom was ordered by his uncle to do '*as he was told, when 'e was told*' at all times or there'd be '*what for*' (whatever that was – though whatever it was it didn't sound pleasant). His uncle needn't have worried, for Tom was determined to stay comfortingly close to the deadly old duffer at all costs. And so, with said deadly old duffer plucking a hefty metal-tipped cane from the umbrella stand, they had waited at the gate of One Punch Cottage until the enormous and plodding shape of Police Constable Tuggnutter loomed into view at the end of Black Lion Lane.

Constable Tuggnutter resembled a sturdy wardrobe (carved from granite) with a large, blond (granite-like) potato balanced on top of it for a head.

'Morning, Tuggers,' offered Uncle Cornelius, in jovial greeting, only for the massive policeman to visibly wince, grunt something unintelligible in reply and then escort them to the waiting police van.

In three minutes they were at the scene of the attack – the area already having been cleared and cordoned off from prying (i.e. *civilian*) eyes.

The Hound, with the hood of his duffle coat drawn up (as if that would somehow draw attention away from the fact that he was seven-and-a-half feet tall, had a shaggy tail poking from beneath the hem of his coat, and a gargantuan black nose and spiky yellow whiskers sprouting from the rim of his enormous hood), strolled over to a solitary figure huddling like a bullied schoolchild in the doorway of the Bystander Café.

'Good morning, Mordecai,' said The Hound, warmly. 'Are there any further developments to report?'

Inspector Mordecai Jones smiled, but somehow managed to retain a gloomy and haunted expression.

'Must say how very pleased I am to see you, Mister Hound. You too, Professor,' he said, and then turned his attention to Tom. 'And who's this then?' he asked.

'This is Tom, my ... relative,' replied Uncle Cornelius. ''E's doing some ... er ... work experience with us, so to speak.'

Inspector Jones smiled at Tom. Tom smiled back. Despite the dourly morose countenance of the Inspector, Tom sensed a good heart.

The seventh son of a seventh son, Mordecai Elijah Jones was a short, slight, dark-skinned man in his early fifties, with closely cropped and grizzled hair and the faintest hint of a Northumbrian accent when he spoke. The haunted stoop of his neck and shoulders had developed in childhood when his "gift" had first manifested itself; for Inspector Jones possessed what is commonly called "The Sight".

His first memory of this "gift" was when his mother (newly arrived to the frozen wastes of Northumberland from the glamorous heat of the West Indies) had taken him for his very first day at his new school – a terrifying first day, at a terrifying new school, in a terrifying new country. '*If 'e misbehave 'imself,*' he had overheard his kindly mother tell his new teachers in her warm Caribbean accent, '*'it him, the young rascal.*' [!?!]

While his mother had nattered pleasantly with the teachers and the other mums, young Mordecai was approached by two painfully thin, unnaturally pale, and ragged-looking children.

'Best be'ave thyself,' they warned the saucer-eyed, trembling young Mordecai. 'If'n thou don'st be'ave thyself then they'll beat thee! Beat thee till thou can'st misbe'ave na mo'e.'

(Mordecai later learned that, many years before, the school building had once been a workhouse, where orphaned children had often been worked, thrashed and beaten to death by the ruthless owners and their sadistic staff.)

Things never really got much better for young Mordecai. Wherever he went he was sought out by the dead, who seemed hell-bent on introducing themselves (due, in fact, to Mordecai's uncommonly friendly and pleasant aura; perhaps, like Tom, they could sense that young Mr Jones had an exceptionally *good heart*, and that was, that is, an attractive and wonderful rarity). His school reports continuously commented on his nervousness and lack of focus – but really, you try concentrating on your O-Level Geography paper whilst the ghost of a mangled twelve-year-old boy named Jed (unjustly killed by the workhouse's pitiless machinery one hundred and twenty-two years ago) sits on your desk and sobs onto your shoulder, wailing for his long-lost mother.

On leaving school, Mordecai stumbled from one dismal dead-end job to another (no pun intended), all the while haunted by the ghosts of the deceased; the moaners, the droners, the curious, the furious and, worst of all, the lonely. There was no end to them. The dead were everywhere.

In an attempt at normality, Mordecai sought the refuge and shelter of "*The System*" and the last sanctuary for the ambitious yet academically underachieving – Her Majesty's Metropolitan Police Force.

For the first time in his life his "gift" became of practical use. He was able, in secret of course, to speak to murder victims directly and find out the truth of the unfortunate matter at hand.

His rise through the ranks was, to put it mildly, meteoric.

This, of course, attracted much attention – but where there is attention, jealousy soon follows. One night, after one too many pints of Timothy Taylor's, at a *Policing in the Community – meet-and-great* – charity-do, he unburdened the full weight of his *terrible* secret to a seemingly sympathetic colleague, who, in turn, bleated and repeated it, with joyous relish, to all and any who would listen.

Mordecai Jones's shining career faltered to a halt.

Shunned and ridiculed by his peers, mistrusted and ignored by his superiors, he was on the verge of leaving The Force (having successfully auditioned for a job as a rhythm guitarist on a Caribbean cruise liner – how many ghosts could there possibly be on a brand new boat in the middle of the ocean?), when his (then) commanding officer (in an attempt to get rid of "*the strange, awkward and miserable little man*") suggested that he might like to "apply his talents" to a mysterious case – concerning the murder of several first-rate fortune-tellers working on Brighton's, then, Palace Pier – which was currently baffling the *yokels* (i.e. the Sussex Police Force).

Mordecai jumped at the chance and within days (after a few extremely civilised conversations with some very interesting, expressive, open-minded and laid-back *dead people* – "Didn't see that coming," was the humorous retort of one poor unfortunate) had the whole matter sorted.

It was noticed and, however much they didn't like his methods (it was, *technically*, cheating, after all – asking dead people what had happened to them, rather than having to work it out for yourself) they had to respect the fact that Mordecai Jones got results.

The local Chief Constable offered Jones a permanent position, giving him free rein to investigate all matters ... "*unnatural*". Mordecai snapped at the opportunity, and so the D.S.C. (the Department of *Special Cases*) was born.

Not long after his arrival in Brighton, Mordecai had come into contact with The Hound and felt that, in some way, his meeting with such a well disposed, polite, educated and (most importantly) undeniably real creature of the supernatural had confirmed the fact that he hadn't been stark-raving bonkers for the whole of his life.

In short, Inspector Mordecai Jones, in terms of vocation and location, had found a home.

'We've got *The Suspect* trapped in Clifton Street Passage, between Terminus Place and Railway Street,' the Inspector grimaced, nodding in the general direction of the curious incident. 'Wouldn't mind giving us a hand apprehending the shifty bugger, would you?' he asked, offering The Hound a haunted but cheeky smile.

'Be delighted, old chap,' The Hound replied, delighted.

The Suspect was hemmed between two groups of extremely nervous-looking policemen – one placed at the top of Terminus Place and the other at the top of Railway Street.

As Tom reached the bottom of Railway Street (walking along the side of Brighton Station – where the full moon was mirrored, with perturbing spookiness, in the station's glass roof) he couldn't help but think that you'd never know that there was a passage (another *twitten* – the aforementioned Clifton Street Passage) connecting the squat little streets; both looking (to the uninitiated) like confirmed dead ends.

As they walked up the short and stubby Railway Street, a pale and slender young woman, in ill-fitting and faded black clothes, broke away from the huddle of policemen and walked towards them.

'Sergeant,' nodded Inspector Jones in greeting. 'What have you got for me?'

Sergeant Hettie Clem was the strangest-looking police officer that Tom had ever seen. Her thick curly red hair was pulled fiercely back into a severe ponytail, her face was covered with metal studs and piercings, and her eyes were circled with heavily applied 'Goth' eye-liner. She looked like an orphaned art student whose grant had run out a couple of terms ago. Tom couldn't help but think that she was doing everything she possibly could to hide the fact that she was, in fact, extremely beautiful. What he didn't know, just yet, was that Hettie Clem was also a psychic – a psychic of the first and highest order – and that she, together with Inspector Jones and Constable Tuggnutter, made up the highly-rated, but seldom talked about, D.S.C..

Sergeant Clem gave The Hound and Cornelius a nervous, bereft of eye contact, nod of recognition and then ran a fleeting appraisal over Tom. Tom felt his pulse quicken a little and his face (embarrassingly) turn an embarrassing shade of scarlet.

'He's old, Mordecai,' she replied, in a deep and husky voice, turning her attention back to the Inspector. 'Very old. And he's enjoying himself – immensely. But beyond that, I can't get a handle on him. Feels human ... but somehow ... not. Some kind of *Imp* or *Bogie*, possibly? Dunno. Out of our depth a little on this one.'

She cast an almost imperceptible nod towards The Hound.

Inspector Jones turned to The Hound and Uncle Cornelius.

'By the look of the quivering of the *thin blue line* up yonder,' he winced, indicating the jittery huddle of police officers stealing squeaky glances from The Hound to the trapped *fiend* and back again, 'I'd say that they'd be rather relieved to be relieved of their duties.'

He gave the faintest of smiles and hunched his shoulders even more. 'All yours, Mr Hound.'

'My pleasure, Inspector,' replied The Hound, licking his lips and excitedly rubbing his hands together. 'Dandy, if you, along with Sergeant Clem, could seal off the exit to Terminus Place,' he growled, eyeing the moonlit terrain and sounding all businesslike, whilst removing his duffle coat and handing it absent-mindedly to Constable Tuggnutter (who grunted something low and unintelligible in reply). 'Tom, you'll accompany your uncle and the good Sergeant.

'Inspector, if you and Constable Tuggnutter would be so kind as to position yourself up there on Clifton Street Passage, I'll go and have a little chat with our friend. Chop-chop, tickety-boo, that's the ticket.'

When all concerned were ready and primed in position (with the 'regular' officers having been removed from the field of operation – 'They can't seem to get a grasp on the subtleties of a case like this and so tend to balls it up,' the Inspector whispered to Tom, as he gently and kindly shepherded the relieved and slightly abashed-looking constables away from the scene), The Hound trotted up and slowly entered the passage between the two streets at a nonchalant saunter.

'Hello, *Jack*,' he purred. 'How's tricks, my fine fiend?'

FOURTEEN
The Curious Chase Of Spring-Heeled Jack

A pair of eyes like constipated fireballs turned and glared at The Hound with a maddened curiosity.

"Jack" stood over eight feet tall, with long (almost impossibly elongated) legs, fingers tipped with vicious metallic claws, and was dressed in a Victorian-style morning suit and cape. His jet-black hair was oiled back from his lean, impish white face and teased into tufts (like short, backward-facing horns). A dapper moustache and forked goatee beard completed his *carnival devil* appearance.

The demonic creature cackled with a manic laughter (that could have been inspired by surprise, fear or excitement), vomited a long, wicked blue flame in The Hound's direction, and then effortlessly backward somersaulted over the eighteen foot high garden fence behind him.

'Flipping Heck!' whistled Inspector Jones, lifting his neck from his hunch like a tortoise watching a firework display.

'Game on, chaps!' cried The Hound, gamely. And, pinning back his ears, he followed after the still cackling 'Bogie' – taking two enormous strides and vaulting over the garden wall like a gleeful carnivorous hare.

Tom heard a startled cat cry out in (understandable) terror, followed by the sight of the giggling *Jack* appearing and disappearing like a well-dressed bouncing ball as he hurdled the garden walls and headed in a south-easterly direction.

There was a scrabble of claws and The Hound poked his massive, pointy snout over the fence.

'Do try and keep up, my good fellows,' he chuckled with jovial delight, and then he sprung away in blissful pursuit.

Cornelius turned and bolted down the narrow twitten, with Sergeant Clem and Tom following hot on his heels. Inspector Jones and Constable Tuggnutter sped back down Railway Street, jumped into a sleek, grey Alfa Romeo that was parked at the bottom of the road, and were frantically revving the engine as Tom dashed past them.

'Stay with me, Tom,' his uncle barked over his shoulder (already outpacing both Tom and Sergeant Clem), twirling his hefty walking cane under his arm as he sprinted gracefully after the diminishing sight of the two giant, bounding creatures; who were currently disappearing under the eerie light of the full moon like the leading runners in the *'02:15 from Brighton – Monsters From Your Very Worst Nightmare – Steeplechase'*.

The gibbering fiend scissor-jumped back over the last garden fence, dashed out of Clifton Street Passage, and sprinted down the hill.

The Hound followed, snapping (quite literally) at his heels.

The were-hound tore along the narrow pavement on Camden Terrace, ears eagerly pinned back and with what could have been a joyous grin (it was hard to tell) shaping on his thin black lips, steadily gaining on his quarry. There was little in Hell, Heaven or Earth, in the Faery Lands or The Nine Realms that could outrun him in the chase, and it was this kind of work that thrilled him the most. He was, after all, born and bred for the hunt.

Dogs awoke and began to bark as the two monsters hammered down the narrow twitten. Bedroom lights flicked on, but by the time the bleary-eyed and puzzled tenants squinted out of their windows the speeding nightmares had long since sped past.

Could it really be him? The Hound mused to himself, as they bolted past the tiny houses. *Really? How thoroughly delicious!*

The fleeing, cackling figure (bounding like a jackrabbit before him) certainly fitted the profile (and from Inspector Jones's description, via the earlier phone call, The Hound's suspicions had already been aroused) but he had never, in all his wildest dreams, ever thought to meet the *legend* that was *Spring-Heeled Jack.*

Spring-Heeled Jack had "terrorized" Victorian London back in the 1830s, attacking and molesting young women and generally making a nuisance of himself. There were no reports of him ever having actually killed anybody (apart from one poor chap who allegedly died of a heart attack when confronted by the fiend), and the assaults seemed to be more for amusement and devilish delight than genuinely malicious. There had been the occasional incident reported outside of the capital, but, as far as The Hound could remember, the last recorded sighting was in Liverpool, way back in the early 1900s.

At the time of Jack's first attacks, The Hound had been out of the country (working, in fact, on a rather problematic incident in Ingolstadt – to wit, some idiotic, harebrained aristocrat [who obviously fancied himself as a bit of a scientific genius] had been dabbling, with an alarming recklessness, into the possibilities of reanimating dead tissue [and therefore, presumably, lording it over *Death* itself] only for [wonder of wonders!] the whole shebang to go frightfully wrong and not turn out quite as well as the irresponsible cretin had hoped) and therefore had never had the chance to pursue the case properly. However, he and Dandy had, over the ensuing years, spent many a quiet winter's evening discussing the mysterious appearance and possible identity of the legendary creature. Man or monster? Practical joker or Demon? Or (as suggested by Sergeant Clem) Imp or Bogie? Well, here was an unparalleled – and totally unexpected – opportunity to uncover the truth about one of the most intriguing and unsolved mysteries of the modern supernatural world.

But, if it was Spring-Heeled Jack (and it certainly looked like it was), why the devil had he chosen to reappear after an absence of over a hundred years? And in Brighton, of all places?

The Hound gained another yard on his fleeing quarry and lashed out with a lightning-fast paw, but the dapper brute managed to spring and twist away from his grasp, howling in anger and, to The Hound's satisfaction, not a little fear.

As he coursed after his prey the were-hound's mind whirled with observations.

Fear; yes he could sense it. Apprehension ... but excitement too. The thrill of the chase perhaps? He could scent that the fiend had fed on blood within the last few days. *That was interesting. But there was also a fragrance – redolent – making him feel somehow agitated and angry at the same time ... a familiar odour that was masked with strange perfumes ... and ... what else? ... Paraffin? ... Perhaps? ... Definitely not Hell-fire ... Come on. Think, Percy, think!*

What was that smell? It was tantalizingly just beyond his recognition. There was also a slight whirring sound emanating from the creature, too high for human ears to detect. Electronic? Possibly. That and a slight creaking sound when the creature leapt and landed during its impossibly long leaps.

They hurtled up Centurion Road; Spring-Heeled Jack bouncing intermittently between the garden railings, pillars and houses on the opposite sides of the street like a demonic pinball.

The well-dressed rogue suddenly twisted, changing direction in mid-air like a circus acrobat, and aimed a murderous spinning roundhouse swipe at his pursuer with a fistful of razor-sharp talons. The Hound effortlessly voided the assault and lurched forward with a stuttering pounce, managing to tear a piece of the short cloak from the creature's shoulders with his teeth.

Jack spun, mid-bounce and twelve feet high above the ground, and spat an arrow of fire at him.

The Hound stopped short and dodged his head, snarling in frustration as the flames licked his muzzle and seared his whiskers.

Jack hit the ground, turned, and pelted at lightning speed down the narrow alleyway called Mount Zion Place.

His nose overwhelmed by the disturbing smell of his own singed fur, the were-hound cursed, spat the burning piece of cape to the floor and followed hurriedly down the twitten.

There was no sight or scent of his quarry.

He sprinted to the end of the passage and looked about him.

It was as still and as quiet and as deserted as one would have expected at a quarter past two on a Wednesday morning.

'Damn it!' barked The Hound, angrily punching a wall in irritation and sending a shower of brick flying in all directions.

'Oy! Keep it down, mate! Some of us are trying to sleep!'

'What!' snapped the were-hound, whirling round to see the back of someone's head – barely visible beneath the swaddling of blankets and plastic shopping bags that was heaped against the entrance of a small passageway running behind the houses to his left.

‘Keep your dog quiet, that’s all I’m asking,’ a man’s voice said, quite reasonably.

The Hound snorted disdainfully and scouted about, trying to collect a scent – though all he could pick up was the smell of immortally unwashed clothing and cheap liquor.

‘Wait a minute. You haven’t, by chance, seen anyone else come this way recently have you, old chap?’ he asked the reeking pile of bags and blankets. ‘Tall fellow, long legs, red fiery eyes, white face, dressed in a dinner jacket, spitting fire and leaping like an Olympian kangaroo on steroids?’

‘You mocking me?’ came the indignant response. There was a short pause. ‘Don’t suppose you could spare a little change could you, mate? Two quid’d go some way to getting me a spot of breakfast in the morning.’

‘Two pounds!’

The Hound distractedly fumbled through one of the pouches in his belt, only to find a couple of *Gravy Bones*.

‘I’m afraid not, sir. My apologies.’

‘Oh that’s charming, innit? Wake a bloke up with a snarling mutt and then bugger off without a by your leave. Well, it ain’t your problem is it, mate? It’s people like you that make me siAAAAAAGHHH!’

The long strangled cry of the would-be beggar was on account of his turning to face his *tormentor* for the first time (having thus far been ‘scaving’ on autopilot) and seeing a seven-and-a-half foot tall were-wolf (he knew no better) looking down its snout at him, with an arched eyebrow and lips drawn back into a snarl that revealed a set of teeth that would have made a tiger shark self-consciously pull his gums over his gnashers.

‘Woof,’ whispered The Hound, softly.

The tramp/down and out/homeless person/knight of the road (a familiar resident of Brighton’s streets, who was known by the rather colourful moniker of’ *Tye-Dai Taffy*) faded into unconsciousness, to awake in the morning with the faint remembrance of a truly horrible nightmare and a newfound desire for abstinence.

The Hound jogged back, in irritation, to Centurion Road to collect what remained of the *Springer’s* cape.

Tom was wheezing like a dog-chewed squeaky toy by the time that they headed up Kew Street. (*Up!* he thought. *Why was it always up?*) Uncle Cornelius waited impatiently at the end of the street, frowning like a disappointed P.E. teacher on cross country training day, for him and Sergeant Clem to catch up. (The smug old swine didn’t even have the decency to look out of breath.) Hettie Clem, hampered by gothy *Frankenstein* boots with four inch heels (most definitely not Police regulation issue), was only a few paces behind Tom.

Tom crumpled to the floor, while Sergeant Clem wilted against the wall of the delightful-looking house on the corner of Church Street and tried her best not to be sick.

'Come on, young'uns, let's keep it moving,' pleaded Uncle Cornelius, with annoyingly encouraging pluck.

Tom pulled his head from between his knees, sucked in air, and nodded with a sodden, grim determination.

At that instant Sergeant Clem's walkie-talkie buzzed and she (gratefully) pulled it from one of her many zipped pockets.

'Inspector?' she hacked. '... On our way. And Inspector ... next time ... I ... get to sit ... in the car.'

She sucked in a couple of deep breaths.

'Suspect's been spotted at the top of Buckingham Road,' she wheezed to the eagle-eared, bristling-whiskered Uncle Cornelius and the jelly-faced, jelly-limbed Tom.

'Is it far?' Tom managed to gasp.

'Just up the hill,' grinned Cornelius, keenly.

There he goes again with the 'up', thought Tom.

They ran up Church Street, passed a small alley called Mount Zion Place on their right (Brighton, Tom observed – and he was not the first to do so – seemed to abound with back-passages) and the Church of St. Nicholas to their left, and took a right turn onto the eternally rising slope that is Dyke Road.

As they rounded the corner a tall, morning-suited figure (with the moustache, forked goatee beard and the features of a carnival devil) howled like a monkey on a pogo stick and then disappeared into a narrow slit in the wall on the opposite side of the road (that was the entrance to a tiny, and rather charming, twitten named Vine Place).

'Oy!' cried Uncle Cornelius as he sprinted after him, waving his cane like a Whirling Dervish who's just got a job as a tourist guide.

Hettie Clem followed twelve paces behind.

As she urgently gurgled into her walkie-talkie a sleek, grey Alfa Romeo sped past along Dyke Road and skidded into the next left turn above Vine Place.

Tom was gasping like an evicted goldfish (in his defence it had been an exceptionally long and exhausting day).

Think, Tom, think!

He knew that he couldn't hope to keep up with his uncle, but he felt a keen duty to do his damnedest to help out.

Before him, running parallel with Vine Place, was a wide, posh-looking street called Clifton Terrace – steps leading up to a raised pavement and swanky houses on one side, and a private garden on the other. He could take that road, he reasoned, and then, if the creature took a left turn at the end of the twitten, he would spot it and see where it was heading. And if it doubled back, then he could ... well, he'd cross that bridge if and when he came to it.

Uncle Cornelius sprinted halfway down the high-walled, narrow little alleyway and then slowed to an aggressive walk.

Patiently waiting at the end of the twitten stood the creature, looking for all the world like Spring-Heeled Jack himself.

Cornelius shifted the heavy cane in his hand, dropping the weighted head towards the ground, and rippled his fingers along the shaft as he readjusted his grip.

Now, if I remember my studies correctly, he thought to himself, *old Springald over there's s'posed to be bullet an' stab-proof. So, let's just see 'ow 'e 'andles a good old-fashioned wallop.*

Hettie Clem pulled up breathlessly at his shoulder and peered around him and at the monster waiting at the end of the passage (currently inspecting his silver nails with a practised nonchalance).

'What's he doing, Professor?' she rasped anxiously, as she lifted her walkie-talkie to her mouth. 'Suspect's at the Powis end of Vine Place ...' she whispered into it. 'Roger that. Approach with extreme caution.

'Professor!' she hissed, as Cornelius slowly began to un-cautiously approach the fiend. 'Professor, stay back! He's up to something. Stay back!'

But Cornelius was tipping the brim of his hat back with a jaunty and determined poke of the finger, and a grin like a summer sunrise was sprouting and blooming beneath his enormous moustache. If there was one thing that Professor Cornelius 'Dandy' Lyons liked above all else, it was a good old-fashioned tear-up with a good old-fashioned super-sized supernatural monster (didn't have to hold back if they were supernatural, he reasoned) and this one, he was very pleased to see, was far too sure of itself for its own good.

Spring-Heeled Jack bowed and gracefully lifted open his jacket, like a magician about to pluck a rabbit from his waistcoat pocket.

Uncle Cornelius stopped in his tracks.

Hettie Clem craned her neck a little further forward.

With an exaggerated theatrical motion, Jack produced what could only be described as a *cartoon bomb* – black ball with a short funnel and lighted fuse.

The well-dressed scoundrel gibbered hysterically.

And then the world exploded in a stunning flash of blue-white flame.

Cornelius staggered back, blinded.

Hettie dropped to the floor clutching her mouth and eyes.

Tom jogged down the middle of Clifton Terrace clutching the terrible stitch in his side. Suddenly, from behind the houses to his right, the sky lit up with a hazy blue-white flash. And then he heard an almighty sucking boom, like a damp firework going off. Instinctively he ducked behind a parked car and put his hands over his head. When he looked up again, he saw a nondescript white van speed by with an impossibly quiet purr to its engine. Tom stuck his head out from behind the parked car and watched the van disappear silently around the corner.

There was something most unusual about that van: as he tried to read the number plates (like a good apprentice detective should), Tom found that he couldn't seem to focus on the digits – it was as if they were dancing around, jiggling in and out of focus. He blinked and shook his head. Perhaps he was slightly discombobulated by the flash.

Then the possible consequences of the explosion hit him and he was dashing back down the road at full tilt, and up towards Vine Place, calling out desperately for his uncle

'Bugger!' cursed Cornelius, when he could see and breathe properly again. 'That was my favourite cravat!'

But now, with the exception of the hacking Hettie Clem and the gently smouldering Cornelius Lyons, Vine Place was completely deserted.

A sleek, grey Alfa Romeo skidded to a halt at the end of the alleyway. The doors flew open and out dashed Inspector Jones and the lumbering Constable Tuggnutter.

'Any sign of the shifty so-an'-so, Jonesy?' rasped Cornelius, patting out the smouldering embers on his neck-tie and whiskers.

'Looks like we missed him, Professor, I'm sorry to say. You OK, Hettie?'

Hettie nodded. 'Where's Mr Hound?' she spluttered.

Uncle Cornelius glanced at her. ''E'll be all right. But where,' he asked, with a look of concern, 'is young Tom?'

Tom literally stumbled into his uncle's arms as the old man was sprinting out onto Dyke Road.

Cornelius looked a little scorched but otherwise none the worse for wear.

'Tom, are you all right?' the old fellow asked, grasping the boy by the shoulders with his massive mitts.

Tom assured him that he was.

'I thought I told you to stick close to me at all times!' he growled. 'Where were you? That's the second time that you've –'

'I couldn't keep up, Uncle, I'm sorry,' bleated Tom, feeling angry and upset, as if he'd somehow let the old chap down.

'No harm done, Professor,' said Inspector Jones, as he walked up behind them. 'Did you see anything that might be of interest, Tom?' he asked calmly.

'I went down Clifton Terrace, thinking that if I couldn't keep up then at least I might be able to see something if he got away from you.'

'Smart thinking, Tom,' smiled Inspector Jones, kindly. 'And ...?'

'I don't know, it might be nothing, but I saw a white van racing along the street just after the explosion.'

'Did you now?' frowned the Inspector, thoughtfully. 'Good work, Tom. That might just about be the best clue that we've got to this whole unsavoury matter.'

Uncle Cornelius ruffled Tom's hair and grinned warmly at him.

'Come on, son, let's see what 'Is Nibs is up to,' he said.

And with that, he pulled from his waistcoat pocket what could best be described as an old-fashioned referee's whistle and blew sharply into it twice – once long and once short. It didn't seem to work, because Tom couldn't hear anything ... but a few heartbeats later he heard a deep, yip-yip-yap cutting across the blue-grey sky and then he saw The Hound gracefully trotting up Buckingham Road to join them.

Ten minutes later (after one last futile sweep of the area) The Hound was squeezing himself into the back of the D.S.C's. sleek, grey Alfa Romeo (which groaned considerably under the combined weight of the substantial Constable Tuggnutter and a seven-and-a-half foot tall, three hundred and seventy-five pound were-wolf-wolfhound) and, along with Inspector Jones, began to head back to One Punch Cottage.

Tom, Uncle Cornelius and Sergeant Hettie Clem walked down Dyke Road to the Clock Tower and then turned left down North Street and through The Lanes until they arrived at Black Lion Lane.

How beautiful and peaceful it all looks, thought Tom, as he stared up at the almost perfectly circular moon. *Who'd have thought it? What a night!*

The Hound had been right – no one would ever believe him if he told them what had happened. Then (much to his embarrassment), he caught himself staring, moon-eyed, at the strange and beautiful Emo police officer walking at his side and felt his face flush hot.

The three of them trotted excitedly up the stairs of One Punch Cottage and into The Study, where The Hound, Inspector Jones and Constable Tuggnutter awaited them – piling into a small mountain of corned beef and mustard sandwiches (stoically watched by an ever-hopeful Bess). The alarmingly gurning Missus Dobbs poured everybody cups of steaming hot coffee, whilst nattering incessantly to all and sundry about the strange weather that they'd been having lately.

Tom looked about him at the most peculiar collection of *people* that he'd ever seen in his life (all, bizarrely, gathered together in one room) and couldn't help but giggle to himself: somewhat miffed and disappointed-looking Elizabethan wolfhound-were-wolf; geriatric, slightly singed, bewhiskered, tweed aficionado and homicidal lunatic; flatulent, ever-optimistic, gigantic wolfhound; skinny, beautiful, psychic, wonderful, shy, lovely, gothy, gorgeous policewoman; Northumbrian-Jamaican spirit-talker and police detective; burly, awkward, silent and Troll-like* police constable; wrinkly, apple-cheeked, gurning, kindly, tea-poisoning and eye-poking House-Fairy. And, to quote a well-known song, Tom could only think to himself – *what a wonderful world.*

'Come on, Tom,' chirped The Hound, 'get stuck in, lad, before Dandy and Tuggers here scoff the lot. Then it's down to business, all hands to the pump, while all's still fresh in our minds.'

Tom smiled and grabbed a sandwich.

He was starving!

(* Tom was later to discover that Constable Tuggnutter was in fact half-Troll, being a descendent of the famous Tilly Tuggnutter [*Ten-Ton-Tuggie]*, the first [and only] Troll star of the Edwardian Music-Hall – whose signature tune

"*Who's that coming over the bridge? Is it my Monster*?" became an overnight sensation; telling, as it did, the tragic story of a lovesick Troll-Maiden waiting for the return of her true love from the brutal Troll Wars, only to be harassed, persecuted and finally evicted by a gang of hooligan Faun brothers [lead by the infamous construction industry racketeer – Geiss Brookbower].

"From underneath my bridge
I hear a little clatter
Of tiny cloven feet
I wonder what's the matter?")

FIFTEEN
A Very Victorian Vignette

Piles of old case files and yellowing newspaper cuttings lay scattered about The Study floor, as *The One Punch Cottage Crew* sat and recounted to each other the extraordinary events of the extraordinary night. Inspector Jones, crouched in a haunted huddle on the tatty footstool, frantically scribbled notes into a small notebook, while The Hound paced around the room, hands behind his back, running his immense tongue over his immensely impressive choppers.

'Right then,' sniffed Inspector Jones. 'Let's see how this all fits together.

'At 01:53 hours – a group of students are assaulted outside the Bystander Café (on the corner of Guildford Street and Terminus Road) by an assailant who can best be described as being of a "diabolical appearance". No serious injury occurs and there was no attempt at robbery, but two of the girls have their clothes slightly torn and describe the touch of their assailant as being "cold and clammy".

'On being confronted by a couple of passing off-duty security guards, the assailant (from here on known as *The Suspect*) spits blue flames at them before leaping away with incredible speed – jumping *humanly impossible* distances – and then remaining on and around Terminus Road and loitering about in a disrespectful fashion.

'At 02:02 – two police vans turn up, with eleven officers in total, followed, moments later, by myself and the other members of the Department of Special Cases (Sergeant Clem and Constable Tuggnutter). *The Suspect* is then herded by the assisting officers and trapped on Clifton Street Passage, between Railway Street and Terminus Place. All attempts to approach him are met with hostile, violent and dangerous resistance; to wit, spitting fire, and slashes with sharp metallic claws.

'At 02:06 – I make the call to Mr Hound and Professor Lyons asking for their assistance.

'At 02:13 – Mr Hound, Professor Lyons and young Master Dearlove arrive at the scene.

'At 02:19 – *The Suspect* is approached by Mr Hound and violently resists his (Mr Hound's) attempts at appeasement. *The Suspect* then leaps over the garden walls (by means of a very impressive backward somersault) and hops away in a south-easterly direction. Mr Hound gives chase – followed by Sergeant Clem, Professor Lyons and Master Dearlove. Myself and Constable Tuggnutter, in an attempt to follow and outmanoeuvre *The Suspect*, head for an undercover police motor vehicle (a rather lovely Alfa Romeo 156).

'Mr Hound pursues *The Suspect* down Guildford Road, along Camden Terrace and then finally through Centurion Road where, around 02:20, an altercation takes place – Mr Hound receiving slight burns to the snout and whiskers, while *The Suspect* has part of his cape torn away.

'Mr Hound then loses *The Suspect* somewhere along Mount Zion Place.'

(The Hound blew his cheeks out in huffed annoyance at what he evidently saw as his own, inexcusable, failure.)

'Mr Hound then makes a sweeping search of the surrounding area – including St. Nicholas Churchyard, St. Nicholas Rest Gardens, St. Nicholas Playground (known collectively as the St. Nicholas Green Spaces) and the streets immediately around the Dyke Road area.

'At 02:21 – myself and Constable Tuggnutter spot *The Suspect* making his way along Buckingham Road and heading towards Dyke Road. We turn the vehicle around and give pursuit, but lose him after he jumps onto the rooftops of the adjacent houses and disappears from sight (though not before hurling some very offensive, and quite frankly hurtful, gestures in our direction).

'Meanwhile, Professor Lyons, Sergeant Clem and Master Dearlove reach the corner of Kew Street and Church Street and, via radio-communication, I inform them of our sighting.

'At 02:23 – Professor Lyons and Sergeant Clem spot *The Suspect* and chase after him, pursuing him down the narrow alleyway called Vine Place – while Master Dearlove (showing remarkable initiative and resolve) heads along Clifton Terrace in order to observe and cut off *The Suspect's* possible line of flight. Myself and Constable Tuggnutter drive down Powis Grove in an attempt to apprehend *The Suspect* at the southerly exit of Vine Place. However, on finding Powis Grove blocked by road works, we are forced to reverse and take the next turning (Clifton Hill) thereby delaying our arrival, and with it the possibility of apprehending the vile fiend.

'At approximately 02:24 – Professor Lyons and Sergeant Clem confront *The Suspect* and are attacked with what can only be described as a firebomb. *The Suspect* again escapes.

'Seconds later, Master Dearlove spots a white, unmarked van – with unusual and highly suspicious number plates – travelling at high speed along Clifton Terrace and then turning right onto Dyke Road.'

Inspector Jones flipped shut his notebook and looked at Tom.

'I've phoned in the description of the van, Tom, and our chaps are checking the CCTV cameras as we speak.

'All *unnecessary* information will of course be erased, Mr Hound,' he added, turning to The Hound.

'Good work, Inspector,' muttered the were-hound, distractedly tapping his snout with a finger like a parrying dagger. 'Sergeant Clem, you said that you detected that the creature was old and that it "*felt human but somehow ... not*", am I correct?'

'That's right, sir,' replied Sergeant Clem. 'And he was most definitely enjoying all the attention.'

'Hhhhmmm,' mused The Hound. 'Well, I can tell you that he most certainly moved with a superhuman, or supernatural, speed. And, furthermore, his scent was one of ... decay and fire and ... and something more. A smell that is quite familiar to me, I'm sure of it, but for the life of me I can't quite seem to put my nose on it.'

He paced the room in silence, while the others held their breath in anticipation.

'I feel that there can be little doubt as to the identity of *The Suspect*,' he continued at last. 'It is unequivocally Spring-Heeled Jack himself (whoever or whatever he may be).'

'Or perhaps someone very much wishing us to believe that it is him,' offered Inspector Jones, with a morose shrug of the shoulders.

'I'd put money on it being 'im,' growled Uncle Cornelius. 'Ticks all the boxes. But why 'ere. An' why now?'

'Ah!' exclaimed The Hound. 'That is indeed the very question.'

They spent the next few hours going through all the reports and newspaper articles, collected over the years by The Hound and Uncle Cornelius, appertaining to the mystery of Spring-Heeled Jack, in order to create a profile of the mischievous and mysterious fiend.

Tom flicked open his copy of *Greymorris' Field Guide* and read out loud –

SPRING-HEELED JACK

[Species unknown]
Other names include -
'THE SPRINGER' & ***'SPRINGBALD'***
Possible association with:
The SHEFFIELD PARK GHOST {late 1700s}
The SOUTHAMPTON GHOST {early 1800s}
The BLACK-FLASH OF CAPE-COD
PEREK – The Spring Man of Czechoslovakia {both mid 1900s}.

SPRING-HEELED JACK: A mysterious, humanoid creature. Reportedly standing anywhere between six & ten feet tall, Spring-Heeled Jack possesses the ability to leap incredible heights & distances, & to breathe (or 'spit') fire. He is known, on occasion, to attack young women, but would appear to cause little or no harm (other than the obvious psychological trauma). The assaults tend to be of a mischievous rather than sinister nature & there are no accounts of fatal or even serious injury.

Jack was most active during the Victorian era, mainly around London's East End (though there were other incidents reported

around the country). The last verified sighting was in Liverpool in 1904.
However, *Spring-Heeled Jack-like* creatures have been continually spotted around the world – from as far afield as the USA (the first verified report being in 1880), Eastern Europe & India.
As to the identity of Jack – it is certain that many of the sightings have undoubtedly been hoaxes, but the *actual* Spring-Heeled Jack would appear to be some kind of mischievous **IMP**, **BOGIE**, **DEVIL** or **PHANTOM**.
[Also see – **BALTIMORE-PHANTOM**, **LA VIDA**]

The mystery was an old one.
As early as 1808, a letter sent to *The Sheffield Times* reminisced that –

> *Years ago a famous Ghost walked and played many pranks in this historic neighbourhood ... He was a human ghost, as he ceased to appear when a certain number of men went with guns and sticks to test his skin ... the name of the prankster was The Park Ghost or Spring-Heeled Jack ...*

Around 1817 there began to appear a spate of nationwide sightings and newspaper reports of a "peculiar leaping man".

The first *officially* recorded sighting and attack by the creature now known as *Spring-Heeled Jack* took place on Clapham Common in October 1837, when a young servant girl by the name of Polly Adams was assaulted one night whilst walking home from work. Her "*demon-like*" attacker was seen a few days later, stalking the area around Ms Adams' home in Battersea, before "melting away into the shadows".

A few months later another servant girl, Lucy Jane Aslop, aged 18, was attacked on the 19th of February 1838. She was pulled to safety by her sister. When passers-by came to the two girls' assistance, Jack was chased through the streets and, in the following pursuit, dropped his cape, but this possibly important clue was "picked up by an accomplice" before it could be retrieved.

Nine days later, on February 28th, Jack attacked yet another young serving girl. The victim, Miss Scales (also called *Lucy Jane* and also aged 18), was assaulted, along with her younger sister, on Green Dragon Street in Limehouse, London. Jack spat fire into Miss Scales' face, leaving her temporally blinded and so terrified by the assault that she lay on the floor having uncontrollable fits for the next few hours.

All three women were understandably shaken, but, apart from a few minor scratches and burns, were otherwise physically unharmed by the incidents.

Reports and sighting continued over the next few years, mainly in the East End of London but also, on occasion, nationwide – ranging from Brighton ("Spring-Heeled Jack Finds His Way To The Sussex Coast!" being the dramatic headline of the *Brighton Gazette* on April the 13th 1838), to East Anglia (mid-1840s), the Welsh borders (late 1840s), and Scotland (1850s). There also appeared to have been a connection with the 60th Rifles Regiment, who seemed to have been plagued by *Jack* between 1877 and 1878 during their various postings at Aldershot, Colchester and Lincolnshire, respectively. The last confirmed sighting was of Jack leaping along the rooftops and streets of Everton, North Liverpool, in 1904.

However, a creature of similar appearance was to terrorize Provincetown in Canada between 1938 and 1945 – a fiend known locally as "The Black Flash of Cape-Cod". His one recorded victim was a woman by the name of Miss Janet Polza. Similarly, a character fitting Jack's description, known as "Perek" or "The Spring Man", was upsetting the good citizens of Slovakia between 1939 and 1945 – the most noted attack being an assault on one Lucinda Selaks.

As to Spring-Heeled Jack's identity, or even species, there has been much speculation but little or no conformity; being invariably described as – a Devil (an evil spirit/denizen of Hell), an Imp (a type of lesser demon), a Sprite (a type of nature-spirit), and a Bogie (an evil faery-like creature; generally found hanging around dark, damp places – bogs and the like [hence the name "Bogie"], although in recent times they have been known to urbanise, being occasionally found in cellars, attic rooms, communal dustbins and even large wardrobes).

There had been considerable speculation during the mid-1800s that the whole *Spring-Heeled Jack phenomena* was nothing more than a cruel hoax devised and played out by Henry de la Poer Beresford (the Marquis of Waterford) and his ne'er-do-well cronies (to whom we are forever indebted for the well-worn phrase "painting the town red" – after their boisterous celebration of a successful fox hunt, when they decided to decorate Melton Mowbray High Street with tins of red paint), but as the attacks had continued long after Beresford's death (in 1859) the theory had, quite naturally, petered out.

Over time Spring-Heeled Jack had entered into the public consciousness – becoming a character, and sometimes even the hero, in several sensational works of popular Victorian fiction (known delightfully as "Penny Dreadfuls"), full-blown novels and plays.

There appeared to be no rhyme or reason to Jack's attacks and no obvious patterns of behaviour (apart from an apparent penchant and delight for mischief, and scaring the living daylights out of young women). All in all – as The Hound succinctly summed it up – an intriguing, but rather minor mystery.

The musical strains of Genesis' "Suppers Ready" suddenly broke the silence and (accompanied by an arching of metal-filled, pitying eyebrows from Sergeant Hettie Clem, and the bristling of dismayed whiskers from Uncle Cornelius) Inspector Jones hastily pulled his mobile phone from his jacket pocket with an embarrassed and haunted grin.

'Inspector Jones, D.S.C.,' he huffed gruffly, resolutely avoiding all eye contact.

He listened with a look of deep concentration for a few moments before replying. 'Well thanks for trying, Hamish. I owe you one.'

The Inspector returned the phone to his pocket and stood up to stretch his legs.

'CCTV cameras pulled a blank on the van. Tracked its movements down Dyke Road and then it seems to have just ... vanished into thin air,' he said, shaking his head in disbelief.

The Hound pursed his lips.

'Well,' sighed the were-hound, 'I'm not sure that there is anything more to be gained by us staying up any longer. It is entirely possible that this latest manifestation by Spring-Heeled Jack is a one-off event that, in all likelihood, will not be repeated again for decades. And I can see no way to pursue the investigation any further at this point in time. We will, of course, stay on the alert for any additional activity. And, should it occur, pray that we have better luck. But, apart from a minor assault and a deepening curiosity into our mysterious jumping friend's identity, no real harm would appear to have been done.'

'... Er ...?' er-ed Tom apprehensively, chewing the end of a pencil and hesitantly looking up from his new notebook. 'It might be nothing ... but, all the same ... it's a bit *odd* ... really.'

'An' what's that then, Tom?' asked Uncle Cornelius, curiously.

'Well,' began Tom, as Bess heralded his announcement with an eye-watering trump that the gathered members of the D.S.C. tried, gamely, to politely ignore, 'if you take the names of two of the original victims – Lucy Jane *Scales* and Lucy Jane *Aslop* and then spell their surnames backwards ... well, *Scales* becomes *Selacs*, which is very close to ... almost the same really ... as *Selaks*. And if you reverse *Aslop* ...'

'You get *Polsa,* which is near identical to *Polza!*' interjected The Hound, excitedly pounding an enormous clenched paw into his palm.

'And this is taking us ... *where* ... exactly?' grimaced the slightly perplexed Inspector Jones. 'You're not suggesting that the Victorian serving girls, Lucy Jane Aslop and Lucy Jane Scales, are one and the same as the mid-twentieth century women Lucinda Selaks and Janet Polza are you? ... Are you?'

'*Possibilities* is where it's taking us, Inspector,' growled Uncle Cornelius, with a hungry look in his eye. 'In our line of work the improbable is always a possibility. Let us just suppose that the two *Lucy Janes* were, in actual fact, 'magic-folk'. Then it might very well be that they are indeed one an' the same as Selaks an' Polza. Many such people can live for centuries, in some cases virtually unaltered in their appearance, an', as we know, it's not un'eard of for some *Fae Folk* to change their names over the years.'

'Good grief!' gasped The Hound, grinding the heels of his palms together. 'What if the answer has been looking us in the face all along? Suppose, for one moment, that the collection of sightings of the mysterious creature known as *Spring-Heeled Jack* are not the random, mischievous play of some devilish Imp, but rather, something altogether more purposeful. What if his attacks and seemingly haphazard manifestations are calculated? To be more precise –

focused? What if the mystery lies not with the *perpetrator* but with the *victims*?'

'Like some sort of quest you mean?' frowned the Inspector. 'But for who? Or what?'

'Could very well be something to do with the individuals that we've mentioned, or perhaps even their families – it's worth remembering that many magic-folk pass on their family name through the maternal line,' mused Uncle Cornelius, chewing the edges of his moustache.

'So what's his purpose?' asked Sergeant Hettie Clem.

'A blood feud per'aps?' speculated Cornelius. 'Or maybe some form of retribution?'

'So, are you saying that Spring-Heeled Jack is some sort of Faery assassin?' gasped Inspector Jones.

'Bit bloody useless if 'e is,' snorted Cornelius. 'Could be some kind of curse though? Who knows? It's all far too open to speculation at the moment.'

'Inspector,' snapped The Hound, excitedly, 'what were the names of the students who were attacked this morning?'

Inspector Jones rifled through his notebook. 'Summers, Burne and Malik,' he said. 'No connection that I can see there.'

'Might it be worth checking out if they're in any way related to any Aslops or Scaleses?' suggested Hettie Clem.

'Mordecai,' asked the were-hound, 'is it possible that you could look into the prospect of uncovering more substantial documents on the incidents that we've discussed this evening? Follow up the lines of investigation on Janet Polza and Lucinda Selaks? See if there is any more background history to be discovered about Lucy Jane Aslop and Lucy Jane Scales? Perhaps there is a connection between them. And while you're at it, would you be so kind as to take a look into what's known about Ms Polly Adams, as well.'

'I'll do my best, Mr Hound,' muttered the Inspector, sounding unhopeful. 'But these are old cases, and the more recent ones took place in other countries. Do you really think that there could be some sort of connection?'

'It is, at the very least, worthy of investigation,' The Hound replied, licking his lips. 'There are a few lines of enquiry that I wouldn't mind following at this end too. Leave that with me for the moment, old fruit.'

'All right, we're on it,' scowled Inspector Jones, standing up and walking towards The Study door, whilst gently motioning his team into action. 'I'll be in touch as soon as we have anything worth a mention. And we'll put that piece of material that you tore from *The Suspect's* cape under analysis, see what comes up.'

As the Inspector reached the door he turned to face Tom.

'Good work, Tom,' he said, smiling a warm yet haunted smile. 'You've all the makings of a damn fine detective, if I may say so, young man. A damn fine detective.'

Tom returned a smug smile as the Inspector left the room.

Sergeant Hettie Clem followed, momentarily pausing to look Tom up and down.

'Well done, Half-Pint,' she said, with a smirk that seemed to touch her eyes and sparkle off her piercings.

Tom could feel himself blushing uncontrollably under a beaming, idiot-grin.

Constable Tuggnutter grunted something low and unintelligible as he loomed past, closing the door heavily behind him.

When they had left, The Hound clapped his hands together excitedly, his tail wagging furiously in delight.

'Good work indeed, Tom!' he declared, full of mustard. 'So far you've been nothing but an asset to *The Firm*. Top drawer! Keep it up, young man, and there's no telling what you could accomplish.'

Uncle Cornelius smiled broadly and slapped Tom heartily on the back – slightly ruining the moment by making Tom stumble forwards and topple over an armchair.

'Been a long an' productive day, Tom,' he said. 'More than enough kinds of adventure, excitement an' whatnots going on for any one evening, I reckon. You done well, son. Proud of you. Now, it's almost five in the morning, so I suggest that we all 'ead off to bed an' get some well-earned shut-eye.'

As Cornelius gently hauled Tom to his feet, both Bess and The Hound raised and swivelled an alerted ear.

There was an urgent knock at the front door.

Boom! Boom! Bo-Boom!

Moments later Missus Dobbs appeared in a state of near ecstatic agitation, pulling off a blood-splattered apron and hastily wiping her bloodstained hands and forearms on it. (Tom could only assume that she'd been butchering the – *most emphatically not poached* – deer, but, then again, you could never be too sure with Missus Dobbs.) She speedily began gathering up the untidy stacks of papers and files from the floor.

'Oh my! Oh my!' she giggled, in an excited panic. 'The Pook hisself is here to see you, Mister Hound. The Pook hisself!'

SIXTEEN
The King Of The Downlands

The Hound hastily donned his red silk dressing robe, fumbling hurriedly with the belt.

Uncle Cornelius did his utmost to improve his singed demeanour, frantically brushing all signs of ash from the seat of his armchair.

'Who's *The Pook*?' asked Tom, all at sea on ill-informed tenterhooks.

'The closest thing to royalty that you're ever going to meet, son, an' that's a fact,' replied Uncle Cornelius, casting a critical eye over Tom's appearance and seemingly reaching the resigned conclusion that it would have to do.

'Alberich Albi, the Nineteenth Pook of the Pharisees,' interjected The Hound, wrapping a spotted silk cravat about his neck.

'The *Pook* being their elected king, so to speak; though that don't really do justice to the *Pookiness* of it,' offered Cornelius to the still mystified Tom.

'Is he an Israelite?' asked Tom, quite reasonably.

'*Pharisees* not *Pharisees*, you numpty!' scolded Cornelius. 'You know, *Pharisees* – the Sussex *Fair Folk*.'

'Uh?'

'Faeries, you daft so-an'-so,' his uncle continued in a hushed, harsh whisper. 'Elves. The Pharisees are the Elf tribe of Sussex.'

There was a gentle rap on The Study door, and then Missus Dobbs – adorned in lipstick (that looked as if it had been hastily applied by an octogenarian sloth) and a matching set of pearl earrings and necklace (that a Caribbean buccaneer would have refused to wear on account of them being too garish) – opened the door, gracefully bowed, and offered entry with an elaborate twirl of her arm.

Alberich Albi, the Nineteenth Pook of the Pharisees and Lord of the Southern Elbi, entered the room. He was small, fine-boned, peculiarly handsome, and radiated strength and grace with every elegant movement that he made. He looked old (but how old Tom found impossible to tell), with long, finely crafted features encased within a gently curling mop of soft white hair and massive mutton-chop whiskers. At one ear (which, much to Tom's delight, was ever so slightly pointy) he sported a thick hoop of gold. He was dressed in a dark and battered three-piece suit, a white collarless shirt, and wore sturdy workman's boots. On the lapel of his suit jacket was a beautiful golden brooch that implied the essence of a wild hare. In his right hand he carried a thick knob-headed walking stick, made from twisted wood that looked like polished iron, along with a squished-up yellow baker boy cap. All in all, he exuded the earthy dignity that only earthy, dignified people can exude.

'Percival. Corneliuz,' he said, in a voice as warm as roasting chestnuts (speaking with what Tom would have taken for a West Country accent if he hadn't already been severely chastised by Uncle Cornelius for making the same assumption regarding his [Cornelius'] accent [though his uncle's accent was nowhere near as thick as The Pook's]: it was, he had been very sternly told, a Sussex accent, which was now all but extinct due to the constant onslaught of modern media and continual influxes from "*that London*").

'I, Alberich Albi, Nineteenth Pook of the Pharizeez, guardian of all the land zouth of the Downzez – from the Devil'z 'Umpzez in the wezt to Mount Caburn in the eazt (an' beyond*), do azk you, 'umbly, for your 'ozpitality,' he proclaimed, using the ancient protocol and self-effacement required to be shown by all Pooks at all times.

(* This last bit – the rather vague sounding "in the west [*and beyond]*" – was added because, over the centuries, the Pharisees territory had shifted and shrunk like a tide with the various invasions and encroachments of modern peoples and modern living. In order to compensate for this unstable state of affairs, they had settled on something big and unmovable somewhere in the general direction, so that they didn't have to keep changing their traditional introduction every few years.)

'Our house is your house. Our hearth is your hearth. Please be seated, friend; rest a while and take refreshment,' replied The Hound, using a variation of the time-honoured response.

'Ta very much, Percy. No, no tea thankz, Mizzuz Dobbz,' he added, pulling a lightning-quick horrified gurn in Tom's direction. 'Cuppa coffee'd go down a treat though. Got any 'Obnobz?'

Missus Dobbs whimpered gleefully and left The Study with a giddy backwards shuffle, curtsying every few steps (and rattling like a set of bingo balls in a biscuit tin in the process) until she reached the door.

''Oo'z the liddle feller?' asked the Pook, smiling at Tom with sparkling green eyes (perched as keenly as a hawk's over his long aquiline nose).

Tom thought that this was a little rich coming from someone who couldn't have stood more than five-foot-two inches tall in his hobnail boots, but royalty must have its way, he supposed.

'This is Tomas. Tom Dearlove – a relative of mine,' replied Cornelius, enthusiastically.

'Dearlove?' mused the strange little man, casting a glance as wise and unfathomable as a mercurial silver minnow darting through a moonlit river. 'Good name there, Tom. One to live up to. It iz a great boon for a man to 'ave a ztrong name.'

The Pook reclined in Cornelius' armchair and artfully dunked a Hobnob into his coffee.

'Must say 'ow much I'm looking forward to *The Ex'ibition* next week,' cooed Cornelius, excitedly.

'You an' the rezt of Upper Albion, I reckonz. We'z all 'oldin' our breath, that'z for zure. An' I dare zay all of Lower Albion iz az well,' answered Alberich, between mouthfuls.

''Ow's Ned? In good shape I 'ope.'

'You know Ned, Dandy, fit az a flea an' twice az keen. Bezt fighting-cove we've 'ad in nigh on three 'undred yearz. Mind you, I probably would think that – 'im being my nephew an' all. Juzt wish 'e could a done a bit more training with you an' Percy 'ere, but what with youz twoz being azked to officiate, well, wouldn't be right now, would it?'

'I'm sure that Alberich hasn't come to see us at five o'clock in the morning to discuss the upcoming contest, Dandy, however intriguing and exciting that may be,' interrupted The Hound, through a steeple of rippling fingers. 'Without wishing to appear rude in any way, Alberich, my dear friend, may I be so forward as to ask you the purpose of your unexpected, but always most welcome, visit?'

The Pook put down his coffee mug, stashed a couple of Hobnobs into the pocket of his suit jacket, and took a deep breath.

'Been a *dizturbance* up at 'Ollingbury Park – acrozz The Ring an' down to The Giant'z Foot,' he growled. 'Az you know, that'z old ground. Zacred ground to uz.'

'What kind of a *disturbance*?' asked the Hound, his curiosity aroused – for Alberich Albi, Pook of the Pharisees, was not one to ask for help from outsiders lightly.

'Zhenaniganz, that'z what. Old magic ... an' new.' (By which he meant *modern technology*.) 'There haz been blood, Percival. Perhapz ritualz ... ritualz of a dark an' dezperate nature. Ned an' Alfie are poking about right now, zeeing what'z to be found, but I'd be mozt 'appy if you wouldn't mind taking a noze, zo to zpeak.'

SEVENTEEN
The Mysterious Incident Of The Hunters Of Hollingbury Ring

Uncle Cornelius pushed Old Nancy, at top pootle, up and along the gentle rise of Ditchling Road and on towards Hollingbury Park. The Pook had taken a night bus down to One Punch Cottage at the first opportunity, as he didn't drive but wanted to talk to The Hound as soon as he possibly could.* ('You getz a free buz pazz when you'z getz to be zixty; zo, me being four 'undred an' twenty-eight next year, I reckonz that I'z iz entitled to one,' as he had quite reasonably explained to Tom.)

(* As a matter of course, Tom discovered, very few Elves hold a driving license or can even drive, as they consider it an affront to their "bountiful Mother the Earth" to pollute Her with exhaust fumes and "*mutilate her skin*" with roads [which they call "scars" – hence *Ditchling Road* becomes *The Ditchling Scar*]. However, being practical and resourceful folk, they are not above scavenging a lift or taking the bus when occasion serves, hence Alberich Albi's use of public transport that morning to contact The Hound as quickly as he could.)

As they chugged along *The Ditchling Scar*, past sleepy-looking houses and deserted streets, Tom wondered how it was that he didn't feel the least bit tired?

What a night! he thought. Harassed by ghosts, then giving chase to the legendary Spring-Heeled Jack, and now, here he was, sharing a car ride and a packet of Hobnobs with a four hundred and twenty-seven year old Elven King! No surprise that he felt wide-awake, really, if you stopped to consider.

He opened his (fast becoming invaluable) copy of *Greymorris' Field Guide* and flicked to "F".

FAERIE

The name given to various *races* of 'magical' humanoid beings. Some are well disposed towards Humans, whilst others are not at all and appear to be inherently evil. All, however, would seem to share a common ancestry (although there is immense variety in their various forms).

The name Faery – *Fair One* [OE] - is most commonly applied to the Elves & Goblins of the British Isles ... [See – **BOGGART, BOGGIE, BROWNIE, DULLEN, ELF** ...]

ELF

[***Aelf***: *OE*]
FAERY or ***FAIRY*** – [Fair One]
'The Children of the Light'
ELBI **(**or ***ALBI*)** – [Britain]
SIDHE – [Ireland]

The name given to the ancient humanoid race that inhabits, and once dominated, the British Isles before the coming of 'modern' Humans.
There are two closely related groups:
1. the **ELBI** – of mainland Britain
and
2. the **SIDHE** (pronounced "Shee") – of Ireland and (later) Scotland.

1. **ELBI**
The Elves of Mainland Britain.
The Elbi, or Albi as they call themselves [lit. '*The People of this Land'*], thus gave the name ***Albion*** to the island now comprised of England, Scotland and Wales.
Though once the dominant people of the islands, the Elbi have been in long and steady decline over the last few millennia – to the point of near extinction. Their waning can perhaps be traced back to the division of the legendary ***Crown of Albion*** (at the end of ***The Second Age***) and the arrival of Humans (at the beginning of ***The Third Age***).
After their defeat at the hands of the early Britons many of the Elbi fled the lands above ground to inhabit the land below, whilst others remained and eked out an existence as best they could. Thus Albion became divided into two distinct parts – (a) **Upper Albion** and (b) **Lower Albion.**

(a)
UPPER ALBION
Of the Elves who stayed above ground, all that remain today are several small but distinct groups. Over the centuries there have been some confusing (and, on occasion, downright baffling) exchanges of land between the *Elbi* and their close relatives the

Sidhe (sometime amicable, sometimes not), but the rough lie of the land is as follows:

(1) The TRIBES

(i) The **ELLYLLON** [***the Fair Family***] occupy most of Wales
(ii) The **FERRISYN** inhabit the Isle of Man. [Originally a colony of *Sidhe* – though now fully, and indistinguishably, integrated with families of *Elbi* origins]
(iii) The **PHARISEES** [***the Fair Folk***] whose territory is roughly the south-eastern English county of Sussex
(iv) The **PISKIE** [***the Strange Folk***] inhabit the south-west English counties of Dorset, Devon and Cornwall.
(The ***Piskie Nation*** is made up of a number of distinct clans and, in some ways, may best be viewed as a confederacy. The origin of the *Piskie Union* dates back to the rise of the legendary Goblin war-chief **Blue Bonnet** [of *Clan Pixie*] and his attempt to create a Piskie Empire [see Dr Martin Raphael's authoritative work "*Blue Bonnet and the Pixie Wars of Expansion"* – Cambridge, 1902]. The dominant element is the aforementioned ***Pixie Clan*** but other sub-tribes include the *ancient* ***Portunes*** and the giant ***Spriggans***.)

[Also see **GOBLIN**]

(v) The **SITH** [***the Wild Ones***] of Scotland.
Although now totally independent, the Sith are in origin a colony of ***Sidhe*** who began to inhabit Scotland at the beginning of the 17th century, after the native northern Elbi (***The Gentry*** – see below) abandoned that territory.

(2) The INDEPENDENTS

OAK-MEN
Small communities of Elves, scattered across the British Isles, who maintain no allegiance or ties to the Tribes.

(3) The *EXILED* ONES

(i) The **GENTRY**
[***the High Ones***]
A tribe of Elbi who originate from the north-west of Scotland, but, sometime around the beginning of the 1600s, emigrated to the north-east of Ireland – possibly after an exchange of land with

Sidhe colonists, or possibly during a simultaneous invasion by the two tribes. [See below – ***The Sidhe: The Elves of Ireland***].

(ii) **SEA ELVES**
[***the Astrai***]
The nomadic and rarely seen *Elves of the Sea* were once known as ***The Red Clan*** – before taking to the waters in and around the British Isles, sometime after losing their ancestral lands in a territorial dispute with the Piskie [see Dr Raphael's "*Blue Bonnet and the Pixie Wars of Expansion"*].

(b)
LOWER ALBION
With the ascendancy of Man, those Elbi who left 'the lands above' created a kingdom beneath the earth, which in time became known as ***The Hidden Realm***, or – to those Men who still remembered the power of the Elves with fond reverence – ***Avalon***. (In the ancient Elbi tongue the letters 'V' and 'B' sound almost identical, thus *Avalon* [more correctly *Alvilon*] = ***Albilon*** [lit. ***Albi*** = '*The people of this land*' + **lon** = '*below*', as oppose to '***Albion***' which can be translated as '***Albi***' = '*The people of this land*' + '***on***' = roughly translating as '*here*'].)

THE AELFRADI
[*the Hidden-Ones – the Proud Ones*]
The Elbi of the Eastern Kingdoms – once the most powerful of all the Elven tribes, and the ones who thought most highly of themselves (thus earning the nickname 'The Proud Ones') – could never bring themselves to come to terms with their loss of power (especially to a species who they regarded as being barbarous and downright backward) and fled the *world-above* in disgust, relocating themselves beneath the earth, to become known, over time, as 'The Hidden Folk' or 'The People of the Mound'.
Over the ages they became renowned for their bitterness, hostility and ferocity towards their conquerors – the *Humans* (whom they consider an evil race of half-demons) – and during the ensuing centuries their underworld kingdom became a haven for many of the disaffected Fae Folk and 'magical beings' of the British Isles and beyond.

Eventually they began to call themselves, or became known (to the *Anglo-Saxon* immigrants of *Upper Albion*), as the ***Aelfradi*** (lit. the '*Nightmare*' - *OE*).
But no matter how grand and majestic the subterranean palaces that they built, or the success and savagery of their above-ground raids of retribution (see ***Wild Hunt***), they have never been content with their situation. Their hatred of all things Human is ferocious, and their resentment towards the other kingdoms of the Elbi is still tangible. To this day, with the power of the over-ground tribes broken, only a fragile truce of mistrust exists between the Aelfradi and the Elbi who remained above.

2. **SIDHE**
The Elves of Ireland ...

Uncle Cornelius parked Old Nancy in the small car park that nestled off Ditchling Road and on the edge of Hollingbury Park.
'Right then,' said The Pook, 'Bezt *tranzform* yourzelf, Percival, till we getz to the woodzez behind the cottagezez. Don't want to go zcaring the *Big Folk* now, do we? We'z got a glamour ztarting from 'bout there, an' zo you'll be fine from that point onwardz.'
'A "glamour"–' Uncle Cornelius began to inform Tom (politely holding The Hound's breeches, as they politely waited while the were-hound changed form in the back of the car).
'Is an "Elven spell of masking, misdirection and/or hiding" – yes I know,' cut in Tom, slightly smugly.
'Good lad,' smiled Uncle Cornelius, with a chuckle. 'You keep on reading them books, son.'

They walked along a small '*scar*' towards four terraced cottages set in the middle of, and dissecting, Hollingbury Woods. To an outsider, it might have looked like any *normal* family out on a jolly early-morning jaunt: Dickensian henchman out for a stroll with his hatchet-faced midget brother, gangly teenage grandson, and monstrous pet buffalo-retriever.
Then they continued through the rather delightful and wild-growing woods that, Tom noted, had obviously, at some point in its past, suffered severe storm damage (*The Great Storm of 1987* to be exact), as there were several large trees toppled on their sides and covered with moss and other dense vegetation. The Hound stayed in dog-form and kept his nose to the ground as he skirted about the meandering pathways – made by generations of walkers picking their way through the woods over the years (so-called 'wish-paths' or a '*wapple way*' in the local dialect).
The Pook led them over part of a rambling golf course and past a few desperate, angry-looking people, commonly called "*golfers*".

‘Bloomin’ golferz!’ snorted the Pook, disdainfully, deliberately slowing down a little to make the waiting players wait some more.

‘*A good walk spoilt,*’ chipped in Cornelius.

‘Uzed to be a beautiful an’ powerful place back in the day. Afore the buggerz decided to put thiz ’ere. Mind you, I zuppoze if’n it weren’t ’ere the daft zodz would ’ave tarmacked the whole bleedin’ zite by now.’

At the top of a gently rising hill stood a circular(ish) rampart of earth known as “Hollingbury Ring” – sometimes called, by the locals, “Hollingbury Castle” or (incorrectly) “The Roman Camp” (it being, in fact, all that remained of an *oppidi,* or hill-fort, dating back to the time when the Elbi were masters of the land).

Tom stood on the turf rampart, the wind buffeting him like an angry hairdryer, and looked back towards the sea. You could see for miles. The English Channel shimmered like a glistening blanket beneath the newly risen sun, while the whole of Brighton stretched out idly before him. To his right and to his left the beautiful South Downs sleepily swayed and rolled, disappearing lazily into the morning mist like a lumpy patchwork duvet.

As Cornelius, Tom and The Pook made their way towards the centre of the Ring, The Hound dipped behind a gorse bush (breeches clenched firmly in teeth) to morph back once more into humanoid-form, before hurriedly catching up with them.

Waiting for them, standing stiff-legged and with thumbs hooked into a wide leather belt, was the figure of a tall man with long greying-brown hair pulled back loosely into a ponytail, and with a thick golden hoop at his ear.

He looked like he might have been about fifty years old, was wearing faded jeans, a hand-knitted grey jumper (that had seen a few too many years of service) and brand new boots. On his back was a golf bag with a small collection of golf club handles sticking out of it. Tattooed in green on the side of his neck was a small, vibrant image that implied the essence of a wild hare.

He turned to face the approaching party.

‘Morning, Archie,’ said Cornelius.

Archie broke into a wide, snaggle-toothed grin.

‘Morning, Dandy! Mizter ’Ound,’ he replied cheerfully. ‘Good to zee you both. Been far too long, that’z a fact. Who’z thiz you got with you then?’

‘This is Tom; newest addition to *The Firm,*’ announced Tom’s uncle, proudly. ‘Tom, this is Archie Swapper.’

Archie took Tom’s hand and looked him over with clever, good-humoured eyes.

‘Could almozt be one of uz, Dad,’ he said to The Pook.

‘Don’t be zo daft, zon,’ came the swift response from Alberich.

Tom was a little surprised to hear that the two were related. They looked so different. Archie had none of the fine features of his father. And, besides that, was at least a foot taller.

In fact, Archie Swapper was The Pook's adopted son. "Adopted" was perhaps too generous a word for it – "stolen" was nearer to the mark.

It had once been quite a common practise among the *Fair Folk,* to steal a human child and raise it as one of their own, but it was now no longer heard of, no longer thought acceptable. Better, it was now believed, to fade into the darkness without making a fuss. For the Elves, like all *magic-folk*, were in decline and had been for centuries. For some reason, they had grown as infertile and as poisoned as the land that they cherished and mourned for. No child had been born to *The Children of the Light* for almost a hundred and fifty years, and though they were, when compared to the lives of men, a long-lived race (the average life expectancy of an Elf – should he survive tribal warfare, persecution and motorways – was around four hundred and ninety-odd years) their numbers were rapidly dwindling.

As their womenfolk had stopped giving birth, some had pleaded with their men to fetch them a human child, so they could raise and cherish it as they would have done their own. In consequence, a healthy human baby had on occasion been taken (swapped in the middle of the night and replaced with a sad, lifeless, tear-stained little bundle) and when the human mother awoke in the morning she found, to her horror and despair, that her beautiful baby had died in the night – shrunken, pale and strangely deformed by some horrible and mysterious disease.

The *stolen child* was generally raised in ignorance of its true birthright and could only wonder why they towered clumsily above their siblings, and (though time spent with *The Children of the Light* would extend their life far beyond the normal expectancy of a human) why they withered and aged as those around them stayed young, vibrant and beautiful.

Alfie had been *adopted* back in 1927.

Taken from a poor couple from Angmering, who struggled to feed themselves and their other four children, Alberich had *lifted* Alfie one night from his cot and swapped him with the lovingly swaddled body of his own stillborn son (little Aelfling) – along with a purse of gold coins uncarefully *hidden* under a *broken* floorboard.

Although Alfie knew *what* he was and *where* he came from (Alberich Albi, being the kind of Elf that he was, had told Alfie the truth about his heritage as soon as he thought that the boy was able to understand) he never once felt the need to return to his natural family, being, in his mind and those of his foster family, a Pharisee – an Elf of the Downlands – a good one at that, and damned proud of it.

'What have you got for us, Alfie?' asked The Hound, crouching down and examining the ground around them intently.

Just then, a trendily dressed, middle-aged couple walked around the corner and towards them, followed by a bounding Irish Setter with an insane grin wobbling across its slobbering chops.

''Ow do,' chirped Alfie, all smiles.

Tom looked on in horror, his chin dropping like a hangman's noose and his head flitting back and forth – like a concerned spectator in the front row of *The Wimbledon, International Live-Grenade Lobbing Championships* – between the nice-looking, well-to-do dog-walkers and the seven-and-a-half foot tall monster dressed like a hirsute Walter Raleigh on his summer holidays (currently hunkered down on his haunches and probing around the bushes with his fearsome snout, with one murderous paw balanced, rather elegantly, on hip).

'Good morning,' the dog-walkers replied, in cheerful chorus, obviously totally oblivious to the were-beast in their midst.

Uncle Cornelius doffed his hat and Alberich tugged a forelock.

The Irish Setter lolloped over to The Hound and started to huff playfully. The Hound scratched its ear then silently shooed it away.

The woman smiled at Tom, who could only simper back a polite, open-mouthed idiot-grin.

'What a lovely day,' she offered, kindly.

Tom gibbered something unintelligible in reply.

'Come on, Jimmy,' called the woman.

The Irish Setter, tail wagging furiously and eyes excitedly fixed on The Hound, reluctantly followed after her.

'Isn't it wonderful that they take them out and about in the fresh air ...' Tom overheard the nice-looking woman say to her partner as they disappeared from view.

Tom, of course, had already been told that a *glamour* had been put in place, but it was one thing to be told and quite another to see it in action. Alfie, seeing Tom's expression, laughed a little and then explained that people would only see what they wanted to see and expected to see. Besides, Hollingbury Hill was an old and powerful site, a magic place, so it was easy to make the whole area 'safe' – the Pharisees' spells and charms becoming naturally enhanced.

Alfie Swapper led them over to an area of ground within the turf walls of the Ring, stopping beside a small grassy mound.

'What do you think, Mizter 'Ound?' he asked, scratching the back of his head.

Looking at the ground around said small grassy mound it was obvious, even to Tom's untrained eye, that something *athletic* had taken place here. The earth was churned dramatically and one of the bushes nearby was unnaturally flattened.

'Zhow 'em what you'z found, Alfie,' growled The Pook.

Alfie put down his golf bag and, reaching into it, pulled out a large spearhead attached to the remains of a snapped metal shaft.

(Of note, the remaining 'implements' of Archie's bag were also, Tom found, of some particular interest; including, as they did, not only a hefty-looking *4-Iron* but also two *golf club shafts* with murderous [and decidedly unsportsmanlike] razor-sharp steel heads [rather like the bastard offspring of a tomahawk and a pickaxe]. Thus, Tom concluded, making Archie Swapper quite possibly the most unsought after caddie in the whole of Sussex.)

'Lookz like zomeone tried to bag 'emzelvez zomething gurt an' nazty,' scowled Archie.

'*Gert*?' hissed Tom to his uncle in alarmed suspense, his eyes widening like a firmly squeezed owl's. 'Who the frickin' hell is Gert?'

''E means "big", son,' the old man whispered back, unreassuringly. 'An' mind your language, Tomas Dearlove, or you'll be getting a clip round the ear'ole.'

Alfie handed the spearhead to The Hound, who, taking it gingerly with the very tips of his ferocious claws, examined it closely – first sniffing along the remains of its shaft and then cautiously testing the metal with his teeth. A grimace rippled over his black lips as he passed the weapon to Cornelius, then he bent down to study the scuffed earth around them.

Tom bustled forward, craning his neck to have a look at the impressive object in his uncle's hands.

The spearhead was a wicked-looking thing – long, hefty and barbed, with swirling lines and symbols etched on its blade. It looked very functional and very ... *unpleasant*.

'Silver,' muttered Cornelius.

At which the Pook shook his head ruefully and pursed his lips.

(In many tales and legends it is often commented upon that Elves have a fear of metal. This is only partially true. More correct would be to say that –

(a) They just don't like it very much [apart from gold, which they adore] as it reminds them of the painful time, long ago in their history, when they lost the battle for their beloved Albion against the early *Britons* – who, being armed with bronze and then iron weapons, were at an unfair advantage over the Elbi [who were equipped with weapons made of stone and wood]. To this day Elves generally tend to use knapped flint for knife-blades, spearheads and arrow-tips. [However, Alfie, not having *Elf blood* in his veins, was very happy to touch and use metal weapons; hence his rather romantic nickname among the Elbi of the *Two Albions* of – '*Silver Spear*'.]

(b) They often can't afford it, and besides, well-knapped flint being almost as good and far, far cheaper [excluding, of course, the Elf-hours, and skill, that it takes to make them], there seemed little point.)

''Unting weapon,' muttered Cornelius. 'Modern design, I reckon. Don't recognise the script on it, but I'd take a punt an' say that it's a spell of *'arm* (for the prey) an' *protection* (for the 'unter).'

'Well, that part didn't seem to work,' snorted The Hound, rubbing his index finger and thumb together, sniffing them and then dabbing his fingertips with the tip of his tongue. 'Blood,' he frowned. 'Human blood.'

The were-hound stood up keenly and, scenting the air, walked towards the flattened gorse bush.

'There's more of it here too. A lot more. But this ...' he mused, switching his attention to a small dark stain on the grass and arching an eyebrow, 'isn't.'

'Isn't what?' asked Tom, urgently.

'Human.'

The Hound looked excitedly around him, reading the ground like Tom would have read a newspaper (if Tom read newspapers, that is, which he didn't – apart from the cartoons).

'Archie, whereabouts did you find the spearhead?'

'Down be'ind that zquazhed buzh what you'z juzt been looking at, Mizter 'Ound,' replied the changeling.

'Well, Archie,' said The Hound, 'I fear that you might be right. It does indeed appear that there has been some sort of hunt ... and a rather unsuccessful one at that.

'Here we have the tracks of a small group of people: four or five in total (one of them possibly a woman). They are moving on the balls of their feet – so presumably with caution (or stealth), and thus primed and ready for action of some sort.

'Then there is this print here,' he cried, jabbing a poniard-like digit towards a compressed piece of grass with scraped furrows in front of it. 'This is the footprint of something large, heavy and in possession of fearsome talons.'

The Hound sniffed the air, pouted, and held his breath in thought.

'So what can we deduce?' he continued at last. 'Their quarry was big and clawed and therefore, we must reason, a carnivore – a predator in its own right.'

''Ere, Alberich? There been any reports of predation on local livestock recently?' asked Uncle Cornelius.

'Not to my knowledge there ain't,' replied The Pook, biting his lip and shaking his head.

'Then we must conclude,' sighed The Hound, 'that the *hunt* was for pleasure – for sport, or perhaps for ceremony. The fact that the creature was being stalked with spears instead of firearms would suggest a ritual or a rite-of-passage, perhaps even some kind of cruel and savage game.'

The Hound started walking around the scene, elaborating his hypothesis as he paced.

'The hunters approach from the Ditchling Road end of the park. Their quarry from the direction of Wild Park (known locally as *The Giant's Foot*). They confront each other here, on Hollingbury Ring. There is a brouhaha. One of the huntsmen is badly wounded (perhaps killed) and is thrown (or falls) onto this bush. His companions succeed in driving the *assailant* away, drawing blood from the creature – who then flees in the direction of Burstead Woods, to our left. However, the hunters do not pursue their game but lift their wounded companion, carrying him or her back in the direction from which they came.'

'Any idea what it waz what did the damage?' asked The Pook, scratching his chin and asking the very question that had been anxiously bothering Tom.

'The ground is too churned for any of the prints to offer positive identification, I'm afraid to say. Some form of large cat, perhaps?'

'Like the *Beast of Bodmin* you mean?' suggested a rapt Tom.

'Just so,' answered The Hound. 'Though I would hazard a guess that this is something far larger.'

'No big catzez around 'ere,' muttered Archie. 'Well, not for nigh on forty yearz.'

'S'pose it's possible that one could 'ave strayed 'ere though – an unwanted exotic pet, or perhaps an escapee from a circus or some such like,' posed Uncle Cornelius. 'Could even 'ave been released on purpose; there's some wicked so-an'-so's about, an' no mistake about it.'

Cornelius paused and pursed his lips.

'Was a full moon last night, though, 'Aitch,' he added, cautiously.

'Yes, I'm well aware of the implications, Dandy,' The Hound responded, gently.

The implications, it rapidly dawned on Tom, was that the *quarry* was a "*creature of the curse*" – a were-beast of some description. Tom had learnt that those poor unfortunates who changed form, often against their will, with the passing phases of the moon – so afflicted either by an attack from a were-beast or a curse from a witch or sorcerer – could be affected for anywhere between one night (the full moon) to a quarter of a cycle (from *waxing gibbous* to *waning gibbous*).

The Hound cocked an ear and nodded in the direction of the Ditchling Road.

Archie leapt up onto the small grassy mound and waved his hands above his head.

'Ned!' he called. 'Over 'ere.'

And into the clearing trotted Cousin Ned.

Ned Leppelin, the last born of the Pharisees, was a younger, even more handsome version of his uncle, The Pook. By looking at him Tom would have guessed his age to be around twenty-two (but being Elf-born that would have made him over a hundred and fifty years old). He moved with the grace of a polecat – with an ease and surety of purpose in his stride. He had a long tussled mane of curly golden-white hair and woolly sideburns, was dressed in a brightly coloured shirt (opened to the navel) and faded flared blue jeans. Around his neck, tied on leather-string, was a beautiful golden pendant that suggested the spirit of a wild hare. Like his cousin, Alfie, he had a golf bag strapped across his back, with the carefully wrapped handles of three *golf clubs* (ha!) visible. (Unlike Alfie's, the shafts of Ned's *clubs* where made of wood and looked like they might have been purchased sometime back in the early 1920s). All in all, he looked, Tom thought, like a cross between the hero from a Norse saga and an early 1970s rock star.

Tom felt the beginnings of what might become hero-worship stirring within him.

'Ned,' grinned Cornelius, giving the dapper little fellow a hearty handshake. 'You looking after yourself, I 'ope. Big day next week, an' all.'

'Don't worry, Dandy, I'll be bringing *The Prize* back Zouth again, you can bet your 'at on it,' replied Ned, with a smile like fresh honey dripping from a golden sunrise.

'None of that now, young Ned,' The Pook chastised him. 'We can celebrate when the job'z done an' not afore'and. You knowz better 'an that. *Louie Lew Llewellyn ap Lew Louie Llewellyn's* a fine Elf, an' a grand champion – won't pay to be takin' 'im lightly, I can tell you that for nothing.'

When all the introductions and welcomes had been made, The Hound asked Ned what, if anything, he had uncovered.

'Theze trackzez 'ere,' replied the young Elf, indicating towards the footprints of the *hunters* (almost imperceptible to Tom's eye), 'come from, an' then go back to, the Ditchling Zcar. Couple of motorcarz drove up an' parked on the grazz at the edge of the golf courze; zmall ones, but fazt, I reckon.'

'Zportz ... I mean, sports cars?' offered Tom, helpfully.

'That'll be them,' replied Ned, with a smile. 'They definitely made off in an 'urry though,' he added.

'I bet they did,' growled the Hound, almost to himself.

The were-hound dug around in one of the pouches of his belt and pulled out (much to Tom's amazement) a large, swanky-looking mobile phone, and speedily tapped in a number with a pointed claw.

'Ah, Mordecai ... I'm sorry, I haven't woken you have I? ... I need a favour ... Could you contact all hospitals, surgeries and private clinics in and around the Brighton area for me ... Yes. We're looking for a patient who would have been brought in a few hours ago, suffering from the type of injury that might have been sustained from an attack by a large predatory animal ... No, that's all I can tell you at the moment ... Yes, do keep me informed on that front too, old stick ... Oh, by the way – have there been any circuses in town recently? ... No. Not to worry then. Toodle-pip, old boy. And, Inspector ... happy hunting.

'Now then,' he growled, pocketing the phone and walking over to the stain of *not-human* blood on the grass, 'let's see just where these other tracks lead us.'

They walked out of and beyond the confines of the hill-fort and past a golf-green that jutted out like a polished peninsula into a sea of ragged woods. All the while The Hound scented and scoured the ground around them, carefully picking a trail (though, he had to concede, the strong winds blowing over the hills made the scent vague and almost impossible to track with any absolute clarity). They passed through a densely packed wood (made up of thin, short, spiky and spindly trees), eventually coming out onto a clearing with a dew pond set at the edge of a large field.

The Hound asked them all to stay back while he walked down and examined the muddy ground around the edges of the pond.

'Ah ha!' he exclaimed at last, calling them over and carefully directing them to stand around a large, deep indentation in the mud.

It was the huge imprint of a foot-like paw, with deep claw-points pressed into the ground before it. Next to it was the impression of a large human-ish hand, where the creature had obviously balanced itself as it either drank from the pond or perhaps washed its wounds.

'Zo it iz a *man-beazt* what they waz after,' frowned Alfie Swapper, quietly whistling to himself.

Cornelius looked from the monstrous prints to The Hound, lifting his hat with one hand and scratching his head with the other.

'What you reckon, 'Aitch? Ever seen a print quite like that before? Don't look like no regular were-wolf track to me. Not one that I've ever seen, anyways.'

Tom wondered just how many were-wolf tracks his uncle had come across over the years?

'It'z gurt – eight, maybe nine-feet tall, judging by the length of itz ztride,' said Ned, from the other side of the dew pond. ''Eavy too. Three 'undred, three fifty-pluz poundz, I reckon. Trackz lead thiz way.'

They followed Ned into yet another closely pressed wood, comprised of more short, thin, spindly trees. Startled birds heralded their approach with panicky warning cries. The trail, however, seemed to evaporate. Ned, The Hound and Alfie made ever-widening circles in an effort to pick it up again. Eventually they converged on a spot where a large beech tree lay, growing on its side. Over the years its root ball had formed into a solid bulbous mound coated with moss. Its branches stretched upwards, still bursting with life despite its horizontal aspect. The Hound dashed along the upward-tilting trunk and into the heavy branches, cocking his head to one side, ears erect and listening intently.

'There!' he cried at last, pointing up towards the very edge of the woods. 'Up there, Ned. Do you see it?'

Moments later Ned had shimmied, like a golden polecat, up a slender tree and was examining a slim grey box – about the size of a small bar of chocolate – which was fastened to the top branches.

'What do you want me to do with it, Mizter 'Ound? Zhall I bring it down?'

'No, don't touch it, Ned,' replied The Hound, fumbling through the pouches in his belt. 'I knew I could hear something; a faint buzzing noise – almost imperceptible.'

He drew a small spray-can from his belt and squirted the area around the tree with the box in it. There, just visible to the naked eye in the early morning sunlight, was a lattice of red beams of light, casting a net-like wall for a hundred metres either side of the tree.

They traced the line of the "invisible fence" and found another box grafted high onto another tree, and then another, and then another; building an imperceptible boundary – starting at the top of the golf course, by Hollingbury Ring, and sweeping around to the edge of *The Giant's Foot* (which, it turned out, was a small valley that cut into the surrounding wooded hills, with a path running around the base of the valley in the vague shape of a giant foot – hence the name – though Tom thought that it looked more like a giant's wobbly sock; anyway, he preferred the parks more commonly used and official name of *Wild Park,* it certainly seemed more fitting).

'Zome zort of barrier, I zuppoze?' sniffed Alfie. 'Though how it workz iz beyond me. 'Ere, Mizter 'Ound? Doezn't 'ave any effect on you, doez it, if you try to pazz through it, I mean?'

The Hound chewed his lip and then stepped gingerly over the threshold and through the lattice of beams. To his obvious relief, he informed them that he felt no ill effects.

'Told you there waz *new magic* in the air,' grimaced The Pook. 'Old magic too. I can feel it.'

When an Elf King tells you that there is magic in the air you tend to believe him.

The Hound could sense it as well.

Near the entrance of Wild Park they discovered tyre tracks made by a large, sturdy vehicle – a pickup truck or van of some sort. It had arrived heavily laden and then left much lighter (about three hundred to three hundred and fifty-plus pounds lighter, by Ned and The Hound's reckoning!). Also to be found were the footprints of another small party of people, trailing the flight of the "man-beast" into the trees and up through the hills leading to Hollingbury Ring.

After an extensive reconnaissance of the area (mapping the perimeter of the "invisible cage" as they went) the six of them sat on the walls of Hollingbury Ring, passing a flask of hot tea and a packet of Custard Creams between them.

'Will you stop that!' barked Cornelius, scowling in exasperation towards The Hound.

'Stop what?' replied the perplexed were-beast.

'Eyeing up my biscuit. Looking at me begrudgingly, like I just bought it with your stolen pocket money, that's what.'

'I never was!' huffed The Hound, indignantly.

'Will youz twoz cut it out,' chuckled The Pook. 'Let uz try an' ztay focuzed on what it iz what'z needed to be done 'ere.'

'You are quite correct, Alberich. Our apologies,' sniffed The Hound, shooting a baleful grimace in Cornelius' direction. 'Let us take this moment to assess the facts as we can see them.

'A van (or similar vehicle) is driven into Wild Park – in which is carried a large, dangerous, humanoid creature. The creature is released into the woods around us, which have some kind of high-tech security fence in place around their perimeter – presumably somehow capable of stopping the poor creature from straying or escaping from the '*field of play*'. The beast is then harried towards Hollingbury Ring, where another party of hunters await it.

'There the creature meets with the hunters, wounding or killing one of their number. The creature, in turn, is also wounded. Both parties – the hunters and their quarry – flee from the scene. The hunt is ended, leaving the creature, we must assume, still in the vicinity'

'Why here? Why Hollingbury Park?' asked Tom, looking around at the woods, nervously imagining that the mysterious *monster* might be watching them this very second.

'Well, it's a comparatively small area, but contains a natural landscape, thereby providing some sort of cover for the beast, but not so much as they might not never be able to find it,' suggested Professor Cornelius *Dandy* Lyons.

'Alzo, it'z a place of power, zo az any magic – zpellz an' the like – what they might need to make, to mazk their activitiez or contain their *prey*, would be amplified,' said Alfie (*Silver-Spear)* Swapper – *The Stolen Child.*

'An' not many people come up 'ere at night. It'z izolated, but alzo cloze to the centre of Brighton. Zo that makez it eazy to get to an' from,' added Ned Leppelin – *The Last of the Pharisees.*

'Zomeone'z playing a game. A right dangerouz one at that. Gurt-Game 'unting; monster 'unting; trophy 'unting, by the lookz of thingz,' said Alberich Albi, *Nineteenth Pook of the Pharisees, King of all the Elf-lands south of the Downs – from the Devil's Humps in the west, to Mount Caburn in the east (and beyond).*

'So what do we do now?' asked Tomas Dearlove – *The Boy Bereft of a Romantic-Sounding Title.*

'We return here tonight,' growled Mr Percival Percy (The Hound *Who Hunts Nightmares*), keenly and sternly (and possibly smugly). 'I have no doubt that the *hunters* will return to finish off their despicable *game* and tidy up all loose ends ... and when they do – *we* shall be here, waiting for them!'

EIGHTEEN
Were-Lions! Were-Tigers! Were-Bears! Oh My!

By the time that they got back to One Punch Cottage, Tom was virtually asleep (despite all his best efforts to stay awake). By the time he made it to his bed, he was all but unconscious before his head hit the pillow.

He awoke in the afternoon (feeling gloriously refreshed) and made his way down to The Study, to find The Hound poring over a collection of old books and manuscripts.

'Ah, good afternoon, Tom,' said the were-hound, lifting his nose from a hefty tome. 'I do hope that you are feeling reinvigorated. Cornelius is out walking Bess; he'll be back shortly. There's some coffee and sandwiches over on the desk. Do help yourself, old stick.'

Tom poured himself some coffee.

'What are you doing?' he asked.

'I'm trying to identify exactly what type of creature our *friends* were after last night. But there's nothing that I can seem to pinpoint,' he huffed, with an intrigued sigh.

'So what have you got so far?' asked Tom.

The Hound looked at him for a moment and then closed the book, steepled his fingers and tapped them lightly against his snout.

'Nothing of any certainty, I'm afraid, but it is a most fascinating and intriguing area of study; one that has always been of great interest to me.

'It is, we can conclude, most definitely a biped – a humanoid creature. If it is a *were-beast,* a *therianthropic* entity (and the presence of silver weapons on the night of a full moon would seem to point us in that direction), then it is most certainly some form of large predator.

'The beast is probably too heavy to be a were-wolf (unless one at the very top end of their known weight range). Besides, your uncle is correct – the tracks are completely wrong, and so this line of enquiry can be dismissed. It is possible, I suppose, that it could be some sort of a *were-cat* – though what one would be doing in Southern England one can only hazard a guess ... but still, in the modern age, everything seems to become *possible*. There do exist *were-lions* (although these always adopt the animal-form and can therefore be discounted). *Were-tigers* have been reported from time to time in India and Southeast Asia – always the result of a curse from a malicious warlock or enchantress. In South America there is a cult of *were-jaguars* – warrior-fanatics – similar in nature to the *Ulfhedinn* wolf-warriors of Scandinavia. In ancient histories there are recordings of a mysterious *cat-people*, the *Naravirala*, but these have surely become extinct, for there have been no sightings of them, to my knowledge at least, for over a thousand years, and besides, they were, reputedly, a race of slight build – far too delicate to fit our profile.

'Moving further afield we have *were-hyenas*, the so-called *Bultungin* – usually found exclusively in the West of Africa (of interest, their transformations are not restricted by the phases of the moon).

Similarly there are *Gnoles* – a race of *hyena-headed 'men'*; savage folk, it is true, but, for the last three hundred years at least, they have shown little interest in the affairs of man.

'Then there is, I suppose, the remote possibly that it could be a *were-bear*, but the tracks seem a little small, and no one in their right mind would consider hunting such a creature for fun – and most certainly not when armed with nothing more than spears.

'Again, one cannot dismiss the possibility that it could very well be some other species of creature; one with which I am, to date, unfamiliar with.'

The Hound spread his enormous hands out over the desk, patted the books and let out an enormous sigh.

'No, I'm afraid to say that, for the moment at least, I am at a loss. There is only one way to find out – and that is to go and observe the poor beast for ourselves.'

'And then what?' asked Tom, trying to hide his growing unease.

'That is indeed the question, Tom. My wish is that we can discover the poor creature before the *hunters* do, help it in its escape, and then return it to a safe and suitable environment.

'Let us hope, for all concerned,' he added, 'that it is a creature that can be reasoned with.'

NINETEEN
The Battle Of Hollingbury Hill

Sundown found the *One Punch Cottage Posse* back on the ramparts of Hollingbury Ring, awaiting the coming of the moon.

The Hound was bristling with excitement, had been all day, in fact. Uncle Cornelius was dapperly dressed in dark hunting-tweeds (with matching silver tie pin, cufflinks and knuckle-dusters) and with an ancient and punchy-looking snub-nosed revolver ('Don't often 'ave to use 'em, an' of course you 'opes that they ain't never needed, but when you do need 'em, you *really do* need 'em, if you get my drift.') loaded with six silver bullets and stuffed casually into his jacket pocket (the other pocket being crammed with a large brick-like package of cheese and piccalilli sandwiches, carefully prepared and wrapped in greaseproof paper by Missus Dobbs). Tom, to his annoyance and dismay, had been given no weapon at all, just an old whistle and a large silver charm to be worn around his neck – with the vaguely alarming promise that it might do some good if things *"got a bit hairy"* (!!!!).

They met with The Pook, Ned and Alfie and a couple of other Pharisees; Fred – slight (even for an Elf), handsome, raven-haired, good-natured and silent; and Ollie – a dour, tough-looking, raw-skinned redhead. The Pook and Ned both carried long hunting bows, and were armed with sturdy knob-stick and flint-headed *golfer's tomahawk* respectively. Archie, Fred and Ollie were all equipped with long-bladed cutting spears, slightly taller than they were, with a thick golden-hoop at the butt of the shaft – the head of Archie's spear being made of silver, while those of Fred and Ollie were expertly knapped from a bluish and wickedly sharp flint.

They gathered solemnly together in a tight circle to discuss tactics for the night's jolly jape; The Hound squatting down in the middle, like the over-exuberant captain of the school's first team rugger fourteens giving a pep talk at the final of the 1909 All England National Championships. Tom began to wonder if his job would be to administer the *magic sponge* and hand out oranges at half-time, but, to his relief (and excitement) he was told to shadow Ned.

Ned and he were to watch for the arrival of the *hunters* from a vantage point overlooking *The Giant's Wobbly Sock* (Wild Park), while Ollie would keep a lookout for their (the *huntsmen's*) approach from The Ditchling Scar end of the grounds. Uncle Cornelius and Fred were to patrol the southern side of the 'arena', whilst The Pook and Alfie would take care of the north side. The Hound was to rove freely, as he saw fit. A carefully arranged system of calls was agreed upon in order to be able to keep in contact and abreast of matters at hand – a fox yip for a sighting of the *hunters* and an owl hoot for a sighting of the *monster* being just the beginning of it. Tom did wonder out loud why they couldn't just use mobile phones, and was informed, rather touchily, that the reception was pretty iffy in the woods and so mobile devices were considered to be too untrustworthy. He was then told (comfortingly) to blow on his whistle like *Gabriel having a coughing fit at the gates of Jericho*, if he found himself in any sort of danger.

Tom and Ned were soon making themselves as comfortable as they could, as they took to their post and concealed themselves within the undergrowth at the top of the steep hill that overlooked the valley of *The Giant's Foot/Wobbly Sock*. From their hidden position they could easily see any approach made from the Lewes Scar end of the park – bar the two extreme wings of the woods on either side of the valley, which were out of their line of vision. These, however, were where The Pook and Alfie, and Cornelius and Fred, respectively, were scouting – just in case the mysterious *hunters* entered via the woods rather than the through the open park.

The moon appeared as if summoned by a sorcerer, and Tom felt himself shiver with a mixture of excited anticipation and more than a little fear. But all he needed to do was to take a look at his heroically handsome and capable companion crouched beside him – bow in hand and murderous putter strapped to his back – to feel comforted. Add to the mix a seven-and-a-half-foot tall were-wolf-wolfhound prowling through the woods, his lethal and deadly uncle, plus a war party of homicidal Elven caddies, and he couldn't help but almost feel a little sorry for the *hunters* (whoever the unsuspecting and irredeemable tossers might be).

The wind built up force and rattled the tops of the trees.

The Hound nestled himself at the edge of the woods next to the dew pond.

The creature, he reasoned, must, most likely, be thirsty, and would therefore, at some point, come to the pond to drink. He couldn't help but wonder what he would have done if it were he in the same situation as this unfortunate soul: lie up during the day, thereby avoiding detection, and then, with the coming of nightfall, try to find an escape from this invisible and truly abhorrent cage? He felt an enormous sympathy for the poor creature and hoped that the matter could be sorted out peaceably.

It was entirely possible that the *hunters* had given up on their quest. Maybe the injury, or death, of one of their number had put them off the idea of this repulsive form of entertainment. Inspector Jones had phoned this afternoon with a negative on any reports of a patient being brought in and treated for the type of injuries sustained from an attack by a large carnivore. So, either the hunter had died of their wounds or his or her companions had the means to treat him/her without any outside help. This he did not doubt. The technology that enabled them to somehow seal off a vast tract of land and pen in a *monster* (and, presumably, ship one in) must have been immensely expensive – that kind of kit couldn't be cheap, and so, by comparison, the hire of a private doctor and small medical facility would be small-feed. And, one would presume, a necessary precaution.

The Inspector had also received the lab report on the piece of material torn from Spring-Heeled Jack's cape last night. All that they could tell was that the garment was over a hundred and fifty years old and was probably made somewhere in Northern Italy.

Just then the ultrasonic ringtone of The Hound's mobile phone went off. He hastily retrieved it from his belt.

'Hello, Inspector,' he whispered, briefly wondering how strange it was that just when you were thinking of somebody they quite often phoned you or you bumped into them. (He also couldn't help feeling a tad embarrassed that he hadn't thought of supplying the whole team with mobile phones, as Tom had suggested.)

'Mr Hound, sorry to disturb you,' said the Inspector, his haunted-sounding voice clipping into the chill night air, 'but there's been another sighting of Spring-Heeled Jack'.

'Good Lord! What's the devilish fiend up to now?'

'Been seen pestering the good ladies of Aldrington. Wouldn't mind giving us a hand again, would you?'

'Sorry, Mordecai, old chap, on a case at the moment. Hush-hush and all that. I'll give you a call when all's cleared up this end. Until then, I'm afraid you're on your own, old fruit.'

Ned gave Tom a gentle nudge with a remarkably sharp elbow.

Tom, pretending that he hadn't been falling asleep, followed the direction of Ned's extended finger and saw three sets of headlights (one high and two low) swing into the park.

Ned shot him an excited grin.

Tom peered cautiously over the bush that they were sitting behind.

The lights of the cars blinked out, but the moonlight made everything astonishingly clear. Nine figures walked from the vehicles (two expensive looking sports cars and one large transit van) and huddled together in a circle, obviously deep in discussion. Tom would have loved to have been able to hear what they were saying, but almost immediately the huddle broke and they were on the move.

Two figures remained with the cars while the rest began to fan out in a line and head towards the trees. Tom could see the moonlight bouncing off the spear-tips that three of the sinister figures held. Two of the others looked like they might be carrying rifles, and the remaining two appeared to be unarmed, but it was a little difficult to tell at this distance.

Ned lifted his head and gave a perfect imitation of the harsh yip-yipping of a fox.

The two *unarmed* figures immediately looked up and locked directly onto the direction of the call. They seemed to be staring straight at Tom and Ned!

Tom felt his cheeks flush and his blood run cold.

'That ain't right,' muttered Ned, sounding a little worried.

And then the two *unarmed* figures were running straight towards them at an impossibly fast, jerking pace.

'This way, Tom!' hissed Ned, urgently tugging Tom's arm and leading him, at a crouch, further up the hill and into the dense woodland behind them.

By the time that they had reached the trees, the two chasing *huntsmen* were halfway up the hill and showing no signs of slowing. Ned dragged Tom along, and they sped like startled deer through the thin, spiky greenwood. They swiftly came to an area of woodland dominated by storm-felled trees, and Ned silently directed Tom to hide under and behind the furthest and largest of them, whilst he himself disappeared like a spirit into the undergrowth.

The Hound heard the yip-yapping call of a fox piercing through the night and pricked a swivelling ear.

'... So sorry Mordecai, must dash. Be a brick, and try to monitor the *Jack's* activities as best you can. Toodle-oo, old pip. I'll speak to you shortly.'

He pocketed the phone before Inspector Jones could even reply, and was making to move towards the direction of Ned's warning call when his eye was caught by the slightest of movements among the trees on the far side of the dew pond.

There, slipping out of the cover of the woodland – as silent as a shadow and as cautious as a ghost – stepped their mysterious quarry.

With his heartbeat pounding in his ears, Tom tentatively peeped through the mesh of branches and twigs, and saw, to his utter dismay and horror, two sinister figures approaching towards him with unerring resolve.

The *hunters* paused in the centre of the fallen ring of trees, scanning the area and showing no signs of being even the slightest bit out of breath. They were tall and thin, with strange and somehow unnaturally jerky animations to their movements.

Tom held his breath and peered through undergrowth. He noticed that both *hunters* were wearing white balaclava masks, each with a blood red star-shaped ring drawn around the left eye. They wore long coats with long white floppy hoods, with what looked like a pair of small spiky dog-ears sown on at the top – one milk-white and the other blood red.

One of the grisly figures slowly turned and looked Tom directly in the eyes.

Tom's heart froze with fear.

She must have been almost eight feet tall, muscled like a wrestler, yet as lithe and as graceful as a ballerina.

Elegant. Beautiful. Deadly.

The Hound had never seen one such as she before, few had, and for a moment he was slightly overcome by her appearance, for, even for her rarest of species, she was remarkably uncommon.

She came forward, warily making her way to the water's edge; black-grey stripes cut over a moonstruck and shimmering blue-grey fur.

A were-tigress.

The dreadful dog-hooded *huntsman* started to walk towards him. Its cold eyes held Tom's in a terrifying and hypnotic grip. And then there was a soft hiss and the *hunter* spun full circle and sank to his knees with an elf-arrow piercing through his neck. The *hunter* slowly rolled onto his back, shuddered momentarily, and then lay motionless on the ground.

Another arrow thudded into a tree, narrowly missing the second sinister *huntsman,* who, with lightning reflexes, dodged the shot like an angry viper. The second *hunter* snarled softly beneath its mask as Ned appeared into view and let lose a hail of arrows. The unearthly figure casually swatted each dart aside, catching the last arrow with an effortless and unnatural grace, before nonchalantly snapping it in two between its long slender fingers. Ned, having loosed his last arrow, turned and fled into the woods, drawing the ghastly creature after him and away from Tom.

Alfie and The Pook were silently heading towards the direction of Ned's yipping fox-call when they heard the sound of people approaching (in attempted stealth) through the woods to their left. The two Pharisees melted behind the trees, invisible to anyone unless they were to walk directly into them.

A tall man – wearing a long white hood (with two "wolf" ears sown on it – one blood red and one milk-white) pulled over a white mask with red markings drawn around the right eye – guardedly appeared through the trees. In his hands he carried a long, powerful hunting rifle. A few steps behind him came two more huntsmen – one tall and stocky, the other shorter and slighter. Both were dressed in camouflage clothing. The taller of the two wore a black balaclava with a red face, whilst his companion wore one identical, save that its face was green. Both carried long-bladed hunting spears of the same design as the one that Alfie had found earlier that morning.

The white-hooded hunter turned to his two companions and silently signalled to them that he was going up and around, whilst they should carry on directly towards the top of the hill. His two colleagues nodded, gave him the thumbs up, and cautiously continued on their way as the rifleman silently vanished into the trees.

Mr Green and *Mr Red* furtively made their way forwards and between the trees that Alfie and The Pook were hiding behind. When they had passed by, the Elf King and his son seeped back into view and silently nodded to each other. The Pook indicated with graceful, fluid hand gestures that he would follow the rifleman. Alfie nodded and, pointing in the direction that the other two had gone, gestured – with a pulling-down and grasping motion of his fist – that he would take care of them.

The two Pharisees evaporated like smoke into the undergrowth in silent pursuit of their respective targets.

The Hound stepped out from behind the trees and into full view.

The were-tigress leapt six feet into the air like an electrocuted ... cat(?) ... and let out a high-pitched snarl that was a terrifying cocktail of surprise, fear and rage. She landed on her feet like a ... cat(?) ... immediately falling into an aggressive hunting stance – head sunk deep into her shoulders, massive arms held out wide, with claws like butcher's knives sprouting from the fingers of her colossal hands like the springs from a broken mattress. She hissed furiously, showing canine teeth that a canine could only dream about.

'Good evening, Madam,' offered The Hound, as reassuringly and as politely as he possibly could (however, under the circumstances, he was only too aware how impolitely unreassuring he must look). 'Is there any way in which I might be of some assistance?' he asked, hopefully.

Mustering all of his courage, Tom cautiously crept from under the fallen trunk and edged his way towards the dead hunter. He stood stiffly over the prostrate figure, feeling both terrified and numb. He had never seen a dead person before (apart from a headless horseman of course, but somehow that didn't seem to count in quite the same way) and now he'd just seen somebody actually killed, right in front him.

He felt sick.

The *hunter* opened his eyes, sat bolt upright and reached over with his right hand to pull the arrow completely through his neck with a horrendous and nauseating sucking sound.

Tom tried to scream but his voice seemed to have disappeared, along with his ability to breathe.

The were-tigress exploded towards him like a missile – a pouncing, snarling, hurricane of teeth, claws and bristling fury. The Hound met her murderous assault with two perfectly timed straight left leads, jolting the creature's head backwards and making her stagger and momentarily lose her footing.

The Hound deftly snapped back out of range.

Instantly, the tigress regained her poise and balance, slightly shaking her head as if to clear her vision.

'Madam, I can assure you that this is all most unnecessary ...' growled the were-hound, as he rolled under and around a lethal roundhouse swipe.

The were-cat snarled and threw a juddering downward blow – like a strongman testing his strength at the fairground with a five bladed mallet.

'Desist, Madam! Immediately!' roared The Hound, in exasperation, side-stepping around and behind her, and sending a wickedly painful shovel-hook into the short ribs of her right flank.

The tigress howled in agony and annoyance, and sprang out of distance – her tail lashing furiously with a homicidal rage.

Alfie noiselessly circled around and in front of the two spearmen and pressed himself against the trunk of the large sycamore tree that stood at the crown of a wide, flat clearing at the top of the hill.

Mr Green and *Mr Red* entered into view, looking attentively to their left and right. The moonlight caught the silver tips of their spears and sparkled like stardust.

Both men suddenly pulled up short, shocked and bewildered by the sight before them.

Alfie Swapper stood nonchalantly at the end of the clearing, the thumb of one hand elegantly hooked into his belt, while his other hand rested on the butt of his beautifully weighted weapon (which he was balancing casually, and rather rakishly, across his shoulders).

'Evenin',' he smiled chirpily, with a wink.

Tom was bombing through the woods, zigzagging through the trees in what he knew must be a futile attempt to outpace his *undead* pursuer. Bolting like a rabbit with a rabid zombie-whippet up its bum, he vainly tried to blow the whistle that his uncle had given him, but somehow, when he needed it most, he seemed devoid of the necessary puff to perform such a basic task and could only manage a painfully pathetic (and alarmingly inaudible) 'tttthhhh' 'tttthhh' noise.

A corpse-like hand grabbed at his coat (a plain, military-style khaki green combat jacket, beloved by Tom) and Tom, to his credit – without the slightest pause or falter of step – slipped his arms through the sleeves and kept on running (offering a silent prayer of thanks that he rarely followed his mum's advice and did his coat up), leaving the baffled *hunter* holding the empty jacket.

The white-masked *huntsman* laughed coldly, then greedily lifted Tom's jacket to his face and buried his nose in it.

Tom could hear the *hunter* hungrily sniffing the garment.

Against his better judgement, Tom turned to see his pursuer fling his beloved coat to the floor and then chortle in a voice like an echo from a cave – 'Coming to get you, little boy. Ready or not!'

The duel of spears was fast, furious and deadly.

Alfie managed to keep himself outside the immediate line of attack at all times, thereby placing his immediate assailant in the middle – and thus assuring that the 'spare-man', so to speak, had always to get past his unbalanced comrade before he could offer a blow to The Pook's changeling son.

Alfie blocked a vicious downward cut from the murderously barbed spear of *Mr Green* with the butt of his weapon and, transporting his adversary's spear towards the ground, swept a devastating downward blow to the hunter's knee with the flat of his blade. *Mr Green* crumpled like a tin can under a bus wheel, whimpering softly to himself, while Alfie sprung out of distance before *Mr Red* could launch an assault.

Alfie and *Mr Red* circled each other – partners in an awful dance of death. Slowly and silently, they stepped like watchful predators through a shimmering net of shadows – their ferocious weapons engaged, wicked-blade to wicked-blade – as the moonlight bathed them both in a silvery, ghostly glory.

Mr Red suddenly chuckled.

Out of the corner of his eye, Alfie suddenly caught a glimpse of a small red dot of light that was dancing on his chest. He felt a dull, heavy blackness of agony ... and then, as he spun round in a circle, heard the noise of the rifle shot, followed by the rasping sound of a surprised cry of pain.

Tom could see the edge of the woods just yards before him, the moonlight dappling a path mercifully clear of obstructive vegetation beneath his feet. He made a desperate dash along it and came out from among the trees at full speed and into the clearing by the dew pond. He was tearing across said clearing and towards the other side – like a man wearing cricket whites with a sudden attack of diarrhoea in desperate search of a public lavatory – when something soft and leathery fluttered against his cheek.

From somewhere his voice suddenly made a remarkable return.

'AAAAAAAAAAAAAAAAAAAAAAAAAAAAAAAAARRRRRRRRR RRRRRRGGGGGGGGGGGGHHHHHHHHHHHH!!!!!!!!!!!!' he squealed, manfully, as he stumbled to the floor, rolling and desperately wiping and swiping his face.

He looked up, terrified, only to see a small black flurry of wings shooting upwards and arch in silhouette against the cold silver disc of the moon.

Phew, he thought. *No need to panic. It's only a bat.*

He hauled himself to his feet, looked towards the clearing, and almost fell over again in renewed horror.

'AAAAAAAAAAAAAAAAAAAAAAAAAAAAAAAAARRRRRRRRR RRRRRRRGGGGGGGGGGGGGHHHHHHHHHHHH!!!!!!!!!!!!' heard The Hound, as he dodged – with a shuffle of his feet like an Elizabethan dance step – the wicked fistful of gutting hooks that was hurtling towards him with lethal intent. Foolishly, he glanced round to see Tom crumple gracelessly to the floor clutching at his face.

A spiked furry hammer of fury raked across the were-hound's flank like a car crash. Instinctively he skipped out of distance with a yelp, grimacing with pain.

He looked down at the bleeding gash in his side and lost his temper.

'That's it! You've had your warning! I tried, Madam, oh I tried. But would you listen? Oh no. Oh no!' he ranted. 'However, I will control myself,' he snorted, struggling desperately to regain his composure and master his murderous rage. 'I can promise you that, at least. No teeth and no claws! We must, if nothing else, be civilised!'

The were-tigress yowled, clawing at the air in fury.

The Hound tucked his chin in, *put up his jooks*, and shuffled lightly forward.

The white-hooded rifleman toppled out of the tree, dead before he hit the floor, with two flint-headed arrows protruding from his chest.

Alfie Swapper rolled to his feet, clutching his bleeding arm.

The Pook stepped into the clearing, notching another arrow and aiming for *Mr Red*, but before he could take the shot the spearman had vanished into the woodland.

It was then that they heard an unworldly scream.

‘AAAAAAAAAAAAAAAAAAAAAAAAAAAAAAAAAAARRRRRRRRR RRRRRRRGGGGGGGGGGGGGGHHHHHHHHHHHH!!!!!!!!!!!!’

‘That zoundz like Tom,’ muttered the Pook. ‘You all right, zon?’ he asked, patting Alfie’s cheek tenderly.

‘I’m all right, Dad. No need to fuzz. Come on, let’z zee what’z ailing young Tomaz.’

The Hound threw two straight lefts – one like lightning, the other slowed ever so slightly – quickly followed by a feinted right-hook to the head. The were-tigress, bloodied around the nose and with a wobbly canine tooth and a slightly dazed ‘*whatever have I got myself into*’ look about the eyes, lifted her left hand high to ward against the blow. In that instant, The Hound shot forward like a locomotive, passing with his right foot and sinking a piston-like left-hand uppercut into the mid-riff of the were-cat.

She sank in slow motion to her knees, gasping for a breath that wouldn’t come.

Ooh, thought Tom to himself, as he watched in admiration like a stuffed carp, *that’s the Fitzsimmons Shift*.

‘Now, Madam, let that be an end to it!’ gruffed The Hound, tetchily.

Tom looked at the were-tigress, awed by her beauty … and then somewhat perplexed by the red dot that had suddenly appeared and was wibbling over her heart. The Hound seemed to notice it too, for he paused and turned his head around.

The were-cat was spun off her knees and landed on her back with a thudding thump before the sound of the rifle shot was even heard, a hole the size of a fifty pence piece in her chest.

The Hound snapped back to look at her, his face (quite possibly) appalled.

Then Tom noted, with ever-mounting horror, that there was now a red dot dancing on the back of the were-hound’s head.

‘NO!’ he cried out, just as a volley of gunshots filled the air like deep barks bouncing through the trees.

The red light was snatched hastily away from The Hound’s head, and Uncle Cornelius was rushing into the clearing (the remains of a piccalilli sandwich smeared across his bristling whiskers), revolver blazing away at the woods behind them.

Ten minutes later found Alfie (arm bandaged and in a makeshift sling), The Pook, Ned Leppelin, Tom, Uncle Cornelius and The Hound gathered around the fallen body of the were-tiger. The were-wolfhound, with his midriff heavily bandaged (but already showing remarkable signs of healing), was kneeling beside his fellow were-beast, tenderly and sombrely stroking her strange, bluish fur.

Ned had arrived moments after the shooting, with the tale of how he had been relentlessly pursued through the woods by the white-hooded, white-masked dog-eared hunter.

'Weren't 'uman, that'z a fact. Not conzidering the way 'e ran an' moved. When I turned to face the razcal, 'e juzt vanizhed like that,' he scowled, clicking his fingers. 'Queer businezz all round, no miztake 'bout it.'

Tom could sense that The Hound was obviously furious with himself, as if he took the death of the were-tiger as his own personal failure.

'Did your best, 'Aitch,' said Cornelius, softly. 'Ain't nothin' more you could 'ave done. Weren't you 'oo chose to 'unt 'er – poor thing.'

That the "poor thing" had been trying her damnedest to rip the life out of The Hound only a few moments beforehand seemed to have been forgotten, Tom noted. All that was left among them was a feeling of failure, and the knowledge that they'd let her down. Not only had they failed to keep her alive, they had also let her tormentors get away; for when Ned and The Pook had returned to find the body of the fallen rifleman – that the Elf King had undoubtedly killed – nothing was to be found, except for the trail where he had been carried back to the, now long gone, cars in Wild Park.

They watched over the were-tigress with a silent, solemn respect as she gently morphed into the form of a young and slender woman of Southeast Asian origins. Tom could only look on with a horror and a pitying wretchedness; mesmerized by her sad and beautiful, but now lifeless, eyes.

Just then Ollie turned up.

He sent a fleetingly intrigued and world-weary look in the direction of the prostrate body of the dead woman, and then he managed to cheer them all up.

'Fred'z captured one of 'em baztardz,' he announced gruffly.

TWENTY
The Prisoner

In the brightly lit room of One Punch Cottage that was especially reserved for such unfortunate affairs, Missus Dobbs gently pulled up the pristine white sheet and covered the face of the delicate human form that had once been a were-tigress.

'Not much to be said, I'm afraid, Ducks,' she gurned sadly, pulling off a pair of yellow washing-up gloves. 'Cause of death – a silver bullet through the heart. Would have been instant at least; about the best that you can say about it, I suppose. Alfie was lucky that he only got clipped; would have lost his arm otherwise.'

Inspector Jones shook his head ruefully and looked around the room with a haunted expression.

'Well, wherever she is, her spirit isn't here,' he grimaced. 'At least I don't think it is,' he added hastily. 'And if it is, then she doesn't want to talk to us.'

'Is there anything more that you can tell me about her, Missus Dobbs?' asked The Hound.

'Not a lot. Hard to be exact, but I'd say she's only a slip of a thing, not even a hundred years old. No distinguishing features – tattoos, birthmarks or the like.' She shook her head and tutted. 'Nothing out of the ordinary – not that I can see at any roads, Ducky.'

'Apart from this,' frowned Sergeant Hettie Clem, looking slightly paler than normal (if such a thing was possible) and holding up a penny-sized silicon device between a pair of hair tweezers.

'What is it, Hettie?' asked the Inspector, peering closer and wrinkling his nose in a mournful fashion.

'We removed it from the back of her neck. Surgical implant – just below the base of her skull. Not sure exactly what it is, but it appears to be some sort of tagging device. And it looks like it's capable of giving off a very powerful and very unpleasant electric shock. High-tech stuff. Never seen anything quite like it before. American military, perhaps? Could be Russian. Possibly Chinese. Not really my field. But one thing's for certain – it's cutting edge technology.'

'I'll bet my teeth that it's connected to the devices that were creating the "laser barrier" around Hollingbury Park; somehow penning the poor creature within the boundaries of their despicable hunting arena,' rumbled The Hound, sniffing the tiny device intently with his great black hooter, and in danger of snorting it up a nostril.

'I'll send it off to the lab for a report, but my guess is that the *lab rats* will be as baffled as we are,' said Hettie, with a shrug. 'Looks way beyond their level of expertise. Maybe we should send it off to boys at MI Unseen?'

The Hound curled his lip.

Inspector Jones nodded thoughtfully.

'Not sure what we can do as to identifying the body, Mr Hound,' he said. 'I can make some enquiries among the local Southeast Asian communities, see if any young women have been reported as being missing recently,' he offered. 'Not that I fancy our chances much, but there's a lot of new groups of immigrants coming into the country these days, and who knows what kind of magic they're bringing in with them.'

'Yeah, bloody Zaxonz,' hissed The Pook, bitterly. 'An' you better not get me ztarted on the bloomin' zo called *Celtz*!' he added, with a soft sneer.

'Well, it certainly does need to be looked into, Inspector,' sighed The Hound, distractedly. 'But if I were you, I'd start by checking to see if there's a community in the UK with connections to the Fujian Province of Southern China.'

'OK ... How's that then?' asked the Inspector, trying to mask his bafflement, and worried that he might have missed some obvious clue that a good detective should have picked up on.

'While in were-beast form, the poor lady's pelt had an unusual blue tint to it. A very rare anomaly, and one that is, or should I say (sadly*) was*, most commonly reported in the South China Tiger [*Panthera tigris amoyensis*] of the Fujian Province; a subspecies of tiger that is unfortunately believed to be all but extinct in the wild. However, the last reported sighting of a *Blue* or so-called "Maltese Tiger" was recorded way back in (or around) 1910, if memory serves me correctly.'

'Do they have tigers in Malta?' asked the Inspector, wide-eyed and hastily rethinking his holiday plans.

'Rest assured, Inspector, the word "Maltese" is used only in reference to the creature's colour and not its place of origin: the term being assigned originally to any domestic cat whose fur could be called "blue" in hue,' The Hound explained. 'However, no sighting of the *Blue Tiger* (or *Blue Devil,* as it is known by the local tribesman) has ever been decisively authenticated, in the West at least, and the truth of its existence remains shrouded in mystery.

'But my point is this: as were-cats are usually "turned" by sorcery, it would therefore seem reasonable to assume that there might be a connection with the region so famed for such a fabled cat – one with such a distinctive feature as shared by our ill-fated friend.'

'Well, I'll do my best to see if I can get in touch with the Fujian Police Department, but it might take some doing,' puffed the Inspector, doubtfully.

'It is a long shot indeed, Inspector,' agreed The Hound, 'but we must pursue every avenue available to us. In my experience, all were-creatures can be said to fall into one of two distinct camps. Firstly, there are those who shun all human contact, tending to live in the remotest of wildernesses; and secondly, there are those (like myself) who live in and among the society of men and therefore, by necessity, need outside help to exist from day to day and thus escape the unfortunate, but perhaps understandable, persecution that our existence arouses. If she is of the former, then we will undoubtedly find ourselves staring down a dead end. If the later, then it is quite possible that someone, or something, is missing her and quite probably searching for her. One can only speculate, with dread, as to how long she was held captive by her tormentors.'

The Hound looked over once more to the lifeless, slight form lying beneath the white sheet and let out a gentle huff.

'Would you be so kind as to see to the necessary arrangements for this poor unfortunate soul,' he asked Sergeant Clem. And then he was silent for a moment, lost in his own unfathomable thoughts.

'What happened last night, Mordecai, with Spring-Heeled Jack?' he asked softly, staring out of the room's solitary window.

'We managed to catch a fleeting glimpse of the scallywag, skipping along the platform at Aldrington Halt, but, after I'd spoken to you, Mr Hound, there was neither sight nor sound of the rascal,' sniffed the Inspector.

The Hound shrugged, turned and slowly walked towards the door.

'A mystery indeed, Inspector,' he said.

'Well, Alberich, Mordecai, my old friends,' he continued, as he paused to hold the door open for them, 'I think that it is high time that we had a little chat with our newfound *acquaintance*, don't you?'

''Ere's a cup of tea for you,' said Uncle Cornelius, sliding open a small hatch in the door of the Wild West-style gaol (situated in the corner of the Muse-asium) and pushing a small cup of tea through it.

He turned his back on the inmate and gave Tom a quick wink that said – "*that'll teach the rotten so-and so*" (or words to that effect).

Inside the gaol sat *Mr Blue* (as they had christened the prisoner), bereft of his blue-faced balaclava, slightly bruised around the eyes and lips, and doing his very best to look unflappable.

He must have been in his mid-thirties, Tom thought, and looked very fit and very well manicured, despite the events of the last few hours.

'How quaintly *English*,' he sneered (in what Tom guessed to be a posh and well-educated American accent), scowling at the back of Uncle Cornelius' head and then briefly sending withering looks to both The Pook and Inspector Jones. (He chose, it seemed, to ignore Tom's presence – which was absolutely fine by Tom.)

Mr Blue lifted the teacup and sniffed it cautiously, turned a little pale, and then dashed the cup violently to the floor, sending shards of bone china and sploshes of tea in all directions.

'Just what kind of hideous people are you?' he gasped, in genuine disgust.

Uncle Cornelius removed his jacket and slowly and carefully rolled up the sleeves of his white cotton shirt, before turning around to face *Mr Blue* once again.

'So, son, you still determined that you don't want to tell us nothing?' he asked, reasonably.

Mr Blue considered Cornelius very seriously – looking like he didn't know quite how worried he should be – and then (much to his credit, thought Tom) managed a tough-sounding, nonchalant laugh.

‘And what are *you* going to do about it, *old man*,’ he scoffed, arrogantly, ‘beat it out of me?’

Uncle Cornelius held the prisoner’s gaze firmly for a moment or two, as if considering the possibility.

‘Not my style, son,’ he said, softly.

‘I ain’t telling you a goddamned thing!’ growled *Mr Blue*, contemptuously (although Tom noted that he did look more than a little relieved). ‘Nothing, do you hear me. Nu-thing!’

Cornelius smiled, humourlessly.

‘I want to speak to my lawyer!’ demanded the American.

‘An’ just where do you think you are, son?’ asked Cornelius, with genuine interest. ‘Does this look like the ’olding block of the local village constabulary to you?’

Mr Blue looked through the bars of his cage and hastily scanned the room, taking in the polished weapons gleaming menacingly on the walls; the bizarre suit of armour; the ancient, grief-stricken, punchbags; the well-worn, blood-splattered boxing ring. He swallowed hard before locking onto Inspector Jones.

‘You!’ he barked, in a voice that was obviously used to being obeyed. ‘You’re a police officer, aren’t you? Surely you’re not going to stand by and watch while this sadistic old lunatic tortures me? We’re in a civilized – if commercially backward – country, Goddamn it!’

Inspector Mordecai Jones smiled a desolate smile and shrugged his shoulders unhelpfully.

‘I’m an American citizen! I demand to see my Ambassador!’ snapped *Mr Blue*, hysterically, seizing the bars frantically with both hands and pressing his face into the gap. ‘NOW!’

Uncle Cornelius slowly opened the seal on a new packet of Bourbon biscuits (the crown prince of the biscuit world), took a couple and passed the packet on to The Pook (who procured a couple for his immediate consumption and then quickly secreted a few more into the top pocket of his suit jacket), never once removing his eyes from the seething *Mr Blue*. The old man pulled up a wooden chair and set it down in front of the cage directly opposite the prisoner. Taking his time, he slowly sat down, arms folded across his chest: thus making the scene look a little like some macabre theatre performance – with The Pook, the Inspector, Tom, and he, all sitting and facing the captive like a row of homicidally unimpressed critics from *The Guardian* at the Edinburgh Fringe Festival.

‘I do ’ear,’ sniffed Uncle Cornelius, very softly and very deliberately, whilst looking briefly at the thick curtain that covered the dividing wall of the adjacent cell, ‘that you like to fight monsters.’

Mr Blue raised an eyebrow and followed the old man’s gaze, but stayed silent.

‘You must be a big man, son. An ’ard man. A brave man. Certainly got some bottom, I’ll give you that.’

Mr Blue was watching Cornelius intently, slightly confused, eyeing the dangerous-looking old codger suspiciously, and growing ever more worried.

'Let's find out shall we?' smiled Tom's uncle, suddenly clicking his fingers.

On the given signal, Tom pulled on the chord that he was holding (thus drawing open the curtain that divided the two cells) to reveal ... The Hound sitting cross-legged, with his back pressed against the far wall of the gaol, and gnawing on a large thigh-bone (taken from the fallow deer procured during their recent excursion to Petworth Park – a fact, however, that *Mr Blue* wasn't to know).

Mr Blue's face turned to the colour and consistency of a hard-boiled egg, and his eyes looked as if they were in danger of flying out of their sockets like burning crumpets popping from an over-sprung toaster.

The Hound might have smiled briefly (it was hard to tell) before he leapt with truly terrifying speed towards the trembling *Mr Blue*, slamming his full weight, with full force, into the dividing bars of the cell (making the whole basement shudder horribly) and snarling, salivating and snapping his horrendous jaws like a pack of Hellhounds trying to catch a wasp.

Everyone in the room – bar Cornelius, who casually snapped a Bourbon biscuit in half – leapt about three feet into the air.

Mr Blue, to use a polite medical term, "*came away from himself*".

And then he spent the next hour *singing like a canary*

TWENTY ONE
The Society Of The Wild Hunt

His name was Charles Heaton Dunkerton, aged thirty-three, from Manhattan Island, New York. A Wall Street banker, working for a very successful and very well-regarded partnership – with too much money to spend, too much time on his hands and, it would seem, an appalling lack of ethics and principles.

A self-confessed adrenaline junkie, Dunkerton had developed a passion for extreme sports – extremely risky and extremely expensive ones, that is. Which, until recently, had apexed with an unhealthy obsession for the hunting of large, dangerous (and endangered) predators; grizzly bears in Canada, polar bears in the Arctic, white wolves in Russia, lions in Kenya and jaguars in the Amazon, being his proud and despicable list of trophies to date.

About three months ago he had been approached by a mysterious individual representing the interests of a certain *influential* set of "sportsmen", and discreetly asked if he would, in exchange for a quite ridiculous sum of money, be interested in taking part in the most dangerous type of hunt possibly known to man – the hunting of *supernatural* monsters.

It had sounded more than a little preposterous, like something out of a horror movie – "Bankers vs Predators" – and he had, of course, been highly sceptical, almost dismissing the matter out of hand immediately. However, the nature and the manner of the offer, along with the bearing and *unusual* demeanour of the messenger, had intrigued him, and so, almost to his own surprise, he found himself insisting on a meeting.

The mystifying group – who kept their individual identities concealed from him at all times – was known as *The Society of the Wild Hun*t. He was, unsurprisingly, cynical at first, but, after accepting an invitation to observe a *Society hunt*, he swiftly lost any doubts that he might have had regarding their authenticity and became near obsessed by *The Society of the Wild Hunt's* power, influence and, above all, vocation.

He had been flown by helicopter – blindfolded, of course – to a remote country house situated somewhere in the forests along the Atlantic Seaboard. (He would take a wild guess at New England, but couldn't be sure and had no possible way of retracing his steps if he ever felt the desire to find it again). Whoever *The Society* were, they were very secretive, very professional and very thorough.

There he had met with *The Society's official* membership – thirteen in total: twelve men and one woman. Also present were two other potential clients. Everyone, including himself and the other prospective *customers* (*Huntsmen*), wore masks at all times. *The Wild Hunt's* leader (known only as *The King of the Wild Hunt*) and the woman (known only as *The Queen of the Hunt*) both wore Venetian carnival masks in the *grotesque* style, whilst the remaining members (known respectively as the '*Lurchers*' and the '*Tumblers*') wore masks resembling the heads of hunting dogs – with milk-white faces, bar one red ear and one red eye: the *Lurchers'* masks bore a red left ear and red right eye, thus distinguishing them from the *Tumblers*, whose masks bore a red right ear and a red left eye. However, the distinction was hardly necessary; for the *Tumblers* were of an extremely *unnerving* disposition, and whenever he was in their company Dunkerton always felt extremely ... *uncomfortable*.

He had been escorted, along with the other prospective clients, by the *King* and *Queen of the Hunt* to observe four *Huntsmen* (wearing coloured masks – red, blue, green and yellow, respectively), accompanied by the remaining members of *The Society* (who acted as 'beaters' and offered protection to the *Huntsmen* should the adventure turn sour), as they pursued their unnatural and hideous quarry, by the light of the full moon, through an enclosed arena set deep in the wild, untamed forests surrounding the house.

Their prey was strange and terrifying indeed. A razor-thin, human-like monster standing almost seven feet tall, with impossibly long and awkward limbs, a bald head, pointed ears, teeth and face like a carnivorous rat, and talons like a bear. A creature of the undead. An odious thing – that Dunkerton had previously considered to exist only in myth, legend and movie. A vampire! (To be precise an ancient, rare and grotesque type of vampire of the order known, among people who knew about such matters, as – *Nosferatu*.)

The hunt had been thrilling and deadly: one *Huntsman* and two *Lurchers* killed, and another *Huntsman* terribly wounded. The 'winning' *client* had struck the evil head from the repulsive creature's neck (with a silver-bladed executioner's sword, especially crafted for the delightful occasion) as the gruesome horror writhed, screamed and pleaded with its captors (two *Tumblers*, almost as terrifying in aspect as the *Nosferatu* itself, who held the monster steadfastly in place).

It was the most singly petrifying and exhilarating experience that Dunkerton had ever witnessed in the whole of his life. The world suddenly became a greater, less boring and more magnificent place than he had ever imagined it to be. It was as if someone had let him in on the most explosive secret in the universe – *monsters did exist*! And, with the right connections, and for the right amount of money, a man could track them, hunt them, and kill them.

Dunkerton had willingly arranged to hand over the down payment (in cash, naturally) to be able to participate in the next hunt ('More money than any of you sons-of-bitches will ever see in your miserable lifetimes!') and fervently awaited news.

A week ago he had been contacted by *The Society of the Wild Hunt*, informed of the nature and identity of *The Hunt's* next quarry, and asked if this was – (a) acceptable, and (b) if he still wished to participate.

Six days ago he had eagerly made the final payment (again in cash).

One day later he was flown, by private jet, to a small island somewhere off mainland Europe. Once they had landed, he had joined the rest of the party – rendezvousing on a large, unmarked yacht. From there they had sailed to

England (he had known it was England because of the white cliffs, but as to his exact location he was completely ignorant).

All members of the party wore masks whenever in company, and nobody's identity was ever disclosed or discussed. All mobile phones, laptops and any other such means of communication having been confiscated long beforehand – before the flight to Europe had even taken off. And he, along with the other three *clients*, had spent the whole time, from their arrival to the time of the hunt, below decks.

The night before last, *The King of the Wild Hunt* had divided them into two groups – one *Tumbler*, two *Lurchers* and two *Huntsmen* per team (Dunkerton's party being completed by 'Mr Green'). Then they had then been driven (blindfolded) to the site of the hunt – or the 'killing ground', as his "hosts" preferred to refer to it.

The hunt had ended swiftly and in disaster.

Within ten minutes the '*Mr Yellow* and *Mr Red* team' had been ambushed by the were-tiger – *Mr Yellow* receiving sickening injuries. There had been a brief fight with the monster before the creature had escaped. *Mr Red* had lost his nerve and demanded that they see to the health of *Mr Yellow*. They all agreed to postpone the hunt for the time being, but to complete it the following night.

They had carried *Mr Yellow* back to the cars, but he (though *he* turned out to be a *she*) was dead by the time that they got there.

The rest of the story, Dunkerton conceded, they probably knew better than he did.

TWENTY TWO
An Extraordinary Elizabethan Enigma

After Charles Heaton Dunkerton had been (gratefully) escorted from One Punch Cottage by Inspector Jones (via the secret tunnel that led from the cupboard under the stairs down to the seafront – where Constable Tuggnutter awaited them in the D.S.C.'s sleek, grey Alfa Romeo), The Hound suggested that they all retire to the kitchen for a spot of lunch before continuing with any further discussion regarding the night's dreadful and appalling incidents.

Seated at the kitchen table, Tom found that he had little appetite and surreptitiously smuggled piping-hot chunks of stewed meat to (his newfound best friend) Bess. The others, however, heartily tucked into the thick, rich-brown venison stew served up by Missus Dobbs.

'So what's to be done now, do you think, 'Aitch?' asked Uncle Cornelius, mopping the gravy from his third helping of stew with a thick hunk of bread. 'Bad business all round. It's a new one on me. What a world we live in. To think that there are people 'oo'd actually pay money to 'unt down so-called "*monsters*" for sport. Well, the very nature of it, the calculated cruelty, comes as a bit of a shock, an' that's a fact – though I do suppose that I should know to expect no better by now. Makes me wonder just 'oo the *monsters* really are?

'Reckon we can track down the rotten so-an'-sos before they split the country, 'Aitch?' he continued. 'Assuming that they 'aven't already, that is.'

'Got more money than zenze,' sneered The Pook, smuggling a chunk of bread into the inside pocket of his jacket. 'Could be all the way back 'ome to the Americaz by now.'

The Hound, who had been remarkably sombre and quiet throughout the meal – despite having (pardon the expression) wolfed down seven bowlfuls of stew – licked his plate clean with his enormous and dexterous tongue, before leaning back into his chair and stroking his whiskers thoughtfully.

'This is a most troubling and intriguing situation,' he sighed. 'And I'm all too sorry to say that it brings to mind a very serious and sinister episode that took place (not far from here, in fact) many, many years ago. A ghastly affair indeed. One that I had all but forgotten about.' He shook his great head ruefully and sucked his terrifying gnashers. 'But the similarities are too striking, too peculiar, to ignore. Though, for the life of me, I dread to think of the connection.'

They withdrew to The Study, where the Hound busied himself searching intently through the bottom drawer of the most ancient-looking of the filing cabinets, randomly tossing out battered old files, rolled-up parchments and tattered scraps of yellowing paper. At last he cautiously pulled out a wooden box (the beautiful walnut wood aged to a shiny blackness) and, carrying it carefully (one might almost be tempted to say "tenderly") to the writing desk, gently laid it down. With a barely audible sigh, he teased open the chunky metal catch that held the lid firmly in place. Lovingly, he wiped the lid free of dust with the back of his monstrous and hairy hand, before slowly lifting it open.

Tom tried to sit up as tall as he could to get a glimpse of the box's contents. His curiosity was fired further still as The Hound removed, in turn – a huge dog-collar (the cracked brown leather decorated with hefty and blackened metal studs); a tattered (and much chewed) leather ball; a lock of grey hair, clumsily tied with a faded blue ribbon; a leather-bound notebook, almost perished with age and over-use, with the name "*Percival*" written unevenly on the cover in a clumsy, childlike scrawl.

Tom couldn't be sure but he suspected that The Hound might be blinking away a tear as he set each *treasure* gently to one side.

Finally, the were-hound pulled out a thick packet of papers, neatly wrapped in a plain and simple piece of cloth. The Hound teased the package open, unwrapping the protective covering and leafing through the yellowing folios until he found what he was looking for. Drawing the required pages aside, he quickly scanned through them, and then, once satisfied that he had found what he was after, sat in his great armchair, resting the selected leaves on his lap.

He took the briefest of moments to compose himself.

'The events described in these archives took place in Sussex during the winter of 1587,' he began. 'I would have been two at the time, in human years at least. And, having been *transformed* by the bite of the were-wolf, Will Shirley, only a matter of a few months previously, was thus at the very beginning of my *secondary* education.

'The papers that I hold in my hand are a record of a most peculiar and potentially catastrophic incident; one that almost brought England into a disastrous war with both the *Kingdom of Spain* and the *Holy Roman Empire* – in short, the full wrath of the combined Hapsburg monarchies would have swallowed England in the flash of an harquebus pan. The episode, however, was never brought to public attention, due to the highly sensitive and irregular nature of the whole diabolical affair.

'I have here a recorded account of the extraordinary matter, as noted by my dear friend – the great Dr John Dee.

'The *Doctor* had been recruited by Sir Francis Walsingham – good Queen Elizabeth's *spy-master general* – to be part of a secret and exceptional team that was charged with *sorting out* this very unusual and problematic wicket, and I, due in part to my ... shall we say ... *unique* potential in the field-of-play, was brought into the squad as a bit part player (a secret weapon among the secret agents, if you will).

'They, we, were unofficially known as "*The Gentlemen Good Friends*", and our number consisted of the afore mentioned Dr Dee, the infamous spies *Lettice Montegue* and *Christopher 'Kit' Marley* (or Marlowe, as history has chosen to remember him), and the so-called "*Italian*" masters of fence – my good friend *Vincentio Saviolo* and his companion and teaching assistant, *Jeronimo*.

'It was, I suppose, my very first case (if you exclude the Will Shirley episode, of course).

'The bare facts of the incident were this: a young Hapsburg princeling, Don Juan of Frinburgh, whilst on a secretive, and somewhat *delicate,* visit to England, had been "accidentally" shanghaied by what was believed to be an underground group of recusant nobles. (I say "accidentally", for it was Dee's firm belief that the Prince's kidnappers had no idea of the importance of his personage, or they would have left well alone – for it was his celebrity that would eventually bring about their downfall. However, that is of no relevance to our current situation.) Their sole reason for his capture was in order to use him as a participant – for their cruel and iniquitous amusement – in a most ungodly and wicked sport.

'The name that the group of kidnappers gave themselves was ...' growled The Hound, dramatically, '*The Society of the Wild Hunt.*'

'Bloomin' 'eck!' eeked Uncle Cornelius.

'Exactly', rumbled The Hound, arching an eyebrow and peering fiercely down his snout at his captivated audience. 'But the similarities, I am almost afraid to say, go much further than that.

'If I may be permitted to read from the dear Doctor's *unofficial* report to my dear Lord and Master – Henry Percy, the ninth Earl of Northumberland.

> *"The motive & nature of The Societie of the Wilde Hunte was one of truly harrowing & infernal concerne & I can only praye that we never see its like againe, for it doth most surely emphasize the depravitie, wickedness & frailtie of the Human condition.*
>
> *Sir Francis W. had contacted me to ask my advice regarding the delicate nature of the unfortunate incident, &, in so doing, informed me that over the previous yeare there had been numerous reports of servaunts, soldiours & mariners disappearing – mainly from around the Sussexe & Kente area. The curious nature of their abductions having thus recently been drawne to his attention (& what matters of curiositie <u>ever</u> escaped the attention of Sir Francis?) through the miraculous adventures of one such abductee – Captaine Hans Meyer, the last surviving member of the unfortunate young Prince Juan's personal bodyguard.*
>
> *It had become most regrettably apparent that a group of debased & depraved English Noble-men were amusing themselves by forcing skilled men-at-arms to fight to the death in gladiatorial contests. The poor unfortunate survivor of these abhorrent tournaments (the 'unlucky winner' – if you will) was then hunted like a beaste beneath the light of the full moone, & then*

murderously slaughtered (his beating heart cut out & eaten!) by the devilish participants of the Hunte.

Sir Francis was of the confirmed opinion that the grizlie spectacle was nothing more than Sporte – Sporte aimed at satisfieing the unnatural & degenerate inclinations of the English aristocracy. (However, it woulde bee wise to remember that Sir Francis was never one who cherished the Great & Noble Families of our most enlightened & Majestic Kingdom, especially if hee thought that they had Catholic sympathies – & to bee honest, Sir Francis suspected everybody of having Catholic sympathies [common sense protect us all!]; having once described them (our noble aristocracy) as (& I quote) –

"As depraved a bunch of criminals who ever craved power!"

(I feel it necessary to add that these are not, & have never been, views shared by myself! I have always thought myself most fortunate & blessed to have been born in a realm that boasts such enlightened princes of power, & of such an inquisitive & naturally generous spirit – & thus do gratefullie receive all patronage & financial rewarde for my ever-more ~~expensive &~~ consuming pursuit of knowledge, enlightenment & illumination.)

But such was Sir Francis' opinion – & again I am forced to quote my erstwhile commander, My Lorde, but must stress that his views in no way represent my own patriotic feelings of love, thankfulnesse & dutie towards my beloved Patrons, past, present & (God willing) future. However, I have no wishe to tainte the vaulted reputation of the ~~swine~~ sadly missed Sir Francis – bearing no malice towards him whatsoever (despite the deceitful, underhand & downright sneakie manner in which he sullied & besmirched my good name & reputation at The Courte, & so cast me from the glorious light of my most beloved Queene). But I digress. To return to my purpose & to ~~quote the oaf~~ recount faithfullie the words of Sir Francis Walsingham –

Sir F.W. - "I can well assure you that most of them [the English Aristocracy] would leap at the chance of watching grown men fight to the death for their [the English Aristocracy's] own amusement, & pay a Queene's ransom to participate in a genuine 'man-hunt'. Rascals, the damn lot of them [the English Aristocracy]! Scoundrels [the English Aristocracy]!"

I, however, formed a different theory than Sir Francis (& hopefully one more educated & enlightened) – I suspected WITCHE-CRAFTE.

It is my beliefe that The Societie of the Wilde Hunte was enacting some kind of ghastlie pagan ritual & engaging in a diabolical form of symbolic sacrifice.

It was, My Lorde, all most fascinating:

Foure Gladiators – who fought Three Contests – resulting in One 'Winner' – who, in turn, became 'The Thirteenth Man' (the 'Champion'), who, having proven through feat of arms that he is worthy, is then offered, by way of a ceremonial hunt, to the Old Gods (i.e. The Devil!).

The number of the Wilde Hunte was Thirteene – the same number (as My Lorde, I am sure, is in no need of reminding) as a Witches' Coven – & consisted of members known as:

The King of the Wilde Hunte
The Queene of the Wilde Hunte
The Huntesmen [x4]
The Servants of the Hunte [x6]
The Thirteenthe Man
[=13]

According to Captaine Meyer's report, all of the participants of The Hunte (barring the poor unfortunate Thirteenthe Man) wore masks at all times – partially, I believe, to conceal their identity & partially for ritual & symbolic purpose.

The Huntesmen wore masks of differing coloures (Blue, Greene, Yellowe & Red) & were the 'paying guests' of the Society (thereby funding their devilish pursuits) & were made up of members of our Noble families with more monie than sense.

The Servants of the Hunte wore masks of a most intriguing designe: white-faced dogge masks – with one red ear & a line of red drawne demonically over one eye. This, to my mind at least, would seem to represent Yeth Hounds (also known locally as 'Wish Hounds'); in the mythology of the common people these being the hunting dogges of the Faery Folk (& are invariably described as milk-white hounds with blood-red ears, who never faile to catch their hapless quarrie).

The 'moone-mask' worn by The Queene of the Wilde Hunte might then represent the Moone Goddesse, or perhaps her priestess. (All of the ghastlie hunts, if you will recall, My Lorde, were conducted by the light of the full-moone, & therefore could well have been held in Her honour).

The mask worn by The King of the Wilde Hunte would seem to be a stylised representation of a Stag, & so, to my mind at leaste, certainly suggests an allusion, at the very leaste, to either Herne the Hunter, Cernunnos (the ancient British 'god of the dead' &, most interestingly, the 'king of the hunt') or perhaps – SATAN Himself!"

'That's a new one on me, 'Aitch,' frowned Uncle Cornelius, when The Hound had finished reading. 'Never 'eard you mention anything 'bout that one before.'

'It was so very long ago that I'd all but forgotten about it, Dandy', confessed The Hound. 'I was very young at the time, and very awkward in my new form. In truth, it's all a bit of a blur.'

'What happened?' asked Tom. 'How were they stopped? And whatever became of *that Society of the Wild Hunt*?'

'Well,' continued The Hound, 'on that fateful night, all members of the *G.G.F.* (*The Gentleman Good Friends*), bar Dr Dee and myself, had infiltrated the diabolical fiends' latest meeting, managed to scupper the festivities, and were in the process of rescuing poor Prince Juan. My only involvement was at the very end of the affair when I spotted *Marley* – dressed, for some reason, in drag (all a bit odd, but he was like that, you know) – being relentlessly pursued through the woodlands between the ancient villages of Kingston and Falmer by *The King of the Wild Hunt*, who in turn was being tracked by young Jeronimo.

'I followed them, unseen by all (you must understand that, at that time, I was painfully self-conscious about my appearance and the effect that I seemed to have on people), and caught up with them just in time to discover Jeronimo lying sprawled on the floor (obviously concussed, and with bent and broken weapons lying willy-nilly about him) and *The King of the Wild Hunt* standing over the prostrate Marley – with an ancient war sword raised to the moonlit sky – and undoubtedly about to do him *no good*.'

'Then what?' gasped Tom, enthralled.

'Well, as you can well imagine, I dashed from the trees, appalled by what I was seeing. I'm pretty sure that I might have tried to say "*Steady on, old chap, surely we can talk this through*", or something equally brilliant – though I'm afraid that it would, at that early point in my education and development, you understand, have sounded like nothing more than a confusing series of rasping snarls and growls.

'*The King of the Wild Hunt* turned to see me approaching, staggered away in shocked terror and tripped backwards, falling down a ravine. Marley passed out (quite naturally, I suppose) and Jeronimo came-to, just in time to see my approach, and then proceeded to bury his head in his hands and start sucking his thumb – clasping one ear and gently rocking himself back and forth. I followed the direction of *The King of the Wild Hunt's* descent, but I could detect not the faintest sign of him. He simply seemed to have vanished into thin air.'

'Zeemz to be an awful lot of that going on recently,' sniffed The Pook, thoughtfully. '*Vanizhing into thin air*, that iz.'

'Indeed,' agreed The Hound, through a steeple of rippling claws.

'So what became of the members of this *Society of evil so-an'-so's*? An' 'oo were they?' asked Uncle Cornelius.

'Well, by the time that Walsingham and some of his lads had arrived, along with the local militia, the whole shebang was done and dusted. As I recall, four Peers of the Realm were arrested. However, they were never full-members of *The Society* – rather, as Dee reported, they were a paying clientèle, and their only chargeable crime was their despicable tastes and contemptible behaviour.'

The Hound scanned through the pages on his lap.

'Let me see ... three *Servants of The Hunt* killed ... two captured – a man by the name of Frizer and another by the name of Cheese. The so-called *Queen of the Wild Hunt* was arrested and was revealed to be one Lady Jane Buckleberry. The rest of the rascals regrettably escaped ... It would appear that Lady Buckleberry was detained in the Tower of London but somehow managed to escape on the morning of her intended execution.'

'An' their Leader? Thiz zo called *King*, what of 'im?' scowled The Pook.

'Not a trace. His identity, if it was ever indeed known to them, was never revealed by his followers. I do recall, however, that a few years later Vincent told me that Jeronimo, who was no mean swordsman (possibly a bit hasty in his use of a *counter time* action for my liking, and with an eye a little too keen for the ladies – which is what eventually got him killed of course, but that is neither here nor there), had said that whoever this *King of the Wild Hunt* was, he fought like Lucifer himself – managing to punch a hole through Jeronimo's metal shield with a blow from a steel-gauntleted fist.'

'Well that indicates a man of extraordinary strength, I'd say,' pondered Cornelius. 'Might even suggest that 'e weren't even 'uman?'

'It becomes a very distinct possibility,' concurred The Hound.

'But the masks, the names, they're ... they're the same? The same as this ... this new *Society*,' gulped Tom, trying to piece it all together.

'Indeed they are, Tom. Indeed they are,' replied The Hound, nodding and giving Tom an intent stare. 'Therefore, the question becomes this: is this a new incarnation of the original *Society of the Wild Hunt*, or the very same one? If the latter, then it has survived (underground and hidden) for nigh on four-and-a-half centuries.'

'An' iz thiz zo called *King of the Wild 'Unt* one an' the zame man (or zupernatural entity)? Or could it zimply be the name adopted by the *Zociety'z* leader, like zome kind of 'ereditary title?' mused The Pook.

'But, supposing that this 'orrendous an' 'orrible society *'as* survived for over four 'undred years ... why 'aven't any of us ever 'eard of it?' asked Uncle Cornelius.

'Alzo, if this King of theirz is a zupernatural being, as zeems more than likely, what about them otherz what chazed Ned an' young Tom tonight? Zoundz like they might be of the zame ilk, don't you think?' frowned The Pook. ''Ere, Tom, when you waz being chazed, did you manage to notice if your purzuer 'ad a red ear on the left or right zide of 'iz 'ead?'

Tom looked at the Elf King for a frozen moment.

'Oh, I'm sorry,' he finally managed to reply, 'I was so surprised at seeing him rise from the dead, pull an arrow through his own throat and then chase me through the woods like a demented axe-murderer with haemorrhoids, that I quite forgot to check which way round his frickin' ears were coloured!'

'Language, Tom!' hissed Cornelius.

The Pook chuckled and shook his head.

'Does sound like them *Tumblers* what our *friend* Dunkerton spoke of, though,' growled Uncle Cornelius.

'Zupernatural folk,' nodded The Pook, as way of a statement.

'They could have been some sort of super-soldier,' offered Tom, hopefully. 'Performance-enhancing drugs, bionic limbs ... that sort of thing?'

'Quite possibly so, Tom,' sighed The Hound. 'But, if we consider what we know about these two *hunters,* there is another explanation – one that is perhaps more dreadful, but, in my experience, much more likely.'

Tom looked on, all ears.

'We know from yours and Ned's observations,' continued the were-hound, 'and from those of Mr Charles Heaton Dunkerton, that these '*Tumblers*' would seem to possess superhuman strength and speed. They also displayed extraordinary senses in immediately pinpointing yours and Ned's location. One of their number receives an arrow through the neck (an injury that should have killed any *ordinary* man outright) but rises and chases after you with no visible signs of ill-effect.'

'Meanwhile, 'is devilish companion chases Ned through the trees,' reflected Uncle Cornelius. 'No mean feat, that – to keep up with a good Elf in good 'ealth, if you catch my drift; 'specially in woodland.'

'And then,' The Hound picked up, 'when Ned confronts his pursuer, he simply "vanishes" – as does yours Tom, when you reached the clearing were I was *engaged* with the were-tigress.

'Tell me, Tom, when you ran into the clearing, what exactly did you see?'

'Nothing really,' replied Tom. 'Just you and the were-tiger having an ... altercation.'

'And you are quite sure that you saw nothing else?' asked The Hound, keenly.

'Well ...' mused Tom, desperately trying to piece together his actions. 'I did see a bat flying upwards ...'

Tom felt the colour drain from his cheeks as he looked, first to The Pook (who sat grimly staring at the back of his hands, which were slowly grinding away at the head of his walking stick), then to his uncle (who stared back at him expectantly, through arched and beetling eyebrows) and finally to The Hound – who might have been trying to give him (it was hard to tell) an encouraging smile.

'You can't mean ...' gasped Tom, in horrified disbelief (despite all the horrifying events that he had recently witnessed), 'vampires!'

TWENTY THREE
The Dark Curtain

'But why would vampires want to hunt other ... *monsters*?' asked Tom, once the unpleasant feeling of perturbed queasiness had eventually subsided, and Missus Dobbs had cleaned the vomit from the carpet. 'And why would they be offering *normal* people the opportunity to do so?'

'Money, that's what,' snorted Uncle Cornelius. 'Ain't many creatures in the supernatural community 'oo are so obsessed with money as what vampires is (save, of course, for some of the Princes of 'Ell). Bunch of bloodsucking capitalists, if you ask me, always 'ave been. Probably what got 'em *turned* in the first place. Selfish gits.'

'Let's please not bring politics into this, Dandy,' sighed The Hound, wearily.

'So they'd hunt their own kind just to make money?' grimaced Tom, almost appalled. 'But what do they need money for if they're dead ... undead?'

'Well, they've got to *exist*, same as does everybody else. Ain't cheap being undead. Costs a lot of money if you want to 'ave an 'igh standard of un-life,' reflected his uncle, sourly. 'An' as to them 'unting their *own*, well, let's just say that they ain't the most moral of creatures, if you know what I mean.'

'There are near infinite varieties of vampire, Tom,' interjected The Hound. 'They would appear, in some form or another, to have been with us for as long, if not longer, than human history itself. The *Nosferatu* mentioned by Dunkerton, for example, is of a species that is but only distantly related to the more *common* form of vampire. The *Nosferatu* (*The Child, or 'Get', of Lilith)* tends to be a solitary creature, extremely long-lived and very powerful, it is true, but slow in its reproduction and therefore their numbers are thankfully dwindling. Other, more common types of vampire (*The Get of Cain* – the *Count Draculas* of this world), would bear little feelings of kindred or loyalty to them, and indeed often try to eradicate them if they come into conflict over the same piece of territory.'

'Zo you thinkz that thiz iz vampirez what iz be'ind all thiz?' asked The Pook, unsuccessfully suppressing a look of disgust.

'The facts would seem to point towards some involvement, yes,' replied the were-hound. 'However, it just doesn't seem to be in the style of *The Families*,' he added, shaking his head in puzzlement.

'*The Families*?' asked Tom, ominously. 'What do you mean "*The Families*"?'

'Well,' sniffed Uncle Cornelius, 'vampires are possibly the most organised "monsters" on the face of the planet, Tom. Most probably be'ind a lot of powerful companies, governments an' even religious organisations, if even 'alf the rumours are to be believed. 'Ave you ever noticed 'ow – in a lot of recent books, movies, television programmes an' the like – vampires are becoming portrayed as being almost benign? Sometimes even shown as creatures to be pitied, an' sometimes even depicted like some sort of super'ero. There are even people nowadays – sad desperate folk, 'oo ought to know better – 'oo 'ave a great craving to *become* vampires themselves; thinking that some'ow it's a grand, desirable an' attractive thing to be immortally undead. Stupid idiots, is what I call 'em. 'Owever, ask yourself this – could it be that it's all a conspiracy to make them (vampires, that is) an' their despicable customs more acceptable to the general public?

'I can't say with any certainty, doubt that anyone could, but it's been suggested that vampires 'ave been manipulating an' shaping 'uman 'istory for centuries, perhaps even millennia. An' now that we live in an age of immediate communication, so to speak, what better way of reaching out to people than through "feel-good films" an' the like? Anything can be made to look agreeable, even attractive, if it's presented to the right types of people in the right types of ways – ways that'll make 'em feel good about 'emselves. It's propaganda really, if you think 'bout it.'

'Long ago,' The Hound resumed, 'the oldest and most powerful vampires and their "*Gets*" (the victims that they have chosen to "*turn*" – their "blood-line" or "offspring", if you will) came together and reached an agreement, a truce; firstly with each other, and then (if the hushed whispers are to be believed) with various governments and powerful organisations They agreed not to increase their number above an allotted quota and to perform their diabolical activities behind a so-called "*Dark Curtain*" – never attracting too much attention to themselves, but slowly, over the years, ever gaining more and more power and more and more influence over world affairs.'

'Now, as we stand today,' picked up Cornelius, 'there are twelve *Families,* spread out over the world, each one with a specific an' carefully understood an' respected territory. Used to be a thirteenth *family* but that *Get* was deemed to 'ave overstretched the mark, so to speak, an' over the years was eradicated by the other *Families,* in one way or another. *Vlad Tepes* – the infamous *Count Dracula,* 'oo we spoke of before, 'e were of that *Family,* so I 'eard. Made too big a noise of 'imself back in the 1890s, if I recollect correctly, tried to snatch 'imself some notoriety an' power, an' was quickly taken out of the picture by the *dark powers that be* an' their agents. Of course, there 'ave been, an' still are, other "*rogues*" – vampires 'oo exist outside of the laws of *The Twelve Families* – but they're usually small fry an' tend to get themselves switched off (if you'll pardon the expression) pretty swiftly. Which makes me wonder just 'oo these *Tumbling* buggers might be?'

There was a knock at the door and Missus Dobbs tentatively poked a gurning face around the door.

'Sorry to interrupt, Ducks,' she croaked, bowing so low in The Pook's direction that she almost concussed herself by headbutting the carpet, 'but that nice young Sergeant Clem is here to see you. Says she's got some interesting news. Now, can I get anybody a lovely cup of tea?'

'NOT FOR ME THANKS, MISSUS DOBBS!' came the swift and heartfelt chorus of reply.

TWENTY FOUR
The Sinister Threads Of A Most Diabolical Tapestry

Sergeant Hettie Clem sat, dwarfed in The Hound's great armchair, looking like *Little Red Riding Goth* come to visit the *Big Bad Were-Wolfhound.*

Tom found himself surreptitiously trying to improve his appearance, which was, indeed, in need of surreptitious improvement – he had, in his defence, been up all night, being chased through the woods by the despicable and thoroughly unfriendly undead.

'Well, it might be nothing, but both Mordecai ... I mean Inspector Jones ... and I thought that it was worthy of note,' she said, pulling her hair back and rearranging it into an even tighter and more severe ponytail. 'The Inspector is still busy trying to sort out what's to be done with Mr *All-Money-and-No-Morality* Dunkerton, so he asked me to come straight over and see you.'

'What 'ave you get for us, 'Ettie?' asked Uncle Cornelius, cracking open a packet of Rich Tea biscuits and offering them round.

'So,' began Hettie, gracefully declining a biscuit, 'I asked a couple of the lads at the Station to check up on the old Metropolitan Police files – see if there was anything of note left out of the *official* incident reports connected to Spring-Heeled Jack. I also asked them to try and trace the two "Lucy Janes" via online ancestor sites – see if we could make any connections between them and the girls who were attacked the other night.'

'Oh that was a good idea!' squeaked Tom – sounding, to his immortal horror, like an over-eager and newly recruited Boy Scout trying to impress his world-weary "Sixer" – instantly blushing a deep shade of scarlet and feeling like a complete and utter twit.

Hettie turned and briefly held his gaze, looking at him as if she couldn't quite decide whether he was mocking her or just a total prat.

'What did you find, Hettie?' asked The Hound, saving Tom from what seemed like a slow eternity of embarrassment.

'No connections that we could find with the students ... but ...'

'Go on,' growled Uncle Cornelius, blowing a small gale of biscuit crumbs from his whiskers as he spoke.

'Well, it might be no more than a collection of coincidences, but it looks more than a little bit iffy to me,' frowned Hettie, opening the small Moleskine notebook that she pulled from her jacket pocket. 'See what you think.'

'In our line of business,' commented The Hound, 'things are rarely coincidence. Please continue, Hettie.'

'Firstly,' she began, 'Polly Adams – couldn't find anything that can definitely pinpoint her. There were a lot of *Polly Adams'* in service in London during the 1800s – bit like trying to find a *John Smith* in a blacksmiths' graveyard.'

Tom, to his absolute dismay, let out an overloud guffaw.

Hettie Clem shot him a look of mild concern and carried on regardless.

'However,' she continued, 'and this is where it begins to get interesting, a *Pollyanna Adams* did marry a sergeant of the 60th Rifles (the regiment which, if you remember, was subjected to a number of *episodes* involving Spring-Heeled Jack) by the name of Matthew Keane – and was stationed alongside him, working as a garrison cook, during the late 1870s. She seems to have separated from her husband and quit her position in 1878, shortly after the Spring-Heeled Jack sightings and attacks ("Jack-Attacks" as the boys at the Station have taken to calling them) –' [Tom chortled raucously] '– on sentries of the 60th Regiment were reported in Colchester.

'Now, according to the *Illustrated London News* of February 28th 1903, a *Mrs Polly Keane* was found dead on Clapham Common, killed after (as the reporter put it) a – "*gruesome and harrowing attack by what can only have been an extremely large and savage dog*", having had her throat (and I quote) "*quite literally torn from her delicate body*".'

Uncle Cornelius snapped a Rich Tea in half with dramatic effect. 'Interesting,' he muttered, swapping meaningful looks with The Hound, who was pacing up and down the room (loudly munching on a Rich Tea biscuit of his own).

'Gets better,' smiled Hettie. 'Connected to the Spring-Heeled Jack sightings in and around Norwich and Kings Lynn, in East Anglia (1844-1846), is the name of one Miss *Lucinda Slakes*. Also of note is that, in 1855, a *Ms L. J. Sellacks* was the victim of a "Jack-Attack" that took place in Edinburgh. Sound familiar?'

'Lucy Jane Scales,' growled The Hound, thoughtfully tapping a biscuit against the end of his snout.

'But here's where it gets even weirder: according to the Slovakian Police's *Unusual and Unsolved Crimes Department* (who obviously don't sleep, or have nothing better to do), in 1961 a *Miss Lucinda Jane Selakz* was found by her neighbours and taken to the local hospital after being the victim of what looked like an attack by a large and ferocious wild animal. The bizarre thing was, however, that she lived on the thirteenth floor of a tenement block in the heavily urbanised city of Bratislava. She died shortly afterwards from her wounds.'

'Fascinating,' rumbled The Hound, glowering intently at the biscuit in hand.

'And finally there's this:' purred Hettie, coming close to sounding excited, 'a *Miss Janet Althrope* was mentioned in association with three related sightings of the "Spring-heeled-one" along the Welsh Borders during the summer of 1848.'

'Lucy Jane Aslop!' cried Tom, brilliantly (slightly ruining the effect by breathing in biscuit crumbs and having a coughing fit).

After a suitable pause – while Uncle Cornelius fetched the poor lad a glass of water and some tissues to wipe away the crumbs that had somehow managed to escape through his nose (plus the tears streaming from his crimson eyes) – Tom, red-faced and wheezing, made his apologies and begged Hettie to continue. Sergeant Clem dragged her horrified expression from Tom's mortified face and attempted to carry on as if nothing had happened, while Tom tried to melt into the stool like a toad in a frying-pan. (The moral of this episode, Dear Reader, is this – never [never, never, never] tackle a handful of Rich Tea biscuits, in company, without having a drink close to hand.)

'The name of one *Miss J. L. Althorpe,*' continued Hettie, unabashed, 'is to be found among the passenger list of the Ocean Liner S/S Cedric, of the White Star Line, sailing from Liverpool to New York on February 19th 1904, only a matter of days after the last authenticated sighting of Spring-Heeled Jack in the UK.'

'Which also just 'appened to be in Liverpool,' added Uncle Cornelius, showering poor Hettie with a dramatic tempest of Rich Tea crumbs.

'We also found a *Mr Allsop*, a *Mrs Allsop* and a *Miss Allsop* travelling together on the R.M.S. Carpathia from New York to Liverpool, on October 1904,' continued the D.S.C. sergeant, stoically. 'Not sure if, or how, that might be connected, and again it all could be just coincidence.'

The Hound stopped pacing and stared intently out of the window, hands clasped behind his back, and, with some difficulty, swallowed a dry mouthful of biscuit.

'It's all pretty weird, right?' said Hettie Clem.

'It is indeed,' agreed the Hound, staring out of the window at the approaching sunrise and furtively smacking his lips in an attempt to get some moisture back into his mouth.

Hettie closed her notebook and leaned forward expectantly.

There was a long silence and then The Hound turned from the window and spoke.

'So let us hypothesise,' he began, lowering his snout and making a biscuit disappear beneath a dry cough. 'Presuming that they *are* the very same people – and therefore assuming that they are all, in some form or another, "magic-folk" – *Polly Adams, Lucy Jane Scales* and *Lucy Jane Aslop* would appear to have been hounded the length and breadth of Britain by Spring-Heeled Jack for a period of over sixty years.

'*Polly Keane*, née *Adams*, is killed, allegedly by a "large and savage dog", on Clapham Common – the original sight of her first recorded meeting with Jack.

'*Lucy Jane Scales* would appear to have travelled through England, making her way to Scotland, and then finally to have fled Britain altogether, in what, we must assume, was an attempt to make a new life for herself in the then Czechoslovakian' – (not an easy word to say when a quarter of a packet of Rich Tea biscuits is sapping every last ounce of saliva that you might have once possessed) – 'city of Prague. In the 1940s, whilst the city is occupied by the Germans, during World War Two, she is repeatedly harassed by a "Jack-like" creature known locally as *Perek, the Spring Man*. In 1961 she is attacked, and killed in Bratislava (now the capital city of Slovakia) by what is reported to have been a "*ferocious wild animal*".

'*Lucy Jane Aslop,* after making her way through the Welsh Borders and then to Liverpool, flees to America in 1904, presumably to escape her pursuer, (possibly, or possibly not, returning to England later in the same year). However, if it is indeed the same person, one Janet *Pozla* is attacked by a *Jack-like* creature – known as the "Provincetown Phantom" or "The Black Flash" – in Provincetown, New England, in 1939. If she is still alive, then her whereabouts remains unknown.'

The Hound, rather unwisely, examined and then snaffled the last of his biscuits.

'But,' croaked Uncle Cornelius, through a painfully dry mouthful of Rich Tea, 'akch Khrpring Hcheeled Kchack 'akch been kchighted in Brighton for the lakcht two nightkch running, might it not be a fair guekch to kchuggekht that 'e might rekchently 'ave moved 'ere, to Brighton (or even 'Ove), to purchue 'ickh quarry?'

'Yekch, Dandy, I think there ickh indeed every pokchibility,' replied The Hound, (dare one say) dryly.

''Ere?' scowled The Pook, who had been sitting quietly and listening intently throughout the whole proceedings (whilst stealthily stashing Rich Tea biscuits into various pockets). 'You don't by any chance mean the Lucy Jane zizterz, do you?'

'I'm not quite kchure that I follow you, Alberickh,' responded the were-hound, with arching curiosity.

'The Lucy Jane zizterz: Lucy Jane Aelfzkalzka an' Lucy Jane Aelfzophia. 'Ad an older zizter called *Pollyanna*. Old 'Arry-Ca-Nab'z daughterz.'

Cornelius raised an eyebrow.

'I kchay, you don't mean Harry Ca-Nab, the kchelf-kchtyled "Devil'czh Hunkchman" do you?' gasped The Hound, in disbelief.

'That'z the one. Well, that'z what 'e liked to call 'izzelf, at any roadz – the flazh git,' scoffed Alberich Albi, Nineteenth Pook of the Pharisees, King of the Elf-lands south of the Downs – from the Devil's Humps in the west, to Mount Caburn in the east (and beyond).

''Arry Ca-Nab, the *King of The Grabbers*?' rasped Uncle Cornelius, after (thankfully) taking a sip of Tom's water.

'Er ... who are *The Grabbers*?' asked Tom.

'The Grabbers,' his uncle informed him, 'are the descendants of the Elven tyrant, Oberon the Third – Nab of The Gentry, or *Snatch-'and Nab* as 'e's most commonly remembered.'

'It'z coz of 'im that *The Crown of Albion* waz broken up,' grumbled The Pook. 'Terrible ruler 'e were. Murderin' an' a ztealin'. Far too greedy an' zelf-obzezzed to be an 'Igh Pook, that'z for zure. When 'e waz finally overthrown, 'iz family an' their retainerz, rather than accept their lot, decided to ztrike it out alone, zo to zpeak. Never zettled to any one place, juzt travelled about az bezt they could.'

'Like Gypsies you mean?' offered Tom.

'A little,' replied Cornelius, mercifully passing the glass of water to the gratefully waiting were-hound. 'But they've always 'eld a grudge against the rest of the Elbi for 'aving 'ad all of their power an' finery taken away from 'em. Always thought of themselves as the *rightful* kings *of All Albion*. Bitter folk they are, or should I say, *were*. Ain't nobody 'eard a peep 'bout The Grabbers for aeons.'

'Daft Buggerz,' sighed The Pook, with a rueful shake of his head.

'So, let me get this right, Mr Albi;' scowled Hettie Clem, 'you're saying that *Adams*, *Aslop* and *Scales* are all related? All sisters?'

'Well, Pollyanna waz an 'alf zizter. If I recollect correctly, 'er mother waz an Aelfradi Princezz.'

'You're telling me that Polly Adams was Princess 'Eartsong's daughter?' spluttered Cornelius, in disbelief.

'Pollyanna Adamzbane – that'z the one,' replied The Pook, giving Uncle Cornelius a hefty look.

'Well, well, well,' muttered the old man, clearly taken aback and grimly brooding into his whiskers.

'Who's *Princess Artsong*?' asked Tom, desperately trying to keep abreast of matters.

'Heartsong, Tom, Heartsong,' corrected The Hound, shooting a sideways glance in Uncle Cornelius' direction. 'She was a princess of the Aelfradi; banished from her homeland, many years ago, and never heard of again.'

'Disowned for marrying 'Arry Ca-Nab, is what she was,' growled the clearly flabbergasted Cornelius.

'And what about the two *Lucy Janes*?' asked Sergeant Hettie Clem, excitedly looking up from her notebook.

'Well,' continued The Pook, '*Lucy Jane Aelfzkalzka* an' *Lucy Jane Aelfzophia* are ... waz ... twinzez, from 'Arry'z zecond wife.'

'The newspaper report of 1837 stated that Lucy Jane Aslop was pulled to safety and away from Spring-Heeled Jack by her sister,' mused The Hound.

'An' that Lucy Jane Scales was attacked on Green Dragon Street along with 'er younger sister,' pondered Uncle Cornelius.

'That'd be 'bout right,' sniffed The Pook, thoughtfully, 'if'n they waz talkin' 'bout Lucy Jane Aelfzophia, that iz. If I've got my factz ztraight, Lucy Jane Aelfzkalzka waz the older of the two by a couple of 'ourz or zo.'

'So Spring-Heeled Jack *was* targeting specific victims – the daughters of Harry-Ca-Nab! Incredible.' reflected The Hound. 'But why?'

'And why have they both got the same names if they're zizterz ... I mean, sisters?' asked Tom, a little confused but excited nonetheless.

'Elven tradition to give twins the same names,' replied Uncle Cornelius.

'Old zuperztition,' said The Pook. 'Alwayz uzed to be thought to be bad luck to 'ave twinzez,' he frowned, shaking his head sadly. 'Not anymore though it wouldn't, I reckon.'

'So what's the story behind that?' asked Hettie, frantically scribbling down notes.

'Well, the ztory goez that when Old Nick, Lucifer 'izzelf, waz collecting zoulzez, he didn't account those of the Elvezez to be worth much; them not being the zonz of Adam (an' zo not 'aving zo much of a grudge againzt uz, I zuppoze). But 'Im and the *Big Fellow*, for zome ztrange reazon only they alone knowz, came to an agreement that the combined zoulzez of a zet of Elf twinzez would count az one. Zo, zuperztitious old twoddle that it iz, Elf parentz, if they had twinzez, would give 'em both the zame, or zimilar zounding name in order to trick Old Nick, zo to zpeak, for fear that 'e (The Devil) would zend 'iz zpecial Elf-zoul-catcher, *Ter-Tung-'Oppity*, to cut the tonguezez from the babiez' mouthzez.'

'Their tongues?' grimaced Tom, in enraptured delight. 'Why their tongues?'

'Old Elven belief, Tom,' explained Uncle Cornelius. 'Whereas 'umans once thought that a man's soul lived in 'is 'eart, the Elves believed that their souls resided in their tongues.'

'Worzt thing that you could ever do to an Elf iz to cut 'iz tongue out,' scowled The Pook, with a shudder, absent-mindedly stowing the last of the Rich Tea biscuits into his jacket pocket.

'It's what old *Snatch-'and* was notorious for – taking an' collecting 'is enemies' tongues,' huffed Cornelius. 'Was said that 'e wore a necklace made of 'em.'

'Barbaric brute! Nazty bit o' work,' spat The Pook, dryly, as he lightly touched the golden hare brooch on his jacket, as if for protection.

'This *Ter-Tung-Hoppity*?' asked The Hound, with a growing and suspicious curiosity, 'what is the nature of his appearance, perchance?'

'Well,' said The Pook, wrinkling his nose in concentration, 'according to the old lullaby what we uzed to zing to the little onez ... let me zee ... 'ow'z it go, now?'

The Pook stood up, cleared his throat and started singing, accompanied by a sinister little dance with creepy hand gestures and facial expressions (as, in fact, are most musical routines designed to entertain young children).

'Onezez. Twozez. Threezez. Fourzez.
'Oo'z that knocking at my doorzez?
A well-drezzed gentleman, pale az zinzez,
'E'z 'ere – to znip – the soulzez from the twinzez.
Fivezez. Zixez. Zevenzez. Eightzez.
'Oo'z that leaping over my gatezez?
It'z Ter-Tung-'Oppity, zpitting fire,
'E'll rip the tonguezez – from your dezirez.
Ninezez. Tenzez. Elevenzez. Twelvezez.
'E's come – to zteal – the zoulzez of the Elvezez.
Clawz of zilver, eyez of red,
Run up the ztairs an' into your bedz
Or 'e'll ... ZNATCH YOU!'

'Zomething like that,' muttered The Pook, sitting back down in his chair. 'Been a few too many yearz zince anybody'z 'ad the chance to zing it, mind,' he sniffed, grimly.

'Good grief!' gasped Tom. 'That sounds just like ...'

'Psychological child abuse?' whispered Hettie Clem, trying to lose the appalling image of a breakdancing Rumpelstiltskin that was flashing through her mind after The Pook's horrifying performance.

'... Spring-Heeled Jack!' snarled The Hound.

'Nah!' snorted The Pook. 'It'z juzt a legend, that'z all. A ztory to frighten the little Elflingz.'

'But it does sound uncannily like our leaping friend;' pouted The Hound, his ears twitching in excitement, 'smartly dressed, pale complexion, red eyes, silver talons, spits fire, and is capable of jumping enormous distances.'

'So what exactly does all this mean?' asked Hettie Clem, still traumatised by The Pook's musical turn.

'Of course, we cannot be certain, but it might mean this:' growled The Hound, fiercely stroking his whiskers and with a hunter's look smouldering in his black-rimmed, almond-shaped and walnut-coloured eyes, 'that, for whatever reason, *Lucy Jane Aelfsophia Ca-Nab* has come to Brighton. And, if that is indeed the case, then her life, perhaps her very soul, is in the utmost peril.'

TWENTY FIVE
The Witches Of Frederick Gardens

Tom was awoken from his slumber by what sounded like a herd of cats being lassoed by a posse of Wild West desperadoes, and then twirled vigorously in the air by their tails. He was out of his bed in a flash and making his way towards the hallway, even though he had a sinking feeling that he already knew what the godawful noise was.

The "music" was emanating from The Study.

Bess sat in the hallway, ears pinned back. She rolled her eyes to Tom with a "please do something about this" look carved onto her face.

Uncle Cornelius bounded jauntily down the stairs in full training togs.

'AH, TOM!' he beamed, hollering above the din of the hurdy-gurdy. 'WAS JUST COMING TO WAKE YOU UP, SON! JUST TIME FOR A QUICK BLAST IN THE OLD GYM 'FORE WE START OUR DAY IN EARNEST!'

Tom wiped the sleep from his eyes and hurried to get dressed.

At least the *Muse-asium* was soundproof.

''Elps 'im concentrate,' offered Uncle Cornelius, as they made their way down the stairs and towards the basement. 'Gets a difficult an' mystifying case like this one an' there ain't nothing 'e likes better than a good old blast on the good old 'urdy-gurdy to make 'im think straight.'

After a blistering forty-five minutes of intensive training (in which Tom was taught *the true art* of how to shift and swap his stance – and therefore the lines of attack and defence – via nifty little patterns of footwork) he and Uncle Cornelius sat down (with Bess drooling expectantly on the kitchen carpet, and the sound of the hurdy-gurdy grinding away in the background like a flock of geese slowly drowning in boiling butter) to a rather unusual breakfast of chicken livers on crumpets followed by jam roly-poly pudding with custard.

'GET THIS DOWN YOU, TOM, AN' THEN WE'RE GOING TO START DETECTING! SEE IF WE CAN GET TO THE BOTTOM OF THIS 'ORRIBLE MYSTERY!' bellowed Uncle Cornelius over the droning, squealing and squeaking hurdy-gurdy.

'WHAT'S THAT?' yelled Tom, through a mouthful of custard.

'DETECTING!' roared his uncle. 'SEE IF WE CAN GET TO THE BOTTOM OF THIS 'ORRIBLE MYSTERY!'

'YOU WHAT? GET TO THE '*WHAT*' OF THIS '*WHAT*' MYSTERY?' screamed Tom.

''ORRIBLE! BOTTOM!' bawled Cornelius, just as the hurdy-gurdy stopped and Missus Dobbs was bending over to pick up a fallen teaspoon.

What sounded like a choir of squirrels with their tongues stapled to the wheels of a speeding go-cart, wound slowly and drearily up again to reach an agonising full-pitch.

Uncle Cornelius rose purposely from the kitchen table, made his apologies to Missus Dobbs, grabbed his coat from the hallway, ground a large flat cap to his head (thus making him look even more like Bill Sykes' more dangerous, and more successful, older brother than normal) and beckoned Tom to follow him as he made hastily for the front door.

They strolled along the pleasant, meandering (and blissfully quiet) streets of Brighton's North Laine at a spry pace – Cornelius occasionally twirling his cane and doffing his cap to the trendy and imaginatively dressed passers-by.

Only in Brighton, thought Tom, *would the old fellow be able to walk through the streets in broad daylight without getting odd looks – or locked up.*

The whole place was a myriad of people dressed in the distinct fashions of their respective subcultures, all rubbing along together more or less harmoniously: Emos; Crusties; Hippies; Rastas; Punks; Steam-Punks; Cyber-Punks; Neo-Punks; ageing Punks. Tom was especially taken with a dapper young *Chap* – who looked like he was nursing the mother of all hangovers, and who bore more than a passing resemblance to the old-time movie star, David Niven – dressed in Victorian sun-goggles, trilby hat and a long film noir style trench coat with the high collar turned up.

It was a wonder that The Hound even bothered shape-shifting when out and about, thought Tom, for he honestly believed that no one in this crazy town would even bat an eyelid at a seven-and-a-half foot tall were-wolf sauntering through the busy streets whilst doing a spot of window shopping.

'Where are we off to?' asked Tom.

'Same place as we always go when we don't 'ave a clue as 'ow to go forwards with a case,' replied his uncle.

'And where's that?' enquired Tom.

'We go ask the witches.'

They were, he was informed, off to see Old Maggs – president of the *South East Counties Coven of Witchcraft, Wicca and Alternative Medical Practises* – and her cronies. According to his uncle, Maggs was quite probably the oldest living human in the British Isles, and so Tom was, quite naturally, intrigued to meet the ancient crone.

They eventually came to a tiny terraced cottage nestled along a thin streak of a twitten called Frederick Gardens. Uncle Cornelius opened a small wooden gate, ducked under an arched trellis crammed with bright flowers in full (and unseasonal) bloom, led them the full half-a-pace up the garden path, and then jauntily rapped on the door with his cane.

Ba-ba-ba-bam!

Thick curtains twitched and a large brown eye briefly appeared at the window, before vanishing like a spider down a plughole.

'That you, Dandy?' croaked a high-pitched, yet warm and friendly voice from within.

'It is, Maggs. Just dropped by to see if you an' the girls 'ad managed to find out anything of interest regarding those *matters* what I spoke to you about the other day?' replied Cornelius, as he leant in closer to the door.

The door creaked open, and there stood the ancient witch, Old Maggs, squinting suspiciously at them through her left eye, with bony hands on bony hips, dressed like a refugee from the *Summer of Love,* and chewing thoughtfully on the stem of a long, unlit clay pipe.

Old Maggs was old – *Obviously over forty*, thought Tom (with slight disappointment) – but nowhere near as ancient-looking as he had hoped or expected. Her hair was a mass of long raven-coloured curls that spilled over her shoulders, and her skin was the colour of drinking chocolate. She must have been, Tom imagined, very beautiful in her youth. It was only when she smiled (which was often) and her face folded into a thousand gleeful creases that she gave the impression of any great age.

'You haven't brought *The Mutt* with you, have you?' she enquired, cautiously poking her head around the doorframe and suspiciously scanning the vicinity.

'No, 'e's busy, Maggs,' replied Cornelius, with a nervous little laugh.

'Last time he was here, I swear that one of my cats went missing. Poor old Gemma – you remember her, the pretty black one with the white spot on her chest?'

She glowered at Uncle Cornelius, accusingly.

'Ha-ha. Whatever are you suggesting, Maggs?' beamed Cornelius, with overcooked good humour. ''E's very ... *fond* of cats, as you very well know.'

'Can'nae manage a whole one, though,' came a creaky Scottish voice from within the darkness of the cottage, followed by a cackling chorus of laughter (like a recycling bin full of glass being emptied).

Old Maggs' face creased into possibly the friendliest smile that Tom had ever seen.

'And who's this fine young gentleman you've got with you?' she asked, winking at Tom.

'This is a relative of mine. Tom. Tom Dearlove.'

Old Maggs took Tom's hand and squinted deeply into his eyes.

'*Dearlove* ...' she mused, thoughtfully. 'I knew a Dearlove, once – Nettie was her name. Good woman, she was. Very kind. Good witch.

'Best come on in then, loves,' croaked Old Maggs, cheerfully opening the door and ushering them in.

There were two other women sitting in the dimly lit cottage (both, Tom presumed, witches) along with half a dozen or so geriatric cats (sprawled, *geriatrically,* over the furniture). One of them stood up (a witch that is, not a cat – the cats simply scowled at the new intruders with eyeballs like polished marbles, seething with disdain) to greet them. She was a petite and very beautiful woman, immaculately dressed in velvet (if such a thing is possible), with perfect porcelain skin, long golden hair, eyes like sapphires and a smile that would have melted the marble heart of a despot's statue.

'This is Ginty,' said Cornelius to Tom. 'Dame Ginty Parsons.'

Dame Ginty Parsons smiled and waved enthusiastically.

'Not *the* Dame Ginty Parsons who wrote "The Book of Spell Recognition"?' asked Tom, possibly awestruck.

Dame Ginty Parsons blushed ever so slightly and fluttered a slender hand dismissively.

'Oh, that little old thing,' she replied, in a polite and well-mannered voice.

'I think that it's a ... er ... *wonderful* book,' gushed Tom. 'I'm studying it at the moment, in fact. It's very ... uhmm ... thorough.'

Ginty smiled at him – and somewhere in the world buttercups turned to face the newly risen summer sun.

A gruff cough hacked through the darkness of the room like a rusty axe.

'Oh, and this is Cutty,' smiled Cornelius, introducing the remaining woman in the room. 'Cutty Sark.'

Where Maggs and Ginty were quite, quite lovely, Cutty Sark looked (to Tom's mind at least) like a witch ought to look – razor-thin mouth, hooked nose, long straggly jet-black hair, and an enormous hairy wart on her chin (which Tom struggled to keep his eyes from). From the neck down she looked as fit and as lean as a poacher's greyhound, but from the neck up she had a face like the proverbial bulldog chewing a lemon-coated wasp.

Cutty Sark looked Tom up and down for a moment, considering him as one might consider a slug discovered in your salad bowl, and then grunted what might have been a hello.

'Can I get you a glass of grass?' asked Ginty, her sparkling eyes boring into Tom like cut-crystal.

'Beg pardon?'

'Grass,' she explained. 'Wheat-grass. Juiced. Good for you.'

'Errrr ...' began Tom, not wishing to appear rude to the only famous author he had ever met.

'Course 'e would,' growled Uncle Cornelius, suppressing a chuckle. 'Old Tom, 'ere, is on a bit of an 'ealth kick at the moment. Ain't you, Tom?'

'Errr ...?'

'Oh, how splendid,' cooed Ginty. 'I'll put some fresh ginger in it for you, then. Add kick. Good for blood.'

'That'd be grand,' chortled Cornelius, smiling wickedly at Tom, and clearly enjoying himself.

'I'll make you one too, Cornelius. I know how much you like my little concoctions,' she cried, enthusiastically, as she disappeared from view, skipping merrily towards the kitchen.

The smile on Uncle Cornelius's face slowly curled southward.

'Take a seat then, Gents,' croaked Old Maggs.

Tom and Cornelius eased their way gingerly between the assortment of moth-eaten cats that seemed to dominate every chair in the tiny room, glowering fiery resentment at the intrusion of the two unwelcome visitors.

Ginty returned (bouncing with excitement) with two tumblers full of a dark-green (grass-coloured to be exact) liquid. She handed one each to Tom and his uncle, and stood by, crackling with anticipation, obviously waiting for them to sup up immediately.

Uncle Cornelius, looking like he was about to swallow a mugful of slimy maggots, sniffed the glass and then, with a look of stoic heroism, downed his tumbler in one gulp and sat for the next few minutes looking like his teeth were stuck on a particularly sticky toffee.

'Hhhhmmmm!' he managed eventually, under Dame Parsons' enthusiastic gaze – all the while nodding his head, winking and chewing manfully. 'Hhhhmmm! Hhhhmmm.'

Tom sniffed his glass with consternation and slowly took the smallest of sips. To his amazement it wasn't at all bad, and he gleefully drained his glass, giving his uncle a cheerful thumbs up as he did so.

Cornelius returned a smile that started and finished at the lips.

'Tea anybody?' asked Ginty.

'Yes bloody please!' blasted Cornelius, hastily correcting and calming himself. 'I mean, yes, yes please, that would be bloomin' marvellous.'

Ginty smiled – and somewhere in the world bees hummed with heartfelt happiness.

'Peppermint; liquorice; jasmine; elderflower; loganberry? Or would you perhaps prefer some Japanese mushroom juice?'

'Got any coffee?' fired the old man, quickly.

Ginty's eyes lit up.

'Well, funny you should ask, Dandy. I've just recently received a delightful batch of very rare coffee from Vietnam. Absolutely wonderful! Very distinctive!' she clucked, excitedly.

'Sounds grand,' replied Cornelius, with a barely concealed sigh of relief.

'Before being harvested, the coffee beans are first fed to the *Asian Palm Civet*, matured in the digestive tract, and then defecated out whole.'

'Got any *tea* tea?' meeped Cornelius, looking pale and close to tears.

Dame Ginty sighed.

'Assam, Lapsang Souchong, Earl Grey, Lady Grey ...'

'Builders?' sobbed Cornelius, hopefully.

'English Breakfast it is, then, Dandy. One for you too, Tom?'

'Could I have a liquorice tea, please, Dame Parsons,' replied Tom.

Cornelius shot him *a look* (known throughout the classrooms of the world) that sneered – "teacher's pet!".

Tom smiled back sweetly, in the pleasant knowledge that he was scoring points over the old nudger. (He was, if truth be told, a veteran of the 'Hippy-tea world', his mum having cupboards packed full of the grisly stuff back home.)

'Of course you can, Tom,' eeked Dame Ginty Parsons, with barely suppressed delight. 'And you must call me *Ginty*.'

They sat huddled in the darkness, waiting for Ginty's return – Tom wondering why they couldn't open the curtains a little, while his uncle and Maggs nattered away, the array of cats slouched sinisterly like hairy serpents with legs, and Cutty scowled in the corner like a simmering toothache.

Ginty returned once more, carrying a tray with an enormous teapot and a beautiful set of bone china cups and saucers upon it. (Tom's liquorice tea was, of course, served in a tall glass.) She carefully poured Cornelius's tea and offered him a biscuit. Cornelius greedily took a giant bite and Tom watched in fascination as the old fellow's eyes snapped open like sprung mousetraps and his whiskers bristled in a most alarming fashion.

'Cabbage, sprout and chilli. Raw,' announced Ginty, proudly. 'Made them this morning. Biscuit, Tom?'

Uncle Cornelius stifled a gag.

'Oh no. No, I mustn't, Dame Parsons, I mean ... *Ginty*,' he beamed. 'As my uncle so rightly said, I'm on a bit of a health kick and I shouldn't really eat biscuits. But thank you, they look ... *lovely*. You can have mine, Uncle,' beamed Tom, smiling like the Cheshire Cat after a change in wind direction.

His uncle shot him a look that could have withered a street lamp, took a great swig of tea and swallowed with stoic manliness.

'So, ladies,' sniffed Cornelius, swilling a large gulp of tea around his mouth and trying surreptitiously to stuff the remains of a biscuit under a sleeping cat, 'what did you find?'

'Well, Ginty and I were up on Hollingbury Ring this morning, with Alfie and young Ned,' began Old Maggs. 'There's magic up there, and no mistake. Old magic too – not Elf-magic but good old fashioned *witchcraft*.'

'A *Binding-Spell* mixed with a *Repulsion-Hex*,' injected Dame Ginty. 'Old ones, executed in a most unusual manner.'

'What do you mean by that?' frowned Cornelius.

'Well, Dandy, it was very well done, if (forgive me for saying so) slightly ham-fisted,' continued Dame Ginty.

'Weaved by a powerful witch, though, Ginty, make no mistake about that,' squinted Old Maggs, drawing heavily on her unlit pipe.

'Powerful indeed,' continued Dame Ginty, 'but one who has not perhaps fully finished her education. But the making of the spell was, well, *old-fashioned*, I suppose you would say. It's just not done like that anymore. Hasn't been for centuries.'

Tom couldn't help but wonder just how old these people were?

'It's not a spell-print that I recognise, anyway, Dandy,' mused Old Maggs, thoughtfully. 'I can usually distinguish what witch has made what hex – a bit like recognising a saxophone player by his individual tone and fingering style. The spells are English in origin, possibly Kentish, I'd say. But as to who made it? All I can tell you is *that it's nobody I know*.'

'What about you, Cutty?' asked Cornelius, turning to the old sea hag – who was loitering like a stale fart in the corner. 'Find anything?'

Cutty Sark sucked in her cheeks and looked as if she was about to spit out a newt (which would have delighted Tom, but he was to be disappointed).

'Well, Cornelius, there have been unusual comings and goings down along the seafront, mark my bones if there haven't.'

'What sort of things would that be then, Cutty?'

'One of them *posh yachts* has been seen drifting in tae Brighton Marina at sundown, leaving before sunrise, and shifting all kinds of suspicious cargoes. Might be that they're doing a wee spot of sports fishing, I suppose, but, I dinnae ken, there's something not right aboot it. By my tooth, it all smells a wee bit fishy, if ye ask me.'

'An' this yacht,' asked Cornelius, ''as it got a name?'

'Aye,' grimaced the sea witch, 'she's known as the "Buckleberry's Revenge", but that's all I ken.'

'*Buckleberry* ...' mused Cornelius, carefully removing a cat that was determinedly trying to drag its way up his leg like a zombie crawling from its grave.

'That was the name of *The Queen of the Wild Hunt!*' gasped Tom, excitedly. 'Lady Jane Buckleberry!'

'So it was, Tom,' growled his uncle. 'So it was. 'Ere, you ladies don't remember any witches by the name of Buckleberry, do you? Been about 1590, or thereabouts.'

'A little before my time, Dandy,' pouted Ginty, with a look of amused chastisement.

Cutty sneered and shrugged her shoulders.

'Not that I can remember, dear,' squinted Old Maggs, thoughtfully rattling the stem of her clay pipe between her teeth.

'Hhmm,' hhmmed Uncle Cornelius, pursing his lips. 'On a different tack, don't s'pose that you've 'eard anything about *The Grabbers* recently, 'ave you?'

'Grabbers!' cried Maggs, sounding more than a little surprised. 'Haven't heard any talk of The Grabbers for years. Bit of a bolt from the blue there, Dandy. Be surprised if there's any of them that's left.'

'Most of them went their own way long ago, hooked up with the Oak-men or went *down under*. Nae, The Grabbers are long gone, Cornelius,' snarled Cutty Sark, sourly.

'*Oak-men*?' asked Tom, though the name sounded somehow familiar.

'The Oak-men are the Elbi 'oo stayed above ground but, for one reason or another, chose to live outside the protection of the Tribes,' explained Uncle Cornelius.

'Or those Aelfradi who were fed up with life *down under*, as Cutty puts it,' continued Old Maggs, 'and returned to Upper Albion.'

'Or the few Gentry who did nae flee across the water with their sorry tails a'tween their legs,' added Cutty Sark, disdainfully.

'What about old 'Arry Ca-Nab an' his daughters?' asked Cornelius. 'Ever 'ear anything about them?'

'Poor old Harry,' sighed Maggs, shaking her head. 'Don't rightly know whatever happened to his girls. After Harry got himself murdered, well, it was the end of The Grabbers, really. They just drifted apart. Found a different path to follow, I suppose, and a good job too, if you ask me. Terrible thing for folk to be so bitter. Does no one no good to live with a grudge: can't learn anything from history until you can forgive it, I always say.'

'I never knew that 'Arry Ca-Nab was murdered,' growled Cornelius, his eyebrows arching with interest.

'Oh yes, poor old Harry,' sniffed Maggs, wistfully. 'Always up to no good, he was.' She let out a little laugh and shook her head. 'Good fun though, was Harry. Harry Ca-Nab, I haven't thought about him in years. The self-styled *King of The Grabbers.*'

'Well he did like to call himself *the rightful High Pook of all Albion*, if you remember correctly, Maggs,' chuckled Dame Ginty, her eyes sparkling like diamonds.

'Aye, never tae sure if he were a canny wee bugger or just as daft as porridge,' offered the glum-looking Cutty Sark.

'Started running with some very bad sorts, though,' continued Maggs. 'Went a little ... *strange* ... after his first wife died.'

'That would be Pollyanna's mum, Princess 'Eartsong,' offered Cornelius.

'That's right. One of Titania's precious brood. Got herself banished for running off with Harry. Strange folk those Aelfradi – don't like outsiders, as well you know, Dandy. Harry remarried soon after, though. Lovely girl. Can't remember her name. Was a princess of The Gentry, as I remember.'

'Ooh, they all liked tae think they was "princesses", that lot. Putting on *airs and graces,*' scowled Cutty Sark. 'Once folk take a mind tae think they're better than the rest of us it's a rapid road tae ruin, mark my bones,' she added, all but spitting bile.

'Now then, there, lass,' chastised Dame Ginty, startling Tom with her sudden development of a broad Lancashire accent. 'There's nay need for thee to be like that. Bread etten is soon forgetten. Ooh, another biscuit, Dandy?' she asked, switching accents once more, and speaking as if she was serving cucumber sandwiches at a Buckingham Palace garden party. 'No?'

'How did he die?' asked Tom, watching in dismay as Cornelius flustered under the awkward dilemma of refusing offered (yet repulsive) home-made biscuits.

'Well,' rumbled Maggs, 'strange business it was indeed, now you ask. Didn't get much attention at the time, I suppose because it wasn't that long after The Gentry had migrated, and that was all that folk seemed to want to talk about.'

'What do you mean by that?' asked Tom.

'Back in the early 1600s, the Northern Elbi, The Gentry, upped sticks an' moved; lock, stock an' bloomin' barrel. Went over to Ireland. Nobody's ever found out why,' explained Cornelius.

'Aye, weird business,' hissed Cutty Sark, with a sour scowl.

'It is most unusual for Elves to leave their homeland voluntarily,' added Dame Ginty, pursing perfect lips.

'They're *of the land*, Tom,' continued Cornelius. 'Powerful 'urt it must 'ave been to 'ave 'ad to leave it. One of the great mysteries of the supernatural world, it is – why ever did The Gentry forsake their 'omeland?'

'Hasn't anybody asked them?' offered Tom, quite reasonably.

'You ever tried to get information out of a miffed Elf, son? Not an easy thing to do. More than likely to get yourself stabbed. Very sensitive folk, they are. Very private,' replied Cornelius, with a knowing shake of his head.

'Miserable wee sods is what they are, if ya ask me,' offered Cutty, curtly (which, Tom thought, was a little rich coming from such a sweet and lovely ray of sunshine as she).

'Anyway,' sighed Old Maggs, 'Harry was found dead, up in Anglesey, I believe – in what they call the *Little Highlands*. I heard that it looked like he'd been torn apart by a pack of wild dogs. Ripped to shreds, he was, by all accounts.'

Uncle Cornelius and Tom swapped meaningful looks.

'Terrible way to go,' continued Maggs. 'He was a bad lad was Harry Ca-Nab, make no mistake, but I was very fond of him and he didn't deserve an end like that. Poor old Harry. *The Devil's Huntsman*,' she laughed again, fondly shaking her head. 'Always scheming. Always mixing with the wrong sort. Too ambitious for his own good, he was. Far too ambitious.'

'So nobody knows nothing about what might 'ave 'appened to 'is girls, then?' pressed Cornelius, with more than a little urgency.

'Like I said, Dandy, who can say?' pondered Maggs. 'As to Pollyanna, well, everyone, I suppose, assumed she must be dead. The Aelfradi Council did their very best to track her down after all that unpleasantness with Titania, but no hide nor hair could be found of her, as you must be very well aware.'

The old witch shot Uncle Cornelius a slightly suspicious look.

'Just who is this Tatiana that everyone keeps mentioning?' asked Tom, teetering on the verge of becoming totally lost, and taking advantage of the weighty pause in the conversation.

'*Titania*, Tom. *Titania Adamsbane*,' corrected Dame Ginty, kindly. 'She was the old queen of the Aelfradi. Their very last ruling monarch, in fact.'

'And the two *Lucy Janes*, Aelfsophia and Aelfskalska, whatever became of them?' pushed Cornelius.

'The twins? Who knows, Dandy,' reflected Old Maggs. 'Went their own way, I suppose. Fled into the world of men, most likely, trying to escape whatever shenanigans Harry had got himself involved in, and most probably got swallowed up. You know how it is, dear,' she sighed, giving Cornelius a kindly and sympathetic smile.

'I do indeed, Maggs,' muttered Cornelius (a little sadly, Tom thought). 'I do indeed.'

There was another awkward silence as the three witches shot compassionate glances Cornelius' way.

'Well, ladies,' sighed the old fellow, obviously a little uncomfortable under their combined scrutiny and sympathy, 'I think we'd best be on our way. Much to be thinking on. A pleasure, as always,' he smiled, standing up and sending one cat flying from his lap while another hung from his crotch by a fistful of needle-like claws, a look of grim and senile determination etched on its smug and smiling face.

'Let us know ... if you ... come up ... with ... anything ... else!' hissed Cornelius, through gritted teeth, a tear welling up in the corner of his eye.

'We will indeed, dear,' squinted Maggs, delicately untangling the dangling cat from Cornelius's trousers.

Dame Ginty stood up and came over to warmly shake Tom's hand.

'How lovely to meet you, Tom,' she said, with a smile that blossomed like a summer's day. 'Wait, I have something for you,' she pouted, enthusiastically handing Tom a thick and hefty tome. 'Just a little something that I've been working on.'

Tom thought he heard a little groan escape from the lips of the old sea hag, Cutty Sark.

With a smile, he took the book from the glamour witch and read the cover.

Dame Ginty Parsons'
Succinct Seven-Word *Who's-Who*

He flicked open a page at random and read –

Percy Bysshe Shelley: Poet.
Vegetarian.
Died young.
Talked to cabbages.

'Thank you,' gushed Tom, with a blush, 'I can't wait to read it.'

Ginty smiled and fluttered her eyelashes bewitchingly.

'And here, Dandy,' she beamed, eagerly offering the old man a worryingly large and weighty-looking Tupperware box. 'Can't let you leave empty-handed, can we? You will take some more biscuits with you, won't you?'

TWENTY SIX
The Night Of The Smack Faery

The days that followed proved to be little more than a series of futile searches for fresh clues, or any information whatsoever, that might progress their understanding of either the enigmatic *Society of the Wild Hunt* or the *curious case of Spring-Heeled Jack.*

There had been no more reports of extraordinary *hunting expeditions*, no further detections of the presence of *unusual* or *old-fashioned* magic, the good yacht *Buckleberry's Revenge* had not returned to Brighton Marina, no one had stepped forward to claim or even enquire about a missing *were-tigress*, there had been no further sighting of *Spring-Heeled Jack*, no reports of *vampires*, no more information relating to *The Grabbers*, and no one had seen or even heard of a *Lucy Jane Aelfsophia Ca-Nab*, a *Jane Aslop*, *Alsop*, *Althrope* or *Althorpe* or, for that matter, a *Janet Polza*.

The Hound continued (much to everybody's great delight) to punish the hurdy-gurdy, convinced that he must be overlooking something, but no advance was to be made. It all remained, all in all, a set of intriguing, but thoroughly mystifying, mysteries.

The mood in One Punch Cottage, however, was gradually reaching a crescendo of bristling excitement, for, much to Tom's incomprehension, the night of the "*Exhibition*" was fast approaching and both Uncle Cornelius and The Hound – as respected members of the supernatural community and highly regarded, and first-rate, *martialists* – had been asked to be part of the team of officials.

'So what exactly is this *Skirmishing Exhibition* event, then?' Tom asked his uncle on the morning of *the great day*.

'A rare day indeed, Tom,' beamed Cornelius, rubbing his hands together in gleeful anticipation. 'First Championship Skirmish for over ten years – an' the first one to be 'eld in Sussex for nigh on eighty.'

'Well, that's ... *fantastic*. But what exactly is going on?' pressed Tom, still mystified.

His uncle looked back at him with an equal bewilderment, seemingly amazed and aghast that Tom had no idea of the importance and unparalleled significance of the evening's spectacular occurrence.

'Young Ned Leppelin is challenging the current Champion, Louie Lew Llewellyn ap Lew Louie Llewellyn, for the right to be called "*The Smack Faery of All Albion*", that's all!' gasped Uncle Cornelius, sounding like an older sibling trying to explain the concept of Christmas to his idiot younger brother.

'*Smack Fairy*?' meeped Tom, instinctively ducking his head and looking sharply about.

'The best fighting-cove in all the Fae Worlds,' growled his uncle, with a faraway glint in his eye. '*The* Champion.'

'You mean a boxing match?' asked Tom.

'Nothing so vulgar,' snorted The Hound from behind his morning newspaper. 'Rather it is a contest of *Exhibition Skirmishing* – a much more satisfactory and civilised manner of displaying martial skill and prowess.'

Uncle Cornelius looked a little put out by that last remark, but let it go and tried to explain the rules to Tom.

'Its 'eld over five an' an 'alf *Courses*,' he began.

'You what?' groaned Tom, wincing in dismay at the thought of watching some kind of full-contact culinary competition.

'Each *Course* consists of two rounds of three minutes apiece, with thirty seconds rest between 'em, an' each *Course* being contested with a differing martial form. For *The Championship*, that begins with unarmed combat, then progresses to sword, then sword an' dagger, followed by sword an' shield, on to cutting spears, an' then finishes with the last, or "Open", round, which goes back to being unarmed combat again.'

'This being because,' The Hound explained, putting aside his newspaper, 'the *true* art of "fencing" (which much misused term has its origins in Elizabethan slang for "of-*fence*" and "de-*fence*" – and has little to do with the uncouth spectacle of two petulant competitors dressed in skin-tight white suits, leaping at each other like suicidal salmon) begins and ends with the body.'

'It all sounds very dangerous,' grinned Tom, growing slightly more interested.

'Quite the contrary, dear boy,' replied The Hound. 'One should fight only with one's enemies and not with one's friends.'

'Eh?' gurned Tom.

The were-wolf-wolfhound sighed.

'All Elves share a common bond,' he continued. 'Add to that the regrettable fact that there aren't many of them left in the world, so why on earth would they want to break their natural ties of fraternity and endanger their kith and kin by brutally harming one another?'

'Elves don't think like we do, Tom,' interjected his uncle.

'Thank God,' muttered The Hound, as he took a sip of tea.

Uncle Cornelius shot him a withering look.

'Whereas we like to know 'oo's the fastest or 'oo's the strongest, these things don't matter much to an Elf.'

'How do you mean?' asked Tom.

'Well, s'pose you 'appens to be faster or stronger than another chap ... well, *good for you*, they say, but ... *so what*? The way that they reason it is – it ain't because of something that you might 'ave done to 'ave earned it, it's just because that's the way that you was born, that's all. Nothin' to brag 'bout.'

'Uhm?' uhmed Tom.

'Say that you beat somebody in a foot race because you 'appen to be faster than they are, or can lift an 'eavier weight because you 'appen to be stronger than them, well,' explained his uncle, patiently, 'what 'ave you really proved?'

'Errrhhh ...?' errrhhh-ed Tom.

'The Exhibition is played rather like two musicians improvising together,' continued The Hound. 'It is a celebration of the art and philosophy of arms, and thus, in order to achieve this lofty goal, it is "contested" at a tempo that offers the *opponent* every opportunity to see *everything* that his fellow player is doing.'

'In that way speed an' strength don't come into it that much,' chipped in Cornelius. 'Rather it becomes an exercise in technical proficiency – that an' the ability to out-think an' out-manoeuvre your opponent.'

'How much harder, how much more rewarding, challenging and exhilarating, to be able to outscore your opponent, knowing that you have to rely purely on method, principle and learning,' cooed The Hound, excitedly.

'Add to that the fact that you 'ave to 'ave completely mastered the use an' 'armony of your body. An' to 'ave utterly understood the concepts of timing, tempo, proportion an' measure – as well as the use an' 'andling of your jooks an' all other manner of weapons,' beamed Uncle Cornelius, 'an' you got yourself a rare old ding-dong.'

Tom's head was beginning to hurt

'Which is where Dandy and I will be of some value this evening. I have been so honoured as to have been asked to be the *Conductor* for tonight's Exhibition, while your uncle will be one of two *Touch Umpires,*' The Hound declared, proudly.

'Should one of the players be adjudged to 'ave sped up in order to deliver an 'it, or to defend 'imself against one, then a point (or points) is awarded against 'im an' to 'is opponent,' grinned Cornelius.

Tom buried his head in his hands and squeezed.

'Probably best if you just come along an' watch it tonight, son,' sniffed Uncle Cornelius, thoughtfully. 'Pick it up as it goes along, like.'

They parked Old Nancy behind The Swan Inn, in the village of Falmer (North), and walked over a footbridge that led to Falmer (South) – the beautiful, picturesque and ancient village of Falmer (that lies between Brighton and Lewes [the county town of East Sussex and, perhaps of a more peculiar interest, allegedly the Wicca capital of Great Britain] having been [quite brilliantly] dissected in two by a whopping great motorway some decades beforehand; add to that two universities and a football stadium, and you might begin to understand why the good villagers of Falmer were beginning to feel a little persecuted) – and made their way towards an enormous thatched barn that lay on the furthest reaches of Falmer (South).

The *One Punch Cottage Posse* was dressed to the nines: Uncle Cornelius in his best cravat, tweeds and cufflinks; The Hound in a long, elegant black frock coat, top hat and white silk scarf. Even Missus Dobbs had joined them for the occasion – resplendent in evening wear, and staggering under the weight of half a ton of the most tasteless collection of jewellery and knick-knacks seen this side of *The Embassy World Darts Championship*. Even her hobnailed boots had been polished to a shimmer – the weight of which, Tom considered, might be the only thing that kept her from toppling over like an over-stacked hat stand. Tom, too, had done his best with what little he had (he'd still managed so far – to his great relief – to evade the dreaded trip to the dreaded tailors); his best jeans pressed, and his trainers wiped spotlessly clean with a J-cloth and a generous splash of Fairy (how apt) Liquid.

'Oldest an' largest thatched building in Sussex,' his uncle informed him, as they approached the barn's enormous door. 'Dates all the way back to the sixteenth-century, so I'm told.'

From within the barn came the raucous sounds of merriment.

Cornelius rapped three times on the wooden door with his silver-tipped cane.

The door swung outward to reveal a sturdy and dangerous-looking Elf (judging by the golden hare brooch on the lapel of his dark three-piece suit, a Pharisee, if ever Tom saw one) and Constable Tuggnutter (looking uncomfortably uncomfortable in dinner suit and bow tie).

'Evening, Ruben,' chirped Uncle Cornelius to the Elf. 'Tuggers,' he grinned, nodding to Constable Tuggnutter (who grunted something unintelligible in response).

'Evenin', Dandy,' barked Ruben, gruffly. 'Now, you knowz the procedure, gentlemen, Mizzuz Dobbz. Zorry to be a nuizance, an' apologiez for the inconvenience, but it'z a fair old gathering – all zortz of folk from all zortz of placez – an' we can't be zeen to be making any exceptionz.'

'Of course you can't, Ruben,' replied The Hound, stepping forward and unbuttoning his coat. 'No bother at all, and no need to explain. The tradition is a fair and most sensible precaution.'

The "tradition" being that no Elf, or any guest of the Elven tribes, could enter a gathering or meeting *armed.*

Ruben made a quick search of The Hound and waved him through. Then he made a thorough investigation of Tom's pockets before courteously letting him pass. Missus Dobbs (looking like a head-hunter who'd won the lottery) was searched by an elderly Elf-wife by the name of Tilly, who cooed and clucked over the cascade of gaudy jewellery dripping from the sweet little old tea-poisoner's neck, and gossiped incessantly as she checked Missus Dobbs' patent leather brick-shaped handbag. Uncle Cornelius offered Tuggnutter an embarrassed smile before handing over a set of his favourite silver knuckle-dusters; two knives (one a vicious-looking Bowie knife, that was almost of sword length, and the other a wicked little commando-style stiletto number); a snub-nosed revolver (complete with extra rounds); his silver-tipped walking stick (on which, as he handed it over to Constable Tuggnutter, the poor police officer nearly impaled himself on after accidentally pressing the button that flicked out a nine inch silver blade from the cane's tip); a spiked metal ball on a chain and stick (commonly known as a "morning star" by the more historically precise psychopathic lunatic); a brace of meat cleavers; four stun-grenades; a can of pepper-spray; a garrotte made of silver wire; a sharpened wooden stake and mallet (matching); and a hefty torch in the shape of a mace. A lesser man than Constable Tuggnutter might have collapsed under the combined weight.

''Ere, can I 'ave a receipt for those?' asked Cornelius, with a look of genuine concern. 'Some of 'em is of great sentimental value.'

Tom entered the barn and was immediately taken aback by the sheer size of the building. The beautiful thatched roof was supported by a complex series of, seemingly abstractly placed, warped and ancient wooden beams; that gave him the impression of being in some sort of mighty organic cathedral. In the centre of the barn stood a square *ring* marked out by wooden barriers. Around which were gathered possibly two or three hundred *people* – Elves, Brownies, Goblins, and even a couple of Trolls (Tuggnutter's cousins, in fact) – most laughing and joking, but a few looking sour and giving off a general demeanour of vindictive gloom.

In the centre of the ring, Tom could see The Pook and Fred deep in conversation with a snappy-looking, sharp-faced, white-haired Elf elder, who was sporting a long moustacheless beard (which gave him the appearance of an ancient satyr), and who wore a beautiful golden badge in the shape of a heron upon the lapel of his battered suit jacket.

In one corner of the hall Tom spotted Old Maggs nattering away to a group of enchanting Elf-maidens. Sitting next to her was the old sea witch herself, Cutty Sark, looking as happy as a fart in a submarine. Tom was a little disappointed that he could see no sign of Dame Ginty.

'Right then, Tom,' grinned Uncle Cornelius, above the din of chattering voices, 'you stick by Missus Dobbs, while me an' 'Is Nibs go see to our duties. When all's done there'll be a rare old shindig, whatever the outcome. Be a grand chance to introduce you to folk, an' maybe see if we can pick up any more information or clues regarding recent *activities*, if you get my drift. It's an impressive gathering, Tom, looks like there's representatives from pretty much all of the Tribes 'ere. It's as good a chance as any to find out what's what an' 'oo's 'oo, if you follow me. An' stay off Auntie Vi's 'ome made mead,' he warned with a wink, wagging an enormous and cautionary finger in Tom's face, before sauntering off to disappear amongst the crowd.

'Come along then, Ducky,' gurned Missus Dobbs, gently taking Tom by the arm, 'let's get ourselves a good seat before they all get snaffled.'

They sat themselves down next to Old Maggs and Cutty Sark.

'Hello, Tom,' beamed Maggs, her face collapsing into a ball of joyous wrinkles.

Cutty grunted what might have been a warm welcome.

'Hello, Ducky,' croaked Old Maggs to Missus Dobbs.

'Oh, hello, Ducks!' gurned Missus Dobbs to Old Maggs and Cutty Sark.

'Duck,' sneered Cutty Sark, sneering as pleasantly as one could possibly sneer.

'Hello again, me Ducks,' croaked Tilly, coming over from working the door to join them.

‘Ooh, hello there, Ducky,’ said Old Maggs to Tilly.
And then the whole gang of crones, Brownies and Elf-maidens joined in. ‘Ducky.’ ‘Ducky.’ ‘Ducky-Ducky’ ‘Duck.’ ‘Ducks.’
Good grief! thought Tom. *This is going to be an extremely quacksing (ho-ho) evening.*

After what felt like a quacking eternity, a bell was sounded and the gathering quickly fell silent and turned their attention to The Pook, Alberich Albi, who stood in the centre of the ring.
‘Brotherz an’ Zizterz,’ he began. ‘Friendz.
‘For thoze of you who ’ave travelled from afar – welcome to the land of the Pharizeez. We are ’onoured to ’ave you ’ere az our gueztzez. It ’az been far too long zince I ’ave zeen zo many of uz gathered together.’
A chorus of “hear, hears!” swept across the barn.
‘Well, az I am zure there’z no need to remind you, we ’ave come together to zee the two leading Zkirmizherz of our landz contezt againzt one another to zee who ’az the right to be called The Zmack Faery of All the Albionz.’
A roar of excited anticipation erupted from the hall. “Louie! Louie! Louie!” and “Ned! Ned! Ned!” thundered the respective good-natured battle cries from the respective camps of supporters.
‘But before we getz down to buzinezz, I’d like to take thiz uncommon opportunity to make a few introductionz, if I may.’
Polite applause rippled unenthusiastically among the throng (accompanied by the odd groan).
‘Firzt of all, I’d like to extend to everybody ’ere the apologiez from our brother Elbi from over the waterz,’ continued Alberich. ‘Az you well know, The Gentry are not up to travelling much theze dayz. But they zend uz their warmezt regardzez, look forward to ’earing of the rezult, an’ extend an offer (the firzt of many that we will no doubt ’ear tonight) for The Zmack Faery to face their own champion, Benny the Pinch, on their *’ome* zoil.’
A few derisive cheers rattled from among the crowd.
Alberich sternly stared the offenders into silence and then continued.
‘’Owever, I am ’onoured to zee amongzt uz zome of our other brotherz from acrozz the narrow zea; our dear friendz – the Zidhe.’
A crowd of thirty or so Sidhe from Ireland stood up to receive the warm applause of the crowd.
‘Also, we ’ave their cloze kith an’ kin – our friendz from the North, all the way from Zcotland, from the Zeelie Court itself – the Zith.
‘From the weztern landz, I’d like to welcome the reprezentativez of the great Pizkie Confederacy.
‘An’ it iz my deepezt ’onour to prezent to you The Pook of the Ferrizhyn, themzelvez. All the way from the Izle of Man – Robbie Glazhan.’
A huge cheer rose from the barn, and up stood the small, sharp-faced, white-haired and white-whiskered, goat-like Elf whom Tom had seen Alberich speaking to earlier.

Pook Robbie Glashan smiled and proudly bowed to all in the barn. Close by stood his personal entourage of nine Elves and Goblins (known, Missus Dobbs reliably informed Tom, as *The Buggane*s – the Ferrishyn Pook's legendary *royal* bodyguard). Among them was a character of quite extraordinary proportions. His face was distortedly sharp and his huge arms where so long that the gnarled knuckles of his humongous hands almost scrapped along the floor.

'That's the Phynnodderee,' whispered Missus Dobbs knowledgeably in Tom's ear. 'Been the Pook of the Ferrishyn's personal bodyguard for centuries, so he has. Lovely chap ... for a Goblin, that is.'

Tom wasn't quite sure what the difference between an *Elf* and a *Goblin* actually was, and so, not wishing to appear rude and cause any offence by asking, he unpocketed, and surreptitiously leafed through, his trusty copy of *Greymorris'*.

GOBLIN

(i) The name given to the humanoid race who share a common ancestry with the Elves of the British Isles.

In appearance some Goblins can be near identical to Elves – though they tend to be slightly shorter, more slender in build, and have, to human tastes at least, a more *grotesque* appearance. Others, however, can be of a truly monstrous size and form.

It is widely believed that the Goblins settled in the British Isles centuries before the Elbi and the Sidhe arrived and colonised the lands. Over time they appear to have been pushed into the corners and more remote places of the Islands by the arrival of the more sophisticated and technologically advanced Elves. However, many families of Goblin origin are still to be found living among nearly all the Elven tribes, and it is believed that the ***Piskie*** (see **ELVES**) of South-west England are of Goblin rather than Elven descent (thus, possibly, explaining the absence of the Piskie Nation from the division of *The Crown of Albion* (see **CROWNS OF ALBION**).

Goblins, like their Elven relatives, are great practitioners of magic – though Goblin magic tends to be of a darker, and perhaps more primitive, nature.

(ii) The Elbi sometimes use the term '***goblin***' to describe any Elven outlaw or tribeless Elf.

(iii) The term '***Goblin***' is used by some humans to describe any individual or group of 'magic-folk' who are particularly hostile towards them.

(iv) From about the 5th century AD until quite recently, many Elbi, especially those of the Aelfradi Nation, used the term '***goblin***' in connection with their raiding-parties and warrior societies: the most famous and dreaded of these being the notorious ***Redcaps***. Other infamous *Goblin Societies* included ***The Boggarts, The Knockers*** and ***The Blue Hags***. Fortunately, for humanity's sake, these societies are a thing of the long distant past.

A note should be made regarding the ***Hobgoblins*** …

HOBGOBLIN – Hobgoblins are not, as is commonly believed, a distinct race, but are rather the secretive, elitist, and highly regarded metalworking guild of the Elbi.
The practise of working with metals was first seen as a dangerous, blasphemous and barbaric practise by the Elbi, and was originally banned by the then ruling ***Council of Pooks***. (See G. B. Critchley's *'History of the Elbi Nations – volume iii; The Rise of the Oberons'* – Cambridge, 1831.)
However, the legendary Elven-smith, ***Hob of the Hearthside***, ignored the ban and began to explore the art of metalworking (in time making some of the greatest of the Elbi's treasures – among which include the fabled ***Crown of Albion*** and the Championship Sword of *The Smack Faery*).
On the discovery of their practise, Hob and his followers (***Hob's Goblins***) were banished from Albion but soon found sanctuary in the lands of the Sidhe. The fame of the beauty and exquisiteness of their work soon spread and they were eventually invited back by the ***Council of Pooks,*** taking up residence at the Elbi Courts as the most prized and respected of all the Elven guilds.
As a reminder to the ***Pooks*** of their folly, Hob and his followers retained the name 'Hob's Goblins', which, in time, became shortened to its present form of '***Hobgoblin***'.

'An' of courze,' continued Alberich, 'we 'ave a great many of our dear friendz from the *Fair Family*, the Ellyllon, who 'ave made their way eaztwardz to zupport their great champion – *The Champion*, hizzelf.'

A huge roar went up from the mass of supporters of Louie Lew Llewellyn ap Lew Louie Llewellyn, who had travelled down from Wales; dark-haired Elves with cheerful, ruddy faces (most probably from the copious amounts of mead that they were adroitly putting away) and dark brown eyes. Many of them were sporting a golden badge that suggested the essence of an owl – the Ellyllon tribal emblem.

'I 'ave 'ere a perzonal mezzage from Gynne ap Nudd (the Pook of the *Tylwyth Teg*) extending an invitation to uz all to vizit the *Fair Family* afore the year iz out.'

More cheers and hurrahs from the crowd.

'Alzo, I am mozt pleazed to zee 'ere among uz zo many facez from the Oak-men communitiez. Welcome, my friendz. An' let me juzt zay that there will alwayz be a zafe 'aven for you 'ere amongzt the Pharizeez, if you zhould ever find cauze to need one.

'An' finally,' said The Pook, very seriously, 'it is indeed an 'onour to 'ave with uz (an' to remind uz all juzt 'ow important an' 'ow 'ighly regarded the title of *The Zmack Faery* truly iz) our brotherz from *down-under*. A warm 'and please for our friendz from The 'Idden Realm – the Aelfradi.'

A slow, unsteady round of handclaps wafted across the hall as all eyes turned towards four figures who were sitting by themselves at the eastern wall of the barn. Three of their number wore long hoods that covered their features, and cloaks that reached down to the floor. The one unhooded Elf amongst them slowly stood up and stiffly bowed to the Elves of Upper Albion, proudly touching the adder brooch that he wore on the shoulder of his jacket as he did so.

He was, by far, the most intimidating and gruesome-looking Elf that Tom had seen (to date); with cruel and grotesque features (like a clown who'd taken a severe and prolonged beating in a bare-knuckle boxing match), long white hair, and skin that was so pale as to seem unnatural. Even more unsettling than that was the lightness of colour of his eyes – almost giving him the appearance of a blind man, but the fierce manner in which he cast a challenging and unflinching glare over the assembled gathering quickly removed any such thoughts.

Missus Dobbs gently squeezed Tom's arm in a reassuring manner.

'It iz indeed a pleazure to zee you again, Tommy Raw'ead-an'-Bloody-Bonez,' smiled The Pook. 'An' an 'onour to 'ave zuch a great 'ero of the Aelfradi people in our midzt. It was a grand match what you gave our Ned lazt year. This young lad 'oo took your title muzt be one 'ell of a Zkirmizher, Tommy, that'z all I can zay, an' no doubt we will look forward to 'earing 'iz challenge in the near future.'

The Aelfradi idol and ex-champion, Tommy Rawhead-and-Bloody-Bones, bowed respectfully to Alberich and then sat back down amidst a murmur of hushed whispers.

'The great dayz of the Elbi 'ave pazzed, it iz true, but they are not forgotten,' continued The Pook, Alberich Albi. 'An' zo it iz a privilege to zit 'ere among zo many friendz an' reminizce about our former gloriez. But, az the light growz dim on the Faery Realmz, let uz all extend our 'andz in companionzhip, an' 'ere, on thiz rare an' wonderful evening that we 'ave together, let uz believe that the proud 'iztory of our people, an' our dayz of zplendour, might juzt live on forever.'

A rapturous and sincere applause broke out from the assembled Elbi, all bar, Tom noted, the small party of Aelfradi – who kept their heads down and glowered at the rest of the gathering like cornered snakes.

'Zo, down to buzinezz. Az Pook of the Pharizeez it iz my pleazure to play 'ozt to you all. Tradition ztatez that when a worthy contender iz found to contezt the right to be Zmack Faery, the exizting Champion muzt accept the challenge an' travel to the land of the Challenger. Zo let me zhut up an' get on with proceedingz.'

A huge cheer, followed by peals of laughter, jittered from the floor.

'Zo, without further ado, let me introduce your officialz for the evening. Firzt, our *Time Keeper* and *Mazter of Tempo* – Mr Jan Tergeagle; adopted zon of the Pizkie Nation.

'Next, our two *Touch Umpirez*. From Pendle, Lancazhire, I'm very pleazed to welcome the *Ladiez Exhibition Zkirmizhing Champion of Upper Albion* (1912 – 1965) – The Queen of the Glamour! DAME! GINTY! PARZONNZZZZ!'

From out of the crowd stepped Dame Ginty, dressed from head to foot in turquoise velvet. The effect was rather stunning, and more than a few wolf-whistles were to be heard as Dame Ginty beamed and pouted magnificently to the crowd.

'Next,' continued The Pook, 'the only 'uman to 'ave ever 'eld the 'onour of being *Champion Zkirmizher of Lower Albion* – PROFEZZOR CORNELIUZ 'DANDY' LYONNNZZZZ!'

Uncle Cornelius bounded jauntily into the arena, waving and smiling to the crowd – who cheered him to the rafters.

Tom had to admit that the wily old duffer was truly the darkest of horses. He also observed, with interest, that the hooded Aelfradi were clearly upset and irritated by his uncle's appearance, and he watched them, with some curiosity, as they leaned forward to whisper together in a huddle. Perhaps, Tom considered, they didn't like the fact that a *hated human* could once have bested them at their own game. If they *were* upset by such things, Tom thought, then he was truly happy indeed, and he added an extra burst of oomph into his applause for the old fellow.

'An' laztly,' continued The Pook, 'it iz my very great 'onour to introduce to you our *Conductor* for this evening'z match. A *gentleman* 'oo needz no introduction to any of you, I am zure – the legendary The 'Ound 'Oo 'Unts Nightmarez! The one! The only! THEEE 'OOUUUNNDDDD!'

Extremely respectful (and possibly over-enthusiastic) applause bristled through the hall as The Hound made his way into the ring, waving an enormous and terrifying paw to the four corners of the barn. Tom smiled as he felt the audience visibly wince in muted terror at The Hound's approach.

'Now then,' continued The Pook, 'to our Zkirmizherz. Firzt of all – The Challenger. The Champion of the Pharizeez, the undizputed an' number one contender, 'oo 'az proved 'iz right to contezt for *The Title* time an' time again ... NED – 'THE 'AMMER OF THE GODZ – LEPPELINNNN!'

Ned Leppelin swaggered into the ring, accompanied by his Seconds (Archie Swapper and Ollie), and waved confidently to the crowd. He was met with huge cheers and jeers from the respective camps. The three hooded Aelfradi, Tom noted (now fascinated by these strange and otherworldly beings), dipped their heads like predators and scowled menacingly beneath their hoods.

'And finally, *The* Champion ... an' what a grand champion 'e iz. The *Zmack Faery* 'izzelf! Louie Lew Llewellyn ap Lew Louie Llewellyn! LOOOOUIEEE THE LEEEEEWWWWWWW!'

And into the ring, followed by *his* Seconds (who looked almost identical to him – and were, in fact, Tom was unsurprised to learn, his two brothers), stalked a lithe and muscular Elf with thick jet-black hair and long woolly sideburns, with fierce black eyes glowering under fierce black eyebrows. In his hands he carried a mighty two-handed ceremonial sword made of bronze, on whose broad, leaf-shaped blade was engraved the names of every Smack Faery from time immemorial.

The two contestants came together and shook hands warmly, before shaking the hands of The Pook and the four officials.

'Now, before we 'ave the traditional challengez,' smiled The Pook, 'we 'ave in our midzt a couple of great old championz from the pazt.

'From the land of the Pizkie, would you pleaze put your 'andz together for Lenny Knock!'

A very old and doddering Goblin, with hairy ears and thinning white curly hair swept up and over his bald pate, made his way to the ring and milked the applause of the crowd for all it was worth.

'And I am very 'onoured to be able to introduce to you a very dear friend of mine, from the land of the Diane Zidhe, arguably the greatezt Zmack Faery what ever lived, the "Maeztro" 'izzelf – Denny Dearg!'

The barn exploded in cheers of genuine hero-worship, for Denny Dearg, who (Tom was informed by Missus Dobbs) was indeed regarded as the greatest Smack Faery in living memory, and counted among the most skilled of all time – even though his reign had been a comparatively short one (he had retired undefeated, at the request of his then fiancée, a Princess of the Ellyllon).

A sprightly, tall and elegant old Elf, with a full head of greying auburn hair, gracefully entered the ring and took a bow, before embracing old Lenny Knock and then shaking hands with the officials, The Pook, and then finally going to each corner and offering warm encouragement to both of the contestants.

'Now then,' cried The Pook, as the room lowered to a buzz of anticipation, 'it iz time for the formal challengezez to be made.

'Iz there any child of the Fae World in thiz room 'oo wizhez to make 'iz feelingz known az to 'oo 'az the right to be called *Zmack Faery*?'

There was a short pause and then a burly Elf, with a red eye and a face that looked like it had been repeatedly slapped with a nine-pound frying pan, stood up from among the numerous parties of Oak-men.

'My name be Picktree Brag,' he called out, in a husky and fierce voice, 'and I be the champion of all the *travelling families*, on both sides of the water.

Whosoever wins tonight had best face me next if he truly wishes to be called a worthy champion.'

'Thank you, Picktree,' smiled The Pook. 'Now, if there iz any Elf, or creature of the Faery Landz, 'oo thinkz 'e haz a better claim than Mazter Brag then let 'im zpeak up.'

There was an excited hush as everybody looked excitedly about the barn.

Slowly, that hush grew into a low hum of whispers. And then the whispers fell to a ghostly silence. For one figure had stood up and waited, shrouded in cloak and hood, like a shadow of death.

It was one of the hooded Elves from the hidden realm of the Aelfradi.

'My name,' he purred, in a voice as cold and as chilling as cut-glass, 'is Prince Edric Bloodstone Adamsbane – "*The Wild Hunter of the Hills*" – and, as the newly-crowned champion of the Kingdom of Avalon, I lay my challenge before any Elf who would claim to be the *defender* of *The Children of the Light*.'

Slowly he removed his hood and cloak to reveal a sharp, pale face that would have been strikingly handsome if not for the malice that seemed to seep from it. He was young, for an Elf, and looked like he was probably of a similar age to Ned. His long white hair was pulled to one side and braided into a complex knot (in the ancient style of the Elbi warrior). But the collected gasp of horror and surprise that came from the hall was not so much for his war-like hair-do but for the clothes that he wore so proudly and fearlessly – for he was garbed in a dark red cap and wore long boots made of iron.

'*Redcaps*!' gulped Missus Dobbs, in a fearful and horrified shock.

The room broke out into a bristle of hissing confusion, as Old Maggs, her face etched with worry and dismay, explained to Tom that the *Redcaps* were one of the oldest, deadliest, and most cruel of the ancient Aelfradi warrior societies. They took their name from the red caps that they wore, which, in order for the continued membership of each individual, had to be dyed regularly with fresh human blood. The other most famous trait of the *Redcap war society* was their disdain of the typical Elven dislike of iron – and its members wore long boots made of iron, and *hunted* with murderous iron spears, pikes and spikes. But the *Redcaps* had not been heard of for centuries, and all present could only dread to guess what the revival of such a horrible and cruel fraternity could mean – for, surely, it could be taken as nothing less than a declaration of war.

Prince Edric's two hooded companions stood up beside him and they too removed their cloaks and hoods to proudly reveal blood red caps and iron boots of their own. The three Aelfradi looked about the hall with an arrogant, fierce and wild challenge.

Tom could see The Hound glaring inquisitively over at them.

Uncle Cornelius looked visibly agitated, and flexed his hands into fists.

'Thank you, Prince Edric,' smiled The Pook, trying to control his own undoubted surprise and dismay, whilst attempting to restore some sense of calm and normality to the proceedings. 'It 'az been many yearz zince we 'ave 'ad Aelfradi ariztocracy in our midzt, an' we are 'onoured (an' indeed, *jiggered*).

We muzt talk, you an' I, afore thiz evening iz through, for I zee that there iz much to be dizcuzzed.'

Prince Edric slowly nodded his head and sat down, arms folded proudly over his chest.

Tom noted however that the fourth Aelfradi, Tommy Rawhead-and-Bloody-Bones, looked a little disconcerted by his companions and the reception that they had received.

'Now then,' The Pook continued, turning his attention back to the anxious crowd, 'the 'our 'az approached. It iz time for *The Championzhip* to be decided. Long live Albion an' long live the Fae Folk!' he cried, before leaving the ring and making his way to take a seat next to his fellow Pook, the goaty Robbie Glashan.

The room broke out, once more, into a chorus of hearty cheers. As disturbing as the appearance of the murderous *Redcaps* might have been, all here were here to see a display of Exhibition Skirmishing, of the first and very highest order, and nothing could dampen their excitement and enthusiasm for long.

The Hound called the two contestants and their Seconds to the centre of the ring and spoke slowly and clearly to them all.

'Gentle-Elves, you are aware of the rules. Be mindful that all and any infringements will be penalised. Are you both satisfied with the weapons of your fellow player?'

Both parties agreed.

'Then, Louie, Ned, obey my instructions. Protect yourselves at all times. Honour the traditions of your ancestors. And good luck to you both.'

Louie Lew Llewellyn ap Lew Louie Llewellyn and Ned Leppelin shook hands again, then returned to their respective corners and shed their robes. Both wore a heavily padded and high-necked vest (Louie's being a red vest with the golden owl of the Ellyllon emblazoned on his chest, whilst Ned sported a dark green one that bore the chalk-white hare of the Pharisees); thick, elbow-high gloves; long baggy shorts (that looked like pleated skirts); and padded lower-leg and knee protection.

The Seconds left the ring, leaving The Hound, Ned and The Smack Faery himself alone.

The crowd fell to a bristling silence as they waited, with almost tangible excitement, for the sounding of the bell for the opening round of the opening Course.

TWENTY SEVEN
The Art & Science Of Exhibition Skirmishing

'I'm not sure that I quite understand the rules,' whispered Tom worriedly in Missus Dobbs' ear.

The House-Fairy turned and regarded him with a kindly and understanding gurn.

'I'm not sure that anyone understands the rules, Ducky,' she whispered back, and then, after fumbling about in her handbag, handed him a weighty and yellowing pamphlet.

'This might help,' she mused, helpfully. 'Then again,' she added with a shrug of her whiskery mouth, 'it most probably won't.'

Tom unfolded the ancient manuscript and read –

BILLIE BLIN'S

NEW EXHIBITION RULES

of

EXHIBITION SKIRMISHING

to determine who has the righte

to be called

THE SMACKE FAERIE

of All the Albiones.

LONDON

Printed by IOHN WOLFF.

1598.

The Ancient & noble Art of *Exhibition Skirmishing* has beene used since time immemorial to decide who is the fighting Champion of the Faye Realmes amongst Faerie & Magickal Folke alike, & can beste bee described as a non-competitive competition that is played in a courteous & chivalrous spirite – removing (as much as is possible) speede,

strengthe, spite, savagerie & skulduggerie from the exchanges & assaults.
The Exhibition must solely bee a display of *technical skille;* the Match not contested as a bloodye & brainless brawl but plaied as a celebration & examination of the True Arte of Skirmishing – therebye celebrating the martial skills & traditions of the Elbi & Sidhe people, as passed downe by *Biflindi.*
The champion of the Magicke Folke is proudlie knowne & recognised across The Nine Realmes as *The Smacke Faerie.*

Billie Blin's
New Exhibition Rules

In forgone days, many a contest for the righte to bee called The Smacke Faerie has resulted in many a long & (to bee quite franke) mind-numbingly boring challenge. Who can ever forget (however hard they might try) the recent '*epic*' battle between ***Nebless Nibby of Hobbside*** (the current Champion) and **Peggy Powler of the Tees**; an Exhibition that lasted for ***46 days*** without a single point being scored, & during which contest three people died – one from old age & two from boredom (one of those being poor Peggy Powler herself – thus deciding the Championshipe in a most unsatisfactory & alarming fashion).
Billie Blin's New Exhibition Rules ensures that neither participant nor spectator alike is ever in danger of death by tedium. The Exhibition being thus limited to a set of five & a half *Courses ...*

She was right, thought Tom, *it didn't.*
He attempted to hand the booklet back to the sweet little old eye-gouger, but she shook her head and smiled.
'You keep it, Ducky,' she said.
Tom had the strange feeling that she was somehow quite glad to be rid of it.

The bell sounded for the *first round* of the *First Course.*

The hall fell into a hushed, anxious and thoroughly expectant and excited silence.

The First Course was, as tradition demanded, contested in unarmed combat (or "*Hand of the Sword and Shield*" as the Elbi call it). As The Champion, Louie the Lew had to allow his challenger to begin each attack during the opening round of each Course.

Ned and Louie came forward and bowed courteously to each other – offering a salute to the sky, the heart and the earth – and then The Hound waved them forward to commence play.

They came together, arms touching lightly at the wrists, both Skirmishers poised like Victorian pugilists. Ned opened with a *straight-right lead* to the Louie's head, moving so slowly that it looked like he was punching through treacle. Louie parried with a right arm cover, followed by a left hand beat on Ned's forearm, and then delivered a right hand *uppercut* (in blisteringly slow, *Hollywood 'bullet-time'* fashion) to the stomach of Ned, who artfully skipped backwards (at a graceful dawdle) to parry with his left hand, beat away Louie's attack, and then cut loose with a left hand *hammer-blow* (delivered with all the startling ferociousness of an enraged mollusc) directed towards the Ellyllon Champion's nose. Louie, in turn, shifted the heel of his right foot inwards and passed forward with his left leg (heel on floor – toes lifted upwards) to parry with both forearms raised like a wall and then roll his weight onto the ball of his foot as he attempted a second *uppercut* (aimed, with sloth-like ferocity, at Ned's ribcage). Ned shifted his foot and slid away with the grace of a hare moving at the speed of a tortoise with lead weights grafted onto its toenails.

There was an appreciative applause from the audience (all bar one – a thirteen year old boy who looked on in bewildered dismay and disappointment). The connoisseurs of *The Art* nodded their heads sagely – *this,* they purred, *had all the makings of a classic!*

The first round continued in much the same manner; Ned making elegantly deliberate and painfully unhurried attacks, and The Champion defending and returning deadly and grindingly slow counters, until the rally ended with one or the other player voiding out of distance.

By the end of the first round the score stood at a scintillating 0 : 0.

Tom wondered just how (with only another ten rounds to go!) he would be able to contain his excitement, and stifled a yawn.

A sharp, pointy, and allegedly ancient, elbow jarred him in the ribs.

'You're not seeing!' hissed Old Maggs.

Tom – with elbows resting on knees, chin resting on upturned palms, eye sockets resting on the tips of his little fingers – shrugged a shrug void of even the pretence of comprehension or interest.

'You've got to watch for the way that they control their movements. Look how they set up their body positions in order to outmanoeuvre one another. Look to the trees and not just the flowers. Stop being so hasty and concentrate, Tom,' she said, sounding disappointed and giving his hand a playful slap.

Tom nodded apologetically. He would hate to think that he was a disappointment to the batty old crone (no matter how unintelligible she might be) and he leaned forward, with forced intent, to watch the contest.

The bell for the second round rang out to the roar of the crowd, and with Tom trying desperately to blink the feeling of drowsiness from his eyes.

It was Louie's turn to be the *Agent* (the player who starts each attack). Towards the end of the session the exchanges began to slowly increase in tempo, and the round wound-up to a blistering pace that brought a gasp of delight and heartfelt applause from the crowd (bar the odd "expert" or two who could be heard to mutter 'Too hasty!'). Tom's interest, however, was marginally aroused. But still, astonishingly, no points were scored.

The Second Course was contested with swords; long and wide-bladed weapons that looked heavy but which the two *Skirmishers* hefted around one-handed and with remarkable ease. The format followed the First Course, with Ned beginning as *the Agent,* and Louie as *the Patient* (the player who waits [patiently] to be attacked). Tom was beginning to note that the strikes were generally defended by covering with the sword, then beating aside the opponent's weapon with the gauntleted left hand, and then finally delivering a counter-strike with the sword, and he couldn't but help think of the lines from Romeo and Juliet – which he had only recently been forced to learn (not that he minded that much, because he was actually strangely fond of Shakespeare) for an English exam last term –

"Of Tybalt deaf to peace, but that he tilts
With piercing steel at bold Mercutio's breast
Who, all as hot, turns deadly point to point,
And, with a martial scorn, with one hand beats
Cold death aside, and with the other sends
It back to Tybalt, whose dexterity retorts it ..."

Maybe it was something like this that old Will was banging on about? Tom wondered, suddenly remembering a glorious afternoon, bunked off school, watching his favourite old musical – *West Side Story*, and the glory that is *"When you're a Jet"*!

At the end of the fourth round, Louie delivered a cut, aimed at the right side of Ned's head. Ned parried the attack on the forte of his blade (whilst passing forward onto the heel of his left leg) and caught Louie's blade at the hilt with his left hand. The young Pharisee then rolled his weight onto the ball of his foot and delivered a descending thrust that grazed the shifting Champion's side.

The Hound called a halt to proceedings and, after a quick conference with Ginty and Cornelius, awarded one point to Ned – it would have been three points but the Officials agreed that Louie had been *riding away* from the blow and so the extent of the score was reduced accordingly. (Each hit could be valued at up to three points, depending on how severe the Officials deemed it to be). A huge cheer rose from the Pharisee's supporters, along with a gasp from The Champion's followers – it had been a long time indeed since Louie Lew Llewellyn ap Lew Louie Llewellyn had received a hit. Everybody held their breath to see how the Ellyllon would respond, for often one point was all it took to decide The Title.

The Third Course was contested with Swords and Daggers. After the preliminary salute they came at each other again – Ned trying to press the tempo while The Champion tried to slow the pace with a steady and waning rhythm. The pattern followed as before – the attack was covered with the sword, the opponent's weapon beaten aside or controlled with the dagger, and then an attack delivered with the sword (or, occasionally, the dagger). At the end of the fifth round Ned transported The Champion's sword to one side and, trapping the Ellyllion's blade with his dagger's quillons, forced Louie to defend against Ned's counter-attack with his dagger alone. The crowd gasped in anticipation as Ned slowly deceived The Champion's dagger-parry and delivered a downward cut that lightly touched the top of Louie's head.

'Three points to Mr Leppelin,' called out the Hound.

The audience exploded into a chorus of excitement.

Louie smiled, nodding towards his young challenger, fully appreciating the audacity and skill of the hit.

They came back on guard again, just as the bell for the end of the fifth round was sounded.

0 : 4 to The Challenger.

The crowd could feel the title slipping away from The Champion. But could Ned hold his nerve? He was, after all, a young Elf (not even two hundred years old) and who knew if he could maintain his composure and not get too carried away. Oh, the impetuosity of youth!

The sixth round saw Louie bring the pace of the exchanges to a truly astonishing lethargy. It was an old trick, first mastered by the legendary Pharisees champion *Nathan "Slow-Hand" Wold*. At one point it looked like Louie might be dead, but The Hound crouched down, examined him intently and, satisfied that The Champion was indeed both still alive and in motion, waved away the protests of Ned's Seconds.

Beads of perspiration appeared on the brow of Ned Leppelin as he awaited the nerve-racking assault and attempted to match Louie's tempo. A long, descending thrust was eventually delivered – one minute and twenty-seven-and-three-quarter seconds into the round (thereby just creeping into the allotted time allowed for an attack). Ned parried – the hilt of his sword held high and the point low, his dagger hand stretched out before him – surrounded by The Hound, Cornelius and Dame Ginty (who crowded round, watching him like vultures to see if he would alter his tempo in order to defend himself). A drop of sweat fell from Ned's chin and smacked onto the floor of the ring with a brittle "ting" as he smoothly, like a locomotive running through molasses, began a counter-thrust of his own. However, at the last moment of blade-contact, Louie, little by little, turned his wrist and sent the tip of his sword swerving around Ned's weapon and spiralling towards his flank. Ned brought his dagger down, shifting his shoulder and foot as he did so, and stopped the blow.

'Halt!' cried The Hound, and he and the other officials fell into a deep discussion.

'One point is awarded to Mr Llewellyn for *Tempo Abuse* by Mr Leppelin,' he informed the crowd.

Appreciative applause rippled round the hall, along with the cheers and groans from the two Skirmisher's respective supporters.

Archie Swapper hurled the tea towel that was wrapped across his shoulders to the floor with a snarl of frustration.

Llewellyn – 1 : Leppelin – 4

The round ended with Louie attempting another *Slow-Hand* attack, but this time Ned was ready for it and survived the snail-paced onslaught.

The Fourth Course was contested with Sword and Shield. The shields were large, round, and emblazoned with the tribal symbols of the Ellyllon and Pharisees, respectively. The tempo of the exchanges was gradually increased by both players until, by the time the eighth round was finishing, Tom could hardly follow the exchanges, so quick were the strikes and blocks. The room boomed with the sound of sword on shield echoing through the rafters like drums, but no points were scored throughout the Course.

The Fifth Course was fought with large-headed cutting spears, similar to the ones used by Fred and Ollie on the night of the *Battle of Hollingbury Hill*. Louie instantly scored a light touch, clipping Ned's thigh with the butt of his staff, and was awarded half a point.

Louie Lew Llewellyn ap Lew Louie Llewellyn – 1.5 : Ned Leppelin – 4.

At the beginning of the tenth round, Ned lost another point for tempo abuse but immediately scored a half point with a short cut with the blade that clipped the tip of Louie's nose and drew a thin line of blood. In turn, Louie slowly hammered an exaggerated cut to Ned's right cheek, Ned foolishly parried with the blade of his spear and Louie instantly shifted his weight onto his front foot and compassed with his back leg, collapsing Ned's parry and scoring two points as the edge of his blade ruffled Ned's enormous sideburns.

Llewellyn – 4.5 : Leppelin – 4.5.

The crowd was silenced into reverence, and feverishly held its breath for the remainder of the round to be played out. As the bell was sounded, the hall erupted into rapturous and appreciative applause.

Four and a half points apiece, with only the last, or "Open", round to play.

The Hound called the *Skirmishers* together for the eleventh and final round. The two Elves shook hands warmly before assuming their fighting stances. The last round was always fought unarmed (the reasons for which The Hound had previously explained). The role of *Agent* and *Patient* was dispensed with and either player could now begin the attack.

The two Elves circled each other warily. The short dark hair of Louie the Lew contrasting strikingly with the long golden curls of Ned Leppelin. Ned threw a "bear-claw" strike to the side of Louie's head at a medium tempo. Louie parried with his elbow and delivered a *chopper* towards the bridge of Ned's nose. Ned shifted and shuffled backwards. The blow fell millimetres short and, in that instant, Ned rolled in with an undulating combination of *hammer-blows*. Louie blocked. Cornelius called for an investigation.

The Hound called a "Time-Out" and went over to speak with Jan Tergeagle, the *Master of Tempo*.

'No abuse of tempo,' The Hound announced at last to the waiting spectators. 'Continue with play.'

The clock was started again.

Louie tried to position Ned for a back-heel trip, but Ned shifted his foot inwards and compassed safely out of harm's way.

'Twenty seconds left, Ned!' hollered Archie Swapper urgently, for a draw would see the title remain with The Champion.

Ned instantly trundled in with a backhand strike aimed at Louie's right cheek. Louie shifted his right foot outwards, parried the blow with his right forearm, shifted again and transported Ned's arm to the other side with a roll of his elbow, pushed it away with his left hand, and then sent in a vicious knuckle-strike towards Ned's throat. Ned gathered his back foot in time with Louie's initial parry, shifted with his front foot and rolled his left shoulder forward, jabbing his left elbow into the wrist of Louie's attacking hand, and then, with another gather of the left foot, rolled his right shoulder forwards and delivered a right-handed uppercut towards the Ellyllon's solar plexus. It landed with the softest of thuds.

The crowd went mad. Even Louie's supporters had to nod their heads in regretful admiration. Such an audacious and rarely seen manoeuvre was indeed the mark of a true artist.

'Three points to Mr Leppelin,' cried the Hound, struggling to make himself heard above the crashing din being made by the Pharisees' supporters. 'Mr Leppelin leads – seven-and-a-half points to Mr Lew Louie Llewellyn's four-and-a-half points.'

Almost immediately the bell sounded, bringing The Exhibition to its conclusion. The barn exploded into an ear-splattering hullabaloo.

Through the turmoil, Ned and Louie embraced and the dark-haired Ellyllon whispered something in Ned's ear that made the young Pharisee laugh.

Archie and Ollie rushed into the ring and hoisted their Elf aloft, to the growing cheers of the gathering.

A new Smack Faery had been crowned.

Ned Leppelin was *The Champion* of all the Magic Realms.

TWENTY EIGHT
The Devil's Huntsman's Daughter

The night jigged raucously away in celebration – teetering on the edge of collapse under the combined weight of mead, cider and ale. Louie Lew Llewellyn ap Lew Louie Llewellyn presented Ned with the Championship Sword (which representatives of the Hobgoblin Guild had hastily engraved with the dates of Louie's reign and added Ned Leppelin's name to the long and proud list of champions). A few speeches were exchanged and then Ned was carried shoulder-high around the hall, touching hands with each and every Elf and magic-folk present.

Gradually the din of merriment was hushed and an intrigued silence hummed among the revellers, for a soft, dull and insistent pounding was to be heard coming from the barn door. Somebody joked that it must be the *Big-Folk* from the neighbouring houses complaining about the noise, but clearer heads knew that that was impossible, for a *glamour* had been placed over the barn so as not to attract attention from the *outside world*.

Tentatively the door was opened and in staggered a tiny and wretched figure, huddled and wrapped in a ragged and bloodstained blanket.

The swaddle of rags took a couple of steps into the barn and then collapsed in a heap to the floor. A ring of shocked Elves gathered around the petite and prostrate form, as Alberich, The Hound, Cornelius and Old Maggs elbowed their way through the crowd.

Tom, following at Old Maggs' shoulder, peered through the gap of gaping onlookers and down at the ghastly, frail little figure that lay slowly writhing on the ground.

'Good grief! It can't be!' hissed Old Maggs, kneeling down to take the poor creature's mashed hand and wipe away blood-clumped hair from the swollen lump of flesh that was the unfortunate thing's face. 'It's ... it's Aelfsophia Ca-Nab!' she whispered.

The Hound and Cornelius swapped a lightning-quick glance of concerned and curious amazement.

Aelfsophia Ca-Nab's face was a wreck – her cheeks ripped open, her eyes swollen shut, her nose split, and her lips almost torn off. It looked as if she had been mauled by a crazed wild animal.

Old Maggs tenderly opened the blanket that was wrapped around the fallen Grabber, and the whole room let out a numbed gasp of horror.

Aelfsophia's limbs had been broken and twisted into unnatural and agonising positions. Tom, feeling more than a little queasy, could only wonder how the poor creature had ever managed to get here.

Seemingly with that thought, Aelfsophia opened a blackened and swollen eye and fixed Tom with a terrifying and horrified gaze. She lifted her twisted arm, the hand somehow snapped to face the wrong way, and pointed what was left of a finger at him.

'*He is coming!*' she rasped in a hoarse and brittle voice, blood seeping from her mouth as she spoke. '*A new High King ... awaits to be ... crowned. A Dark Lord ... brings ... ruin ... to you all. He knows your secret, Children of the Light. He knows your secret! Forgive me ... forgive us all. Far better if you had let us keep ... the ... Crown ...*'

She coughed blood, twitched for a moment, and then lay still.

Old Maggs felt for a pulse and then looked up at The Hound.

'She's dead,' she said.

TWENTY NINE
The Council Of The Elves

A thorough scout of the vicinity was hastily made, but – beyond the discovery of a fresh set of tyre tracks and the bloodied, twisted and faltering footprints of Lucy Jane Aelfsophia Ca-Nab tottering determinedly towards the barn doors – there was nothing that could be pursued.

The abused and lifeless body of the youngest daughter of Harry Ca-Nab, the last *King of The Grabbers*, was gently wrapped and taken from the barn to be given a proper burial in due time.

Everybody present (Elf, Goblin, Brownie, Troll, witch, were-wolf-wolfhound, bewhiskered tweed-clad lunatic, and terrified thirteen year old boy) was in a state of shock and dismay. Not only had an Elf died (there being so few of them left now that each death became an ever more devastating event; a dreaded moment that was met with a profound sorrow and despair) but she had also been horribly tortured and had clearly died as a result of her dreadful injuries.

It was an extraordinary and appalling occurrence, and one that needed to be discussed and examined immediately.

The barn floor was cleared and a circle was formed so that all present could hear what was said and have their say.

The two Pooks, Alberich Albi and Robbie Glashan, held the centre of the ring, along with the Aelfradi prince, Edric Bloodstone Adamsbane.

The regal *Redcap* disdainfully cast his colourless gaze along the collected rows of faces around him, as if hunting for vermin.

'What right does this ... *Human* ... have to be here?' he demanded (spitting out the word "Human" as if it was half a worm discovered in an apple), indicating Cornelius with a dismissive gesture of his long, spidery hand, not even deigning to meet Tom's uncle's severe stare, and clearly making it known that he thought that the old man was beneath contempt.

'Dandy Lyonz 'az been a great friend of the Elbi for many yearz,' said Alberich, calmly.

'No friend to the Aelfradi!' hissed Prince Edric, bitterly.

'That's a lie,' scoffed Uncle Cornelius, springing from his seat and fronting up to the Aelfradi prince.

Edric turned his head and looked at Cornelius as if he had just noticed a bad smell.

'You'll take that back, Edric Bloodstone,' snarled the old fellow, softly, 'if you know what's good for you.'

Tom had never seen his uncle look so furious – and the fact that his anger wasn't loud and *shouty*, but quiet and almost gentle, made it seem all the more chillingly dangerous.

'Friends,' bleated the goaty Robbie Glashan. 'An Elf-maiden has been murdered. Now is not the time to bring up the hurts of the past. Let us instead work together at this terrible time.'

Alberich nodded his agreement.

'Be zeated,' he snapped sternly, allowing no room for discussion on the matter.

As they were all technically guests of the Pharisees, both Edric and Cornelius backed off. But Tom noted that his uncle glowered at Prince Adamsbane as he did so, and if Tom hadn't been so scared of the Aelfradi prince he might have felt sorry for him.

The Hound settled a calming hand on the old fellow's shoulder and whispered something in his ear.

'And *this*?' continued Edric, oozing disdain. 'This ... *whelp* of Adam? This ... *man-child*?'

To his horror Tom realised that Prince Edric meant him!

He felt the colour drain from his face and his heart pound in his chest like a kick drum.

Not an easy thing for a young "*man-child*" – being under the fierce scrutiny of someone who is not only a prince of a tribe of warlike supernatural beings who have a sworn hatred and history of bloody animosity towards all things human, but who is also a leading light (possibly the club secretary, for all Tom knew) of a gang of murderous and psychopathic goblins who regularly dyed their clothes with fresh human blood just to keep their monthly membership up to date.

What made matters worse was that now every eye in the building was directed, in a questioning and eyebrow-arching manner, towards him.

Tom felt his mouth sapped of any moisture.

He turned to his uncle and saw the old codger bite his lip in concerned indecision.

Tom was also particularly delighted to observe that the other three Aelfradi were also intently ogling him: the two *Redcaps* looked on like a brace of bleached hatchets scrutinizing a freshly laid turd in a laundry basket, whilst Tommy Rawhead-and-Bloody-Bones was studying him with a strange and curiously perplexed expression etched upon his gruesome visage – as if he had just forgotten what he was about to say and was desperately trying to remember what it was.

'He's my apprentice,' lied Old Maggs.

The Elf-prince tore his eyes from Tom and considered the old witch venomously.

'An' a friend of the Pharizeez,' growled Archie Swapper, thumbs hooked elegantly in the belt loops of his fraying trousers, and giving the Aelfradi prince a filthy, unflinching and challenging look.

Ned Leppelin, the newly-crowned *Smack Faery*, stood up and quietly stood beside his cousin.

'Good enough for me,' baaed Robbie Glashan, deliberately walking between the two princes (the *Redcap* and the changeling), before taking a loud sip of beer and easing himself onto a seat.

And with that, the matter was settled and the council was begun.

Alberich Albi stood before the assembly.

'Iz there anybody 'ere who knew Lucy Jane Aelfzophia Ca-Nab?' he asked.

Old Maggs put her hand up.

'I knew her quite well, when she was a young'un,' she said. 'Knew her sisters too, but when old Harry Ca-Nab died they all ... well, they all just disappeared is what they did. Never heard from any of them again.'

'Did anybody know, or 'ear rumour, that Aelfzophia waz in Brighton? Or, for that matter, anywhere in the land of the Pharizeez?' continued Alberich, his handsome face engraved with apprehension.

There was a collective shaking of heads.

The Pook of the Pharisees pulled at his whiskers, deep in thought.

'After Harry Ca-Nab got snuffed out, we had a few of his followers join up with some of our communities,' offered Picktree Brag of the Oak-men. 'But I reckon that they must be all dead by now. Weren't no spring chickens when they came to us, if you get what I'm saying.'

'Others sought shelter in The Hidden Realm,' purred Tommy Rawhead-and-Bloody-Bones, his voice like melting frost on a gravestone on a misty winter's morning. 'But, as Master Picktree says, most were aged Elves when they came to us. I would be most surprised if any are still alive.'

'Whatever did 'appen to Aelfzophia'z zizterz?' asked Ruben, the burly Elf who had been on door duties earlier.

Alberich Albi looked up from his whisker tugging and turned heavily to The Hound.

All eyes followed The Pook's gaze.

The were-hound stood up, towering above the collected gathering.

'In the course of some resent research, in connection with an on-going investigation,' he began, 'it has become apparent that both of Aelfsophia's sisters, Pollyanna and Aelfskalska, are not only dead, but were brutally murdered. By all accounts they suffered injuries not dissimilar to those that might be inflicted by a wild and savage animal – wounds in keeping with those displayed by poor Aelfsophia this very evening.'

There was a low and deep rumble of sadness, shock, displeasure and anger from the congregation of Elves.

'It is also my belief,' continued the were-wolfhound, 'that the Ca-Nab sisters were the victims of a curse; for they were haunted, harassed and pursued across the centuries by a supernatural entity – a spirit known as ... *Spring-Heeled Jack*!'

There was a bewildered silence of non-recognition, though Tom noticed that Old Maggs, Ginty and Cutty Sark all raised a sceptical eyebrow.

'Then perhaps that entity is better known to *The Children of the Light* as ...' The Hound dramatically announced, '*Ter-Tung-Hoppity*!'

There were a few open laughs (quickly stifled as The Hound turned to glower at the perpetrators) accompanied by a smattering of huffs and groans.

'That's just an old ...' (Tom waited excitedly to hear what word would be used in place of "fairy tale") '... scare-story, that's all,' scoffed Picktree Brag, gingerly (and also, to Tom's mind, rather disappointingly). 'Ain't no truth in it. Just a yarn we used to use to frighten the little Elflings with. Used to put the fear of the Devil up my end when I was a nipper, and no mistake,' he continued. 'But it's made up. No such creature exists.'

Like Elves, Goblins, Brownies, witches and a pantaloon-clad were-wolf-wolfhound who talks like he's half swallowed a punnet of plums? thought Tom to himself.

'Then how do you explain the fact that both Professor Lyons and I spotted, and gave chase to, *Spring-Heeled Jack/Ter-Tung-Hoppity* in central Brighton only last week?' enquired The Hound, after waiting for the clatter of dismissive voices to die down.

And then, as a hushed and fearful silence fell among the gathering, the were-hound began to detail the basic line of events concerning Spring-Heeled Jack and their (Hound & Lyons' [established 1895]) on-going (and rather fruitless) investigations into them.

'But, as extraordinary as that may be,' growled The Hound, after he had recounted his tale, 'I feel that it is of the utmost importance that we return to, and consider, the last words of poor Aelfsophia Ca-Nab.'

The giant man-dog sucked his teeth and began to pace about the hall, arms tucked behind his back, pointy snout held high to the rafters, ears twitching in concentration, and muttering to himself under his wiry whiskers.

'The answer to this diabolical play might just be found within her tragic words of warning,' he mused, (probably to nobody in particular, Tom thought, but it sounded like he was expecting answers and, well, to be honest, who really wants to disappoint a seven-and-a-half foot tall cynanthrope?).

His captivated audience set about gurning the best thoughtful expressions that they could muster.

'"*He is coming*",' The Hound cogitated. 'Who is coming?' he boomed, suddenly spinning around to face the circle of startled Elves, who hastily pulled their heads down like guilty schoolboys who have forgotten to do their homework.

An unharmonious chorus of "Errrhhmms?" fluttered across the stillness of the barn like a flock of lost starlings.

The Hound glowered at them with what might have been disappointment, lowered his muzzle, and tried again.

'"*A new High King a-waits to be crowned*"?' he meditated, looking over his nose at them, like a bored Latin teacher terrifying a classroom of under-prepared and under-performing pupils.

'Can't 'appen,' sighed Pook Alberich Albi. 'No Elf can, nor ever would want to, make 'izzelf 'Igh King. An' even if zomeone waz daft enough to want to try it, it juzt ain't pozzible. *The Crown of Albion* waz broken a long time ago – dizmantled for that very reazon.'

The barn erupted into a collection of arguments – with no one being heard, listened to, or making any particular sense (just like the House of Commons, really).

While this unseemly chorus of braying was going on, Tom took the opportunity to open and flick through his copy of *Greymorris*' to find out just what this mysterious *Crown of Albion* was, exactly.

CROWN OF ALBION

This much debated and mythical object plays such a pivotal role in the story of the Elven people that it is necessary to explain what little is known about its history.

In the distant past, at the very zenith of their power, *The Children of the Light* elected from among their number a High King (***High Pook*** or ***Oberon***). To symbolize and unify the combined strength of the Elbi, a magical crown (of purportedly untold power) was crafted by the great smith ***Hob*** (See **HOBGOBLIN**) – it became known as ***The Crown of Albion***.

The first Oberon was the fondly remembered ***Good King Sill,*** and under his rule the Elbi thrived and prospered. However, in time, after the horrendous and tyrannical reign of ***Oberon III*** ('***Nab of the Gentry'*** – or '***Snatch-hand Nab***' as he is remembered by history) *The Crown* was dismantled; the Elbi coming to the belief that so much power in the hands of one Elf was far too dangerous and detrimental to the good of the people and to the prosperity of the land.

The Crown was therefore broken into four parts and divided among the four great tribes of the ***Elbi***.

The Crown of Spring went to the Elbi of the East, ***The Summer Crown*** went to the Elbi of the South, ***The Autumn Crown*** went to the Elbi of the West, and ***The Winter Crown*** went to the Elbi of the North.

The concept would appear to have been that each *kingdom* would dedicate a term, or season, to matters of *High Court*, and then pass on the responsibility of *national government* to their neighbour when their allotted season was up – thereby ensuring that tyranny would never again raise its head in the land of Albion.

However, this division, instead of liberating and empowering the Elbi, appears to have led to jealousy, corruption, infighting and, eventually, civil war.

As the Elbi fought amongst themselves (and against their neighbours, the Sidhe of Ireland) a newly arrived group of immigrants (Humans) prospered, grew and eventually took over as the dominant people of the islands.

Over the ensuing centuries, the legend of *The Crowns of Albion* has become the focus for much occultist attention, for it is widely believed that whosoever makes *The Crown* whole again (by reuniting the four lesser crowns) will become lord of the Two Albions and *master* of all the supernatural powers of the land. In consequence, many a wizard, witch and warlock has dedicated their lives to the discovery of these fabled crowns. All, thankfully, to no avail.

The exact whereabouts of the four crowns remains the most closely guarded secret of the Elbi. *The **Crown of Spring*** was taken below ground by the ***Aelfradi*** millennia ago (and is therefore far beyond the reach of any mortal being). *The **Summer Crown*** lies in the possession of the ***Pharisees*** of Sussex. *The **Autumn Crown*** is guarded by the ***Ellyllon*** of Wales. The whereabouts, or guardianship, of *The **Winter Crown*** is (reputedly) uncertain – some have speculated that it would have been taken across the waters to Ireland by The ***Gentry****;* others contest that this is impossible, for it is tied to the land, and therefore it must lie hidden in the highland wildernesses of Scotland, waiting to be reclaimed once more when the ***High Ones*** return to their homeland.

'"*A Dark Lord brings ruin to you all*" – How?' considered The Hound.

Many sets of Faery eyes looked at each other with flummoxed consternation.

'"*He knows your secret, Children of the Light. He knows your secret*" – What secret?' The Hound demanded.

'How do we know!' whimpered Picktree Brag, articulating the assembled congregation's frantic dismay.

'It's obvious,' cried out a strange, but somehow strangely familiar, voice.

Tom was more than a little surprised, and mightily mortified, to realise that the speaker was none other than himself.

All eyes turned towards him.

'The secret whereabouts of the four Crowns – that must be the ... secret ... that ... she was ...' began Tom, suddenly very self-conscious and feeling like he'd overstepped his station.

'The boy's right!' bleated Robbie Glashan, shaking his head in ruination. 'What else could it be?'

'"Far better if you had let us keep The Crown",' sighed the were-hound, ominously.

'It's not my place to ask,' asked Robbie, 'but the four Crowns are all safe, aren't they?' As a Ferrishyn, and therefore (technically) a Sidhe and not an Elbi (though that was open to debate), the Pook of Mann was not party to such knowledge concerning the treasures of the Elbi.

'Ourz iz,' sniffed Pook Alberich, perhaps slightly defensively.

'Yeah? Only the damned foo-el of a Pharisee would name a tow-en after the place that they've hidden their most important treasure in!' wailed one of the party of Ellyllon – possibly the worse for wear after one too many ales (and perhaps upset at their champion's loss of The Championship).

The room broke out again into a blister of arguments and name-calling.

'What's that all about?' whispered Tom to his uncle.

Uncle Cornelius rolled his eyes and huffed.

'The old name for Brighton is *Bright-'elms-tone,*' he began, 'in reference to *The Summer Crown* of the Pharisees: Summer Crown = Bright Crown = Bright 'Elm'

'Elm? You mean ... like a tree?'

'No! An 'elm! You know, a tin 'at – an 'elmet, like what a knight might wear.'

'Aah, you mean a "helm", Uncle.'

'That's what I said, son. Any'ow, Bright 'Elm = Bright 'Elm Town = Bright Town = Brighton. It's widely believed that *The Summer Crown* is, or was, 'idden somewhere 'ere abouts, but that's about all anybody really knows. Load of 'ot air, if you ask me,' he sniffed, indicating the pandemonium that was breaking out among the tribal factions. 'When people get scared or upset an' don't know what to do, well, they just look to blame someone else, that's all.'

The Hound rumbled a low growl that reverberated around the barn.

Everybody fell quieter than a piglet in a roomful of blind butchers.

'Friends,' he implored, 'this is not the time for petty squabbles. If Alberich says that *The Summer Crown* is safe, then that is good enough for me. If there is anyone here who doubts his word then let them speak up *now*.'

There was a collective and abashed silence.

'The Gentry are not among us to tell us anything regarding *The Winter Crown*. *The Autumn Crown* is, I am sure, safe among the Ellyllon?'

There where hearty affirmatives from the tribesmen of the Fair Family.

'But the whereabouts of *our* crown,' spat Prince Edric Bloodstone, with a ferocious and pained bitterness, 'is unfortunately not so certain. Is it?'

'*The Crown of Spring*, I can assure you, Prince Edric, is in no danger whatsoever. You have my word on it,' responded The Hound, holding the Aelfradi prince's stare with unwavering certainty.

Edric sneered and turned to his companions.

'It is time for us to return to the Hidden Kingdom, my brothers,' he hissed, loud enough for all to hear. 'I have had my fill of these meek and conquered creatures. Let us prepare ourselves for whatever disaster these cowering lapdogs have led us to.'

He turned and glowered at the gathering.

'Once again,' he snarled, 'it falls to the Aelfradi to watch the gates and guard the walls – as we have always done, ever since the coming of the curse-ed sons of Adam. If any of you have any pride, or Fae blood left within your veins, then you will join us. For the war spears of *The Proud Ones* are raised once more, ready to protect our ways.

'All who would seek to threaten us will feel our wrath, for we will unleash such a nightmare as to make the bones of all men quiver to their core. Hear me, *Children of the Light*, for I give you fair warning – we, the Aelfradi, will unleash the *Wild Hunt* upon all our enemies!'

And with his words still ringing through the rafters, the Aelfradi warriors elbowed their way from the barn, stopping only to pick up their iron knives and lances, before vanishing into the night like the shadow of a bad dream.

THIRTY
Three Princesses

'So what happens now?' asked Tom, as they pootled back along the Lewes Road and homewards towards One Punch Cottage.

'The Elves will return to their respective homelands, make sure that their crowns are safe, and take whatever precautions they feel are necessary for their continued protection,' answered The Hound, from the back seat of the car.

'And why did Old Maggs say I was her apprentice?' quizzed Tom, bubbling with questions.

'Ooh, she's a sharp one, make no mistake,' cooed Missus Dobbs, gurning wisely beside the were-hound – and rattling like Marley's ghost as her jewellery clunked with every bump and pothole that Old Nancy found in the road. (Tom thought that the old crock [Old Nancy, not Missus Dobbs] was most probably built before the concept of suspension had even been contemplated.)

'Some of those Aelfradi are truly terrible folk, Tom,' growled Uncle Cornelius, his eyes fixed intently on the road as he drove. 'Not all of 'em, mind, but there's plenty that are. An' those that are, like them what was there this evening, well, they 'ave a powerful 'atred of 'umans, they do. I 'spect that Old Maggs was most probably trying to protect you from too much unwelcome attention, that's all.'

Tom let out a silent *phew* and couldn't help but suppress a shiver as he recalled the chilling glare of the pale-eyed Aelfradi.

'And them being *Redcaps* and all, didn't help anyone's nerves, I can tell you, Ducky,' grimaced Missus Dobbs. 'Brings back some truly horrible memories.'

'They certainly didn't seem to like you very much, Uncle,' said Tom.

'We 'ave 'istory, son, Edric an' me. Goes back a bit. Long story. Always looking for trouble that one. The slimy little twerp.'

'So how do you know him?'

Uncle Cornelius seemed to spend an age considering Tom's question before answering.

'I spent some time in The 'Idden Realm, few years back. That's when I first met 'im.'

'That's right. The Pook announced you as the "*only Human to have ever been champion Skirmisher of Lower Albion*",' gasped Tom, excitedly.

Uncle Cornelius smiled, almost despite himself. 'Aye,' he sighed proudly, as if recalling a fond memory. 'That I was. Champion of Avalon. For a brief while, at any roads. But that was a long time ago, Tom. Another life, or so it feels like sometimes.'

Tom seized the opportunity with both hands. 'So, Uncle ...?'

'Hhmmm?'

'Just how old are you?'

His uncle guffawed.

'Old enough to know better, that's 'ow old,' he chuckled, without much humour.

Tom knew when to drop a lost cause, so he plucked another of the many unanswered questions that were galloping at full tilt around his head.

'So ... what *has* happened to *The Crown of Spring* – the crown of the Aelfradi?' asked Tom. 'And why don't they have it, or seem to know where it is? And why do they think that you do?' he probed, turning excitedly to The Hound.

Uncle Cornelius sniffed.

'A few years ago, Tom, the old queen of Avalon died ... *unexpectedly*, leaving the line of ascension in dispute,' replied The Hound.

'Queen Titania Adamsbane was 'er name, as you no doubt remember Dame Ginty telling you the other day, Tom,' added Cornelius. 'An' she was a frightful an' 'orrible old thing. 'Ated 'umans, she did. Was a sworn an' bitter enemy of all mankind.'

'At the time of her death,' continued the were-hound, 'there appeared to be two possible heirs for *The Throne*, but one of them was too young to contest for *The Crown* and so the Aelfradi had to declare themselves a "*Suspended State*" and pass the safekeeping of *The Crown of Spring* to an outside and trusted party –'

''Is Nibs back there,' interjected Cornelius, indicating the were-hound with a nod of his head.

'– until the second heir came of age and the new ruler of The Hidden Realm could be decided.'

'I don't understand,' said Tom. 'What do you mean "decided"?'

'Ancient Elbi law states that if a monarch dies without naming their 'eir, then all direct descendants of that ruler 'ave an equal claim to the throne,' explained Cornelius. 'An' that the matter can only be decided by combat. Not dissimilar in fashion to the Ex'ibition bout what we saw tonight. Only difference being that this time they use sharps, an' don't go so slow, on account that they 'ave to fight to the death.'

'That's barbaric!' snorted Tom.

'Quite so,' huffed The Hound, softly.

'Maybe it is, but that's their custom. Course, it's only the Aelfradi 'oo keep it up nowadays. Any'ow, until the second claimant reaches his *maturity*, an' is deemed old enough to fight for *The Throne*, the Aelfradi are ruled by an elected council, much to Edric's annoyance, no doubt,' sneered Uncle Cornelius.

'So where is this other prince?' asked Tom.

'In 'iding.'

'Whatever for?'

'Well, you've met Prince Edric,' grunted the old man, curling his lip in disdain, 'an' would you trust 'im not to arrange for some nasty little *accident* to 'appen to 'is only rival to *The Crown of Avalon*?'

Tom had to concede that he wouldn't, and then wondered to himself just how old an Elf had to be before they were considered to have reached *maturity*.

If you took it as roughly seven human years for every Elf year (like 'dog years', but in reverse) then they'd have to be about a hundred years old!

Good grief! he thought. *Imagine having to be told what to do and being treated like an idiot for a century*. The very idea made him feel slightly queasy.

'It all sounds a bit messy,' whispered Tom, mightily glad that he wasn't an Elven prince.

'Bloody shambles, if you ask me,' sneered Uncle Cornelius. 'Queen Titania 'ad three daughters, see – *'Eartsong*, *Bloodstone*, an' *Spiritweather*. All of them married *badly*, I s'pose you'd say, an' all three of them, sadly, died in childbirth. Would 'ave broken the old Queen's 'eart, if she'd 'ave 'ad one, that is.

'*Princess 'Eartsong* (the eldest) ran off an' married our old friend 'Arry Ca-Nab, the self-styled King of *The Grabbers* (though in actual fact 'e was no more than a rogue an' a vagabond, if you ask me). An' now we know that they 'ad a daughter, 'oo, it just so turns out, 'appened to be –'

'Polly Adams!' cried Tom, quickly joining up the dots.

'That's right, son,' growled Cornelius. '*Pollyanna 'Eartsong Adamsbane Ca-Nab*, 'oo was murdered all those years ago on Clapham Common.

'Now, Princess Bloodstone, she married an Aelfradi brigand an' *goblin* renegade by the name of *Iron-Shoes*. 'E got 'is comeuppance only quite recently, so I 'eard. Got *done in* by some American paranormal investigator over in Ireland – back in '63, I think it was.'

'I think you'll find it was 1961, old chap,' corrected The Hound, languishing artistically in the back seat and staring absent-mindedly out of the window as Old Nancy bimbled along the motorway.

'Whatever. Iron-Shoes were the brother of old Raw'ead-an'-Bloody-Bones, 'oo you met this evening. Any'ow, 'fore she died, Princess Bloodstone an' Iron-Shoes 'ad a son – Edric (the snotty-nosed little git what you 'ad the great misfortune of meeting at the Ex'ibition tonight), 'oo was taken back to The 'Idden Realm as a lad, an' raised in full pomp as an Aelfradi prince.'

'And *Princess Spiritweather?*' asked Tom, utterly intrigued.

'Well, Spiritweather married outside of the "Family" so to speak,' continued Cornelius. 'An' she too gave birth to a son, the last thing that she ever did – an' a more 'orrible an' unpleasant a *goblin* never existed. Any'ow, for some reason, old Queen Titania took a shine to the nasty little brute, an' 'e, so it was said, became 'er favourite. An' everybody assumed that it would be 'e what was named as 'er 'eir. But 'e – due to 'is wicked, wicked ways – got 'isself *switched off* (thank the Gods). So that was the end of 'im (an' good riddance, if you ask me).'

'So that makes Prince Edric the only surviving heir, doesn't it? And ... therefore ... the rightful king? Right?' asked Tom, becoming more than a little confused.

'Nope,' sighed his uncle. ''Cause afore 'e got 'isself rubbed out of the picture, so to speak, Queen Titania's favourite grandchild – the 'orrible, foul creature 'oose name I can't even bring myself to say – found 'imself a wife (God alone knows 'ow) an' they 'ad a son.'

'So,' continued The Hound, 'until Queen Titania's great-grandson (Princess Spiritweather Adamsbane's grandson), is old enough to fight for *The Crown of Spring*, Prince Edric has to bide his time and try to amuse himself as best he can.'

'Don't think that 'e's very 'appy about it,' chuckled Cornelius.

'But what if this other prince doesn't want to become king? What if he doesn't want to fight for *The Crown*? Can't he just relinquish his claim?'

'Doesn't 'ave that freedom, I'm afraid,' sniffed Uncle Cornelius, sourly. 'There's all sorts of responsibilities what comes with being royalty. 'E ain't got no choice in the matter. 'E either fights – an' maybe 'e wins or maybe 'e dies – or 'e just gets executed.'

'Doesn't sound very fair to me,' huffed Tom, 'a fully grown Elf warrior versus someone who, by the sound of it, is little more than a child.'

'No it doesn't. It'll be a bloody massacre. *Murder* is what I calls it,' snarled Uncle Cornelius, as if he had a bad taste in his mouth.

'Indeed,' sighed The Hound, 'most regrettable. But what is perhaps a more pressing concern at this present moment,' he continued, changing the subject (much to Tom's chagrin), 'is this: if someone does, as poor Aelfsophia Ca-Nab implied, now know the secret whereabouts of the four *Crowns of Albion* – how did they become privilege to such delicate and secretive information? And, more importantly, what are they planning to do next?'

He tapped his ferocious talons against the glass of the window with a rippling motion.

'Dandy, did you notice that the tyre tracks left this evening (presumably by the vehicle that conveyed poor Aelfsophia to the barn) were identical to those that we found on the outskirts of Wild Park on the night of the recent were-tiger hunt?'

'Is that right?' purred Cornelius, suddenly more alert and enthusiastic than he had been.

'In which case it would seem that there is a connection between *The Society of the Wild Hunt* and whosoever murdered Aelfsophia,' hypothesised the were-hound.

'Prince Edric said that he would "*unleash the Wild Hunt*", just before he stormed out of the barn,' offered Tom. 'Perhaps the Aelfradi have something to do with all that business at Wild Park?' he suggested.

'Not their style, Tom,' said Cornelius, shaking his head. 'Besides, in Elven terms, a "Wild 'Unt" is just the name given to any raiding party made on 'umans. To top it all, it looks like *The Society of the Wild 'Unt* is running along with vampires. Not a thing that any Elf would ever do, no matter 'ow desperate or aggrieved they might feel.'

'It could be *vampire-Elves*?' suggested Tom, helpfully.

'No, I'm afraid that dog won't hunt, dear boy,' huffed The Hound, cracking the knuckles of his long, elegant and lethal fingers. 'It is impossible for Elves to become vampires. Different bloodlines, old chap.'

‘Then what about Spring-Heeled Jack?’ pressed Tom. ‘Where does he fit into all of this? If he killed Aelfsophia Ca-Nab, which seems most likely, then it must be him who wants to make himself High King of the Elves.’

‘However bizarre and improbable that may sound, Tom, it does indeed seem to be the most likely explanation,’ the were-wolfhound reflected. ‘But if so, just what is the devilish swine’s connection to *The Society of the Wild Hunt*?’

‘An’ where, an’ what, an’ ’oo, is the springy old bugger?’ sniffed Uncle Cornelius.

‘Well, whoever did drive poor Miss Ca-Nab to the barn, they were certainly aware of what they was doing,’ gurned Missus Dobbs, sagely. ‘They knew that there was a rare old gathering of the Elf tribes going on, and they knew where to find it. And they also must have known that poor Aelfsophia’s appearance and dying words of doom would travel through the Elven kingdoms, spreading mayhem and alarm, faster than wildfire,’

‘You are most worryingly correct, Missus Dobbs,’ sighed The Hound, burying his humongous nose in the upturned collar of his frock coat. ‘Our best course of action would seem to be to locate the aforementioned vehicle. It is, alas, the only real lead that we have. If we can do that, then at least we may have a chance to apprehend Aelfsophia’s killer – be it Spring-Heeled Jack or some other, as yet unknown, lunatic – and, in so doing, put a stop to this contemptible fool who would make themselves *King of the Fae World*.’

THIRTY ONE
Four Jacks & A Queen

The majority of the next week seemed to be taken up with sweeping walks in and around Brighton, visiting every garage and lock-up that they could find (checking and matching the tyre treads of any likely-looking vehicle), and generally enquiring after – and searching in vain – for the mysterious van.

It was a frustrating and futile search, but at least Tom felt like he was getting to know every nook and cranny of old Brighton Town.

Early one morning – on the following Wednesday after Ned's triumph – just as the sun was thinking about rising, Tom and Uncle Cornelius were again pounding the streets (the whiskery old chap blending into the surroundings, quite marvellously, in a yellow chequered three-piece suit), searching the garages and lock-ups in and around the Preston Circus and New England Street area.

They were just about to head back for their ritual early morning training session, when Tom noticed a large white van parked rather carelessly outside a tower block (that appeared to be home to many an aspiring artist's studio).

Here we go again, thought Tom, having investigated so many white vans in the last few days that he was becoming a bit of an expert (in both white vans and disappointment).

However, as he approached said vehicle, he became aware that, no matter how hard he tried, he couldn't quite seem to be able to read the number plate. A plate was certainly there, and it certainly had numbers written on it, but when he tried to focus on the digits they seemed to shimmer and jump around in a bizarrely unreadable fashion. The next oddity that aroused his suspicion was the natty-looking aerial (which looked as if it would be more at home on a space-shuttle) jutting from the van's roof.

'Uncle!' he hissed urgently. 'Come and have a look at this!'

Uncle Cornelius trotted over and inspected the van.

Only the driver's cabin had windows (all tinted to near blackness). Along with the driver's and passenger's doors, there was a side door and a set of back doors – all locked, and all looking exceedingly impenetrable. Uncle Cornelius put his hand on the bonnet to feel the warmth of the engine, and then jogged to the back of the vehicle and sniffed the exhaust pipe.

'Been parked 'ere for a while, by the looks of it,' he said to Tom.

The old fellow studied the doors, intently searching for a lock. Curiously, none could be seen, and so there wasn't the opportunity for the nifty set of lock-picks that Uncle Cornelius had previously used (with impressive skill, Tom had to admit) to open up suspicious-looking vans on preceding occasions.

Uncle Cornelius looked a little puzzled.

'Ain't seen nothing like this before,' he muttered, shaking his head.

The chequered old cove stole a couple of furtive glances up and down the street, to make sure that nobody was about (whiskers fluttering with an intense vigilance in the gentle morning breeze), and then pulled from his pocket a heavy and particularly nasty-looking set of knuckle-dusters – with broad, shovel-like spikes. After wrapping his yellow paisley-pattern cravat tightly around his wrist and forearm, he gave the back door of the van two sharp wallops with said *dusters*, creating a fist-sized hole next to the handle.

Cornelius removed and pocketed his "can-opener" and gave Tom a wink.

'Let's 'ave a gander, shall we?' he beamed.

The door opened smoothly.

Tom and his uncle exchanged a look bristling heavily with arching eyebrows.

'Bingo!' muttered a triumphant Cornelius.

At the back of the van was a narrow, robust-looking cage, with a set of sturdy manacles and a metal collar attached to the bars. Overlaying the cage was a fine wire-mesh. The only access to the mobile coop that Tom could see was via the side door of the van.

Tom whistled and jumped in to have a closer look.

Uncle Cornelius clambered in behind him, closed the door, and went over to inspect the cage.

'Silver,' he whispered, gently tapping the bars with a fingernail. 'Interesting.'

The only other item in the van was a large aluminium case.

Cornelius knelt down and gingerly opened it.

His eyes lit up like the nose of the poor chap in the game "Operation".

''Ello, 'ello, what 'ave we got 'ere then?' he rumbled.

And from the box he lifted: a prosthetic rubber mask of a pale-faced, carnival-style demon; a black wig, with the hair swept back into horn-like tufts; a set of gloves with sharp metal talons at the finger-tips; what looked like a jogger's water-bottle, with a long bendy straw attached, half-filled with a substance that smelt very much like paraffin; a black opera-suit with impossibly long trouser legs; a pair of three-foot long curved planks, made of fibre-glass, with buckles and a platform at the middle (that looked like you would strap a foot into them), thick rubber traction-soles (like a running shoe or a BMX bike tyre) at one end, and (presumably) knee-straps at the other.

'*Powerbocks*,' offered Tom, knowledgeably.

'You what?' frowned Uncle Cornelius, examining the bizarre contraptions with a look of concerned misgiving.

'*Powerbocks*. You strap them to your legs, like stilts, and then you can run and jump amazing distances – like a gazelle.'

'Or like a *Spring-'Eeled Jack*!' growled Uncle Cornelius.

'Good grief!' gasped Tom. 'So that means ... Spring-Heeled Jack is a fake! It's just someone dressing-up and pretending to be ... no. No, hang on a minute. Nobody could jump the kind of distances or run at the kind of speeds that we saw him move at.'

'Unless they was attached to someone, or *something*, 'oo 'ad supernatural strength,' growled his uncle.

'You mean ... someone who was ... a vampire! Of course!' cried Tom, pummelling a fist into an open palm (in the time-honoured tradition of the plucky sidekick). 'But why would a vampire, who is, after all, a kind of monster, want to dress up as another sort of monster? Do they go in for fancy dress parties much?'

Just then, they heard the soft scraping of soft shoes outside the van.

Uncle Cornelius put a finger to his lips and noiselessly shushed Tom into silence. Then, indicating to Tom that he should stay put, he got out of the van and gently closed the doors behind him.

'Morning, Gentlemen,' Tom heard his uncle say.

Tom crept as quickly and as quietly as he could to the van doors and peered through the gap.

Four large, lean and dangerous-looking *gentlemen* – all dressed from head to toe in black (like a team of crack bank robbers from a low-budget heist movie, tempted out of retirement for one last job) – were fanned out in front of his uncle. They looked very pleased indeed to see Uncle Cornelius, but not in the way that one would ever hope that other people are pleased to see you; more in the manner of a ruthless gang of loan sharks who have just caught up with a particularly elusive *customer,* who has been defaulting on his repayments and spreading rather nasty rumours about their parentage in the meanwhile.

'Wha'ever it is vat you're lookin' for, mate, you've made a *big* mistake,' purred one of their number (a tall blond with an outrageously mock Cockney accent), grinning with wicked confidence.

'Oh Dude!' chuckled another, clearly an American. '*Man*, you have just entered the arena of pain.'

'I'm sorry,' gasped Uncle Cornelius, with enquiring indignation, 'did you just call me ... a "dude"? I'm not sure that I like your implication, young man.'

The cocky American looked both amused and puzzled.

'Per'aps I should teach you some manners, son,' mused Cornelius, ''fore you get yourself into some *serious* trouble.'

'Stop 'aving a natter an' get 'old of the old git! 'Er Ladyship wants 'im. Alive, if possible,' sneered *The Mockney*.

The brash American instantly sprung forward like a coiled viper, swinging a hefty and spiteful-looking fist at Uncle Cornelius' jaw. The old fellow blocked the blow with a hard, ancient, gnarled and (Tom knew from experience) painfully pointy elbow (Tom heard the crack of fingers from where he was hiding, and couldn't help but wince) and then lashed down a hammer-blow onto the bridge of the poor lad's nose (a "chopper" to use Regency slang). Said nose exploded like a tomato being hit with a pegging mallet.

As the American stumbled backwards, one of his companions dived in with a spinning roundhouse kick aimed to the old tweedster's kidneys. Cornelius parried and pushed his attacker's leg upwards, making the dear boy hop and totter backwards, then, while the poor chap was off-balance, the sprightly old codger shifted his weight and threw an uppercut like the hammer of Thor – directed well below the belt. With a wobbly little whimper, the poor little darling dropped like a sack of pulped spuds, and lay writhing on the floor, gulping for air and delicately cupping his mashed (and undoubtedly precious) *family potatoes.*

The Mockney and his remaining companion both paused, perhaps slightly apprehensive as to their next move.

Uncle Cornelius rolled his shoulders and stretched his neck, as if warming up, shot them an encouraging wink and jauntily whistled a few bars of one of his favourite ditties ("*If It Wasn't For The 'Ouses In-between*"). He looked like he was having the time of his life.

The two remaining men-in-black wearily circled him, trying to outflank the chequered old codger.

Cornelius glided smoothly around them.

The two goons suddenly charged in, but Cornelius kept them at bay with the nimblest of footwork and a series of piston-like stiff straight punches.

As the three men circled in their deadly dance, a hand shot up from the floor and grabbed the old man's ankle. The American (nose leaking like a crushed sieve, and with one hand resembling a gaggle of wobbly sausages) clung gamely onto Cornelius' legs like a heroic scrum-half. His colleagues seized the moment and leapt in, trying to get past the whirling fists of the bewhiskered old devil. They rained in blow after blow and slowly, steadily, began to drive the old man to the floor.

Tom burst from the van and swung a *Powerbock* into the back of the knees of one of his uncle's attackers. The man swore (quite possibly in Russian), turned round and backhanded Tom across the face – sending him spinning and thudding into the side of the van. But it gave his uncle the moment that he needed. Cornelius managed to regain his footing and drove a shovel-hook into the ribs of *The Mockney* (forcing the poor boy to his knees, clutching his side and wheezing for breath) and then dropped a knife-punch into the game American's *good* wrist (causing him to holler and release his grip on Cornelius' ankle).

Just then, a sleek, grey Alfa Romeo roared into view and skidded dramatically to a halt.

'Oh, thank the good gods!' sobbed Tom, in joyous relief, his cheek red and smarting, and his eyes weeping from the force of *The Russian's* blow.

Out of the car stepped a tall, elegantly dressed (and if not beautiful then strikingly handsome) woman, who Tom didn't recognise as a member of the *Department of Special Cases*, but, at this point in the game, who cared?

'Just what is going on here?' she demanded, in a soft and musical American accent.

The combatants stopped, like a pack of shamefaced schoolboys caught (by their rather attractive deputy headmistress) fighting over a dropped penny chew outside the college tuck shop.

The tall woman lifted her arm, pointed a pistol at Uncle Cornelius, and shot him point-blank in the face.

The old man dropped like a felled ox.

'Get the brat!' she hissed furiously to the sprawling mass of henchmen. 'And I want this one alive!'

THIRTY TWO
The Brighton Boy

Tom turned and ran, faster than he had ever run in his life – even though his legs felt like jelly, he couldn't seem to breathe, and he could barely see where he was going through the torrent of tears that were streaming uncontrollably from his eyes.

Weeping hysterically to himself, he raced along the wide streets of the newly built Brighton *City* and towards Trafalgar Street and the narrow lanes of old Brighton *Town*. He could hear the sound of two sets of footsteps pounding the pavements hard behind him, but he didn't dare to look round to see who they belonged to. He guessed that it wouldn't be "*The Weeping Nut-Cupper*" nor the mashed and once swaggering American who had had the audacity to call Uncle Cornelius a "dude".

Uncle Cornelius! Uncle Cornelius! He couldn't be dead. He just couldn't! He was ... invincible.

Think, Tom!' he screamed inwardly. *Think!*

He must get back to One Punch Cottage as fast as he could. The Hound would know what to do – and then God help the evil bitch that had just shot his uncle! The thought flashed across his mind that he wasn't far away from Old Maggs' house, but he decided not to try for it. What if she wasn't in? He'd be caught like a rat in a drainpipe. Even worse, what if she was in and she was hurt trying to protect him? No, One Punch Cottage it must be.

Tom dashed through the tiny streets of The Laine (the bizarre collection of odd little streets [crammed with bizarre and odd little shops] named not after their lane-like appearance but after the old tract of land that once stood there), pelted past a plethora of *artisan* (?) coffee-houses, and then chanced a glance over his shoulder. He could see *The Mockney* pelting after him, just turning onto Upper Gardiner Street. Tom couldn't help but observe (with mounting alarm) that the henchman must be made of stern stuff indeed to be running so fast after the wallop that his uncle had just given him.

His uncle ... Uncle Cornelius!

Tom stifled a sob between the huge gulps of air that he was sucking in. He couldn't see *The Russian,* but he guessed that the callous brute would be sprinting down one of the streets that ran parallel, in an attempt to cut him off and intercept him.

Tom's lungs felt like they would burst. He knew that he couldn't run much further.

Think! Think! Think!

He stumbled to the end of Upper Gardiner Street and turned left onto North Road. In front of him was a music shop (tastefully painted bright yellow), and standing adjacent to the corners of its custardy walls were two dull-grey metal junction boxes. Tom leapt towards them and wedged himself behind the one closest to the shop window in a desperate (and probably futile) attempt to hide himself.

That was it! He had nothing left. He couldn't run anymore. Let the bastards do what they wanted with him. It didn't matter. Nothing mattered anymore!

With that thought running through his head, he chanced to look up and saw a bronze plaque mounted on the wall above him.

Embossed on it were two images of the same man – firstly dressed (shabbily) in top hat and cane, and then in the familiar pose of a well-known muscular-looking chap in tights. It read –

TOM SAYER
PUGILIST
CHAMPION OF ENGLAND
BORN 1826
PIMLICO, BRIGHTON, SUSSEX
'IT'S A MAN'S GAME -
IT TAKES A GAME MAN TO
PLAY IT'

It was as if his uncle was speaking to him.

What would dear old Uncle Cornelius have done in this situation?

He could almost hear the old codger whispering words of advice in his ear – *'Stay calm, son. Do what you know you can do. An' above all – keep thinking.'*

The Mockney spluttered around the corner, immediately saw Tom (currently hunched and cowering behind the metal junction box like a wheezing and bull-whipped dog) and slowly and menacingly made his way towards him.

'Don't worry, mate,' grinned the vile henchman, barely out of breath, but with a slight wince as he clutched his ribs. 'I ain't gonna 'urt cha.'

Of course you're not, thought Tom, as he sucked in air through gritted teeth and waited.

The instant that *The Mockney* came within arm's-length, Tom sprung forward and upward, lashing his left arm out like a rapier. *The Mockney* swatted it away, annoyed but surprised. Tom quickly shifted his weight onto his left leg and feinted a right hook to the henchman's jaw. Instinctively *The Mockney* raised his elbow and covered his head with his arm, and in that instant Tom hurled all his weight forwards onto his passing right foot and delivered a left-hand uppercut. It should, technically, have been an uppercut to the solar plexus, but, what with Tom starting his attack from a crouch and *The Mockney* being uncommonly tall, his uppercut landed in a place that would have had him instantly disqualified from any boxing ring and most probably earned him a life-long ban by the British Boxing Board of Control. It was, Tom fleetingly considered, the *Fitzsimmons Shift with knobs on.*

The Mockney crumpled to the floor like a dropped concertina – with a long, high and squeaky hiss like a punctured football. Tom resisted the brief temptation to jig about his fallen opponent, punching the air triumphantly, and, with a salute of thanks to Tom Sayers – *the Brighton Boy* (once the most celebrated Champion of the English Prize Ring) – raced off down the road along Regent Street and towards the Pavilion Gardens.

Within a few strides he heard a mutter of angry voices behind him. He looked around to see *The Russian* and the hobbling *Mockney,* hot on his heels in pursuit.

THIRTY THREE
Dr Chow's Carnival Of Curiosities

Tom hammered down Regent Street. If he could just make it across North Street then he could easily lose his pursuers in the warren of tiny twittens that made up The Lanes (sometimes called the South Lanes and not to be confused with The Laine, or North Laine, that he had just raced his way through), the oldest and most crookedy part of Brighton – the place was like a bloody maze.

By the time Tom hit the end of Regent Street, *The Russian* was only twenty paces behind him (and gaining with every stride!), with *The Mockney* (shambling along like the *Hunchback of Notre Dame* in ill-fitting Speedos) bringing up the rear.

Tom dashed down New Road and onto the lawns and gardens that surrounded the opulent edifice that is the Royal Pavilion – the former holiday home of the famously debauched Prince Regent (who would, in turn, become known the world over as the famously debauched King George IV), which was built along the lines of a Maharajah's fairy tale pleasure palace (but with all the sensitive, understated good taste and refinement that one has come to expect from members of the British monarchy).

One corner of the lawns was sectioned off by a low barrier of fencing, and home to a small circle of large and exotic-looking circus tents. Tom glimpsed an exquisitely elaborate sign that boldly proclaimed "*Dr Chow's Carnival of Curiosities*". He boldly hurdled the picket fence and launched himself through the first doorway that he could find.

It was very dark inside the tent, uncomfortably warm, and smelled strongly of jasmine. Candles flickered – their impossibly long and impossibly blue flames fluttering in an imperceptible breeze, swaying and shimmying like dancers with shimmering veils. The tent was enormously high and the floor was carpeted with thick, lush rugs, embroidered, beautifully, with dramatic and colourful scenes from Chinese folklore.

A very tall, very thin and very old Chinese man (dressed like a pantomime villain – long wispy beard and whiskers, flowing silk robes, and with a pillbox hat perched perilously on his head) sat at a small, round table, on which stood a chubby, but exquisite, green teapot.

The old man slowly turned and regarded Tom with a thoughtful expression.

'Young ... man?' he enquired (with deliberate and enormous pauses between each word). He set down the fine china teacup that he had been holding in his delicate and elegant hands – curiously elongated by the immense and tapering fingernails that clicked against the teacup like dragon's claws. 'Is there ... something that I ... can do ... for you?'

'SOME-MEN-JUST-SHOT-MY-UNCLE-AND-NOW-THEY'RE-TRYING-TO-CATCH-ME!' Tom blurted, unfathomably.

'I ... see,' frowned the old fellow, looking like he'd just received the unexpected and abysmal news from his agent that he'd failed in his recent audition for the role of Fu Manchu. 'Perhaps ... I ... can be of some ... assistance?'

The sound of harsh voices and fleet footsteps could be heard pounding menacingly towards the exotic gazebo.

The tall, thin man rolled his eyes in the direction of the fast approaching disturbance.

'Please,' he smiled, 'kindly step behind this ... screen.'

With a languid and fluid turn of his wrist, the old man indicated a divinely and intricately carved wooden dressing screen.

Tom didn't wait to be asked twice, and leapt behind it.

He crouched down behind the partition and found, much to his surprise, that he could see through it as clearly as if he was looking through glass (though when looked at from the other side the screen had been impenetrable).

The flap of the tent burst open and in stomped *The Mockney* and *The Russian*.

Tom cowered lower and held his breath.

'We're looking for a boy,' squeaked *The Mockney*, in a high-pitched and wobbly voice (still clearly feeling the effects of Tom's withering uppercut).

The old man turned and regarded the intruders with a slow and ancient unflappability.

'A ... boy?' he asked, and then he raised an eyebrow in enlightenment. 'Ah yes, I ... understand.'

Tom felt his heart sink. *Damn the doddering, spineless old git!* He was going to turn him over to the evil, murdering swine just like that! And here he was, trapped like a fart in a sleeping bag.

'Boys!' called the double-crossing tosser, gently clapping his hands. 'Oh, boys!'

Tom was about to give himself up when, just at the moment of his capitulation, two small, slim and elegant young ladies undulated in through a partition in the marquee. On closer inspection, Tom realised that they weren't girls at all but were, in fact, middle-aged men with their faces heavily made-up to look like young women.

They minced over with a feline grace and stood, hands on tilted hips, beside the old man.

'Oh *hello*,' purred one of the *lady-boys* in a hoarse, husky whisper – eyeing up the two henchmen like a hungry cat looking at a couple of caged canaries.

The other *lady-boy* pouted imperceptibly and widened his eyes as if in eager anticipation.

'These kinds of ... *boys*?' enquired the old fellow, inclining his head to one side and observing the two goons with a look of gentle fascination.

'Er ... no, mate, no,' rumbled *The Mockney*, with a look of alarm. 'Sorry to have ... er ... disturbed you ... uhm ... Bye.'

He and *The Russian* fled from the tent at an even faster pace than they had entered it.

Even evil, murderous henchmen must have their prejudices, considered Tom.

The two *lady-boys* giggled and sashayed their way back whence they came.

Tom slowly crept out from behind his hiding place and took a deep breath.

'Thank you,' he said to the tall, thin gentleman – who was standing with his arms folded and with his hands disappearing into the wide openings of his sleeves.

The old man inspected Tom, as if he was studying an abstract painting.

'It is my ... pleasure,' he replied at last. 'My name is ... Dr Chow. May I welcome you, most courteously, to my ... humble ... *Carnival of ... Curiosities*.'

'Thank you, Dr Chow, my name is Tom, but I really need to be going now,' babbled Tom, urgently.

'Ah yes. I recall that you mentioned ... that somebody had been ... shot. Your ... uncle? May I ... respectfully suggest, that it might be of some ... wisdom ... to remain here for a little while ... longer. Your ... pursuers may well still be waiting for you ... outside. It would be best, perhaps, for you to ... stay here, until we are certain ... of their ... departure. For they did not look, to me, like the sort of men who would so easily ... give up.'

He was right, thought Tom, though he hated the idea of waiting and doing nothing. But it was exactly what Uncle Cornelius would have suggested – think before you act.

His uncle. Uncle Cornelius. Tom gave a tiny sob.

'Please,' said Dr Chow, looking a little alarmed, 'have some tea. It is an old Chinese leaf. Very ... calming. Very good for the nerves.'

Dr Chow poured a cup of dark brown liquid from the chubby green teapot and handed it to Tom with a graceful little bow.

Without thinking, Tom took a gulp.

The tea was hot, sweet and delicious, and he could feel its effects working on him almost immediately.

'Please, do not think me ... rude, Master Tom. But I ... am ... wondering why a pleasant young man, such as yourself, is being chased by such ... determined and ... dangerous men ... at such an early hour on a Wednesday ... morning? And why anybody would wish to ... shoot ... your venerable ... relative?'

Tom hesitated between sips of tea. What should he say? He couldn't exactly tell the benign old codger that he and his uncle had been out looking for a van that was owned by a consortium of Faery-murdering, were-beast-hunting vampires who like to dress up as Victorian boogie-men, and that, when they had at last found them, they'd had a rare old *ding-dong,* and then a mysterious woman had pulled up in a car and shot Uncle Cornelius point-blank in the face.

Dr Chow noticed Tom's indecision and frowned.

'Perhaps,' he sighed gravely, 'it is a matter for ... the police?'

Tom took a large glug of tea, which was really rather good and going down a treat. *Yes. Yes he should contact Inspector Jones. Did they have their own office number*? he wondered. Or *did one simply phone 999 and ask for the 'Department of Special Cases'?*

'Ah! I think that I ... understand,' smiled Dr Chow – obviously mistaking Tom's tentativeness for something more sinister – and revealing a set of extremely impressive gnashers in the process. 'The police can be so – oh, how do you say? – ah yes ... *intrusive*.'

'Well actually ...' began Tom.

Dr Chow nodded back sagely and held up a finger like a gutting-knife to gently silence him.

'Since *The Fates* have thrown us ... together, may I take the opportunity to tell you ... why you find I, Dr Chow (and my ... humble ... *Carnival of Curiosities*), encamped in the fair and most invigorating ... seaside resort of Brighton? More tea?'

Tom nodded. The tea was certainly making him feel more relaxed.

Dr Chow poured him another cup.

'It has been many years since I have travelled to Europe, young Master Tom,' he purred, 'but ... circumstance has made my visit, shall we say, ... an unfortunate ... *necessity*.'

'How so?' asked Tom, noisily slurping a great mouthful of delicious cha.

'I have had *something* of ... great ... value ... taken from me. Stolen. And I must get it back, Master Tom. I must get it back.'

'Something?'

'Perhaps I should say ... *someone*.'

Dr Chow tilted his head to one side and looked intently into Tom's eyes.

Tom wondered if the old boy's hat was going to fall off.

'Some*one*?' enquired Tom.

'Her name is Su Lin, and she is ... as beautiful and as ... extraordinary as a lotus flower of the rarest shade of ... *blue*.' Dr Chow's eyebrow briefly fluttered as he nodded nonchalantly at Tom.

Tom felt the back of his neck suddenly tingling.

'She was the ... star attraction of my little travelling show. The finest interpreter of the works of ... Kate Bush in the whole of the Fujian ... Province.'

Tom carefully put his teacup down and matched the unwavering stare of Dr Chow.

'But, she was also a creature of ... two sides,' continued the old man, steadily holding Tom's gaze, 'for she could be as terrible and as ferocious ... as a ....' Dr Chow let his sentence hang in mid-air with an air of expectation.

'As a ... *tiger*?' suggested Tom.

Dr Chow smiled deeply. 'Ah,' he sighed, 'I see that we understand one another. Truly, there is no such thing ... as ... a ... coincidence.'

'Then, Dr Chow,' gasped Tom, sombrely, as the old fellow poured more tea, 'I'm really, really sorry, but I have some terrible news to tell you.'

Dr Chow looked up from the teapot and bowled a worried countenance towards Tom.

'Your friend, Su Lin, if she is who I think she is ... is ... dead,' he gulped. 'Murdered!'

'Oh!' gasped Dr Chow, his mouth a perfect circle of sorrowful surprise. He stared forlornly at the chubby green teapot for what seemed an eternity. 'That is most ... unfortunate news ... indeed,' he said at last. 'Please tell me, how it happened ... and how it is that ... you ... come to know about ... such ... calamitous events?'

'Well, she had been kidnapped by a group of ... well ... *trophy hunters*, I suppose you'd call them. My uncle and The H...er ... his friend ... were trying to stop them and save ... Su Lin, but she was shot and killed before they could rescue her. I think that the men who chased me earlier are part of the same gang who kidnapped and murdered her.'

Dr Chow stood up to his full height, and a terrible flash of anger flittered across his eyes (making Tom momentarily quail).

'It is a great pity that we did not discuss such things a few moments earlier, Tom,' he sighed, grimly, swiftly regaining his calm.

Dr Chow clicked his fingers (no easy thing when you have fingernails like a hairdresser's scissors) and, almost instantly, three muscular, short and agile young men bounded into the tent.

'May I introduce to you, Master Tom, the world famous ... *Caracal Brothers* – Bruce, Chuck and Jackie – perhaps the greatest acrobats in all of ... the Orient.'

The three handsome young chaps bowed courteously to Tom.

'Bruce,' said Mr Chow, addressing the tallest, thinnest and most muscular brother, 'we have just had a ... visit ... from two men. It is believed that they are in some way ... associated with the disappearance of ... Su Lin. Please follow them, and report to me what you find. And Bruce, please be ... discreet.'

The three brothers bowed to the old man, right fists pressed into the palms of their left hands, and then bounded purposefully out of the tent.

'Let us hope that the trail has not grown too ... cold,' said Dr Chow, with a look of kind concern. 'Please, tell me, what is the name of your uncle ... and of his ... *friend*, the *H–er*? I would wish to show them my eternal ... gratitude for their attempt to ... save Su Lin. Complimentary tickets for tonight's show, perhaps?'

Well, Uncle Cornelius is dead, thought Tom, surprisingly insensitively, *so I'm not sure how far that'll get you.*

'Let me just get this straight, Dr Chow,' frowned Tom, wanting to get things straight (if he'd got hold of the wrong end of the stick then this whole conversation could turn in a most alarming and disastrous fashion). 'Your friend, Su Lin, she was a ... *were-tiger* ... right?'

'Ah,' beamed Dr Chow, his eyes flashing like jewels. 'How refreshing ... to be able to speak so ... candidly. Yes indeed, Master Tom, Su Lin was, undeniably, a child of ... two worlds. A ... were-tigress. My rare ... and ... wonderful ... *Blue Devil*.'

'Good,' sniffed Tom, pouring himself some more tea – *Cracking stuff this leaf. Maybe I could introduce it to Missus Dobbs* – 'as long as that's all sorted and understood.'

He took a long deep swig of tea.

Dr Chow watched him intently with smiling eyes.

'Be careful, Master Tom, too much *tea* can make you most ... light-headed. It is a rare and exquisite blend, just as was my dear Su Lin. But, excuse me, please, you were about ... to ... tell me the name ... of your ... uncle and his *friend*.'

'Ah yes,' yawned Tom, nursing his teacup and rubbing his temple with his forefinger. 'Well, my uncle is ... was ... Cornelius Lyons, and –'

'No!' exclaimed Dr Chow, his face illuminated with a genuine surprise. 'Not Professor Cornelius ... 'Dandy' ... Lyons, the famous pugilist and paranormal investigator?'

'Yes, that's him!' said Tom, feeling rather pleased that the delightful Dr Chow knew of his uncle, and enjoying basking in the reflected light of the tweedy old codger's fame.

'Then his friend must be ... The Hound,' cried Dr Chow, excitedly clapping his hands together, 'The Hound Who Hunts ... Nightmares?'

Tom smiled at the old man, nodded with a knowing wink, and took a nonchalant slurp of tea.

'Oh! How ... fortunate and ... wonderful indeed,' clucked Dr Chow. 'Even in my far-distant and ... humble country ... his deeds are spoken of ... and his exploits are ... mentioned ... with a hushed awe ... and ... reverence. To think that here I sit with a ... friend of the most famous and illustrious ... were-wolf in all of ... history.'

'Were-wolf-wolfhound actually,' sniffed Tom, smugly.

'Indeed?' gasped Dr Chow, his eyes widening imperceptibly. 'I stand corrected, educated and ... enlightened. Thank you, Master Tom.'

The old man slowly sipped his tea, his eyes seemingly whirling with indecipherable thoughts.

'My *Carnival of Curiosities*,' he began again, 'is a ... home, a ... *refuge*, for those who are cursed ... (or blessed – as I prefer to say) to live in two ... bodies – the human and ... the beast. CATS!' he snapped loudly and excitedly (making Tom jump out of his skin and almost lose his teacup), clapping his fingertips together and making a reptilian clinking noise with his nails. 'I love cats. Perhaps, while we await the return of the ... world-famous Caracal Brothers, you would honour me by allowing me to ... show you ... the rest of my *Curiosities*?' he asked, enthusiastically.

Tom thought that that sounded like a capital idea, and hurriedly drained his teacup dry.

Dr Chow led him to a large tent with a circus ring within and a small stage at one end. The two "ladies" that Tom had met earlier were jiggling in graceful synchronisation on the stage, wearing matching tight-fitting silken dresses. They immediately stopped as soon as Dr Chow and Tom entered.

The old man beckoned them over.

'You have already met Mae and ... Lu – the legendary "Lady-boys of Siam",' he said, as the two *chaps* smiled and waved daintily at Tom from behind large and fluttering fans.

'Long ago,' explained Dr Chow, 'Mae and Lu were ... cursed ... by an evil sorcerer and ... turned into ... Siamese-were-cats. One day, while in cat-form, they managed to ... escape ... from the wicked old warlock and were found and rescued by a local ... charity for stray felines. Unfortunately, it was the ... policy of that organisation – undoubtedly a good practise at heart, but most unfortunate and ... distressing for my good friends ... Mae and Lu – to ... neuter their animals before ... rehoming them. Mae and Lu were ... obviously most upset and distressed by such an unforeseen and cruel turn of events. However, in every misfortune there is to be found ... happiness ... for it did wonders for their singing voices. Oh, Master Tom, you should hear their rendition of the Shirley Bassey Songbook. It is indeed the wonder of ... the age.'

Mae and Lu giggled behind their fans and broke out into an impromptu, close harmony duet of "*Diamonds Are Forever*".

Tom had to admit that it was ... loud.

Dr Chow cheerfully dismissed them with a subtle wave of his hand.

The *lads* bowed and sashayed their way back to the stage, tittering to each other behind their fluttering fans.

'Who's that?' inquired Tom, excitedly, as he pointed to what must have been just about the ugliest and scruffiest moggy that he'd ever had the misfortune to see.

The hideous creature – jet-black, with ragged battle-scarred ears, eyes like jaundiced haemorrhoids and an expression like an over-curried burp – hissed back at him with breathy indignation.

'That,' replied Dr Chow, with a kindly smile, 'is my dear friend, Mr Tickles (the eighth of his name).'

Mr Tickles, draped like a brooding turd over the seat of a wooden chair, eyed Tom suspiciously and then made a sudden bolt for the exit.

'What does *he* do?' asked Tom.

'Eats ... sleeps ... and shi– ... well, he eats and sleeps, mainly.'

So he isn't ... you know, a ...?'

'A were-cat?' the old man shook his head and smiled, 'No, Master Tom, he is not.'

Dr Chow then led Tom through the backstage exit and into a dark little chamber (a dressing room, Tom presumed) where sat a thickset, imposing man with mottled skin, blue-black hair and an impossibly square jaw. He was sitting at a small table, nursing a half-empty bottle of whisky, and playing cards by himself.

'May I introduce to you, Master Tom, Hector Antonio Sanchez Silvio – The Mighty HASS. A strong-man and ... wrestler of ... extraordinary ... abilities.'

The Mighty HASS didn't bother to look up but continued with his game in a bored, disgruntled and distracted fashion.

'Originally, Hector is from the forests of northern Argentina. He ... came to us ... due partly to his ... *other* nature (his venerable ancestors were warriors ... of the legendary and mystic *Were-Jaguar Cult*) and partly because of his ... obsession and calamitous ... misfortune at ... cards.'

The Argentinian growled a low rumble deep in the back of his throat, clearly not pleased by the turn of Dr Chow's conversation. The old man sharply clapped the back of one hand into the open palm of his other in irritation, presumably at the were-jaguar's appalling display of ill-manners.

Finally Dr Chow took Tom to meet a middle-aged lady with long and tufty hair, who, on their arrival, tilted her head awkwardly to one side. Her eyes were completely white, and Tom realised that she was totally blind.

She purred softly as Dr Chow approached.

'This is Lady Lynx, a ... were-lynx, from the northern province of Inner Mongolia. As you can see, she has, most regrettably, lost her sight, but she can see much, much further than you or I, young Master Tom. For, she can see into any man's ... future. Would you care for her to read your ... fortune, Master Tom?'

Tom, however, found that he was all of a sudden incredibly sleepy, and tried, unsuccessfully, to stifle a gigantic yawn. Dr Chow caught him by the arm as he began to sway a little uncertainly on his feet, and gently escorted him towards a rather comfy-looking armchair.

Tom was thinking that he liked Dr Chow ... a lot. He might even be his new best friend. Not that Tom had ever had a best friend before, but that didn't matter, for now he had one. His eyes felt ridiculously heavy, though, and strange little lights seemed to be dancing in the corner of his vision, and he just couldn't seem to keep his eyelids open for a moment longer.

The old man settled him gently into the armchair and laid a hand upon his shoulder like a perching bird of prey.

'It is most fortuitous indeed that we have met, Master Tom. I had intended only to return to this wet, miserable and ungrateful island to fetch back Su Lin and punish those who had taken her from me – for she was the most precious jewel in my collection. Her killers will, of course, be dealt with most severely for their disrespect, have no fear. But now that she is, regrettably, dead, what would once have seemed an impossible task – to have to try, in some way, to replace her – has become an opportunity to develop and to reach forward to newer and greater prospects. For you, Master Tom, have offered me the possibility to obtain a far, far greater prize.

'Now I will capture the legendary *Hound Who Hunts Nightmares* (the most renowned and famous were-beast in all of the known world) and I will break him and bend him to my will. And, in so doing, make him my star attraction. And you, Master Tom, will be the bait that brings him to me!'

THIRTY FOUR
Kidnapped!

Cornelius awoke with his head pounding like a halibut floundering on a sushi chef's chopping board.

He slowly opened his eyes.

Everything was excruciatingly bright.

His face hurt.

Painfully, and slowly, he sat up and took stock of his surroundings.

He was in a small room, perhaps ten foot by six foot. No windows and no door that he could see, only bright white walls, ceiling and floor. There was a small, gleaming white toilet and a bijou white sink. And he found himself to be sitting on a narrow bed made of white wood, with a pristine white blanket and a white, flat pillow.

White, white, white, white, white.

He held his head in his hands, trying to collect his thoughts and shake the fuzzy throbbing from his skull.

He thought he knew where he might be.

He'd heard the tales (who hadn't?) – of blokes who had travelled to the *Other Side*. Some had even come back. Returned and changed forever, with terrifying stories of their terrible journey. He'd seen strong men, hard men, broken by the experience. Men who'd once enjoyed active, healthy and independent lives became shattered husks of their former selves, who now sought only the solace, comfort and refuge of the alehouse and the bottle.

'Bloody 'ell!' he groaned to himself, through a fuggle of despair. 'I'm in Ikea!'

A small hatch snapped open and a faintly familiar voice chirped 'Say "cheese" mate,' and suddenly there was a bewildering flutter of blinding flashes and whirring clicks and then the hatch was snapped shut and Cornelius was alone. Alone and naked – save for his (no longer lucky) lucky blue and white striped "pirate" long johns and (matching) vest.

He lay back down on the bed and cracked his knuckles.

THIRTY FIVE
The Visitor

The Hound paced restlessly back and forth around The Study in the foulest of moods. It had been three days since he'd last seen Cornelius or Tom. There had been no word, no sightings and, on investigation, not even the slightest trace of a clue regarding their whereabouts – nor any signs or reports of a struggle that might have given some indication as to what might have happened to them. He was worried, as worried as he'd ever been. Again, he cursed himself for letting them go out on their own. He knew that he was being irrational to think so. Dandy was more than capable of taking care of himself and, over the years, had out-thought and out-fought some of the most terrifying monsters that the supernatural world had to offer. But even that knowledge was of little comfort. Dandy and Tom must be either dead or, at the very least, in serious danger.

He had spent the last two days and nights out on the streets (in dog-form) with Inspector Jones as his "escort". They had found nothing, not even the slightest of scents. The one curiosity that had presented itself was that a mysterious circus had pitched up on the Pavilion Lawns in the early hours of Wednesday morning, only to be evicted by the local council shortly before midday for not having the necessary permits. All enquiries along that line of investigation had so far led to nothing – the circus had seemingly vanished without trace.

The Hound had set a whole network into motion, all out looking for Dandy and Tom – the witches, the Pharisees, and the D.S.C., to name but a few. He had even asked the sea hag, Cutty Sark, to try to send word to Danny Blackflower, the captain of the elusive Sea Elves*, to ask for their help in finding the mysterious yacht known as "Buckleberry's Revenge", following the theory that Tom and Cornelius had been abducted by *The Society of the Wild Hunt* and were being kept, imprisoned against their will, out at sea. But the *Elves of the Sea* were hard to find, rarely ever coming onto dry land these days.

(* Of interest the Sea Elves, or *Astrai*, had been driven from their homelands and onto the oceans, many centuries ago, after a short and bloody war with the Piskie [during *the Blue Bonnet Wars of Expansion*]. The last, and decisive, encounter having been fought [and lost, by the Red Clan – as the Sea Elves were then known] at the legendary *Battle of Buckland St Mary*, in Somerset.)

The Hound had spoken to The Pook, Alberich Albi, earlier that morning. The Pharisees were diligently scouring the woods and hills searching for clues that might lead to the whereabouts of Dandy and Tom, or of the enigmatic circus. Emissaries had been sent to the hidden lands of the Aelfradi, just in case it was they who were behind the abductions. (They also needed to find out just how serious, or even committed, *The Proud* Ones really were to Prince Edric's threat of war).

He had also talked to his old friend, in depth, about the threat posed to *The* Crowns of Albion. Alberich had reassured him, rather unreassuringly, that *The Summer Crown* (the hereditary crown of the Southern Elves) was safe – tucked securely away in a biscuit tin under his bed.

Sometimes The Hound despaired. It was as if the Elves had given up the ghost, as if they couldn't be bothered anymore; knew that their days were finally coming to an end and just let everything wash over them. Maybe they didn't really believe that anyone could succeed in pulling *The Crown of Albion* together again – it was a far distant memory of their great-great-great-grandparents when a High King had last ruled over them. Perhaps, deep down, they even secretly wished that someone would try – maybe that would slow, or even stop, the long and painful decline of *The Children of the Light*.

But, The Hound couldn't help but wonder, how many creatures of the supernatural were there even left in Britain? And would it even be worthwhile having power over them? The world was changed. What could anyone hope to achieve in these days of blistering technological acceleration? The time of the "magic-folk" was, if not over, then nearing its end. Was somebody really trying to give them one last huzzah?

There was a sharp knock and Missus Dobbs stuck her head around The Study door.

'There's a ... a *lady* here to see you, Mr Hound,' she croaked, sounding alarmed, tense and surprised. 'A ... human lady. Says she has "*important information for you*", Ducky.'

'Indeed?' replied The Hound, with interest. 'And does she have a name, this ... *human lady*?'

'Calls herself *Madame Buckleberry*,' gurned Missus Dobbs.

'Does she, by God?' rumbled The Hound, running an enormous tongue over an enormous canine tooth. 'Well, keep her waiting for five minutes, Missus Dobbs, and then send her up.'

Think, think, think, thought The Hound, as he wrapped and rewrapped his red silk dressing robe tightly around him. *Don't get impatient, and don't bite her head off ... as tempting as that might be at the present time. Let her wait and let her sweat. She must be excited to be here, and she wouldn't be human if she wasn't more than a little nervous. Let her stew in her own juices for a while and then let's see what mistakes she might make.*

The Hound artfully arranged himself in his armchair, took a moment to compose himself, crossed his legs elegantly, picked up his morning newspaper, and waited.

Missus Dobbs knocked again and led in a tall, immaculately dressed, and if not beautiful then strikingly handsome woman, who smiled pleasantly to the clearly agitated House-Fairy.

The Hound busied himself with pretending to read the sports page of his broadsheet and waited for the new arrival to make the *"excuse me" cough.*

The were-hound casually glanced over the top of the newspaper and set it slowly aside.

'Ah, *Madame Buckleberry,* I presume?' he smiled, as kindly as he could manage. 'Please, take a seat,' he continued, indicating the shabby footstool.

Madame Buckleberry sat down in the armchair opposite him and smiled back.

'It is a great honour to finally meet you, sir,' she purred, in a rich, musical and refined American accent (Virginian, The Hound deduced). 'Your reputation is –'

'Of little importance,' The Hound completed, with a bored sigh.

'Oh, quite the contrary, I can assure you,' replied the American, with an easy confidence.

'You are, I assume, a descendant of Lady Jane Buckleberry?' enquired the were-hound, sticking his enormous snout through the steeple of his terrifying forefingers.

Madame Buckleberry looked a little surprised and then let out a rather delightful and breathy giggle.

'I *am* impressed, sir,' she said, with the slightest nod of her head. 'You most certainly do live up to your reputation.'

The Hound returned the slightest of dismissive gestures with his hands, as if her opinion was of no consequence to him (which it wasn't – and besides he wanted to do his best to annoy her, then perhaps she might be goaded into revealing more than she intended).

'I am rather busy at the moment, Madame Buckleberry. – Such an interesting choice of title, wouldn't you say? Did you choose it yourself? – What is it that I can do for you?'

'Well, sir,' Madame Buckleberry began, her cheeks rising a little to red, 'I believe that it is *I* who can assist *you* in retrieving something of yours that is *most* valuable.'

'Pray tell.'

'Professor Lyons.'

The Hound raised an eyebrow and suppressed the low growl that was welling at the back of his throat.

'We have him.'

'I assume that, by "we", you mean *The Society of the Wild Hunt*?'

Madame Buckleberry clapped her hands together and gave another little laugh.

'Oh, you *are* good!' she cried. 'But then I guess that Dunkerton liked to talk. City types, all the same – all flash and no pan. Let's talk business.'

'Yes let's!' he simpered. 'You have Professor Lyons, what do you want of me to get him back? And just what else do you have?' he asked, fishing for some news of Tom.

Madame Buckleberry looked a little perplexed.

'There is nothing else, sir. Is not the life of your dear friend and companion enough?'

So, they didn't have Tom, thought The Hound. That was intriguing, more than worrying, and unexpected – but one thing at a time.

'Then tell me what it is that you want? ... Excuse me, I am being *frightfully* rude, could I offer you some tea?' he asked, pleasantly.

'That would be most kind, sir,' smiled Madame Buckleberry. 'I do so love your quaint English notions of hospitality.'

The Hound might have smiled back sweetly (it was hard to tell).

'Missus Dobbs,' he called.

The House-Fairy instantly poked her head around the door (clearly having been eavesdropping all the while).

'Ah, Missus Dobbs, would you please be so kind as to fetch *Madame* Buckleberry a nice cup of tea.'

Missus Dobbs nodded and vanished to the kitchen.

'Please,' said The Hound, 'continue.'

'My business partner –' she began.

'Your *master*,' corrected The Hound.

Madame Buckleberry smiled again.

'He'll never *turn* you. You do know that, don't you?' sighed the were-hound, almost sympathetically. 'And I'm quite sure that you know the reason why,' he added, with an almost bored relish. (The Hound had absolutely no idea as to why, but it was always worth a try. All he did know was that vampires hardly ever, if at all, "*turned*" their *familiars* – no matter how much they might promise it, and no matter how loyal and hard-working the desperate, pathetic and misguided fools might be, nor, indeed, how much they might beg and wish for it. But The Hound felt it his duty to try to probe and unsettle this hateful woman as much as he possibly could.)

'– wishes to meet you in ... "*person*" ... (so to speak) ... and discuss terms,' continued Madame Buckleberry, trying her best to ignore the were-wolfhound's distractions (and doing a very good job of it).

But more importantly, The Hound noticed, she hadn't even flinched when he'd hinted at the subject of vampires.

'And how do I know that you do indeed have what you say you do?' The Hound enquired, reasonably.

Madame Buckleberry took a moment to dissect his sentence and then popped open the slender black leather briefcase that was resting on her lap, took out an A4 Manila envelope, and gingerly handed it to him.

The Hound left her with her hand outstretched, just a little beyond politeness, before taking the envelope and opening it. Out slid a photograph of Cornelius, stripped down to his stripy lucky long johns and vest (matching), and with a hefty bruise below his right eye, looking bewildered, startled and confused, and sitting on a narrow bed in what appeared to be a small white room.

'He is ... *mostly* unharmed, for now,' said Madame Buckleberry. 'As soon as he recovers from the effects of the tranquilliser he'll be right as rain ... as long as you cooperate, that is.'

'And just *who*, exactly, is it that you're working for?' asked The Hound. '*Spring-Heeled Jack*? *The King of the Wild Hunt*? Or are they, I wonder, one and the same?'

Madame Buckleberry sent a confidential pout in his direction and tutted. 'As I have already told you, sir, my business partner wishes to introduce himself to you in person.'

The Hound raised an eyebrow and tried to stare her down.

To her credit, Madame Buckleberry effortlessly held his gaze, but then, The Hound presumed, she must be quite used to dealing with all manner of monsters.

'Where?'

'St Nicholas' Graveyard. Tonight. Midnight.'

The Hound nodded thoughtfully.

'An unusual choice of location ... for a vampire,' he mused, arching an eyebrow. 'He must be very old and very powerful. And, one must assume, beyond the normal constraints of the *Council of The Twelve Families*.'

Madame Buckleberry grinned, arched an eyebrow of her own, and leaned forward.

'Oh, you have no idea,' she purred, with a proud smile. 'Now,' she continued, 'I'm sure that this is unnecessary for me to say, but I'll do it just the same, just so as we are completely clear on the matter and know *exactly* where we stand. You understand how these things work. – If there are any attempts to, shall we say ... *disrupt* the meeting, or any untoward episodes that might be intended to swing proceedings back in your favour, then I'm afraid that Professor Lyons will meet a most unfortunate, unpleasant, and painfully slow end. Do I make myself clear, Mr Hound?'

The Hound sucked his teeth, leaned back in his seat, entwined his fingers, and slowly counted to ten in his head, just to keep his temper in check.

'Absolutely,' he replied, calmly.

'There's a good boy,' smirked Madame Buckleberry.

The Hound leant slowly forward and spoke extremely softly into her ear.

'So, now that you have delivered your message, *little girl*, what makes you think that you are going to walk out of here alive?' he asked, gently.

Madame Buckleberry suppressed a petite giggle.

'Down, *Fido*,' she whispered. 'You so much as touch one hair of my head and the old fool gets it.'

'And just what makes you believe, for one moment, that you, a mere ... *messenger*, are of greater value than the ambitious plans of your ancient and ruthless master?' he asked, almost tenderly, licking his lips like the villain from the *Three Little Pigs*.

Madame Buckleberry blanched a little.

The Hound allowed himself an inward chuckle. It never failed to amuse him that the more immoral a person was, the more they were willing to believe the worst of others.

Just then, Missus Dobbs entered the room with a steaming cup of tea balanced precariously on a tray.

The Hound slowly sat back and eyed the American like lunch.

Madame Buckleberry eagerly grasped the teacup and took a huge, calming gulp.

Her eyes bulged like hard-boiled beetroots and she spluttered with a contorted grimace, spewing out a mouthful of tea, holding her throat and gagging painfully.

'Oh dear. Did it go down the wrong way?' enquired The Hound, reaching down to pick up his newspaper, his voice void of any concern whatsoever. 'Missus Dobbs, if you would be so kind as to show our ... *visitor* the way to the bathroom before escorting her from the premises.'

The moment the door was closed behind them, The Hound dashed the newspaper aside and pounced on the briefcase left by Madame Buckleberry. He held it cautiously in his hands and sniffed it intently from top to bottom, before gingerly opening it.

The case was completely empty.

Missus Dobbs came back into The Study.

'She's gone,' she said.

'Good,' snarled The Hound. 'What a truly ghastly woman.'

He set the case down and sniffed the seat that the American had been sitting in.

'Now, Missus Dobbs,' he growled, his eyes ablaze with a ferocious intensity, 'it is time, at last, to meet the despicable puppeteer of this most objectionable drama.

THIRTY SIX
We Are Siamese If You Please

Tom awoke, feeling like his head was submerged in mud. His hands were bound in front of him and he found himself to be lying on the sawdust-covered floor of what appeared to be an old-fashioned circus cage – the type used by old-school lion tamers to transport dangerous and depressed animals. He tried desperately to drag himself to his feet, but the ceiling was so low that he couldn't stand up properly and so he flopped to his knees and leant his back against the cold bars of the cage.

He felt hungry and shaky, his mouth was dryer than a sand lizard's armpit, and he had absolutely no idea as to how long he had been here (although he had vague and murky recollections of visits and muffled interrogations instigated by the villainous Dr Chow).

He caught a sudden shimmer of movement in the corner of his eye and turned to see Mae and Lu slinking gracefully towards the cage, jauntily waving and smiling at him.

'Hello, Mister Tom,' they chirped cheerfully, like two disturbingly over-glamorous chambermaids come to change the bedding at a pleasant five-star seaside B&B.

'How are we feeling today?' purred Mae.

'You look *so* much better,' added Lu, happily.

Better than what? thought Tom.

He glowered at them, trying to make himself feel brave.

Mae pushed a bowl of rice through the bars and Lu prodded an opened and battered tin of condensed milk after it. They both stood back, gaping at him like two cruel and inquisitive children let loose in the hospital wing of a monkey sanctuary.

Tom was both famished and parched but, in a futile act of defiance, made himself stay where he was and not make a move towards the proffered meal.

'Eat,' said Mae. 'Keep yourself strong.'

'Please, do not worry,' added Lu. 'Food is not drugged.'

After a brief show of reluctance, Tom hungrily reached out for the containers and ravenously snaffled them dry. The two were-cats looked on with pleasant but small grins (if they smiled too widely their make-up was in danger of cracking).

'The poor boy is thinking – "*Whatever will become of me*?"' tittered Lu to Mae in his singsong little voice, as if Tom couldn't hear or understand them.

'The poor little cub must be terribly afraid,' agreed Mae. 'Perhaps we, the world famous Lady-Boys of Siam, should rescue him?' suggested Lu.

'Please! Let me go!' pounced Tom, his voice sounding dry, frail and desperate.

'Oh, we would like nothing better than to set you free, Mister Tom,' smiled Lu.

'But we are too afraid,' confessed Mae. 'If Dr Chow were to discover that we had helped you ...'

'His anger would be too terrible, too dreadful, to even contemplate,' gulped Lu.

'We would be punished,' gasped Mae.

'And we have already risked so much,' chirped Lu.

'So much,' agreed Mae.

They both leant closer to the bars and whispered to Tom in a confidential manner.

'It was we who released Su Lin, you know,' sniffed Lu, in a conspiratorial tone.

'If he even, for one moment, suspected that it was us, then we would be killed, most unpleasantly!' hissed Mae, rolling his eyes with theatrical horror.

'You helped her escape!' cried Tom, in hushed excitement. And, bless them, now, surely, he could convince them to help him. They were on his side!

'Oh no,' sniffed Lu, 'not *escape*.'

'We sold her,' said Mae, casually.

'You what?' choked Tom, appalled.

'We sold her – the stupid little bitch,' spat Lu.

'Not so little,' sighed Mae, and they both giggled.

'Why?' Tom asked, in disgust.

Mae and Lu regarded him for a little while before answering.

'All part of our plan,' said Lu.

'Our revenge,' added Mae.

'We will kill the old fool one day, for what he did to us, and then we will set up a travelling show of our own,' continued Lu. 'An extravaganza!'

'One that is dedicated to the excellence and celebration of song, dance and music,' expanded Mae. 'No more of these vulgar *variety acts*.'

'Sooo last century,' tittered Lu.

'But to do that –' begun Mae.

'We need money,' finished Lu.

'We heard –'

'We hear many things, Mister Tom.'

'– that a foreign gentleman was looking for exotic and ferocious *beasts of two worlds* (if you comprehend our meaning) and would pay most handsomely for them,' explained Mae.

'And Su Lin was far too full of herself,' sighed Lu, bitterly.

'Thought that she was the bloody star of the show!' scowled Mae.

'Too big for her boots, that's what she was. Thinking that she was all that! Jiggling around in her bloody leather bikini!'

'And her voice was, well ...'

'Ghastly,' tutted Lu.

They both began to sing (badly) a quite extraordinary version of Kate Bush's

"Babooshka' – whilst skipping about and waving their hands like wide-eyed, over-enthusiastic veterans of the village amateur dramatics society, before falling on each other with peals of laughter.

'Truly terrible,' sniggered Mae.

'Most distressing,' agreed Lu.

'So, now we will bide our time until the hour for our revenge walks to us,' said Mae, very seriously.

'That story of his – "*There once was an evil old sorcerer" ...'* scoffed Lu, his eyes blistering with rage.

'*He* was the evil old sorcerer!' growled Mae.

'And as to the fiction about the "*stray-cat rescue charity*" ...' sobbed Lu.

'He is a big fat stinky liar!' stomped Mae.

'We wanted to be Bing and Frank!' simpered Lu.

'And now we're the bloody Andrews Sisters!' snarled Mae, angrily.

They suddenly locked arms and broke out into a cat's chorus of the Irvin Berlin classic "*Sisters*".

'Why don't you let me help you?' pleaded Tom, trying to seize the opportunity. 'I have friends who will –'

'Oh no,' tutted Mae, cutting him short with a wag of his perfectly manicured finger.

'The time is not yet ready, Mister Tom,' hissed Lu. 'Dr Chow is far too powerful. It is far too dangerous for us to make our move just yet. But things will change, in time.'

'I am afraid, Mister Tom, that you must walk the path that Fate has set you on,' sighed Mae, with a sad nod of his head.

'But if you all rebelled against him – HASS, the Caracal Brothers, Lady Lynx – he wouldn't stand a chance!' begged Tom.

'The *Carnival of Curiosities* is far too uncertain and far too divided to act so hastily,' frowned Lu, ruefully.

'Split,' agreed Mae.

'The Caracal Brothers adore Dr Chow, they would kill us like rats if we even hinted at rebellion, Mister Tom,' puffed Lu, sounding alarmed.

'And as for *Lady* Lynx, she has blindly doted on the evil old fool for decades,' growled Mae.

'She love him,' sighed Lu, gossiping through the bars.

'What about the Mighty HASS? He'd be on your side, wouldn't he?' Tom pleaded.

'Ah, the Mighty HASS,' considered Mae, shaking his head sadly and fluttering enormous false eyelashes.

'Mister HASS is on nobody's side but his own. He is, regrettably, lost, Mister Tom,' sighed Lu, with a regretful smile. 'To tell the truth, he is nothing but a sad old drunk. Though he is still dangerous. But to whom, Mister Tom? To whom?'

'Many years ago, Dr Chow win Mister HASS in a game of poker,' prattled Mae. 'Now Mister HASS is bound and tied by an invisible chain.'

'The stupid "honour-code" of the gambler. Imbecile! Now Mister HASS just drink himself into oblivion,' grimaced Lu. 'Mister HASS is too obsessed with his own troubles. He is not to be trusted.'

'We trust no one, Mister Tom.'

'But what's going to happen to me?' demanded Tom.

'Oh, who knows, Mister Tom? No one can read the future. Not even Lady Lynx – no matter what she might have you believe,' smiled Mae, with a confidential giggle.

'I think that half of the time she just make it up,' confessed Lu.

'Maybe Dr Chow turn you into a were-cat?'

'Lucky news.'

'Maybe, when you have outlived your usefulness, he just kill you?'

'Not so lucky.'

Mae clapped his hands together jovially.

'Must be going now, Mister Tom,' he said, with a little bow.

'Oh, so lovely to see you again,' cooed Lu.

And with that, they gathered up the empty bowl and the battered condensed milk tin and left Tom alone with his growing feelings of dismay, despondency and despair.

THIRTY SEVEN
The Reunion

Two hours to go before the meeting with the mysterious *King of the Wild Hunt* found The Hound squished in the back seat of the D.S.C.'s sleek, grey Alfa Romeo, and Inspector Mordecai Jones hunched anxiously in the driver's seat. They were parked halfway along St. Nicholas Road, waiting while Dame Ginty and Constable Tuggnutter checked out St Nicholas' Churchyard (situated at the far end of the street) for booby traps – magical or otherwise.

Inspector Jones stole a glance at the were-hound in the driving mirror and shook his head in an uneasy fashion.

'I do wish you'd let us stakeout the site, Mr Hound. Place a couple of officers discreetly at hand, in case of any trouble,' he said, a hint of doom hanging on his every word.

'We've already had this discussion, Mordecai,' replied The Hound, softly but firmly, 'and there is nothing more to be said on the matter. And nothing you can do to convince me that I should respond otherwise.'

'We'll be waiting for a signal, just the same,' insisted the Inspector, with a resigned and dour expression of hope.

'Do as you think best. Just make sure that you stay out of sight and in no way jeopardise the meeting. The rescue of Professor Lyons, and hopefully news regarding the plight of young Tom, depends upon me playing this completely by the book. I expect you to understand that, Inspector, and act accordingly.'

They could see Ginty and Tuggnutter heading back towards the car. Inspector Jones shunted over to the passenger's seat. St Nicholas Road was a one-way street that had a complete pavement on only one side – the other side being, predominantly, made up of the wall of a school. That being the case, they'd had to park on the 'wall-side' of the street – thus making it only possible to access and exit the car via the driver's side.

The glamorous witch and the police-Troll discreetly opened the doors and slinked into the car (well, Ginty slinked and Tuggnutter flopped next to the Inspector with all the grace of a fridge-freezer being tipped from a removal van). The Alfa Romeo groaned a little under the addition of Tuggnutter's exceptional weight. Dame Ginty squidged apologetically past and over The Hound – both of them trying to retain some level of dignity and decorum during the process.

The were-hound couldn't help but wonder why the Sussex Police Force couldn't get round to buying the D.S.C. a bigger car?

'Well?' asked Inspector Jones, with gloomy expectation. 'Did you find anything?'

'There's a complex enchantment around the whole perimeter of the graveyard,' replied Dame Ginty. 'A *Spell of Repulsion, Concealment and General Disinterest*. Anyone deciding to go for a stroll, or to cut through the graveyard, on approaching the churchyard boundaries would feel most unpleasantly *uncomfortable* and decide that they just didn't want to be there after all. And,' continued the beautiful witch, 'unless I'm very much mistaken, it was woven by the very same hand that fashioned the spell of *Binding and Repulsion* that we found up in Hollingbury Park not long ago.'

'Madame Buckleberry!' growled The Hound under his breath.

'It's a powerfully crafted hex, a little overcooked perhaps, not subtle by any means – she appears to have thrown the kitchen sink at it – but very ... *effective*,' pouted Dame Ginty, with a look of barely concealed concern directed towards the were-hound.

'How ... *American*,' muttered Inspector Jones.

Constable Tuggnutter mumbled something unintelligible.

The Hound drew a long, deep breath. There was nothing more to be gained by waiting here any longer.

'Inspector,' he said, 'if you would be so kind?'

The Inspector nodded. He and Constable Tuggnutter got out of the car. Dame Ginty crawled back over The Hound (they really hadn't thought this through very well) and stood beside the two D.S.C. officers – all of them politely studying the pavement while there was a five second cacophony of harsh crackles, pops and crunches from within the car as The Hound morphed into "dog-form".

Inspector Jones opened the door for him, and then stooped in and grabbed The Hound's baggy pantaloons and belt from the seat.

For the briefest of moments Ginty rested her hand on the great dog's head.

'Do be careful, dear,' she said.

'Come on then, Mr Hound,' sighed Inspector Jones, 'I don't like it one bit, but let's get this over with.'

And he walked beside the giant wolfhound, *escorting* him to the graveyard.

As they were approaching the Church Street entrance to the church, they saw a group of local Emos mooching along with an air of practised dissatisfaction towards the churchyard, clutching fistfuls of beer cans and cider bottles as they moseyed. On reaching the gateway, Mordecai saw them suddenly stop and look at each other a little uncertainly.

'Nah. Don't fancy this place tonight, man,' goobed their leader, looking rather pale(r). 'Boring! Let's go down the beach. Yeah?'

His friends heartily agreed that that was an absolutely first-class ticket of a proposition, and so they nonchalantly skirted the graveyard and sauntered purposely onwards towards the seafront.

As Inspector Jones and The Hound drew near St Nicholas', the Inspector was himself overwhelmed by a growing feeling of apprehension and nausea. Dame Ginty was right – there was no mistaking the strength and power of the spell.

'I need to stop here,' he grimaced, feeling more than a little queasy. 'Look after yourself, Mr Hound. We'll be waiting for you if you change your mind and you find that you do need some help. Just give us a howl or something and we'll be straight there. And, Mr Hound, ... good luck.'

The Hound looked up to Inspector Jones, gave the briefest of nuzzlings against his hand, and then entered the graveyard.

The were-hound could, of course, feel the witch's enchantment (like the glow from an over-heated lamp) – he was, after all, a creature of the supernatural – but he assumed that Buckleberry would have woven her spell in such a fashion that he would not be too greatly affected by its potency. It would, he had to admit, have been only too easy for her to collect a few of his hairs on her visit to One Punch Cottage earlier this morning (he tended not to moult much – thank the gods – but there would always be the odd shedding) and for a truly first-rate sorceress (which he had no doubt Madame Buckleberry was, despite Dame Ginty's concerns about her lack of finesse) that would be ample to craft the complex *exemption hexes* required.

The Hound made a quick sweep of the churchyard. It appeared to be completely void of anything remotely suspicious, save for a large plastic shopping bag stuffed with three long black leather coats (interesting, but in all likelihood completely innocuous), and so, after marking the bag and coats with his scent, he decided to leave them where they were.

Fully satisfied that everything was as it seemed, he sought out the furthest and darkest corner of the graveyard and, with a display of absolute mastery in the art of concealment, settled down to wait.

Since Cornelius and Tom's disappearance, The Hound had managed to knit together a few pieces of the puzzle. The strange but oddly familiar scent that he had picked up from Spring-Heeled Jack on the night that he gave chase to the fiend, he now irrevocably knew was the base smell of vampire. It had been skilfully masked – no doubt to deliberately put him off the scent (quite literally) – but he could have kicked himself for having missed it, all the same. The exact same fragrance had been on poor Aelfsophia's body on the night of her appearance at the Exhibition, and again, more clearly, on the briefcase and clothing of Madame Buckleberry when she came a-calling this morning. But if Spring-Heeled Jack was indeed somehow connected to the mysterious *Society of the Wild Hunt*, and if indeed he was some strange sort of vampire, then his behaviour was, to say the least, most baffling.

The church of St Nicholas of Myra (known locally simply as *St Nick's*) is the oldest church in Brighton. The current building dates back to the mid-fourteenth century, though there has been a church recorded on the site as far back as the Domesday Book, and local legend would have it that even before the coming of the Saxons and then the Christian Missionaries it had been an ancient Druidic site of sacred importance. (The South Saxons were supposedly the last people in England to convert to Christianity – hence the old saying *"Silly Sussex"*, which has its origins in the *Middle English* phrase *"Seely*

Sussex", which in turn was a corruption of the Anglo-Saxon word "saelig" [meaning "*holy or blessed"].* The term was applied, presumably, because of the vast number of churches to be found in the county; built en masse, no doubt, with the fervour of the last people to join the party – or, perhaps, to understand the joke.)

The churchyard was spookily beautiful by night; eerie, atmospheric and, well ... as silent as a graveyard. A line of tall trees stood patiently, in dark silhouette, against the inky grey sky. The church itself squatted like a flint-knapped toad at the top of the gently rising hill, oozing Protestant gloom, and lit, in exquisite broodiness, by four tall street lamps.

The minutes ticked by.

The Hound waited.

If anybody had entered the graveyard they might have mistaken him for a stone gargoyle that had tumbled from the church roof and been placed at rest among the sparse smattering of crumbling tombs that lay dotted about the sloping ground.

Out of the corner of his eye he caught a darting movement and watched as two large cats (Siamese?) scurried playfully across the grass to disappear behind the row of aged and unreadable gravestones that were propped, like waiting deckchairs, against the far wall.

The Hound felt secure that he had taken all the precautions that he possibly could. One Punch Cottage was at this very moment being guarded by Missus Dobbs, the mighty Bess, Sergeant Clem and the witches – Old Maggs and Cutty Sark. He was a little concerned that, having already found the cottage so easily, *The Society of the Wild Hunt* might make some sort of a raid on the premises while he was otherwise distracted (it's what he would have done in their position). The Pharisees were out guarding the hills, woods and roads, ever-watchful for any suspicious comings-and-goings, and keeping an ear to the ground for any rumblings that might be heard from The Hidden Realm.

Now it was up to him.

He wondered, once again, just who this mysterious and ambitious vampire might be? Not a member of *The Twelve Families*, he was certain. He'd made enquiries (he had his spies), and the heads and councils of *The Families* seemed totally oblivious and ignorant as to what had been going on.

Great Britain held a unique status among *The Families* (due, in part, to its recent imperial past and cultural importance), and was seen as something of neutral hunting ground by the three North American *Families* and, more directly, the two powerful clans that *ruled over* Western and Central Europe (the *Della Morte* clan holding sway over most of the Mediterranean territories, and the *Nachzehrers* lording it over most of the *Germanic* countries).

Whatever it was that was going on, it just didn't have the usual *vampire feel* about it.

Midnight.

The sky hung like a smudged and crooked watercolour. A timid, nearly full moon peeped tentatively from behind dark-grey clouds.

The Hound crackled into were-hound-form, donned his pantaloons and buckled his belt (*Strange how "nudity" was fine in dog-form, but somehow oddly uncomfortable in his human[ish]-form*) just in time to see an unusual swirl of mist seep up through the graveyard's most southerly entrance, shuffle along the path, and finally gather in a swirling cloud around the base of the tall octagonal stone pillar that stood close to the doors of the ancient church.

Like an old photograph being developed, the shape of a dapper, slender man (dressed in a knee-length, high-collared film noir-style trench coat) formed from the vapours and stood, hands in pockets, looking up at the beautifully and exquisitely crafted, aged and wind-lashed stone carvings that were just visible at the top of the monument – (four in all: one, of a pious-looking chap [presumably St Nicholas of Myra]; the next, of a saint, or angel, armed with sword and shield, stomping [with great delight] on the head of a dragon [possibly *St. George and the Dragon*, or, more probably, the *sword-angel* Michael expelling Lucifer from Heaven]; the third was of the Madonna and child; and the last image was of the same child, some thirty-three years later, being crucified).

The Hound held his breath and silently stalked up behind the elegant figure, suppressing the almost irresistible urge to leap onto the nasty little creature and shred this horrible, kidnapping monster into a thousand pieces.

But tonight was not a night for revenge.

Tonight he needed answers.

He stopped his snout inches away from the vampire's willowy neck and gently let go his breath. It was a favourite trick of his and usually did a cracking job of scaring the (un)living daylights out of anyone, human or supernatural alike.

'Ah, there you are, old boy,' chortled a cultivated, extremely engaging and pleasant voice. 'I was beginning to think that you wouldn't show.'

The vampire half-looked over his shoulder and up at The Hound, smiled and then turned round fully to reveal a handsome, charismatic face under a crown of short wavy hair and a somewhat rakish pencil-moustache.

'Would offer you my hand, old chap, but I'm not sure that I'd get it back,' he joked, with affable charm.

The Hound glowered and huffed his cheeks. This wasn't what he'd been expecting. The swine exuded decency, good taste, propriety, and an impeccable display of tailoring. God damn him!

The dapper little vampire turned back and studied the plinth again.

'I've been following your career for centuries, you know. Always knew our paths would cross ... again.'

'We've met before?' snarled The Hound. 'You will forgive me, but I have absolutely no idea who, *exactly*, you are.'

'Course you do,' chuckled the vampire, with an excited giggle. 'That ghastly *Don Juan of Frinburgh* palaver, back in ... oh, when was it now? ... 1588? ... 91?

Saw you leaping out of the bushes straight for me. Almost soiled my breeches. Was in a rare old state for weeks afterwards, let me tell you. Believe me, I couldn't look a poodle in the eye without breaking into a cold sweat for decades afterwards.

'Well, between you and me, old stick, it hadn't been the best of days. Nigh on ten years of scheming and planning down the drain, and all because of that infernal oaf Walsingham and his intrepid band of ne'er-do-wells. Bloody Puritans! You've got to laugh though, old boy, don't you? Go mad if you didn't. No, no hard feelings there, old chum. Just the way *the cookie crumbles,* as our colonial friends like to say. But as to *you* having absolutely no idea as to *who*, exactly, *I* am ... well, all I can say is, quite frankly – *good*.'

The Hound wasn't quite sure what to say.

The vampire walked backwards (the were-hound having to sidestep rather rapidly to avoid the debonair little rake backing into him), his eyes firmly focused on the plinth as he leisurely sat down on the low, coffin-shaped tomb opposite it. He looked up at The Hound, winked and playfully patted the tomb's lid, clearly proposing that the were-hound come and take a seat next to him.

The Hound looked about, and then, not really knowing how to react, sat down, towering awkwardly above the slender and stylishly elegant fellow.

'I knew you before that, though,' grinned the exasperatingly suave little bloodsucker, giving The Hound a delightfully warm and charming smile.

'You did?' gasped The Hound, annoyingly intrigued despite all his misgivings.

'I am so sorry! Where are my manners? The name is *Manfred de Warrenne. Manny* – to my friends.'

'*Mr* de Warrenne,' sniffed The Hound, stiffly.

Manfred de Warrenne chuckled.

'That's the ticket, old son,' he chortled. 'But if you really want to keep it formal, it's *Lord* Manfred de Warrenne, but I don't really abide with all that nonsense, so plain "Mr" is just fine by me,' he smirked, with pleasant good humour.

'You said that you knew me before. Where? How?' demanded the were-hound, racking his brains and feeling gallingly charmed as well as enthralled.

Manfred de Warrenne regarded him intently for a long time before he carefully answered.

'Knew your mother,' he said.

It was the last thing that The Hound had expected to hear and he gave a little choked cough in surprise.

'Grand girl she was. Bit naughty. But I loved her dearly. Hope she felt the same way.'

'I beg your pardon!'

'Well, how shall I put it, old chap, without it sounding ... insensitive?' considered de Warrenne, delicately. 'She was my ... dog ... I mean, I was her ... well, I was her *master,* I suppose you'd say. By the way, whatever happened to dear little Dindrane?'

'Errh? I ... Uhmm? You wh...? Wh...! J...Just what the deuce are you saying?'

'Look,' said de Warrenne, raising both hands in a show of placation, 'back in the day, I was running around with some of the – shall we say – "wilder" members of the Elbi aristocracy. One night, dear old Bella (that was your mum's name, by the way; bless her) ran off and must have ... well, at the risk of sounding indelicate – *coupled* with one of the Aelfradi's hunting hounds.'

The Hound was aghast to feel a tear coming to his eyes and surreptitiously swiped it away, whilst trying desperately to control his wobbling bottom lip.

'Anyway,' continued de Warrenne, pretending not to notice (*Blast his good form!* blithered The Hound, inwardly), 'a few months later, out you pop. I didn't know what to do with you; was too busy, nipple-deep in diabolical scheming, to give you a decent home or life-style – so I gave you, along with your sister, as a gift to Henry Percy, the then newly titled Earl of Northumberland.'

'My father was a Faery Hound?' hissed The Hound, totally wrong-footed.

'Suppose that goes *some way* to explaining why, when you were given the old "*chomp*" (so to speak) from that nasty little were-wolf, you ... "changed". First and only time in history that that particular little cocktail's come about, I'm guessing,' laughed de Warrenne with a shake of his head. 'Didn't turn out too bad, though, did you, by gad! Just look at you. All grown up. Extraordinary!'

The Hound ran a ferocious paw over his ferociously furrowed brow.

Lord Manfred de Warrenne patted him comfortingly on the knee and stared up again at the plinth.

The were-hound struggled to regain his composure. He was losing his focus and looking like an over-emotional idiot to boot. It was all ... well, it was all ... intolerable, is what it was!

Compose yourself, Hound! he cursed silently to himself.

'What's the fascination with the monument?' he snarled, in an attempt to swat the ball away from his own unexpected discomfort and firmly back into de Warrenne's court.

Manfred wrinkled his nose and brushed his dapper little tache with elegant and manicured forefinger and thumb.

'They do say that this is the spot where she dropped down dead,' he sighed.

'Who dropped down dead? My *Aunt Peggy,* I suppose?' sneered The Hound, sounding a little harsher than he had intended to.

The vampire looked down glumly at his exquisitely expensive handmade Italian loafers, gnawed his lower lip for a moment, and shuffled his feet.

'No,' he said at last. 'My darling lady. Edona.'

The Hound tapped his snout. This was rapidly getting a little weird.

'Do you know the story of how this church came to be built?' asked Lord Manfred de Warrenne.

'Which *particular* version?' scoffed The Hound.

The vampire stared around at the church and thoughtfully sucked his pointy teeth.

'Back in the 1300s,' he began, 'my father – the 4th Earl de Warrenne – was locked in a bitter feud with the Lord of Pevensey. One thing led to another and things came to a head, and what the tongue had started the hand would finish, as they say. (You must understand that it was a brutal and quite often foolish and childish age). Anyway, to keep things short, dear old dad and Lord Pevensey decided to sort out their differences in a grown-up, civilised manner, and so agreed to try and murder each other in a duel – up at Lewes Castle in the merry month of May, so I was told, anyway.

'By all accounts, the *old man* was getting much the worst of it and was eventually cornered by Pevensey, who was all geared to smite the life from dearest Papa with a kiss from his favourite battle axe. However, Mother was watching fretfully from the battlements and offered up a prayer to St Nicholas (she was a grand old witch was Mother, mark my word; if she hadn't have been aristocracy they would have hog-tied her to a smouldering stake quicker than Joan of Arc at the annual *Anglican Bonfire Society's* jamboree) along with the vow that if her husband was spared, their first-born son (yours truly) wouldn't marry until he had made a pilgrimage and laid St Nicholas' belt (which, for some reason, God alone knows how or why – and I always thought it better not to ask – was in my family's possession) on the *Tomb of the Blessed Virgin* in the ancient city of Byzantium.

'Would you believe it, but at that very instant Lord Pevensey lost his footing and slipped. Well, dear old Pater was on him faster than a dose of the clap, skewering his arch-rival repeatedly with his trusty sword.'

'Remarkable,' remarked The Hound.

'Indeed,' indeeded de Warrenne. 'Anyhow, twenty-one years later and there I was, desperately smitten and head-over-heels in love (as only a twenty year old Anglo-Norman noble – with land and titles beckoning, and the comforting certainty of a privileged and brilliant future waiting to drizzle from his bejewelled and noble fingers – could be) and betrothed to the gorgeous and delectable fair Lady Edona.

'On the night of the annual banquet that my father held to celebrate his victory over his bitter rival – and on this occasion a dual celebration (no pun intended) to announce my betrothal to the cracking little stunner, Edona – a ghostly and violent storm raged and seethed with a vengeance through the hall, and a spectral fire flashed like blue lightning along the tapestries. All the guests cowered and watched, in enthralled terror, as a vision of Dad's epic encounter with Lord Pevensey was replayed before their eyes.

'It was a truly remarkable show. And if I was wavering in my belief in the existence of a *higher hand*, then that little demonstration put me right back on the path of the straight and narrow, let me tell you.

'Well, my parents understood at once the significance of this strange and terrible omen. They had failed to live up to their part of the bargain, you see; for there I was, about to marry the scrumptious Lady Edona (and she was a beauty, old boy, my God, wasn't she just!) and I'd been no closer to Byzantium than the odd jousting tournament in Burgundy.

'The wedding was immediately postponed and I was hastily prepared for my quest – with the heartfelt promise that I would marry my ravishing bride-to-be on my return. And so I set sail for the fabled city of Byzantium, the once mighty capital of the Eastern Roman Empire.

'I won't bore you with the details of the journey, but I will say that when I did finally get there (after many a hair-raising adventure, let me tell you) the place was in utter turmoil. The Ottoman Turks looked set to invade and overrun the whole area at any moment, while the rest of Christendom looked on aghast and twiddled their thumbs in martial brilliance. But, more importantly than that (to my mind at least), the belt of St Nicholas had been stolen from me along the way and so I had no way to complete my family's vow.

'Not knowing what to do (couldn't really just head straight back home with my tail firmly tucked between my legs, now, could I?), I offered my services to the Emperor and helped in the slowly crumbling defence of the slowly crumbling city, while I tried to decide my next course of action. But, the thing is, I was getting dreadfully homesick and missing Edona something rotten. And so, after a few months of waging war against the Turk, I decided that I could bear it no longer and that I'd just have to go back home, face the music and make my apologies.

'And then it happened. I suppose you could say that I brought the whole wretched thing upon myself for not fulfilling the vow, but there you have it.

'His name was Alexios, of the most royal and ancient Spartan bloodline, and he was a vampire. He *turned* me. I shall spare you the grisly details, old flower, but, after months of staggering around in full vampirical confusion, I decided that I wanted to get back home to Edona more than anything else in the whole world. And so I managed to secure passage on a ship setting sail back to dear old Blighty. My plan was to get home, meet up with Edona, *turn* her, and then we could spend all eternity (quite literally) in wedded bliss.

'Oh, the innocence of youth,' snorted de Warrenne, ruefully, with a sad little chortle.

'By the time I reached the coast of England, every member of the crew was dead. (It was a long and dreary voyage back in those days, you understand, and I, in my vampiric *infancy*, was in no way able to control my "unnatural" appetites).

'Unbeknownst to me, however, my family, along with my beloved fiancée, were watching for the ship's return from this very hill; having received news of its arrival from the local fishermen. It was the seventeenth day of May ... and I can remember it as if it were yesterday.

'However, I was in a rare old pickle. Well, what was I to do, old pip? Couldn't just turn up on a ship full of blood-drained corpses (with me looking as fresh as a daisy) and claim that there had been a terrible accident. Nor could I throw the inconvenient little blighters overboard and declare that, along the way, they'd mutinied and decided to jump ship, leaving me to manfully struggle home on my tod. No, it just wasn't going to wash.'

'Tricky,' sympathized The Hound.

'Quite. So, rather brilliantly (or so I thought at the time), I decided that the best course of action was to sink the whole bloody boat; thus making it look like there were no survivors. I could swim, wade, walk to shore at my leisure, go and visit darling Edona, and then we could skip off together for a life-eternal as love-struck, undead love-birds. Wonderful!

'The only flaw in my cunning plan was that Edona, on seeing my vessel go down, and thinking that I was thus drowned and so lost to her forever, gave one sigh and sank to the ground, dead from sorrow and a broken heart.'

Manfred picked up a stone and bounced it on the path in frustration.

'Life plays cruel tricks on us all, I suppose ... even the undead,' he sniffed, with an ironic little smile to The Hound.

'Well, what can I say,' stammered The Hound, not knowing quite what to say. 'Awfully bad luck, old chap.'

'Oh, it's all water under the bridge, old fruit. Long time ago. Still miss her though ... sometimes.'

'I'm quite sure that you do, old hen. I can only begin to imagine ...' fumbled the were-hound compassionately, not quite sure how they'd reached this point in their relationship after such a brief acquaintance.

'Anyway, legend has it that Edona was buried here, where she fell. Apparently, Dad never smiled again and lived just long enough to build this church ... as a reminder, no doubt, that one should never welch on a vow.'

'Is all this true?' asked The Hound, giving de Warrenne a sideways glance.

Manfred de Warrenne gave him a cheeky wink.

'Mostly,' he replied, with a chuckle. 'Haven't been here for years. Always like to come and pay my respects, though, whenever I'm in the neighbourhood.'

'And just *when*,' enquired The Hound, '*was* the last time you were "*in the neighbourhood*"?'

Manfred scratched his chin, deep in thought. 'Must have been about 1830-something, I suppose? Amazing how the years fly by, don't you think?'

'Around the time of the *Spring-Heeled Jack sightings*, perhaps?' offered The Hound, helpfully.

'Ah,' chortled de Warrenne. 'Yes. Spring-Heeled Jack.'

'So, just what is with this Spring-Heeled Jack hokum?' growled The Hound. 'Or should I say ... *Ter-Tung-Hoppity*?'

'Oh, you *are* good,' whistled de Warrenne, clearly impressed. 'Alexandra was right.'

'Alexandra?'

'Madame Buckleberry,' said de Warrenne. 'Her family's been in my service for centuries now.'

'Lady Jane?'

'Quite. Ghastly people, really. Amazing how far you can manipulate some folk when they think you've got something that they want. Stout witches though. Very ... *useful*.'

The Hound waited expectantly.

'Right,' de Warrenne chuckled, 'Spring-Heeled Jack. Deception, that's what he's about, old cock. Misdirection.'

The were-wolfhound raised an eyebrow.

'Look, it's tough being an outlaw vampire,' began de Warrenne, 'one who's from the "Get and Set" of dear old Alexios, bless his unbeating heart.'

'Alexios, *father* and founder of the Thirteenth House?'

'Right you are, old pip. Spot on. The other *Families* despised him, you know. Jealous really. He'd always played it *clean*, so to speak. Only ever turned those who he thought would make the right sort of immortal.'

'You mean those with *royal* blood?' sneered The Hound.

De Warrenne guffawed.

'I suppose you're right. Bit of a snob. Made a few errors of judgement, to be fair. Old Vlad for instance. He was a bit of a wild card. Ho ho! Wasn't he just! Ha ha!'

The dapper little cad slapped his thigh in merriment, no doubt recalling the wild, boisterous and hilarious nights out on the tiles that he must have shared with the infamous *Impaler*.

The were-hound looked on with an expression of mild disgust.

The vampire slowly stopped laughing and regained a sombre composure.

'You're quite right. For the best really,' sniffed de Warrenne, apologetically. 'Well, as you seem very well aware, *The Families* finally declared an all-out war on Alexios and his House. Destroyed most of us, as you know. A few of us managed to get away, though, and keep our heads under the radar. Occasionally one of my "siblings-in-darkness" would turn up, get themselves noticed, and then *The Families* would unleash their assassins, or put a price on their heads. Dear old Vlad being a prime example.

'I won't lie to you, Percy – sorry, do you mind if I call you Percy? I named you after my favourite uncle, by the way; cracking chap – I'm ambitious, always have been. But it's not easy being that way inclined when all the doors to promotion and preferment are shut to you, just because of the accident of your *second birth*. Besides, nobody takes you seriously in polite undead society if you're under a thousand years old. So, what's a boy to do, I ask you?

'Keep your head down and give the rotters what for, that's what,' continued de Warrenne, answering his own question before The Hound could get in a pithy answer.

'So, *The Society of the Wild Hunt*?' frowned The Hound. 'This *King of the Wild Hunt* business is just ...?'

'Just a way for me to operate without *The Families* sitting up and getting too interested, stealing my profits, and sawing my head off. They hate the idea of any vampire making a go of it unless he's "connected".'

'And *The Crowns of Albion*?' asked The Hound, folding his arms.

'Very good, Percy,' huffed de Warrenne, clicking his tongue and genuinely taken aback. 'I am impressed. Always knew that you'd come back to bite me,' he sighed, digging an elbow into The Hound's ribs with a jaunty little chortle.

'Listen, why don't we go back to beginning of this whole imbroglio? I'm sure that you're dying to know, and it's a pleasure, a relief and a rarity for me to get the chance to talk to someone about it; especially an old chum from the good old days. I say, do you mind if we walk, old sport?'

'Not at all, old sprocket, was just going to suggest the very same thing myself,' replied The Hound, rising from his seat and looking suspiciously around the graveyard.

Let him talk, thought the were-hound. De Warrenne seemed very keen on bringing him up to speed on matters – which, The Hound considered, however intriguing, was a slightly worrying sign. When villains start letting you into their dastardly plans, it usually meant that you weren't going to be around long enough to blab about them to anyone else. But he was ready for pretty much anything.

Or so he thought.

THIRTY EIGHT
The Grabbers' Secret

The vampire and the were-wolfhound ambled leisurely, side-by-side, around the graveyard – The Hound towering over de Warrenne by at least a foot and a half (excluding ears).

'Britain has never been an easy place for vampires, you understand,' confided the bloodsucker. 'Not really the culture for us over here. What with the power of the Elves and the Goblins and the other *Magic Folk*, it's always been seen as a bit of a fallow field by most of my kind.

'I spent the first hundred years or so living like a fox in a forest full of wolves – always on my guard against the greater predators that lurked around the corner. And when Alexios was murdered by the jealous *Families*, his Get, if they could survive, just had to rub along as best they could and with what little help they could find.'

'Must have been dreadfully awkward,' sympathised The Hound.

'Well, one must muddle along, old brick, mustn't one. Anyhow, as I've already mentioned, I was hanging around with some of the wilder Aelfradi and Goblin outlaws. As I'm sure you're only too well aware, it's a very difficult process outliving everyone that you knew and cared about, and having no *family* support to boot; your old one estranged to you and long since departed, and your new one having been wiped out by their resentful, envious and supernatural rivals. I was on a pretty sticky wicket, let me tell you.'

'Oh, I can imagine,' commiserated The Hound.

'It was then that I first met a young scallywag of an Elf by the name of Harry Ca-Nab. Ha! Good old Harry!'

'Harry Ca-Nab? *The Devil's Huntsman*? Wasn't he the so-called *King of the Grabbers*?' asked The Hound, feigning ignorance.

'That's the chap,' replied de Warrenne. 'Anyway, old Harry was just about to get himself into a whole skinful of bother by eloping with Princess Heartsong, the eldest daughter of good Queen Titania – harridan ruler of the Aelfradi.

'Harry and his wife were on the run for a good few years, being chased and harried the length and breadth of the country by the Elf-Knights and Goblin Clans of Avalon. Anyhow, to cut a long story short, one night, crafty old Harry Ca-Nab came to me and begged me to help him. What he expected me to do I wasn't quite sure, for I had no great power back then (still developing, I suppose you might say) and was only tolerated by the Goblins because they thought of me as some kind of demon (which just goes to show you how uncommon vampires really were over here, back then). I was, at first, rather uncertain as to whether I should get involved with the shameful little rapscallion, when, in a fit of desperation, he told me the *secret* of *The Grabbers*.'

'That they were the descendants of Snatch-Hand Nab and his court?' suggested The Hound, hoping to wee on the vampire's parade.

'Common knowledge, Percy,' tutted de Warrenne, sounding a little disappointed. 'No, there was more.'

'I'm all ears,' growled The Hound, suddenly feeling very self-conscious about his ears; they were red ... red like a ... like a Faery-Hound's!

'When Snatch-Hand was deposed, his only daughter, Ca-Nabitha, swore revenge on the tribes of Albion and made it her life-long mission to discover the whereabouts of the four pieces of the lost and broken *Crown*: the so-called *Crowns of Albion*. Somehow, God alone knows how, she succeeded, and that dearly brought and explosive information was passed down to her descendants, in the sincerest hope that, one day, they, the Ca-Nabs, would be in a position to regain their *rightful* title of *Oberons of All Albion*.'

'And he thought that you could help him?' asked The Hound, trying to mask his disbelief.

'Quite. Harry needed money you see, and I, well, I'd come up with a cracking little scheme for making it. Quite brilliant really, if I say so myself. To wit, *The Society of the Wild Hunt* – having noticed that people seemed to have an insatiable passion for (a) watching (from a safe distance) other people try to kill each other, (b) hunting dangerous and unusual quarry, and (c) all things mystical and elitist.'

'I think that you'll find that not quite everybody is like that,' muttered The Hound, somewhat defensively.

'The ones who are in a position to do so bloody well are, let me tell you. Old money or new, it breeds a certain ... *disregard* for one's fellow being, wouldn't you say?'

The Hound declined to answer.

'Anyhow,' continued de Warrenne, 'if I agreed to help Harry regain *The Crowns*, then he, in turn, would help me set myself up in business. I didn't really believe a word of all this "*whosoever reunites The Crowns will rule over all of the magic realms of Albion*" nonsense, but Harry was full of it. Sometimes I think that he actually believed that he *was* the High Pook of the Elbi. He was a bit dotty really. Good fun though.

'Anyway, Harry's first target was *The Winter Crown* – the crown of The Gentry.'

The Hound pricked his ears.

'Old Snatch-Hand Nab had been a Gentry by birth, you know, and so Harry felt that we should start with the crown that he felt he had the most right to. Bless him. And do you know what?'

'Please, enlighten me,' yawned The Hound, trying to conceal his fascination and sound bored.

'We did it. We *did it*! We managed to steal *The Winter Crown*! It was right there, just where Harry had said it would be.'

The Hound masked a sharp intake of breath. This was explosive news indeed. Harry Ca-Nab and this extraordinary little vampire had stolen *The Winter Crown*! Unbelievable!

'We instantly set about preparing our next target – *The Summer Crown*, the crown of the Pharisees. Harry reasoned that they were probably the smallest of the Elf Tribes, so should offer the least resistance. I liked the idea; Sussex being my old stomping ground, and all that. But now it was time for Harry to fulfil his part of the bargain, and so we set into play *The Society of the Wild Hunt* – Harry nabbing fighting-men from here, there and everywhere, and I, sucking-up to the naturally depraved nature of the English aristocrat.

'We were making an absolute packet, until the harebrained little cretin brilliantly managed to kidnap a fully fledged prince of the Hapsburgs (probably the most dangerous and powerful human family on the face of the planet) and brought the full wrath of the mighty Walsingham down upon our heads!'

'Yes, I remember,' whistled The Hound, softly.

'Of course you do,' grimaced de Warrenne, with refined self-mockery. 'I barely got out of the country alive! And Harry? Harry disappeared back into obscurity – travelling the back roads and byways with his wretched ragtail party of followers and ne'er-do-wells.

'And that might just have been an end to it. I, eventually, made my way to the Americas. And there I stayed for the next hundred-odd years or so, trying to suck-out a living (if you'll pardon the expression); watching with frustration, envy and impotency as *The Families* spread across the New World like a cancer, claiming all the power and privileges that they could lay their cold clammy hands on.'

'What changed?' asked The Hound.

'Well, funny you should ask, old chap, but it was one of those innocuous little incidents that transforms everything.

'I came across an old Goblin-witch by the name of *Black Annis*, who was in self-imposed exile from the mother country. She had recently emigrated to the United States in order to avoid the relentless persecution by over-protective parents that she felt she was being subjected to. Well, you know how it is when you meet a fellow countryman, both being strangers in a strange land, and all that. She filled me in on all the gossip from back home. (As you know, news travelled so slowly back then.) The big story on everybody's lips was that The Gentry had upped sticks, abandoned Scotland, and settled in Ireland. It was, she reflected, the "mystery of the millennium", and nobody had the slightest idea as to what the daft little blighters were about.

'But I knew. By all that is unholy, I knew! Harry had actually been right all along! Unbelievable, but it was obvious: The Gentry had migrated from their native land because they had lost *The Winter Crown*. It had to be! They must have been petrified that whosoever now owned their crown would hold absolute power over them. And so, rather than kowtow to some stranger and do their bidding, they had left the ties of their native land so that they could be free. Now, that is power indeed, Percy. By the Devil's whiskers, that is power!

'I was on the next passage back to England faster than a Dachshund on a dropped dinner. I had to find Harry and make him tell me his secrets. If I could find no way to power and promotion through my own supernatural curse, then what might *I* achieve if *I* could somehow unite all of the Elbi Crowns? What if *I* could become the *High King of Albion* – with all the supernatural and delightfully venomous creatures of Britain bound to do my bidding? Then *The Families* would really have to sit up and take note. And, more importantly, I'd have a ready-made army at my back, capable of matching anything that the spiteful, vindictive and downright narrow-minded swines might send against me. I'd be safe, respected and feared. By God! But why stop at High King? I could be an emperor; lord and master of all the supernatural realms!'

I knew it, thought The Hound, trying an understanding grin, *he's bloody mad!*

'When I arrived back in England the old place had changed beyond recognition! My England, *little old England*, that was once seen as nothing more than a cultural backwater, was now the hub of a mighty and industrial empire – the greatest empire the world had ever seen; the heartbeat of the modern world.

'Anyhow, I eventually managed to catch up with old Harry Ca-Nab. That took some time, let me tell you, and when I did he was in a frightful state. His first wife, Heartsong, had died in childbirth, and his second wife had not long passed away too, after giving birth to twins. I, like the dear old friend that I was, tried to help him drown his sorrows and plied him with more and more drink, in the vain hope that he would let slip the remains of *The Grabber's* secret. But he wouldn't budge and damned *me* for a thief and a fraudster (the cheek and ingratitude of the conniving little bastard!). However, he did blunder into revealing that he had entrusted to each of his daughters the secret location of one of the remaining crowns. Three daughters – three crowns – three secrets. (Bingo, old chap! Game on, I'd say, wouldn't you?)

'We argued, Harry and I. He accused me of betraying him, abandoning him to a life of poverty, and plotting to steal *The Winter Crown* from him (which was true – the last bit at least, the ungrateful little wretch). And I ... well I'm ashamed to say it, Percy, old boy, ... but I lost my temper and made a sorry end of him.'

'You murdered Harry Ca-Nab?' said The Hound, coldly.

'And there's not a day that I don't regret it, believe me. But, as they say, it's a cut-throat business, is *Business*.'

'And with his murder I assume that you came into the possession of *The Winter Crown*?'

Manfred de Warrenne shot the were-hound a cheeky wink, accompanied with a jaunty cluck of his tongue.

'Now all that remained for me to do was to track down Harry's daughters and get the remaining pieces of the puzzle from each of them.

'But England had become an important place, and powerful eyes were watching, desperate to make their move onto the most profitable table in town; frantic to exploit the delicious possibilities of this "*New Rome*". Well, as they say – where there's money there's bloodsuckers.

'I needed to find a way to get about, to make my enquiries and do my diabolical deeds, without attracting the attention of the ever-inquisitive

Families. And then I struck upon the idea of *Ter-Tung-Hoppity* – the Faery boogeyman that legend says terrorises Elf twins.

'Before I knew it, I was a minor celebrity. *Spring-Heeled Jack* was born and entered into the annals of folklore. A little technology added to the gifts of the supernatural goes a long way, old sprout, let me tell you.'

'And so you set about harrying and pursuing the Ca-Nab sisters, murdering Pollyanna and Aelfskalska, in turn, as they revealed to you their secrets,' hypothesised The Hound. 'All the while disguised as Spring-Heeled Jack.'

'Spot on, old stick. Spot on. I chased Aelfsophia for decades, you know. Almost caught her in Cape Cod, but the dear little sprite always managed to give me the slip. Not easy to track someone down when they have the whole of the Americas to disappear into; especially when they're an Elf, a *Grabber*, and the daughter of the slippery old arch-scoundrel, Harry Ca-Nab to boot. Led me a merry dance, I can tell you. And then she finally made a bolt back to England. Why? I'm still not sure. Maybe she had a change of heart and wanted to warn old Alberich Albi and his clan? Doubt it though; they were as bitter and malicious a bunch of scallywags as I've ever had the misfortune to meet, were the Ca-Nabs, the whole oily lot of them.

'Anyway, we, *The Society* (I've kept that little old money-spinner boiling on the stove ever since I first hit America – keeps me in the [un]life-style that I've grown accustomed to), followed hot on her heels, tracked her down to Brighton and organised a *Hunt* to cover our expenses. But there was one big problem. A problem with Brighton.'

'And what, pray tell, was that?' enquired The Hound.

'You,' sniffed de Warrenne, with a sad little half-smile.

'How *inconsiderate* of me,' apologised The Hound.

'Nothing personal, just the way it is, old boy. I needed to catch Aelfsophia and perform the *Hunt*, whilst not raising the attention of the all-powerful *Families* (who are very fond of Brighton, as you very well know) and not arousing the curiosity of one of the local residents – the world famous paranormal detective, Percival T. Hound.'

'And so ...'

'And so I knew, I just knew, that if there was even a whiff of a mystery involving a supernatural celebrity to be solved, you couldn't help but be drawn to it. And thus Spring-Heeled Jack was set to work again. And there you came, like a dog to his master's (spring) heel,' chortled de Warrenne.

'So it was you that I chased the other night?' asked the were-hound, doing his best to suppress the desire to pull odious little toad's head from his shoulders.

'Good God no. That was an ... *associate*. I was far too busy organising *the Hunt*. That, and catching and *questioning* Aelfsophia. It was an absolute pleasure, I can tell you, to finally get my hands on that slippery little bitch.'

'And with the murder of poor Aelfsophia, I assume that you now know the whereabouts of the three remaining crowns?'

'I'll make a grand High King, don't you think?'

'No,' growled The Hound, with an inward leap of the heart, for he knew something that de Warrenne obviously didn't – and it was this: since the death of Queen Titania, *The Crown of Spring* (the crown of the Aelfradi) had been relocated, and only two people were privy to its whereabouts. And of this he was certain – because he was one of them.

'Oh, come on,' snagged de Warrenne, playfully. 'Something's got to be done. Is it right that the *Magic World* goes down before a barrage of inward-facing technology and human arrogance and apathy without a fight? Without a champion? Without a hero?'

'Let's be serious, de Warrenne, you're not exactly anybody's idea of a *hero*,' snorted The Hound.

'Just look at them,' sneered the vampire, ignoring the were-hound and indicating the wider world about them with a majestic sweep of his arms. 'So obsessed with their computer games, television programmes and social networking, that they can't see that something quite extraordinary, quite beautiful, is dying about them. They need to be controlled. They need to be ... (how shall we say?) ... *pruned*.'

De Warrenne stopped walking and looked The Hound in the eye.

'They wouldn't even notice, believe me. Their *reality* is so divorced from reality that they'd have no idea of what was really going on. Probably wouldn't even care if they did. Most of them are stolen from and lied to almost every day of their wretched lives – so what difference would it actually make? Wouldn't it be worth it? Just to try and stop the rot? Even slow it down a little? Tell me I'm wrong, Percival, old chum. Tell me that it's not worth fighting for.'

The Hound said nothing

'I would ask you to join me, but somehow I don't think that you'd go for it.'

'You are most correct.'

'Shame.'

'Now, if you've quite finished soliloquising, can we get down to business?' snarled The Hound, impatiently; he'd had just about enough of this odious, self-centred little rogue. 'Where is Professor Lyons and what do you want of me in order to get him back?'

De Warrenne gave a sharp little gasp.

'Yes, of course. Listen to me: here I am cracking on about all and sundry, and all you're here for is the rescue and safe return of your *dear friend*. How rude of me. Down to business it is, old sport.'

'How splendid!' huffed The Hound in exasperation. 'Professor Lyons, is he unharmed? I do hope, for your sake, *old sport*, that the answer is "yes".'

'Oh he's just *dandy*,' haw-hawed de Warrenne. 'Delightful old duffer, ain't he. We do need to keep sedating him, though, or he starts punching holes in the walls,' he offered, looking slightly apologetic.

'Just tell me what you want!' growled The Hound, losing patience and in danger of losing his temper.

'You are most correct, my dear sir. Best let's not get too chummy, shall we. We've some hard ground to cover.

'You've caused me a lot of trouble, you know, over the years,' sighed de Warrenne.

'Oh I'm frightfully sorry,' sneered The Hound.

'Oh, I don't take it personally, old rhubarb. Just the way it is, that's all. Must crack on, mustn't one,' chuckled the vampire, with jaunty keenness. 'Damned expensive business, though – this *Wild Hunt* hogwash. Last one was a bit of a disaster, as you know only too well. Two clients dead, one in prison, and the *last man standing* ... well, none too happy about the whole experience, let me tell you. Had to give the survivors a bit of a refund. Shouldn't have really, they knew the dangers when they came on-board but, well, always pays to take the lash, as they say.'

The Hound puffed in irritation. *Would this dapper little bloodsucker ever get to the point?*

'Oh, there I go again, how terribly ill-mannered of me. You must be thinking that I'm in love with the sound of my own voice.'

'Not at all,' lied the were-hound, through gritted teeth.

'Look, here's the rub: I need a bit more cash and –'

Ah! Here we go, thought The Hound, a little disappointed. *He's going to ask for a ransom. The vulgar little cad!*

'– I'd like to set up one more *Hunt*. Seems silly not to. Everything's in place, and it all feels a little bit like unfinished business, as it stands. But getting hold of exotic and dangerous supernatural creatures – the kind that rich morons will pay an absolute king's ransom to have a pop at – is not as easy as it once was. Do you know, in the past we've hunted Cave Troll, Nosferatu, were-wolf and *Bultungin*; but how, in Heaven's name, are we supposed to top a rare, blue-pelted were-tigress?'

The Hound had the uncomfortable feeling that he knew exactly how they were going to top a rare, blue-pelted were-tigress.

'And then it struck me. What could be a more exotic and thrilling experience than hunting a bona fide supernatural legend? A truly unique and terrifying creature, famed, and in some parts (I do so hate to be the one to tell you, old ticker) *detested*, throughout the Magic Realms.'

The Hound raised an eyebrow and noticed three bats fluttering across the sky and then disappear from view behind the church.

The stillness of the night was suddenly broken by what sounded like the startled squeals of a choir of alarmed Girl Scouts. Both de Warrenne and the were-wolfhound spun round to see the two (Siamese?) cats that The Hound had seen earlier, bounding up a tree and vanishing across the rooftops.

'You've made some pretty powerful (and deliciously wealthy) enemies over the last four hundred-odd years, Percy, old chum,' continued de Warrenne. 'I've made a few tentative enquiries, and they're literally queuing at the door for the chance to have a pop at you. Looks like I'm going to have to auction the "honour" to the highest bidders. You'll be delighted to know, I'm sure, that I'll be making an absolute mint.'

'So, let me get this straight: you want *me* to participate in your ghastly little game and allow myself to be *hunted* by whosoever pays *you* most handsomely for the privilege?'

De Warrenne nodded enthusiastically.

'That's the ticket, old boy. And in return I'll set Professor Lyons free – unharmed, unscathed, and no worse the wear for the experience. You have my word on it.'

'And how do I know that you'll be as good as your word?' enquired The Hound, pricking his ears at the sound of three sets of light footsteps approaching behind him.

'Percival?' sighed de Warrenne, with a slightly disappointed scold. 'What manner of monster do you think I am? I should be offended.'

The footsteps came to a halt, but The Hound didn't need to look round, for his nose had already informed him that there were three vampires standing behind him, all wearing wee-stained leather coats.

'Who knows, old stick, you might even win.'

'And what would happen then?' growled the Hound.

'Well, to be honest, it's not likely, but I thought I'd just give you the impression of hope,' chuckled the vampire, in the best of humours. 'But if you did, then I'd expect you to come after me like ... well, like a hound out of Hell,' tittered de Warrenne.

'Cornelius will track you down and kill you, you do know that don't you? He's very partial to a good stake. So why should I trust you when you say you'll let him go?'

De Warrenne looked the were-hound steadily in the eye.

'Percy, old chap, I swear, on the blessed memory of your dear mother, that no harm will come to Professor Lyons.'

The Hound scowled and rumbled a low growl deep in his throat.

'There is something else that I need to ask you about,' he said at last.

De Warrenne tilted his head inquisitively.

'Ask away, old chum.'

'When you abducted Professor Lyons there was a young boy with him, a child. What became of him?'

'Him!' choked de Warrenne, with a little guffaw. 'Oh he's a slippery little tyke, and no mistake. Tried to get him, old brick, I assure you, but I'm very sorry to say that he got clean away. We'd assumed that he'd made it back home safely to you, *mother hen*.'

The vampire licked his lips and then had the audacity to pull a concerned expression.

'I say, you mean he didn't make it back? I do hope that the little fellow's all right. Can be a frightfully perilous world out there, old stick, as well you know.'

The fearsome expression on the were-wolfhound's face made the vampire tone down his jaunty concern a trifle.

'I give you my word, Percival,' said the vampire, as solemnly as he could manage. 'We don't have him, and I have absolutely no idea as to what might have happened to him.'

The Hound looked de Warrenne firmly in the eye and then puffed out his cheeks and gave the slightest nod of his enormous snout.

De Warrenne clapped his hands in delight and then reached up and delivered a chummy slap on The Hound's shoulder.

'Good lad. That's the spirit. Always knew you would. Now then, to business. Let me introduce to you my *associates* – my *family*, my *children of darkness*, if you will.'

The Hound turned around to face the newly arrived vampires, who were standing (at a respectable distance) behind him. All three were garbed in long black coats that reeked, quite nauseatingly, of fresh wolfhound pee (and looking none too happy about it), and had all, quite obviously, dressed in some hurry after their entrance and transformation from bat-form.

'Prince Opchanacanough,' smiled de Warrenne, proudly, 'great hunter-warrior of the Powhatan Confederacy, and my eldest surviving "child"...'

The middle of the three vampires, a tall, well-proportioned fellow with a sour expression, gave The Hound a slight nod of his head.

'Okomto – priest-prince of the mighty Ashanti nation.'

The slender African vampire smiled broadly, showing his long canine teeth.

'And my youngest – the *Maharajah-in-perpetual-waiting* – Ajit Singh.'

A young, fierce-looking vampire, with ferocious black eyes and an even more ferocious black beard and whiskers, dipped his head and lightly touched his hands together.

'I'm afraid I lied, old fruit: I am a bit of a snob, after all. One thing about dear old Alexios' *Get and Set* (no matter how detested we might be) is that we only turn royalty: only recruit the best of the best, so to speak. No wonder the other *Families* hate us – indiscriminating and dreary little fuckers that they are.'

The Hound weighed up whether he could take on four vampires at once, but thought better of it. Besides, the act needed to be played to its bitter end.

'As I'm sure that you are aware, Percy, old chum, the next full moon is only a couple of days away. Until then, I'm afraid that I'm going to have to ask that you be our guest, old bean. I'm awfully sorry to insist, but if you wouldn't mind, we need to put a little ... *gadget* ... in you – just to make sure that we can keep you in your place. If you'll allow?'

The Hound gave a low, menacing growl and scowled at each of the four vampires in turn (one smiling a jaunty little smile and the other three looking more than a little uncomfortable – obviously aware of who was going to be doing the "putting").

'Don't worry, it won't hurt, you big old baby, and you'll barely notice that it's there. I do hate to insist, but I'm afraid that it is a condition of Professor Lyons' continued safety,' smiled de Warrenne, apologetically.

Prince Okomto stepped gingerly forward, pulling a long syringe-type contraption from his coat pocket and waving it in front of the were-hound's face.

'If you would be so kind as to turn around, sir,' he said, in a high-pitched, singsong voice.

The Hound gave the approaching vampire his most baleful glower and had the small satisfaction of seeing him blanch.

'All right, do what you must,' he said, looming over and fixing de Warrenne with his most penetrating stare. 'But I have a little condition of my own, de Warrenne,'

It was the dapper little vampire's turn to raise an eyebrow.

'And what, pray tell, is that, old sport?'

'While your nasty little *associate* here inserts his nasty little implant, you'll place your nasty little arm in my mouth.' said The Hound, curtly. 'Sorry to insist, *old brick*, but it's a condition of my cooperation.'

De Warrenne hesitated.

'Or you could, I suppose,' offered The Hound, trying to sound as gentle and reasonable as possible, 'try to do it by force.'

De Warrenne burst out into a giggling laughter and slapped his thigh.

'Oh, all right then,' he guffawed. 'Let's get it over with, you big untrusting lump.'

And with that he placed his arm between the were-hound's massive jaws while Prince Okomto injected the tiny binding device into the nape of The Hound's neck.

'Splendid,' cried de Warrenne, wiping the saliva from his coat sleeve onto the African's jacket. 'Now that all that *unpleasantness* is over with, let's crack on, shall we?'

'Your chariot awaits you, sir,' smiled Okomto, indicating a large white van that had pulled up outside of the churchyard's north-westerly entrance.

The Hound looked hard at de Warrenne, whilst quickly mulling over the evening's extraordinary events. At least Cornelius seemed to be safe, for the moment – though he was sure that these scoundrels were not to be trusted for one minute. But if there was even a hint of an opening or opportunity for escape, then he knew that Dandy would take it. And if he had to risk his life for the slightest hope of helping his friend, then he would do it, a thousandfold. For him; for Dandy.

But what worried him most was Tom.

If these wretched blighters didn't have him, then just what had happened to the lad? And where the devil was he?

The Hound looked away from the vampires and towards St Nicholas Road, and briefly wondered if he should give a signal for Inspector Jones to act upon.

De Warrenne seemed to read his thoughts.

'Oh, don't worry about your chums in the car, old chap. They've been suitably ... *distracted.*'

And with that, the were-wolfhound was politely escorted to the van, invited to take his place in a shallow, sturdy cell in the back (the silver-coated bars stinging his skin like nettles at the touch) and driven away into the stillness of the night.

THIRTY NINE
Hoodwinked

It was almost four in the morning.

Dame Ginty unstitched the last of the spells from around the graveyard and beckoned Inspector Jones forward.

The Inspector, with Ginty and Constable Tuggnutter hot on his heels, dashed into the churchyard and looked around.

It was empty.

Of course it was.

Mordecai swore inwardly and angrily slapped a tomb with the palm of his hand.

They had been hoodwinked.

Inspector Jones had had no intention of following The Hound's orders. Not out of any disrespect for his friend, or a belief that his call of judgement was in any way impaired (he held the were-hound in the very highest esteem), but because he was not the sort of man who could just sit about and do nothing while a dear friend put themselves in peril.

He had intended to give The Hound an hour or so to get himself settled, and then planned for himself and Tuggnutter to discreetly follow and position themselves at a vantage point from where they could pounce at the first whiff of trouble. But it was not to be. Within twenty minutes of walking back to the car, a large dustcart had pulled up and shuddered to a halt beside them. The driver, a tall blond man, had jumped from the lorry and apologised (in an outrageously affected Cockney accent), telling them that they'd only be a few minutes.

Jones had thought little of it, had even joked with Dame Parsons about Brighton Council's bewildering policy of refuse collection. And then, after half an hour had elapsed, came to the awful realisation that the dustcart had been abandoned and that they were now completely trapped within the car – boxed in by the cars parked in front and behind them, the driver's side doors blocked by the lorry, and the passenger's side by the wall of the school. Their police-radio wasn't working and, infuriatingly, none of their mobile phones had any reception. It was only after a police car had turned up to investigate a parking violation (reported by one of the street's irate residents) that they had been finally able to get the truck towed and found the signal-jamming device jammed onto the roof of the Alfa.

Constable Tuggnutter trotted over towards him, carrying a pee-reeking plastic shopping bag at arms'-length.

Inspector Jones kicked a gravestone in frustration.

'We've lost him!' he cursed.

FORTY
Courage & Shuffle The Cards

'I do so enjoy our little ... chats,' purred Dr Chow, gracefully lifting a teacup and saucer with both hands and taking an elegant sip. 'They have been so ... enlightening.'

Tom sat with his back pressed against the bars of his cage, scowling with impotent and fuddled fury at the complete assembly of the diabolic (and decidedly feline) cast of the *Carnival of Curiosity*: Dr Chow (in his long silk robes and perilously positioned pillbox hat); the Lady-boys of Siam – Mae and Lu (smiling sweetly at him, as if they'd just popped by to visit a favourite nephew); The Caracal Brothers – Bruce, Chuck and Jackie (in were-caracal form – five feet tall, lithe and muscular, with sand-coloured fur, golden eyes, huge moth-like tufty ears, long tails, and claws like syringe needles); Lady Lynx – staring blindly towards him, her head ever so slightly tilted to one side; and the Mighty HASS – transformed into something resembling a were-cat (but more man-like than cat-like), with massive canine teeth protruding from his upper lip and hanging down towards his impossibly square and softly-whiskered jaw, colossal forearms, hands (currently clutching a half-empty whisky bottle) with talons like razors, and the patches on his mottled skin somehow more pronounced. Even the repulsive Mr Tickles was to be seen, prowling in the distance like the spectre of a damp fart, glowering at Tom accusingly, and hissing like a vexed viper trapped inside a moth-eaten vintage stole.

Dr Chow took another dainty sip from his teacup.

'I have learnt so much, Master Tom, I must thank you. You have educated me beyond my deepest ... expectations: the venerable Hound, Professor Lyons, *The Society of the Wild Hunt*, vampires, and, most intriguing of all, *The Crowns of Albion*.'

He supped his tea, his lion-like eyes never leaving Tom's.

Tom looked at the teacup nestled in Dr Chow's talonous hands and licked his lips.

Dr Chow slowly shook his head.

'So sorry, Master Tom, but there will be no more tea for you. You have become, regrettably, too ... dependent.'

Tom lifted his head and looked out at the sea of feline faces – watching him like he was an overweight and sweaty gerbil who'd just managed to haul himself out of a bucket of fresh catnip – and felt an overwhelming mixture of fear, disgust and loathing.

'The question to be answered, however, is this: *what is to be ... done ... with you*, Master Tom? Should I ... let you go?' The old sorcerer lightly rippled his nails on the edge of his saucer, making a strange music of chiming clicks and tinkles. 'Or, perhaps, you would be of more ... use ... if I turned you into a ... were-cat?' he considered.

'A Tom-cat,' sniggered Lu.

'A ginger Tom,' chortled Mae.

The Lady-boys giggled.

The old man silenced them with a flash of his hand.

'Or have you reached the end of your ... usefulness? Are you simply ... a loose thread that must be ... snipped?'

Dr Chow set down his teacup and saucer on a little round table and deftly patted his moustache dry with the cuff of his enormous sleeve.

There was a hushed and expectant silence – from both sides of the bars.

Tom's heart pounded in his throat and he struggled against the desperate urge to throw up.

'Lady Lynx,' said the wicked old sorcerer, 'would you be so kind as to look into Tom's future and tell me what you ... see.'

The blind cat-woman teetered slowly towards the cage and seemed to regard Tom for an eternity, her head tilted to one side as if she could hear Tom's heart pounding from the other side of the cage.

'His future, like his past,' she said at last, purring in a voice like gurgled honey, 'is steeped in the bloodshed of others.'

'That's a lie!' hissed Tom, lurching forward and grabbing the bars of his cage.

'I have heard it said,' sighed Dr Chow, coldly, and staring Tom into silence, 'that a man's future is written on his forehead ... for all to see ... but himself.'

'Great power could be his,' continued Lady Lynx, tipping her head to the other side, 'but that path is ... blind to him.'

She smiled, turned and bowed to Mr Chow, and then tottered back to her place.

Dr Chow wrapped one side of his long, drooping moustache around the prodigious length of the nail of his little finger and considered.

'Perhaps it is indeed wisest,' he mused, 'to kill the tiger when it is still but a ... cub?'

For some reason Tom looked to Lu and Mae (as if they could or would lift a finger to help him!).

The Lady-boys looked away.

'I have learnt much from you, Master Tom, it is true. But I have other, more trusted methods of gathering information.'

His eyes cast the briefest of flickers towards the Lady-boys, who purred in appreciation.

'Would you like to know what I have ... discovered, Master Tom?'

Tom glowered back, rebelliously silent but intrigued.

'I have learnt the secret location of the base of operations of this ... deplorable ... *Society of the Wild ... Hunt*. Your uncle, you will no doubt be delighted to hear, is very much alive. Alive ... but a prisoner of the despicable *Wild Huntsmen*.'

Tom almost cried. Uncle Cornelius was alive!

'Did you know that they have also captured your friend ... The Hound Who Hunts Nightmares ... and intend for him to be the quarry in their next vile game? Such a ... waste, don't you think? So ... barbaric.'

The hideous old man watched Tom, like a crocodile eyeing a wounded duckling flapping on the water.

Tom tried to blink away the tears that somehow seemed to be stuck in his eyelashes. This was terrible news. Could it get any worse? Uncle Cornelius and now The Hound! Both captured by the sinister and deadly *Society of the Wild Hunt*. And here he was, helpless and imprisoned by this horrible old man and his circus of feline unpleasantnesses. It was, Tom reflected with utmost concern, what The Hound might have described as an *extremely sticky wicket*.

'What do you intend to do?' he asked, his voice sounding strangely hoarse and distant.

'A very good ... question, Master Tom. What indeed?'

Dr Chow regarded Tom intently and stroked his wispy beard.

'Mae. Lu,' he said at last.

The Lady-boys of Siam snapped to attention.

'You will stay here with Lady Lynx and strike camp as darkness falls. We must be ready to move by the morning.'

'Awww!' huffed Mae and Lu, stomping the ground like rebellious toddlers. 'Why do we always have to do the donkey work?'

'SILENCE!' roared Dr Chow.

The whole room flinched.

Mae and Lu cowered, and bowed their heads repeatedly.

'Bruce, Chuck, Jackie, you will come with me,' the old sorcerer continued, cunningly. 'We will hunt the hunters of the hunted.'

'Eh?' gurned Chuck.

'He means, that we will track down and kill the huntsmen who are hunting the were-dog, you stupid fool!' explained Jackie to his older, and dimmer, brother.

'But we must be careful,' warned Dr Chow. 'Even the lion must beware the hyena when he goes to steal its kill. Once we have ... *rescued* ... The Hound, we will turn our attention fully to the punishment and destruction of *The Society of the Wild Hunt* ... for the shame and ... dishonour ... that they have brought to us. And when they have been ... dealt with ... we shall seek out *The Crowns of Albion* ... and *I* shall become the Lord of the Magic Folk of this tiny, but curiously ... potent, island. And they shall love me, Master Tom, for I shall make them great again.'

'And what about me?' came a voice like warm urine bouncing off a frozen tombstone on a frostbitten winter's morning.

All eyes turned to look at the Mighty HASS, who stood at the back of the tent nursing a three-quarter-empty bottle of whisky.

'Tonight, Mr HASS, you will escort Master Tom to the heart of the woods – So delightful at this time of year, don't you think? No? – and there, Mr HASS, you will ... devour him.'

The Mighty HASS laughed, drained the whisky bottle dry and sent it smashing to the floor as he strode from the tent.

Dr Chow sighed and rolled his eyes in despair.

'Goodbye, Master Tom,' he said, approaching the cage and considering Tom with an almost reptilian curiosity. 'It has been an ... honour.'

He made a low bow and then turned and glided from the tent, followed by the tottering Lady Lynx and the bounding Caracal Brothers.

Lu and Mae peered through the bars of Tom's cage with eyes like excited owls.

'Help me,' pleaded Tom. 'Please!'

'So sorry, Mister Tom,' said Lu.

'What can we do?' shrugged Mae.

'Let me go?'

Lu licked his lips.

'Such a waste,' he sobbed.

'So lovely,' sniffled Mae.

'So plucky.'

'It is a most unfortunate end, Mister Tom,' commiserated Mae.

'But you are so very brave, Mister Tom,' sniffed Lu, cheerfully. 'Everybody say so.'

Well that's all frickin' right then, isn't it!! thought Tom, but he did his best to hide his anger.

'The Mighty HASS, he say, he will take your courage and add it to his own.'

'Well,' considered Mae, 'it is a sad fact that most of The Mighty HASS's courage comes from a bottle, so that is no bad thing.'

'Dutch courage,' agreed Lu, regrettably.

'What are you talking about?' hissed Tom.

'The Mighty HASS like nothing better than to eat the still-beating hearts of his victims ...' began Lu.

'... while they look on,' completed Mae, a constant source of comfort. 'It is the very last thing in their poor, sad, miserable lives that they will ever see.'

'The Mighty HASS chomping on their pumping organ.'

They both tittered.

'A most peculiar preference.'

'He say – *it is tradition*.'

'He say – *it make him strong*.'

'But we say – it just give him indigestion.'

They burst out into uncontrollable peals of laughter that made Tom feel even sicker, if that was possible.

He watched the Lady-boys slink, arm in arm, from the tent.

Only when he was sure that they had gone did he sink his head into his hands and weep.

FORTY ONE
The Wild Hunt

The Hound awoke to find himself lying, sprawled facedown, in the middle of Hollingbury Ring. His head was fuzzy. He staggered unsteadily to his feet. The moon, full and glorious in Her brilliance, dominated the night sky, and the kiss of Her luminosity began to clear his head and free his body from the tranquillisers (and/or spells) that had been used to sedate him. He was, after all, one of Her *children*, and at Her greatest moments of splendour he felt his powers heightened to their full potential.

He had been held for the last few days far out to sea (presumably on the elusive and aptly named 'Buckleberry's Revenge'), confined in a small cabin whose walls were lined with silver. (*Was there no exhaustion to this dastardly delinquent's despicable wealth?*). The Hound had to wonder just how much power and riches it would take to make de Warrenne a satisfied and contented little parasite. But he knew, in his heart, that it wasn't money or power that drove Lord Manfred de Warrenne. It was the desire for the respect and admiration of his peers. He simply thought himself as good a vampire as any of the so-called *Elders,* and could never rest until he had proved it. A little bloodsucker with a big chip on his shoulder. Perhaps, having messed up so tragically in "life", he felt the undying need to prove that his "un-life" was not going to be an equally abject failure?

The first thing that The Hound needed to do was to check the boundaries of the "hunting arena" and test the strength of the walls of his new cage. It was going to hurt, of that much he was sure.

As he approached the limits of the enclosure he could feel the back of his neck tingling. He forced himself to take another step forward, and almost collapsed under the savage pain that slashed through his body like a set of red-hot razor blades. He leapt back, snarling with anger, frustration and pain.

The were-hound took a moment to get his bearings. One thing that was firmly in his favour was that he knew these woods like the back of his hand/paw, had been strolling and hunting in them, on and off, for the past eighty-odd years or so. But were *his* hunters already here? And if not, how long did he have until they arrived? And just who the blazes was he up against?

Over the centuries he had made more than his fair share of enemies, it was true; had ruined the villainous plot of many a supposed master criminal (supernatural and otherwise). It was almost flattering to try to guess who was prepared to pay a small fortune and risk their lives in order to even up the old scoreboard.

Instinctively, he made his way towards the dew pond. It was going to be a long night and he desperately needed to drink. His mouth felt like the inside of one of Cornelius' socks. (*Ah, dear old Dandy. Would he ever be able to surreptitiously riffle through the old fellow's laundry basket again?*) 'Come now,' he chastised himself, harshly. There was no need, nor time, to get maudlin. All that was really necessary was for him to keep out of sight for the night, stay alive, and wait for an opportunity for escape to present itself.

But what might happen if he did remain undetected? Would the hunt be continued the next night? And then the next? Over and over again, until he was finally caught and murdered? Would he become like a champion pug in de Warrenne's grotesque carnival boxing booth – taking on all comers and earning the dapper little swine a fortune, until the inevitable night of his downfall inevitably came?

It was a full moon – surely that would mean something to his friends? Surely The Pook and the Pharisees would be on the lookout, watching over their beloved and sacred grounds? They must be aware that something *untoward* was going on.

But if de Warrenne had been telling the truth, and he did know the whereabouts and locations of all of *The Crowns of Albion*, then, quite terrifyingly, he knew where *The Summer Crown* was being held.

Manfred was a cunning little coyote of a vampire. His whole operation was based on disguise and misdirection – like a conjuror or a cardsharp at a gaming table. Perhaps while this beastly and degrading spectacle was taking place, de Warrenne and his vile crew of the damned were already seeking out the treasure of the Pharisees.

The thought filled him with a chilly resolve.

He took one last mouthful of clayey water before melting like a shadow into the woods.

The Mighty HASS held Tom firmly by the wrist and hauled him from the *Carnival of Curiosities'* camp and into the dense woodland that surrounded it.

Tom tried not to yelp in pain as he felt his arm almost jerked from its socket by the miffed and scowling man-cat.

He turned to look back at the tents, but he could see no sign of the encampment. It was as if it just wasn't there. (Tom had absolutely no idea where "there" even was, but wherever "there" was ... it wasn't there anymore.)

While incarcerated, his pockets had been emptied and he had lost his ear-shaped eye-stone – not that he'd have had the chance to use it, but even so, he felt a strange curiosity to know exactly where it was that he had been imprisoned. Not that it mattered, he supposed. In a few minutes, maybe seconds, he would be dead.

Despite all his intentions to face his end stoically, he couldn't help but heave a little sob.

The Mighty HASS spun round and sneered at him.

'What is it, Little Cub?' he smiled cruelly, the stench of his booze-soaked breath hitting Tom's nose like an over-zealously vinegared chip.

Tom spat in the man-cat's face. The were-jaguar twisted Tom's wrist, locking his arm at the elbow and threatening to break it like a twig.

‘Do not play me so,’ growled HASS softly into Tom’s ear, and Tom could feel the words rumbling through his bones like the thundering of a distant train.

‘Let me go!’ he hissed fiercely, his eyes streaming (both from the pain in his elbow and from the whisky fumes emanating from the were-jaguar’s rancid breath).

‘Bah!’ The Mighty HASS released him and shoved him dismissively to the ground.

‘Look at me, Little Cub,’ he said, glowering down at Tom. ‘I was once the greatest wrestler in all of the Americas – now see what has become of me. Look at me! Here I am; nothing more than a sadistic old conjuror’s hired killer. It is a sad end, Little Cub, for both of us. But I will honour you as best I can. I will eat your heart as it still beats, and then you will be with me forever. It is the best that I can do for you. Believe me.’

He dragged Tom to his feet and pulled him deeper and deeper into the wild woods.

The Hound quickly came to his favourite part of Hollingbury Woods – The *Migrating Forest (as* he liked to call it).

When the *Great Storm* had struck (back in 1987) the hurricane had hit with such force that you could still trace the path of destruction caused by the tempest. A line of ancient trees lay on their sides, as if flattened by an enormous bowling ball – all miraculously still alive. Now, surrounded by young trees and saplings, it looked as if the elders of the forest had decided to leave; to head away from the uncaring and lethal approach of man and hide themselves deeper inland. And so they stretched, arching and rippling like strange and wondrous sea creatures ploughing through an ocean of moss and knee-deep grasses.

The Hound softly hurdled the first line of fallen trunks and lost himself within the comfort and sanctuary of the undergrowth.

By chance, he came to a crouching rest not far from a still warm and steaming pile of fox poo. It was, perhaps, a small and unexpected pleasure, but it was also one of great use in his current predicament, and so he took the opportunity to roll in it with gay abandon.

The were-hound was just contemplating whether or not to shift into ‘dog-form’, when he picked up a vaguely familiar scent and then, almost immediately, caught the slightest of movements from the corner of his eye.

High up in one of the still-standing older trees was a large dark shape, far too big to be a bird’s nest.

With supernatural stealth, he crept towards the base of an adjacent trunk in order to get a better view.

Perched on a slender platform was a man, a human, dressed from head to toe in black, save for his face. He was dark-skinned, and what The Hound had first mistaken for a stripe of war paint across his nose was, in fact, a large plaster. On closer examination both of the man’s eyes looked slightly puffy, and The Hound deduced that he must have been punched really hard in the face quite recently and had his nose broken. Both wrists and one hand were also bandaged, leaving only the thumb and forefinger free. But that was all that was needed for the hunter to pull the trigger of the powerful-looking crossbow that was nestled in the crook of his arm.

The Hound tiptoed to the base of the *hunter's* tree.

The *hunter* stiffened and The Hound heard him sniff.

'Fox crap?' whispered the huntsman.

Not the most heroic of last words, thought The Hound, as he launched himself like a harpoon and dragged the startled *hunter* to the floor by his ankle.

The huntsman lay on his back, the wind knocked out of him and struggling for breath.

He opened his eyes.

They kept on opening as he stared into the savage, salivating mouth of the snarling were-wolf-wolfhound.

Then he passed out.

'Damn it!' cursed The Hound, looking away in frustration.

He had hoped to get some answers out of the wretched little swine. *But still*, he reflected, as he bound, gagged and trussed the unconscious rascal to the underside of a fallen tree trunk (using a length of rope that he'd handily found coiled on the sniper's platform), *the ghastly fellow's equipment might just shed some light onto the nature of what he was about.*

The *hunter's* crossbow was armed with silver-tipped bolts. The Hound also found a long, black leather case. Opening it, he was surprised to discover two swords: one, a silver-edged, military sabre (in the style that might once have been favoured by a nineteenth century Prussian cavalry officer), and the other, a long and slender-bladed, silver-tipped cup-hilt rapier.

Intriguing.

He briefly thought about taking the weapons with him, but both were far too small to fit his hand and so he carefully returned them to their case and hid them in the undergrowth.

On the ground, next to where the *hunter* had been yanked from the tree, The Hound found a white balaclava with a red stripe across one eye-hole, that must have tumbled from the huntsman's pocket as he fell.

So this wretched fellow was a member of *The Society of the Wild Hunt* – one of their so-called *Lurchers*.

According to Dunkerton, the *Lurchers* acted as guides for *The Society's* paying customers. With that in mind, it would reason that there must be other huntsmen close by.

The Hound sprang silently back into the woods and waited amongst the pod of fallen trees.

The Mighty HASS dragged Tom further and further into the woods.

The full moon cast eerie shadows among the trees, making them look like dead men's fingers clawing up from their graves.

Deeper and deeper they walked into the forest, until the trees were so dense that the moonlight could barely seep through the seemingly oscillating roof of branches.

In despair, Tom flung himself to the floor.

He looked up at the jaguar-man scowling down at him – tufts of hair bristling from the man-cat's muscular shoulders; his long canine teeth jutting from beneath his upper lip and pointing downwards like daggers towards his cast-iron, softly-whiskered chin; the rosettes of pigment that stood out on his skin like tattoos (invoking the spirit of the creature that raged within him); his eyes smouldering with a ghoulish green sparkle, that threw back the moonlight like an unholy fire.

The were-cat rolled and cracked his neck, as if warming up for a grappling match.

'What is it now, Little Cub?' he growled in frustration.

'I'm scared,' whispered Tom, stifling a snivel.

'*You're* scared?' hissed the Mighty HASS, looking around and up to the gnarled, moon-scratched and twisted black tree-limbs that coiled and slithered above them like a pack of petrifying pythons, 'I've got to walk back on my own!'

The were-jaguar howled with laughter, hauled Tom to his feet and slung him over his shoulder like a sailor's kit bag.

The Hound smelled them before he saw them – two vampires, treading softly and wearily towards him.

'It came from over here, Rocia,' hissed a musical Italian voice. (The Hound was, of course, fluent in most of the major languages of Europe: you can learn an awful lot of things in four hundred years – if you put your mind to it, that is).

The were-hound peered between the branches of the tree that concealed him ... and saw a short, gracefully lithe and muscular chap moving towards him with the poise of a dancer. He was pale-skinned and had large brown eyes and a halo of long dark curly hair. He looked like he'd just stepped out of a Renaissance work of art, or at least modelled for a Caravaggio painting (which of course, at some point, he might very well have done), save for the fact that he was dressed in close-fitting, state of the art, hunting-fatigues and looked to be bristling with all manner of gadgets and weaponry – the most dominant of which was the hefty silver-bladed cutting-spear that *The Wild Hunt* seemingly gave to all of their *clients*.

The Hound seeped forward a little to get a better view.

Ten paces behind the Italian was a woman (*Rocia*, presumably), stepping lightly through the woods. She was slightly taller than her companion and looked like she might have been born in southern Spain. Spear in hand, she moved with all the dignity and grace of a homicidal flamenco dancer.

Vampires, snarled The Hound to himself. Not that that was a surprise in itself (almost, perhaps, a slight disappointment) but he didn't recognise either of them, which could only mean that they were either hired killers or part of a larger organisation. The obvious choice would be the *Della Morte Family*.

He'd been a constant thorn in the side of that particularly bloodthirsty fraternity for the last two hundred-odd years, had ruined more than his fair share of their more grisly enterprises in his time, and accounted for a fair few of their number as well.

The *Della Morte Family* were vastly powerful. They jealously ran most of the supernatural underworld of Mediterranean Europe. Manfred de Warrenne was playing with fire indeed if he was trying to involve that hideous powerhouse in his gruesome plans.

The Hound waited for Rocia to stalk past his hiding place.

She stopped, yards in front of him, turned her head and sniffed the air.

'*Zorro*?' she hissed to herself, seeming to relax slightly as she said it, and then, cautiously, she followed after her companion.

'What is it, my love?' The Hound heard the handsome Italian vampire ask in his soft singsong voice.

'Nothing, *mi amor*. A fox, that is all,' she replied, with a fond sparkle in her voice.

Her companion laughed softly. 'Ah, *una volpe*,' he whispered. 'But tonight it is a much larger *canino* that we must hunt, *il mio amore*.'

The Hound let himself smile. *Now the hunters would indeed become the hunted.*

Just as he was preparing himself to follow them, there was the sound of a hefty crash in the trees to his left.

The '*Renaissance* vampire' let out a hoarse little cry of excitement, sprung forward, and disappeared into the woods in the direction of the sound.

'Antonio!' hissed Rocia, as she increased her step to follow him.

There was a short, breathless whistle followed by a low thump. Rocia gasped and buckled to the floor, clutching at a sliver-tipped crossbow bolt embedded in her ankle.

A fraction of a moment later came a sharp, loud snapping sound, followed by Antonio's voice crying out for help.

'Help me, my love! I am trapped!' he wailed.

Rocia pulled the bolt from her leg and looked in the direction of her companion's cry; her once beautiful features now distorted in rage – the lower part of her face contorted and extended into a monstrous set of jaws, with elongated fangs and an expression like an electrocuted bat.

However, her attention was soon taken by the sudden flashing blur of twirling silver and steel that exploded from the trees behind her.

Her attacker was dressed from head to toe in black, only his dark and ferocious eyes visible beneath the black balaclava that he wore. In his hands were two great tulwars, spinning around him with lightning speed – like a malfunctioning food-blender. Taken aback as he was, The Hound immediately recognised the gait of *The Wild Hunt* vampire Ajit Singh (a good fencer's walk is as distinctive as a signature), as the swordsman launched himself like a crashing helicopter towards Rocia.

The Della Morte snarled in anger and, snatching up her spear, fended off the dervish-like attack of Ajit with the skill and grace of a matador.

This, thought The Hound, *is all most ... unusual*. What the devil was de Warrenne up to? What kind of dangerous play was he about? Why invite members of one of the most powerful supernatural crime syndicates on the planet to participate in a hunt and then attempt to murder them before the whole affair had barely begun? Even if the identities of *The Society of the Wild Hunt's* membership were unknown to the *Della Mortes* (and The Hound had to assume that they were, or the *Della Morte Family* would have snuffed out the dapper little cad and his crew of iniquity quicker than a row of candles: de Warrenne was right about one thing – *The Families* hated the *Children of Alexios* with a vengeance) now nothing short of the Archangel Michael would now stop them (the *Della Mortes*) from extracting their revenge on whomever had so disrespectfully wronged them.

In a fair contest, a spear-fighter is normally more than a match for any swordsman, but Rocia, as fierce, quick and skilful as she undoubtedly was, was hampered by the wound in her ankle, and Ajit was making sure that he kept her moving about as much as possible over the uneven ground of the forest (the cunning little blighter). Her companion, Antonio, (out of sight and presumably ensnared in some devilish device) was hissing to her, calling for help and demanding to know what the devil was happening; but Rocia was far too occupied to even think about answering, desperately fighting for her (un)life as she was.

The duel raged with a supernatural ferocity.

The female vampire side-stepped one of Ajit's whirling attacks and tried to spring out of distance and away into the woods by launching herself from the trunk of a tree, but her injured ankle buckled under her and she stumbled, sprawling to the floor. In that instant Ajit threw one of his tulwars, catching her full in the chest.

She hissed and wailed like an impaled lizard.

Singh was on her like a rash, pinning her mercilessly to the forest floor with his second blade.

He stepped back and looked down at her.

'Whoever ... you are,' she half-laughed half-screeched, writhing in agony and fury, 'know that you have signed ... your own ... death warrant.'

A second figure approached the scene.

He was tall, armed with a crossbow, and dressed from head to foot in black (like Ajit and the first *huntsman* that The Hound had just recently dealt with).

The newcomer looked down at Rocia and whistled.

'Nice work, mate,' he whistled quietly, in an outrageously faked Cockney accent. 'She's a pretty one, ain't she? Wouldn't mind 'er *turnin*' me, given 'arf ver chance.'

Rocia snarled weakly at him.

Antonio was yelling in confusion and anger, blindly oblivious to the turn of events.

'Come along, sir,' said *The Mockney*. 'Best get on wiv it, ay?'

He took the long, black leather case that was strapped across his shoulders (identical to the one that The Hound had examined earlier) and laid it on the floor. Opening it, he took out a heavy-looking silver-edged sabre, indistinguishable from the weapon that The Hound had found previously.

The Mockney tossed the sabre to Ajit Singh, who deftly caught it and twirled the murderous weapon expertly in his hand. Then, standing over the prostrate and pinned Rocia, with a single stroke of the great blade, the *Wild Hunt* vampire hacked off her head.

Rocia's body thrashed and shuddered and then slowly melted into dry ash, until only an outline of her remained (as if someone had filled in the chalk lines at the site of a police murder investigation with shovel-loads of dust).

Ajit struck the sabre through what would have been her heart and drove it deep into the ground, almost to the hilt.

'Now,' he hissed, not bothering to face his *Society* fellow, 'let us find those other devils.'

The vampire pulled free his own swords and, with a quick nod to *The Mockney*, dashed into the woods in the opposite direction from the trapped and struggling Antonio.

The Mockney looked up and nervously looked around.

'Oy! Dwight!' he whispered, as loudly as he dared.

There was no reply, and The Hound realised that he must be calling for his companion – the *hunter* that he had dispatched moments earlier, and who was now bound beneath the "Migrating Trees" only yards away from them. He held his breath, half-expecting the fallen huntsman to make a cry or a commotion, but there was nothing.

'Bloody Sceptics!' hissed *The Mockney* as he turned and followed the path of the vampire, Ajit Singh.

When they were gone The Hound approached the low mound of ash (that was all that remained of *Rocia of the Della Mortes*) and sniffed the handle of the sabre that was driven into the ground. He might almost have missed it, but a sudden shift in moonlight caught the edge of a lightly engraved emblem just visible on the cup of the guard. The Hound pulled the sword up a little, just enough for him to be able to get a proper view of the design.

It depicted a bat with the head of a man, its wings spread majestically over a circular moon, and a struggling lamb caught in its terrible talons.

The were-hound looked up and towards the direction of the snared and ranting Antonio – who was still frantically hissing for Rocia, imploring her to tell him what was going on.

The Hound knew this symbol – who in his line of work didn't? It was the family crest of the *Nachzehrers*, the powerful vampire clan that controlled the supernatural world of Central and Northern Europe.

What the devil was de Warrenne up to?

By making it look like the *Nachzehrers* had murdered a *Della Morte Family* member he was likely to start a war ... Of course! That was it! The cunning little rascal!

If the two powerful *Vampire Families* of Western and Northern Europe became involved in a blood feud, then they might take their eyes off Britain just long enough for de Warrenne to achieve his diabolical goal of setting himself up as overlord of the Elbi kingdoms. And who knows, if the *Della Mortes* and the *Nachzehrers* weakened each other sufficiently, then de Warrenne might be able to simply walk in and take over their territories too. De Warrenne had told him that he was ambitious but, good grief, he'd never expected the ruthless little rake to be this motivated! And if he succeeded, then, by all the Gods and their unholy mothers, what might follow? With two vampire clans and the power of the Fair-Folk at his beck and call, de Warrenne might very well set about bringing down the rest of *The Twelve Families* and then crown himself as some kind of self-styled emperor!

The Hound had underestimated the dapper little scoundrel. And he would bet his eye teeth that he wasn't the first one to have made that mistake.

So, he mused, *The Society of the Wild Hunt were hunting the Della Morte assassins, and, according to Ajit Singh, there was still at least one other set of would-be hunters prowling the woods, who, in turn, were still, presumably, hunting he, The Hound, who, in turn, was hell-bent on hunting and finishing not only The Society of the Wild Hunt but also these other wretched swines who had paid money to try to seal his end, who, in turn, were unaware that they, in turn, were being hunted by The Society of the Wild Hunt, who, in turn, once their murderous plan was complete, would no doubt come, all spears a-blazing, for he (The Hound).*

Hhhmm? he pondered, brooding over the possible variations and implications.

Interesting, to say the least. But all these deplorable shenanigans might just improve his chances of survival.

It would appear that there were only three members of *The Society of the Wild Hunt* (now down to two) stalking the woods tonight. So where were the rest of the despicable scoundrels? And, more importantly, what were they up to?

The Hound felt a sudden nervousness for The Pook and the Pharisees, and hurriedly tracked the path taken by Ajit Singh and his lackey with a grim and ruthless determination.

Tom was roughly dumped on the ground.

He hit his head on a log and yelped in pain.

'Quiet, Little Cub,' scowled the Mighty HASS. 'Meet your end with courage. Make your last moments worthy of remembering. Be brave. You will taste all the sweeter for it.'

Tom gathered himself into a crouched position, ready to spring. He had no intention of meekly meeting his end like some tethered lamb. And though he was under no illusion that he would last more than a few seconds against the full fury of the were-jaguar, he would at least go down fighting. And, who knew, maybe he would find the chance to make a dash for it. The one thing that his uncle always stressed was, that in times of danger – keep thinking and keep looking for opportunities.

The Mighty HASS looked down at him, rippled his claws and flexed his muscles.

'Are you ready, Little Cub? For the moment your death has come.'

The Hound picked up the trail of *The Wild Huntsmen* and followed them like a ghost flickering through the woods. Ajit Singh and *The Mockney* were moving fast and skilfully through the forest, and he wondered, for the umpteenth time, just who their quarry might be?

There was a soft click as a twig snapped to his left.

He froze, sniffed the air and squinted through the thicket of trees.

'Psssst! Up here!' hissed a voice.

The Hound looked up to see what could only be described as some kind of *were-cat*, nonchalantly balancing on a precariously thin branch.

The creature was about five feet tall, lithe and muscular, with gigantic tufty ears, golden fur and a long swishing tail.

The were-wolfhound racked his brain. *Did he know this creature?* To be honest, he didn't even recognise its species. Some kind of lynx perhaps? Had he ever upset a were-lynx? Or even met one before? It was remotely possible, of course, but for the life of him he couldn't remember if he had.

The strange cat-man smiled and bowed.

'Mister Hound,' he grinned, with an arrogant purr, 'I come to offer you your freedom.'

The Mighty HASS cracked his knuckles and took a step towards Tom; a wicked, pantomime villain grin spreading across his mottled face as he approached.

'I don't think that you want to be doing that,' sniffed a delightfully comforting and familiar voice. 'It might just prove to be bad for your 'ealth, son.'

Both Tom and the Mighty HASS twanged their heads like bowstrings, to see ... Uncle Cornelius – dressed in nothing more than stripy long johns and vest (matching) – leaning against a sycamore tree; his long, sculpted arms folded menacingly across his ample chest.

'And *who*, exactly, *are you*?' enquired The Hound, with polite suspicion.

'My name is Jackie Caracal,' beamed the were-cat, (*Of course*! thought The Hound. *A caracal – like a lynx, and even at one point considered to be a subspecies of lynx, but now ... not.*) 'of the world-famous Caracal Brothers.'

'Forgive me, young Master Caracal, but I'm afraid to say that I've not heard of you ... or your brothers.'

Jackie Caracal looked a little disappointed.

'No matter,' he smiled, 'you will learn.'

There was something in the way that the were-cat said that last phrase that made the hackles on the back of the were-hound's neck rise, and instinctively he spun around to see two more creatures, almost identical to the strange little chap in the tree, fanned out behind him.

'May I introduce to you, Mister Hound, my older brothers,' purred Jackie, proudly, 'Bruce and Chuck.'

Bruce and Chuck smiled and bowed, pressing the fist of one hand into the open palm of the other, but never removing their golden eyes from the were-hound for one moment.

'If you will come with us, Mister Hound, then we will lead you to safety. Away from this dishonourable and most embarrassing spectacle,' said Bruce, with a high-pitched meow of pride and pleasure.

'Or we'll smash your head in,' added Chuck, thickly.

'Shut up, you stupid idiot!' hissed Bruce, punching Chuck's arm in frustration.

Chuck gave a muffled yowl.

'What did you do that for!' he mewed.

'Dr Chow say we should try to get him to come along by asking him nicely, and only smash his brains in if he refused!' explained Bruce, gently.

Jackie Caracal slapped his forehead into his hands. 'Why?' he mused momentarily, before politely and respectfully addressing his older brothers. 'Shut up, you blithering buffoons! You've ruined everything!'

'Eh?' gurned Chuck.

Bruce reached across and pulled a fistful of hairs from his younger brother's chest.

Chuck danced a jig of pain, accompanied with a rhythmical song of "oh-ahs" delivered through gritted teeth.

The Hound looked on in mild bewilderment.

What extraordinary little fellows, he thought to himself, as he turned to walk away.

'GET HIM!' roared Jackie, launching himself at the were-wolfhound like an enraged paratrooper.

Bruce and Chuck narrowed their eyes into evil frowns, meowed like moggies mugged of their catnip, and then bounded forward like deadly rubber balls, aiming spikily-lethal flying-kicks at the were-hound's head and heels.

The Mighty HASS did another double take.

Tom almost sobbed with joy.

'You all right, Tom?' asked his uncle.

Tom nodded.

'Well ... apart from this ... *gentleman* ... proposing to rip my beating heart from my chest and then eat it in front of me ... none too shabby, I'd say,' he replied, all but giggling with relief.

'Was 'e now? An' just 'oo is this ... *gentleman*?' enquired Cornelius, saying the word "gentleman" as if he was spitting out one of Dame Ginty's home-made biscuits.

'My name,' growled the were-jaguar, with theatrical menace, 'is Hector Antonio Sanchez Silvio, better known to fight fans the world over as – The Mighty HASS!'

''Ow do,' snarled Uncle Cornelius, springing forward and hurling a left-jab like a hand grenade at the Argentinian man-jaguar's granite jaw.

The Hound tore a were-caracal from his back and hurled him like a throwing-axe towards a tree. Jackie (for it was he who was so tossed) nimbly absorbed the impact with his legs and ricocheted back at him, tumbling like an acrobat across the floor. The were-hound dodged Jackie's whirling attack, blocked a spinning back-kick from Chuck, and riposted with a countering combination of his own – a swinging "bear-claw" strike and follow-through "scissor-snap" bite with his jaws – but missed and loudly cracked thin air with his teeth. Instantly he received a sharp stamp to the ankle from Bruce and momentarily lost his balance.

A storm of fists, claws, knees, elbows and feet hailed down on him as he struggled to find his footing. He managed to deliver a hammer blow to the skull of one brother (Chuck) and sent the swine reeling through the woods, bumping into trees like a pinball that has run out of oomph.

Jackie attempted a knee-strike to the were-hound's groin (the irredeemable bounder!), but The Hound shifted his leg inwards and blocked the strike with a drop of his elbow (making the youngest Caracal Brother howl in agony and limp away, cursing in language that would have made a Premiership footballer – role models to the youth of the country – blush).

The were-wolf-wolfhound threw a *double jab, right-cross* combination at the remaining were-caracal, Bruce, who parried the first and somersaulted out of the way of the follow-up attacks.

The three brothers regrouped – their tails lashing furiously in anger.

They fanned out and slowly began to stalk back in.

Uncle Cornelius and The Mighty HASS cautiously circled each other. A trickle of blood ran from the man-cat's lip where Tom's uncle had clipped him with a straight left lead.

With HASS dressed in bright-yellow enormous wrestling pants and Cornelius clad in blue and white stripy long johns and vest (matching), it looked like a woefully-conceived scene from the most undesirable *male underwear* photo-shoot for the *Littlewoods Catalogue* that the world has ever seen.

'Stay still, old man, so I can rip your heart out!' snarled The Mighty HASS, unencouragingly. 'With your blood coursing through my veins I will become truly powerful indeed.'

With the words scarce from his lips the man-jaguar pounced with the speed of a ... well, the speed of a jaguar, actually ... at Uncle Cornelius, his fearsome fingers spread out like a 1970's wrestler's.

Cornelius skipped out of distance and shot out a brace of straight punches aimed at the man-cat's fingers.

The Mighty HASS howled in pain and clutched his hand, his index finger snapped and disconcertingly facing the wrong way.

Like lightning, the Argentinian spun, lashed out with his good hand, and tore his claws across Uncle Cornelius' shoulder.

The old man shifted back, gritting his teeth. A rosette of blood bloomed and began to seep down his arm.

The were-jaguar circled around Cornelius, while the old pug held the centre of the "ring" – elbows tucked in, left hand long, right hand short, with his balance somewhat on the back foot. He glowered at the The Mighty HASS, squinting along his raised left shoulder, his head tilted slightly to one side.

'Tom,' said the old fellow, calmly, never taking his eyes from his circling opponent, 'might be an idea if you started running, son.'

Tom picked up a weighty stick from the forest floor and tested its heft in the palm of his hand. He'd had enough. Chased, imprisoned, drugged, interrogated, teased and then threatened with the most hideous of deaths. All that remained within was the empowering urge to extract a little vengeance. Plus, there was no way on earth that he was going to leave his uncle to face this *monster* alone. In fact, he was pretty determined to never leave the whiskery old codger's side ever again.

'I'd rather not, if that's all the same to you, Uncle,' he said.

Uncle Cornelius nodded.

'Good for you, Tom. Shows a lot of bottom, does that. Keep thinking, son, an' do what you know you can do,' said the old man, dry spitting through his whiskers and then closing in on the hissing HASS.

The Caracal Brothers advanced in a deadly slink – crouching low, shoulders hunched, heads craned forward, and sheathing and unsheathing their claws in lethal syncopation (like cast members from a feline version of West Side Story).

The Hound held his ground. He had the briefest of thoughts that perhaps he should run – he was, after all, wasting time on these annoying little blighters, but, well, damn it, he had his pride. He wouldn't be the one to run from a gang of delinquent moggies. He'd never live it down (assuming that he survived this whole deplorable imbroglio, that is).

He wondered, once again, who these odd little chaps were? And just who the blazes was this devilish-sounding *Dr Chow* fellow?

Eight ears suddenly pricked and swivelled simultaneously towards the trees to the Hound's right.

Approaching through the woods came a soft whirring sound of tiny ticks and clicks – like the intricate and delicate clunking of clockwork.

Surely not? thought The Hound, raising a disbelieving eyebrow.

The Caracal Brothers turned apprehensively towards the imminent sound of the approaching ticking tocks.

Out of the trees appeared a lightly-built and sprightly-looking man, dressed in what appeared to be a nineteenth-century hussar's jacket – with a plethora of gold medals pinned across his breast. However, on closer inspection, what at first glance had appeared to have been decorative gold braiding and *martial gongs* was in actual fact a complex series of golden gears, cogs and wheels (all clicking with unerring efficiency, and in a state of perpetual motion) protected by a transparent covering.

The newcomer's bloodshot eyes widened in surprise and excitement.

'Mein Gott!' he hissed. 'So it *is* true. It *is* you!'

'Baron Rudolf Von Bathory!' growled The Hound, menacingly lowering his muzzle, 'How ... *delightful* to see you.'

'Oh, how I have longed for zhis moment!' chirped the Baron. 'Und vhat is zhis I see before me?' he squeaked, scowling in delight at the were-caracals (who were watching him with a startled and, dare one say, cat-like curiosity). 'You have some uzzer furry friends for me to play vit. Here kitty, kitty, kitty. Oh, you are just so cute! It is almost too much,' he twittered. '*Zhe big bad vulfhund* und *zhe zhree little kittens*,' he laughed merrily, though no one else looked like they were in any danger of joining in.

The Baron slowly drew the murderous-looking sabre that swung at his hip, and flamboyantly saluted them with it.

'Now I shall have four heads instead of vun to hang in mein hunting hall.'

He scuttled lightly forward on the balls of his feet, as graceful as a ballet dancer; right leg before left leg, left fist resting gently on his hip, brutal weapon glistening and poised like silver death under the pale moonlit sky.

The Hound supposed that the Caracal Brothers had their pride too, for he observed them launch themselves like bouncing-bombs at the encroaching hussar. He wondered, for a brief moment, if he should join in the looming scuffle – as he watched the Baron swat Chuck away with the flat of his blade and then retreat out of distance (with classically perfect aplomb) from a double spinning back-fist strike delivered by Bruce.

'Oh, how marvellous!' chortled the Baron. 'Come, ja, come, little kitties! Let uz dance a dance of death. Come, sup from zhe soup-plate of honour!' And, with a berserker-like battle cry (that would have warmed the cockles of the great god Woden's heart), he lunged forwards like a greased viper hurtled from a catapult, flicked his wrist and sent his blade swinging like a guillotine towards Jackie Caracal. The were-cat ducked and somehow managed to narrowly avoid the strike ... but not without losing a few tufts of hair shaved perilously close from the tip of his ear. The youngest Caracal Brother squalled in miserable anger and cartwheeled out of distance.

The Hound decided that the best course of action in such an event as this was what he and Dandy had christened "The Lund Manoeuvre".

> ***The Lund Manoeuvre*** – So-named after a visit, by The Hound and Cornelius, to Sweden in order to watch the bicentennial *Helda Gris-Oga Remembrance - Invitation Sevens Tournament (*a particularly brutal form of Troll-rugby played by only two teams in the world – for which read that there were only two teams in the world stupid enough to want to play it).
>
> The challenge was centuries old, however, and had originally arisen out of a dispute over who was the rightful fiancé of the

legendary Troll-beauty Helda Gris-Oga (Princess of the *Jaette Trolls* of Sweden) between the feuding factions of the *Huldrefolk Tribe* of Norway and the *Bjergtrolde Clan* from the mountain regions of Denmark. In the ensuing brouhaha (in which poor Princess Gris-Oga was used in much the same fashion as a sturdy length of rope might be used by two rival tug-of-war teams) the glamorous Troll-maiden's head was pulled clean from her shoulders and a two-day ruckus broke out, in which both sides tried to claim the head and head off home with it.

However, it was decided by the two contending houses that they'd never had so much fun, and that they wanted to repeat the whole palaver, every fifty years or so, in celebration of a damned fine brawl (Trolls love a good brawl). And so they did; contesting the event with the (now sadly shrivelled and thoroughly battered) head of the once beautiful (for a Troll) Princess Gris-Oga, with the winning team keeping the unfortunate, but now immortalised prize (to wit, Helda's skull, complete with tiara), until the right for the grisly trophy could be contested again.

Forty-six years ago Dandy and The Hound had travelled over to watch the spectacle, which was taking place that year in the fair and beautiful university city of Lund, and were just enjoying a post-match supper at a local restaurant – discussing the oft-debated subject of whether 'Lobe-Snorkelling' (the act of ripping off an opponent's earlobes and stuffing them up his nostrils in the attempt of suffocating him [legal, as long as one at least showed an effort to blind-side the referee]) should be banned from the sport altogether, or, if by so doing, one would lose the manliest (or *Trolliest*?) and most sophisticated aspects of the game – when, by unhappy chance, it appeared that both rival teams had accidentally booked the same restaurant for their post-match celebration/commiseration party.

It was carnage (as has already been noted, there is nothing more that a good Troll likes than a good old-fashioned scrap) – chairs, tables and limbs being strewn everywhere.

Rather than steam straight into the fray right away, Dandy and The Hound had decided that the most sensible course of action was to remove themselves from immediate danger and hide themselves under their table – where they could finish the rather good (and rather expensive) bottle of *Barolo* that they had just purchased, and also wait for the battling Trolls to wear themselves out and punch themselves to a standstill (no stamina, your average Troll – thank God!) before they decided to join in the ensuing melee and clean up.

Which they did; thus earning themselves the eternal gratitude of the restaurant's proprietor (and the non-Troll clientèle) and a free meal to boot. Huzzah!

With this thought in mind, The Hound nonchalantly disappeared behind a tree and nestled himself down for a concealed, but excellent, ringside view.

'I will devour you both! First you, you interfering old fool, and then you, Little Cub!' roared the Mighty HASS, though not sounding really too convinced about the whole matter.

Suddenly a beam of light raked across his face, making his eyes glisten like two emeralds in the darkness of the night.

'I don't think that that's such a good idea, sir,' said a familiar and husky voice.

Tom turned to see the delectable Sergeant Hettie Clem – holding a torch with one fist and a revolver in the other, both fixed resolutely on the were-cat.

Tom's heart rose another notch.

They were safe!

The man-jaguar twitched, as if preparing to pounce on her, only to come nostril-to-nostril with the barrel of a gigantic blunderbuss held by the delicate and shapely hands of the glamour witch, Dame Ginty Parsons.

'Oh, I wouldn't do that if I were you,' she tutted, sounding like she was scolding a favourite nephew for sticking his fingers in the organic Brussels sprout and seaweed marmalade.

The Mighty HASS yelped and slowly cowered to the floor, curling himself up into a tight little ball.

Tom couldn't help but notice a dark stain appear in the man-cat's yellow wrestling trunks, but he could find no pity for him.

More thundering footsteps could be heard, and into the clearing pounded Inspector Jones and Constable Tuggnutter, pistols held out at arm's-length and aimed at the cringing and whimpering were-jaguar.

'Blimey! You can't half shift, Professor!' puffed Mordecai, loosening a pair of handcuffs from his pocket.

Uncle Cornelius shot Inspector Jones a smile, and then bounded over and took Tom in his arms – almost crushing the breath out of him, he squeezed so hard.

'You all right, Tom?' he asked.

Tom hugged the old fellow back and buried his head in his uncle's chest.

There was a sudden popping sound and Tom turned to see the final morphing of the *were-jaguar* into a full *jaguar-jaguar* (*Panthera onca* without the "*were*").

Tuggnutter fired a shot, but the great cat was already vaulting away, sprinting through the trees like a moggy with a rocket tied to its tail.

'After him!' yelled Inspector Jones.

'No!' screamed Tom.

All eyes turned to look at him.

'Why ever not, dear?' asked Ginty, lowering the barrel of her portable cannon.

'We don't have time!' babbled Tom, hastily. 'Forget him, he's not important! It's The Hound!' he cried. '*The Society of the Wild Hunt* are hunting him! Tonight! In Hollingbury Woods!'

'Are they, by God!' snarled Uncle Cornelius.

Baron Von Bathory – as unpleasant a vampire as he'd ever had the misfortune to meet, mused The Hound; watching as the undead hussar joyously battled the tumbling were-caracals. Well, he certainly wasn't surprised to see him! They had history, he and the Baron. Bad history.

They had first crossed paths back in the 1880s, when The Hound had foiled a particularly dastardly plan by the Baron and his henchmen to kidnap the (then) young, and outstandingly brilliant, Austrian-Hungarian inventor Nikola Tesla – in a despicable attempt to turn Tesla's exceptional discoveries in the field of electricity to their diabolical advantage ("their" being the powerful vampire clan of Central and Northern Europe – the *Nachzehrers:* Bathory being one of their very finest and most capable captains).

There had been a showdown in a matchstick factory, culminating in a thrilling and top-notch display of swordsmanship – from both sides. (The Hound considered Von Bathory one of the finest swordsmen that he'd ever encountered, and quite probably [with the possible exception of Sergeant Bob 'Hacker' Harrington* – darling of the British Light Cavalry {'*The Achilles of Waterloo'*}, and one-time leading *special agent* of *The Unseen League*] the best sabreur that he had ever seen). In the course of their brouhaha, a fire had started, swiftly followed by an explosion (unbeknown to all involved, the matchstick factory's owners had been expanding their repertoire and were working on a revolutionary new range of indoor fireworks) and the Baron had been struck in the chest by the entire contents of an exploding matchbox.

(* Sergeant Harrington was called "*Hacker*" in much the same way that a fat man is sometimes nicknamed "*Slim*".)

In normal circumstances (for a *normal* person) it might not have been too bad an injury, but for a vampire, fifty miniature wooden stakes embedded in your chest – and all of them working their way slowly towards your heart – becomes a tad worrying to say the least. It had proved impossible to remove all of the offending matches and so a mechanical device had been implanted in his chest that, somehow, managed to keep the tiny stakes immobilized and in a chronic state of suspension. From that day on, much to his annoyance, the bloody Baron Rudolf Von Bathory (who liked to be called *The Silver Sabre* or *The Heartless Hussar*) became known in supernatural circles as *The Clockwork Baron* or, even more cruelly, *The Wind-up Wampyre*.

Bathory held The Hound responsible and had sworn vengeance. They'd met on numerous occasions over the ensuing decades, had had the odd set-to and usually went their separate ways – the Baron's schemes invariably foiled. The

Hound did, he had to admit, feel a slight pang of remorse for the Baron's unfortunate predicament, and from that day on had given up his habit of smoking cheroots whilst duelling evil, sword-wielding, undead maniacs (terrible habit anyway) (smoking cheroots that is, not duelling with evil, sword-wielding, undead maniacs) (though that, on reflection, wasn't the best of habits to acquire either).

The Baron was advancing and retreating with classical perfection, using his leather-gauntleted left hand to swat away anything that managed to get past the serpent-like tip of his flashing blade. The Caracal Brothers (having suddenly realised that The Hound had left them to it) had obviously decided that taking on a highly trained, psychopathic and undead hussar wasn't really the order of the day, and were desperately looking for a means of extricating themselves from the situation.

As one, they back-flipped out of range of the Clockwork Baron's artistic swipes, and formed a triangle around him. Then, like lightning, they struck together: Jackie going in high, while Chuck and Bruce attacked low and from the sides.

The youngest brother – with a look of uncertain terror warping like a smiley face drawn on an over-stretching elastic-band – dodged the vampire's snake-like through-cut and landed a double-footed kick on the startled Baron's chest, just as Bruce and Chuck rolled themselves like bowling balls into the back of Von Bathory's knees.

The vampire fell backwards and landed in a humiliating heap on the floor, whilst the world-famous Caracal Brothers fled from the scene as fast as a troupe of tumbling were-cat funambulists fleeing from a homicidal sabre-wielding vampire.

The Baron rolled gracefully to his feet.

'Scaredy cats!' he howled after the fleeing Caracals, stomping his feet in frustration.

Then his eyes narrowed and he looked about him. The Hound was nowhere to be seen.

He growled in thwarted annoyance and petulantly swung his sword into the trunk of a tree in exasperation; leaving the sabre quivering like a springboard as he bit his fists in frustration.

The Hound, watching from the undergrowth, had half-risen to pounce out and throttle the odious little monster, when a sudden movement behind the Baron made him stop in his tracks.

'You alwigh', sir?' asked a disgracefully affected Cockney voice.

The vampire spun round ... to see *The Mockney* standing behind him.

The Hound noted that the *Wild Huntsman* had swapped balaclavas and now wore the red striped white mask of a *Wild Hunt* 'Lurcher'.

The Hound melted back down into the undergrowth.

'He vas here! Damn him! He vas here und now he has got avay! Again!'

‘We’ll find ’im, sir, don’t worry,’ cooed *The Mockney*, chirpily – sounding like Dick Van Dyke trying to woo Mary Poppins to the pub for half a pint of mild and a packet of Tabasco-coated pork scratchings.

‘Und zhose cats?’ demanded the Baron. ‘You never told me zhere vould be pussy cats!’

‘Pussy cats, sir?’ asked *The Mockney*, genuinely bewildered. ‘I’m not sure vat I follow you.’

The Baron stared at him like he was the scrapings from his knee-length riding boots, and then made to follow him.

‘’Scuse me, sir.’

‘Vhat is it now!’ demanded the Baron, with impatience.

‘You’ve forgotten your sword, mate,’ replied *The Wild Hunt* henchman, sounding like his teeth were stuck together by an unusually sticky toffee.

‘Ah, ja. Danke. I vould forget my own head if it veren’t screwed on,’ chuckled Baron Von Bathory.

As he turned to collect his sabre his eyes bulged like over-pumped balloons.

Ajit Singh lunged and plunged the point of a beautifully crafted silver-tipped cup-hilt rapier into the *Wind-up Wampyre’s* mechanically tick-tocking chest.

The Baron wobbled. The golden cogs on his breast rumbled and shook, straining to turn. But the steel from the rapier’s blade jammed their motion – dead.

The *Wild Hunt* vampire stepped back and watched whilst the Baron clutched at the sword and pulled a face like a man trying to draw breath under water. The Sikh vampire unsheathed a tulwar and turned it deftly and slowly in his hand. Baron Von Bathory sunk to his knees, weakly trying to pull the rapier from his chest and gasping like a hooked cod.

Ajit Singh spun forward, and – with a motion somewhere between a pirouetting ballerina, a Whirling Dervish, and a fast-pace bowler thundering down at Lords from the Pavilion End – lopped the gargling Baron’s head clean from his shoulders with a single swipe.

Von Bathory leached to the floor like a toppled wicket.

Ajit flicked his blade clean, then leant over the prostrate body of the Nachzehrer and pressed his weight on the pommel of the rapier; driving the sword through the body of the fallen Baron and deep into the ground. The skewered Von Bathory melted into a pile of dry ash. The cogs and sprockets from his mechanical chest popped and sprung, eventually falling to rest like flowers on a freshly-packed grave.

The rapier swayed gently in an imperceptible breeze, perfectly skewering, as it did, a beautifully crafted golden gearwheel.

‘Come, we must be gone,’ said the vampire, Ajit Singh. ‘There is still much work to be done this night.’

‘But what about Ve ’Ound?’ asked *The Mockney*.

'Leave him. He cannot escape. We will deal with him soon enough. Either *The Master* will want him dead or he will use him again and make more profit from the vile cur's *precious* pelt.'

The Hound suppressed a rumble.

'An' what about Dwight?' asked the phantom toffee-chewer, with a look of agitated concern.

The vampire considered his question, with the air of someone contemplating the plight of a misplaced mobile phone belonging to someone that he didn't like very much, and then shrugged.

'Look for him if you want, just try not get yourself eaten,' the Sikh replied, emotionlessly.

The Mockney looked around at the moonlit woods with saucer-like eyes.

'But make sure that you bring my things with you,' purred Ajit, in the softest of tones, thrusting his beloved tulwars into the ground, 'or you *will* get eaten.'

Ajit Singh looked briefly up to the sky and then clapped his hands together. His clothes crumpled to the floor and a large bat flew upwards and circled into the night, fluttering, briefly, in perfect silhouette against the frozen moon.

The Mockney stole another wide-eyed glance over his shoulder, muttered something under his breath, hastily picked up Ajit's clothes and swords, and then hurriedly made his way towards the Wild Park playing fields.

The Hound was just about to follow, take down this grisly and wretched little creature and get some answers from him, when there was a burst of movement to his right.

Into the scene raced a very tall and gaunt vampire, dressed in a long black leather World War One fighter pilot's coat.

The Hound momentarily regretted the strange turn of events that had denied him the opportunity to bring a bucket of popcorn with him, for his concealed pew behind this fallen log was proving to be the very best seat in the house.

The vampire's features looked like somebody had described what a human face should look like to a blind alien sculptor. His cheekbones stuck out like numbed razors, and his eye sockets were like pitiless black pools of despair. His thick blond hair was waxed upright, making him look even taller and thinner.

The Hound thought that he recognised the vile thing as an associate of the Baron's. His name might have been Victor Bertrand, but he couldn't quite remember. But what he was certain of was that this vampire was a killer, of the first and highest order, for the ruthless and powerful House of Nachzehrer.

Victor, if that was his name, knelt beside the mound of ashes and unmoving golden gears.

'Baron,' he whispered, with tender shock. 'Who could have done zhis to you?'

And then he seemed to notice the impaling rapier for the first time.

He sniffed the blade and recoiled a little at the smell of silver. Then, with a gloved hand, he pulled the sword from his companion's ashes and examined what appeared to be a maker's-mark on the forte of the blade.

It was the image of a dancing, bat-winged skeleton playing a lute.

Victor looked up at the moon; his eyes deep jet-black wells of vengeful sorrow, his canine teeth stretching and growing horribly down his chin.

'*Della Morte*!' he snarled, snapping the blade in his hands and throwing away the foible end. '*Schweinhunds*! Zhe filthy dogs!'

I say! Steady on, old chap, snarled The Hound, inwardly, as he pondered his next course of action.

Should he leap out and kill this wretched creature and, in so doing, avert a *vampire war*? But *why* should he? If there were to be a feud between these two abominable, criminal, and odious Houses, then that would only mean that there were a few fewer of the despicable bloodsuckers to plague the world. Good riddance!

'Zhey vill pay, Baron,' hissed the tall, blond vampire. 'I swear by all zhat is unholy, zhey vill pay.'

Victor Bertrand rose and looked down mournfully at the pile of cogs and ash, saluted his old murdering companion with what remained of the rapier, and then turned and ran like an express locomotive, disappearing like the shadow of a cloud among the moon-bathed trees.

So that's it? thought The Hound. *I'm here – alone? Until The Society completes its terrible night's work and returns to try to finish me off, that is.*

He wondered, fretfully, how Cornelius was faring. Had de Warrenne been as good as his word? And The Pook and the Pharisees? The Hound had no doubt that they were in for a hard night. And Tom? What had happened to the dear little chap? In their brief acquaintance he'd grown quite fond of the lad, and there were ... well ... there was a lot to be considered.

It was all most frustrating, but for the moment there was nothing for him to do but wait.

But wait! Hang on one second!

He suddenly remembered the Della Morte vampire, Antonio, snared among the "Migrating Trees". And the *Wild Hunt* "Lurcher", Dwight, bound and gagged under a trunk.

He rose and raced back towards the spot where Rocia had been killed by Ajit Singh.

On his way to the site of Rocia's ashes he found the remains of a net hanging from a tree, its silver-coated webbing torn and gnawed to shreds. Not far from there was all that remained of the *Wild Huntsman,* Dwight. His body was clawed and gashed as if mauled by a rabid wild animal – his throat torn out, his chest ripped open and his ribcage pushed aside like a swing-gate where his heart had been removed.

The Hound tracked back to the site of Rocia's death.

The *Nachzehrer* sabre was gone, presumably taken by Antonio to show to his superiors as proof of the treachery of the Teutonic clan.

On the mound of ashes that had once been Rocia, wild flowers had been laid in a circle, and in the middle of that circle was placed a heart – a human heart.

It was, The Hound knew, the sign of undying affection from one undead lover to another.

It was a symbol, a promise, of eternal retribution.

The Hound made his way back up to Hollingbury Ring.

He stood on the brow of the ancient hill-fort and looked down at the flickering lights of Brighton town.

He tilted his snout and bathed his face in the brilliance of the full moon.

She was beautiful and he was Her creature.

He threw back his head and howled.

Down in the sweeping valley, the dogs of Brighton sang back their pleasure, while cats hastily scuttled under whatever cover they could find.

FORTY TWO
False Endings

They found The Hound sitting on the lip of Hollingbury Camp, gnawing on the bones of a freshly caught rabbit and staring, absent-mindedly, at the splendour of the moon.

As soon as he spotted him, Tom raced forwards, waving his arms frantically. The were-wolfhound leapt up and bounded towards him, his mouth open and his tongue lolling to one side, with what was definitely the biggest smile that Tom had ever seen.

He reached Tom and cradled the boy's head in his massive hands.

'You're safe!' cried Tom, out of breath from both his sprint and from the burst of emotion kicking in his heart, as he threw his arms around the giant were-beast.

'As are you, Tom,' replied The Hound, gently patting him on the shoulder. 'As are you.'

Uncle Cornelius soon reached them and the two old friends briefly embraced each other – rather awkwardly and stiffly, it must be said – and then heartily pumped hands.

'You all right, 'Aitch?' asked Uncle Cornelius, his voice suddenly catching in his throat.

'Tickety-boo, old cock,' replied The Hound, his tail lashing the air like a demented whip. 'Tickety-boo.'

With the arrival of Dame Ginty and the D.S.C., they all took turns to recount their extraordinary adventures.

The Hound told of his meeting with the vampire, Lord Manfred de Warrenne of the ruined and exiled Thirteenth House; of the dapper little swine's diabolical scheme to become master of *The Crowns of Albion* and make himself High King of the Fae Folk. He then briefly detailed his subsequent exploits in general since being a *guest* of *The Society of the Wild Hunt*.

Tom told them of his imprisonment by Dr Chow and the despicable *Carnival of Curiosities* – The Hound and Uncle Cornelius both fascinated by the details of his tale.

And Cornelius recounted how he had woken up only a few hours ago, confused and bewildered, with a splitting headache and thinking that he was, for some inexplicable reason, in a launderette.

'There I was, wearing nothing but me lucky pirate long johns, an' all I could 'ear was what I thought was the sound of washing machines. It finally dawned on me that it was actually the noise of what the young folk these days call *music*,' he gave a rueful chuckle and shook his head. 'Then it all came back to me – my abduction, my imprisonment. An' for the life of me I couldn't remember 'aving 'eard them kind of sounds before. Then I noticed a door that 'ad been left ajar. So out I popped, expecting a right old ruckus. An' do you know what? There weren't a soul in sight. Everything was completely deserted.

'I stumbled through a maze of corridors an' soon found myself in the middle of Sussex University campus (in the 'Alls of Residence, by all appearances), with 'alf of the scholars of Sussex partying their merry 'earts out.

'I asked a lovely young couple where I be an' what time it was. To their credit, they were completely unfazed by my appearance – professors creeping around campus in their underwear at twenty minutes to midnight obviously being nothing out of the ordinary these days,' sniffed the old fellow, with a concerned look of disapproval briefly blooming across his battered and bewhiskered visage.

'Anyway, feeling a little abashed, I made my way to Stanmer Park (which the University backs onto) an' it was there that I 'appened to see, in the distance, what looked like a big brute of a man dragging a little fellow into the woods against his will. I didn't know that it was Tom, at the time, but it all looked a bit iffy to me, an' I was in the mood for a bit of conflict, if you follow me.

'There was a group of very relaxed an' friendly students on the edge of the park, members of S.B.U.T.A.S. (The Sussex an' Brighton Universities Tobacco Appreciation Society), or so they told me, for they were sharing a *foreign*, funny-smelling cigarette between 'em. Any'ow, they were only too 'appy to lend me one of them mobile telephones. An' so I calls up Inspector Jones, right away, an' told 'im where I were an' what I was up to, an' 'eaded off in 'ot pursuit of the dodgy-looking cove what I'd just seen. An' the rest, as they say, is 'istory.'

Tom put his arm around his uncle, avoiding the fresh bandage that Ginty had fashioned for the old boy whilst they had raced the short distance from Stanmer Park to Wild Park and then up to Hollingbury Hill.

''Ang on a minute, 'Aitch, I've got something for you,' frowned Cornelius, as he proceeded to rummage around in his vest.

After an intensive furtle, he produced a sweaty envelope – addressed, in a fine and practised hand, to "*Master Percival Percy*" – and passed it over to the were-hound.

The Hound raised an eyebrow, ripped open the clammy envelope with the claw of his little finger, and drew out and unfolded a sheet of expensive writing paper.

It read –

> *Dearest Percival,*
>
> *You know, I almost hope that you get to read this, old stick.*
>
> *If you do, then you'll know that Professor Lyons is safe and unharmed – just as I promised you he would be.*
>
> *I, in turn, will know (should you have survived the night's little ordeal unscathed) that you will be hot on*

my trail in pursuit – ever the good and faithful pooch that you try so hard to be, dear boy.
Our paths will cross again, I have no doubt. When that time comes, then rest assured that the kid gloves will be off. But, just this once, I'll play the "good vampire" and live up to my word.
For her sake, old boy. For Bella.

TTFN.
Lord Manfred de Warrenne

The Hound folded the paper and tucked it into his belt.
'You all right, 'Aitch?' asked Cornelius.
The Hound licked his teeth and nodded.

Inspector Jones then explained how, in their absence, everybody had mobilised themselves in rota – having had at all times one of the witches stationed at One Punch Cottage, another with the Pharisees, and the third roving and investigating with the D.S.C..

'And where are the Pharisees now?' asked The Hound, uneasily.

'They should have been here, Mr Hound,' replied Inspector Jones, sounding both alarmed and surprised that they weren't. 'They've been watching this site for days, looking for any fresh signs of activity.'

'Then we have work to do,' growled The Hound. 'Let us away. First to the house of The Pook, and then on to One Punch Cottage – for I begin to fear the worst.

'If this evening's diabolical events have shown us but one thing, then it is this:' he rumbled, standing up and staring across the rolling Downs with a ferocious look in his almond-shaped and walnut-coloured eyes, 'the game, my friends, has only just begun.'

For more information about the adventures of
the paranormal investigation agency of
Lyons & Hound
and to join the Caractacus Plume mailing list
and receive a free e-copy of the Lyons & Hound adventure
INCIDENT AT FIVE HUNDRED ACRE WOOD
please visit

www.caractacusplume.com

The Tomas Dearlove Chronicles – Book Two

GRENDEL

A MONSTER FROM THE DEEPEST PITS OF HELL:
A DARK SECRET LAID BARE:
AN OLD SCORE TO BE SETTLED.

JOHNNY GRENDEL, the most feared and ferocious Fae in all the Nine Realms, has been freed from his bonds and is hell-bent on exacting revenge on those responsible for damning him to decades of the most cruel and torturous imprisonment – to wit, Mr Percival Percy (THE HOUND WHO HUNTS NIGHTMARES) & PROFESSOR CORNELIUS "DANDY" LYONS.
But as the esteemed paranormal investigation agency of LYONS & HOUND (est. 1895) – along with their newly acquired (and not so quietly quivering) apprentice, TOMAS DEARLOVE – race to stop the monstrous villain before his murderous rampage brings ruin to them all, the war for *The Lost Crowns of Albion* threatens to boil over, as villainous gangs of VAMPIRES, WERE-CATS and GOBLINS continue to battle for the supremacy of the supernatural underworld.

A swashbuckling supernatural detective adventure, continuing the curious case of The Lost Crowns Of Albion.

From The Casebook Of Lyons & Hound

The Undead King Of New York City

The Curious Case Of
The Kensington Kidnapping

Arrow Of The Gods

Incident At Five Hundred Acre Wood

The Goldemar Affair

The Tomas Dearlove Chronicles

The Wild Hunt

Grendel

The King Of Avalon

www.caractacusplume.com

Silvatici Publishing
silvatici@outlook.com

Printed in Great Britain
by Amazon